SOUTHLANDS

LEE HARDEN SERIES

BOOK 2

D. J. MOLLES

To the gentlemen of P.D.,
Who keep me sharp.

SPECIAL THANKS

The more I do this, the more I find myself leaning on a lot of special people. I've thanked you all in person, but I've been a bit remiss about publicly acknowledging what you've done for me. Hell, I might've given the impression that I do all this myself! Nothing could be further from the truth.

To my beta readers, Coty Bradburn, Jarrod Pierce, Maggie Johnson, James Hornback, Jon Carricker, Julie Jane, Ron Paige, and of course my father, Brad Molles, who reads everything I write: I want to thank you all for taking the time to read unfinished drafts and give me your honest opinion on things. You don't know how much it helps for me to have a sounding board.

To Josh White and Randy VanScoten: Thanks for all the medical knowledge from two badass trauma nurses.

To Steve Sellers: Thanks for making Lee look so good, and for my female readership.

To my agent, Dave Fugate: Thanks for always going above and beyond for me.

To my lovely wife, Tara, whose artistic and graphic design skills grace the covers of almost all my books: Thanks for making me look like I know what I'm doing!

And of course, to you, the reader: Thanks for holding this book in your hands right now. If it weren't for you, I'd just be a guy clacking away on a keyboard, with no one to read my crazy ideas.

PROLOGUE

IT WAS THE LAST NIGHT *that they would all be alive and in one place together.*

None of them knew that. But maybe they felt it. A tremor in the strings of the universe. A faint vibration through the chord of their lives that they perceived fleetingly, with a swallow and a shudder of foreboding. And then they ignored it for the impossible superstition that it was.

Lee, Julia, Abe, Nate, and Tomlin, in a circle.

Carl, being his usual curmudgeonly self, had knocked off early.

The rest of them stood around a steel barrel, burning some brush that had been cleared away from one of the fence lines here in the Butler Safe Zone.

It was their one-night stopover in Butler before heading into Alabama.

Their route planned, their mission briefed, and their equipment packed, save for the few items they would need to sleep and rise and set out again, there was nothing left for any of them to do. As the sun set in the west and darkness overtook them, the pile of brush began to dwindle.

Their surroundings went from navy, to black. A damp springtime chill crept up on them. But the fire kept it at their backs. Bathed their faces in yellow, their clothes in warm woodsmoke. Embers meandered up into the sky, and then winked out. Firelight glinted off smiling teeth and eyes as they laughed and talked to one another.

"Didn't mean for y'all to do my brush burnin' for me," a voice drawled.

Lee Harden took his eyes from the pleasant flames and looked to his right. Ghost-lights danced in his eyes for a moment, but he saw the basics of the figure striding out of the gloom. The tucked-in County Brownie shirt. The bowlegged walk, like he'd been on a horse all day. The bright white mustache that seemed to precede the face out of the darkness.

"Sheriff Ed," Lee smiled. "We're just enjoying the fire. Don't let us hold up your work."

Ed's mustache moved, and Lee thought he might be smiling underneath it, by the way his eyes crinkled in the corners. He sidled up to the fire. He had a mason jar full of clear liquid in his hand, but kept it down at his side, as though trying to be inconspicuous.

With his free hand, he waved Lee off. "You just enjoy yourselves. Y'all sound like you got plenty of nasty work ahead of you, headin' out into The Wilds. Might as well take some time to relax a bit."

Lee nodded. He looked into the fire, and then up from the flames, to Julia, who stood directly across from him. He saw the small smirk on her face. She knew how much Lee enjoyed Ed's cowboy ways.

Ed shuffled about, and then made his gift known, holding it up and swishing it around, and then shoving it into Abe's chest, like a football to a running back.

Abe accepted it, then held it up and gazed at it with eager eyes. "Hell yes."

"Well, now," Ed held out a cautionary hand. "I never claimed it was good. But it won't rot your guts out neither. I 'stilled it up myself."

"Shit, sheriff," Abe said, making to hide the jar. "Lawman can't be seen handing out hard liquor like that. It'll scandalize the townsfolk!"

Ed gruffed. "I wouldn't worry 'bout that. All the townsfolk are already drunk on the same stuff."

Abe laughed, then clapped Ed on the shoulder. "Well, thank you for this."

Ed waved it away, once again. As though thanks and appreciation were flies to swat at. "Y'all just have a nice relaxin' evening on me, awright now?"

"Awright now!" Abe proclaimed.

Across the fire, Brian Tomlin turned it into a whoop: "Awright now!"

Ed departed, his eyes crinkled in merriment.

Tomlin clapped his hands together and then made a "gimme" gesture. "You gonna stand there and ogle that shit or sip and pass?"

Abe pulled the jar away. "Whoa. Settle your scrotum there, happy hands. It'll make its way around. Clockwise, as tradition dictates."

A round of banter ensued between Tomlin and Nate. Lee and Abe passed the jar back and forth a few times, with appreciative nods. It tasted like yeast and rubbing alcohol, with a hint of ammonia. It was fantastic.

Time went by to the tick-tock of sip-and-pass. The laughter sometimes grew raucous, as though to defy the darkness, and other times it was almost demur, as though afraid to draw hostile attention.

The pile of brush dwindled some more.

The flames leapt up when they put more branches in, then gradually died down.

Lee looked across the fire at Julia and saw the firelight flickering across her eyes. Her face bore a slight smile. She was content where she was at. And so was Lee. She looked across the fire at him, and something good passed between them in that look.

But it reminded Lee of a time before.

A time several long years ago, when he'd sat around a similar fire in Camp Ryder, and joked with a man named LaRouche. Julia had been there too.

Was Julia remembering that same thing?

The memory was bittersweet. It was another memory in a long list of ones that were attached to a person they would never see again.

Lee found the light smile on his lips grow heavy.

He held onto it only by remembering that this was his last mission. When he finished with this, he was going to start training new soldiers to take the place of the people around this very fire. And then they would all be part of Lee's training cadre. And they could take a much-needed break from the corrosive wear of near-constant combat operations.

Tomlin and Abe were now hurling arguments across the fire at each other about a comic book character. Tomlin believed the character was a pussy. Abe asserted that Tomlin was not only a much bigger pussy, but that he was misogynist to use such terms, and then began trying to enlist Julia in his argument.

Nate, a traditional lightweight, stared into the flames, occasionally laughing at Tomlin and Abe, and swaying on his feet. The jar had been around about five times by then.

Julia sipped, and passed it to Abe.

Abe held onto it for a while, too involved in laying out a five-point syllogism for why Tomlin didn't know what the hell he was talking about. Eventually Lee gave him a nudge, and Abe took a perfunctory sip and passed it.

When it reached Nate again, he held it, staring at it for a moment, and then seemed to come to a sudden decision. He shook his head, and passed the jar without sipping.

"I'm goin' to bed," he announced. "Y'all're too much."

Everyone agreed with the wisdom of heading off to bed, and not finishing the entire jar of moonshine, as much as they would like to pretend that they didn't have to do important and dangerous things the very next day.

And that was it.

Nate left the fire, his back retreating into the darkness, and the orange light chased him, but then gave up as he slipped through its grasp and was gone in black.

Tomlin followed shortly after, with parting shots at Abe, who was off in the shadows taking a piss. Abe yelled something inscrutable over his shoulder so that Tomlin wouldn't have the last wo

That's how it ended.

They all left the fire.

They all left that warm glow, and they walked like ghosts into the night, who've only momentarily slipped into our world, and don't plan to stay. Some of them would be lost forever. Others would go on. But they would never again be in that spot together, to share that moment, or that bond.

They would never again be whole.

ONE

INFECTION

Two women meet.

It is obvious they hate each other.

But there is no one around to witness it. They are alone, in a shaded section of a quiet path between two rows of houses. Those houses belong to a neighborhood that exists in a tiny bastion of human survivors called Fort Bragg. Beyond the high voltage perimeter of Fort Bragg, a hostile world waits. Lurks. Hunts.

One of these women wants to destroy Fort Bragg.

The other is there because her son is a rapist, and if anyone ever found out, she and her son would have to go out into that hostile world. And she knows that they would not last long.

"You better be here to tell me that she's infected," Elsie Foster says. She is the one that wants to see Fort Bragg burn.

"It's not that simple." Taylor Sullivan squirms. She is the mother of the rapist.

"I feel like we've had this conversation," Elsie sighs. "For you and your son's sake, tell me that you did it."

"Yes. For God's sake. I did it already."

"How?"

An audible swallow from Sullivan. "Doc Trent has a primal. He's been...autopsying it or something. I snuck in there. Stuck it with a needle. Then I used that needle to give..." another swallow. Poor Nurse Sullivan is really struggling with this. "...I used the infected needle to give Abby an injection. Into her IV."

Elsie nods along, appearing to picture it. "I wanted results."

Sullivan is so frustrated she stamps her foot. "Those *are* results! What do you want from me? I introduced infected material to her bloodstream! She's almost guaranteed to get it now."

"'Almost' and 'guarantee' don't go together."

"I did what you asked."

"Let's get something straight." Elsie pokes the shorter woman in the chest. "I asked for Abby to be infected by now. Not 'on her way out' or 'in the process of being infected.' Fucking *infected*. Shitting the bed. Biting her mother. Howling at the moon. *Infected*. It's been two days, Taylor. And your time's up."

Sullivan is angry. But more than that, she is scared.

They'd found the body of the woman that had been attacked by the primals two nights ago. Her carcass had been stripped of meat. Just a patch of scattered, bloody bones, still held together by tendons and whatever else the primals hadn't fed on.

They'd even eaten her face off.

And Sullivan keeps thinking, *That's going to be you. That's going to be you and Benjamin, if you're not careful.*

She holds up a shaking hand. "It's done, Elsie. She's infected."

"How long? And don't bullshit me. I'll fact-check what you tell me."

"She'll be symptomatic in twenty-four hours. Completely insane by forty-eight."

Elsie sniffs. "I get proof that you did your job, and the proof against little Benji-Boy goes away. That's the deal. You get me what I want, and you get what you want. Twenty-four hours."

Sullivan's nostrils flare. Her jaw muscles bunch. "You'll get it."

Two women depart.

It is obvious that they hate each other even more.

TWO

WILDLIFE

ALLEN, THE WILDLIFE OFFICER, was sweating bullets, despite being in the air-conditioned cab of the SUV.

Surrounding him, four soldiers laughed and joked amongst themselves, as the driver rolled them through a dilapidated neighborhood outside the Fort Bragg Safe Zone.

Allen thought they were probably as nervous as he was, but they had a better outlet: They knew each other and could laugh to relieve the tension. Allen could only sit in silence, clutching the air rifle in his hands, his sweat glands betraying him.

Allen was in the back passenger seat. There were four soldiers in the vehicle with him. Two up front, one to his left, and one in the far back. The interior of the vehicle was gray. Old. Stained and cigarette-burned. It smelled musty, and also like soldiers, which was a distinct scent. Like old camping equipment—leather and canvas and metal, a layer of body oils and dirt on all of it, with fresh sweat underneath.

11

Outside was a bright, warm, spring morning. A few wispy clouds. A light breeze that smelled like pollen.

They kept the SUV—an old Ford Expedition—moving at about ten miles an hour. And every once in a while, the driver would lay on the horn, and it would blast out into the ghastly silence of the dead neighborhood.

All around them, the houses stared on, their dark, broken windows like empty eye sockets, and their doors hanging open like gaping mouths. Some of them were fire-blackened. Some burned straight to the ground. Others stood in more or less the same condition they'd been left in, except for mold creeping on the siding and brush growing up so high in the lawns sometimes you could barely see the front porch.

"She was a dependapotomus," one of the soldiers was saying. "You can tell just by looking at her."

The driver, whose girlfriend was in question, laughed, but he was getting defensive. "Nah, man. She looks good."

"Pff. She looks good *now*. That's just the rationing done slimmed her down."

"Five years ago," the one in the far back put in. "She was three hundred pounds—guaranteed. You'da gained five pounds by eating her out."

This brought on gales of laughter.

The driver shifted about, getting more irritated. He honked the horn a few more times.

Allen flinched at the noise.

"Y'all're fucked up," the driver mumbled.

The soldier behind the driver nudged the seat in front of him. "Bro, she probably never even left

Bragg. She's been here the whole time. Her last Joe probably went to Greeley, and she's been lurkin' down in the sewers ever since, like the clown from 'It', just waitin' for her next victim."

The corporal, who was in the passenger seat, seemed to detect that they had reached the boiling point with their friend, and he reached across and gave the driver a slap on the shoulder. "Alright. We're all just jealous because Chris is gettin' head on the reg. Good on ya, bro."

There were boos and hisses from the back, but they quieted down.

The corporal twisted in his seat and looked at Allen. "Hey, buddy. You okay back there?"

Allen forced a smile and nodded. "Yeah. Fine."

The soldier behind the driver eyed him, and spoke in a southern plantation accent: "He doth appear to perspire a great deal."

Allen flushed. Which only made it worse. "It's hot, okay?"

The soldier frowned. Went back to his regular voice. "I mean…didn't you say you, like, hunted bears and shit with that thing?"

Allen turned to look out his open window. "I never said I *hunted* bears. Said I shot one. It was up in a tree in a neighborhood."

"Oh damn. Okay." A sly smile. "So what if one of these things is runnin' at you?"

Allen was getting about as irritated as the driver. He was preparing a retort when something flitted between two houses.

Low to the ground. Almost hidden by the tall weeds.

"Shut up," Allen whispered.

13

"Hey, easy. I'm just askin' about your proficiency level with that thing—"

"No, I mean shut up!" Allen snapped, and then jerked the air rifle through the open window. "Three o'clock!"

"Oh shit."

There was a scramble of bodies and a clatter of gear as the soldiers refocused themselves out their windows.

The corporal tapped the driver's shoulder again. "Stop here."

The Expedition rolled to a stop in the middle of the neighborhood street.

"What'd you see?" the corporal demanded.

"I dunno," Allen replied. "Between those two houses there."

"Alright, everyone look frosty. Chris, hit that horn again. Allen, you got one shot, brother. Make it count."

Allen was well aware that he only had one shot. It didn't help to be reminded of it.

He double- and then triple-checked the rifle's load, the bolt, the air pressure, and the safety. Every second his eyes were not fixed on the weeds out there was torture. He refocused himself, with his heart hammering in his chest and his breathing coming on fast.

"Remember," the corporal said, putting his own rifle out his window. "When they come, it's probably gonna be from all sides. So watch your lane."

The air rifle was fixed with a three-power scope. It wasn't much, but the effective range on it was only fifty yards.

An animal could cross a lot of that ground in a very short amount of time. It'd probably eat up half of it before Allen could get a shot off. And then how long before the tranquilizer knocked it down?

He pressed his cheek against the buttstock. Sighted through the scope.

The magnified image met his eyes.

Weeds.

A house front.

"Call 'em when you see 'em," the corporal coached.

"Hey, I got movement at nine o'clock," someone called.

"I got some at six. Shit. Fuck these things…"

Grass.

Leaves.

Eyes.

Allen's whole body locked.

Breath caught in his chest.

Heart stopped.

It stared right at him. Two, big, wild eyes fixed on him over the tops of the weeds.

"Oh, Jesus," Allen squeezed out.

"Whatcha got?"

The thing in the grass charged.

Allen felt his brain short-circuiting. His finger touched the trigger before he meant to, and he pulled himself back at the last second before firing, knowing that he had to wait for the thing to get clear of the grass—he needed a shot at its torso.

"R-R-Right! Right!" Allen gasped out.

Gunfire suddenly erupted. In the enclosed space of the SUV, Allen's hearing went out like a light, and it was all a muddy wash of noise. All he perceived was his own breath hissing in his throat, and all he saw was the primal charging at him.

He saw the chest. The heaving of the fatless muscle. The long, loping arms.

He squeezed the trigger.

Saw the dart hit, dead center in the chest.

"Go! Go! Go!" Allen screamed, jerking himself back into the SUV, and backpedaling away from his open window.

"Drive!" the corporal yelled, but the driver had already hit the gas.

The primal hit the side of the vehicle, then rolled off the side, and Allen lost sight of it.

They were still firing.

"Don't shoot that one!" Allen yelled, though he wasn't sure anyone could hear him over the gunfire, and even if they could, did they even know which one he was talking about?

The one with the red-feathered dart in its chest!

He felt rough hands shoving him.

"Get the fuck off me, man!"

In his haste to get away from the window, Allen had pressed himself against the soldier on the driver's side. Allen tried to get off him, but the driver swerved around a fallen tree, causing Allen to lose his balance again and topple back into the soldier amid a flurry of curses.

The SUV ramped a curb with a bang as loud as a traffic collision, then slammed through an old mailbox, and then tumbled back onto the roadway, going about forty-five miles an hour now.

Allen was propelled back into his seat by the angry soldier.

The corporal shouted: "Take the circle, right here, *right here!*"

The SUV skidded through a hard right turn.

The neighborhood street they were on meandered through houses for a while, but would bring them back to where they'd been. They'd been driving this same circle for the last hour.

"Slow down," the corporal ordered. "Give them some time to chase us." He turned into the back. "Everyone okay? Anyone have physical contact?"

The other four soldiers reported that they were good, and no, they'd driven off before any physical contact was made.

"Allen," the corporal looked at him. "Get the collar ready. We're gonna be back around in about a minute."

That minute zipped by like a bullet.

Allen already had the collar prepped, but he double- and triple-checked it like he had his air rifle. It took him longer than he wanted to fumble through this. His hands trembled.

"Stop here," the corporal ordered.

They rolled to a stop.

The thrumming engine.

The silence of the outside world, cut through by the sound of bugs chirping.

"Hit the horn again. See if we can't draw them further away."

The horn blared, making Allen flinch again.

"Hey." It was the soldier to his left. Not angry anymore. He leaned over and squeezed Allen's shoulder. "Breathe, bro. Take big breaths."

Allen wanted to shrug the man's hand off him, but he resisted the urge. "I'm fuckin' fine."

"There you go. Hardcore."

"Alright," the corporal called. "Chris, hit it."

The SUV lurched forward again, accelerating through a series of turns.

"We got one shot at this, and we need to move fast. If I call 'abort,' get your ass back in the truck, no questions asked."

The SUV turned onto the same stretch of street where they started.

"Jones, you're with me and Allen. Three sixty coverage. Call what you see."

The driver let the Expedition drift down to about thirty miles an hour, then twenty. Everyone's head was on a swivel, searching the grass and the weeds and the places around fallen trees—not just for primals hunting them, but for a body...

"Got him!" the driver yelped, and stomped on the brake.

By the time the SUV rocked back on its chassis, Allen and Jones and the corporal had already spilled out of their doors. Allen clutched the collar in one hand, his eyes sweeping left and right along the roadway.

Great drifts of leaves had gathered against the curbs, and gradually turned to dirt, so that the edges of the neighborhood street were slowly being digested, and the weeds infiltrated that dirt, and in another few years, perhaps the entire road would be engulfed, the planet absorbing and metabolizing the unnatural, returning itself to homeostasis.

Ain't nature grand?

It was there, in a peninsula of dirt and weeds that jutted out into the road, that Allen saw the shape of the thing. Just the head and shoulders, slumped on its side. A few yards past it, Allen saw the tire marks from where they'd sped off.

The primal had rebounded off the back of the Expedition, and kept its feet for another few yards before collapsing.

That was good. That meant the tranquilizer was working as fast as it should.

Hopefully he hadn't tranq-ed the damn thing to death.

Allen rushed towards it, feeling sicker the closer he got. The corporal was in front of him, and Jones was behind.

The corporal reached the body first and barely broke stride, terminating his run with a kick to the thing's torso, to see if it was still reactive, which it wasn't.

"You're good," the corporal breathed out. "It's down for the count."

The corporal hopped over the body and began scanning the weeds and windows and doorways around them, his rifle up.

Allen skittered to a stop, his breath clenched. He'd never been so close to one of these things. It shook him to his core, and he didn't want to touch it but he knew that he had to. He saw the thing's chest rising and falling, so he knew that it was still alive.

What freaked him out was that the eyes weren't closed.

This shouldn't have surprised Allen, but it did.

When he'd tranq-ed the bear in that neighborhood, the thing's deep brown eyes had been half-opened, staring out at nothing. It was the same here. But it was a human's eyes—sort of—and that similarity almost made Allen stop.

What kept him from stopping was the screech that suddenly split the stillness.

Deeper in the neighborhood. A few streets over.

It should've been a comfort—the primals only called when they were honing in on you, but when they had you dead to rights, you never heard them coming. But it slammed his body with adrenaline and all he wanted to do was get his job done and get out of there as fast as possible.

He dropped to his knees beside the thing and shoved it so that it lay on its belly. It was a male, he thought, though he didn't take the time to check the equipment down below. He already had the collar opened up and adjusted to the approximate width of a neck.

"Come on, Allen," the corporal hissed at him. "Get it done! We need to leave!"

Allen didn't reply. With trembling hands, he fed the transmitter collar around the primal's neck, then tried to bring the two buckles together...it was too tight. Wouldn't buckle.

Allen let loose a string of curses under his breath.

"What's taking so long?" Jones demanded.

"Too tight," Allen gasped, removing the collar and loosening it.

He listened for another call from the primals. But they were quiet now.

The damn collar was brand new and stiff as hell. He struggled to get the D-ring to loosen.

"Allen, are you gonna get this done?" the corporal said.

"I'm trying!"

"Contact!" Jones called. "Between those two houses!"

"Shit! Allen! Do it now or let's go!"

Allen shoved the collar down around the thing's neck. It let out a thready grunt and Allen almost jumped back—almost wet himself, too—but managed to keep his hands on the collar, and pulled the two ends together.

Still snug, but he wasn't worried about the primal's comfort at this point. He snapped the clasp together, and then bolted upright. "It's on! Let's go!"

He was already running for the Expedition.

Down the road, less than a hundred yards behind the Expedition, two shapes galloped towards them on all fours.

"Oh Christ, oh Christ, oh Christ..."

Allen's door was still open. He threw himself inside.

"Go! Drive!" he belted out.

The driver didn't drive. He was still waiting on the corporal and Jones.

"Contact, rear!" the soldier called from the back, and then gunfire punched at Allen's eardrums again.

Allen was on the floorboards. His feet still hung out of his door, and it felt like when he was a kid and his feet were outside the covers where the monsters under his bed might be able to get them...

He was peripherally aware of Jones hurtling into the SUV. Jones's boots clambered over Allen's head, but Allen didn't care, not even when Jones cussed him out. Allen curled himself into a ball, trying to get his feet into the Expedition before the monsters grabbed them.

There was yelling, but the language was hard to interpret past the jackhammering of his heart and his dull, aching eardrums.

He felt the SUV lurch forward.

21

Felt doors slam.

And they were driving.

Jones kicked at him. "Get back in your seat, you fucking cherry!" he screamed. "I almost couldn't get in the fucking car because of you, you piece of shit!"

Allen didn't care. Relief flooded him so hard he thought he might lose control of his bladder again. He had enough shame left in him not to let that happen, but it was a close call.

He pulled himself away from Jones, and had enough of a spurt of anger to give the soldier a shove to the chest. Jones gave him a fiery glare and looked about ready to pummel his face.

"Cool it!" the corporal barked. "Jones!"

Jones drew himself up with mighty indignation. "Fucking cherry," he griped, but said no more.

Allen pulled himself into his seat with muscles that felt like they'd turned to pudding. He leaned forward so his sweating face was pressed against the faux-leather of the front passenger's seat.

The engine roared. The driver pulled them through twists and turns.

Safe.

Safe-*ish*.

The tension broke when someone started laughing.

Allen wasn't sure who it was. His eyes were squeezed shut.

The corporal was telling everyone they did a great job.

Amid the laughter, Jones loosened up. He reached over and patted Allen on the back. "Sorry 'bout that. Just…you know how it is. Got a little hot there for a second."

Allen pushed himself off the front seat, wilted back into his own. "It's whatever," he mumbled. Glad to be done. Glad to be heading back to the Fort Bragg Safe Zone. At least until the time came to come back out and start tracking the damn thing they'd just strapped a transmitter to.

But he chose not to think about that right now.

The nervous, cathartic laughter petered out.

A few giggles, like troublesome schoolboys in the back of a classroom.

The engine thrummed on.

All was silent for a while.

The driver started fidgeting in the front seat again. Started glancing over to his corporal as though he had something to say.

The corporal watched this for a few seconds. "What?"

The driver huffed through his nose. Gripped the wheel and rung it in his hands.

"I mean," he said, plaintively. "How can she be a dependa when there's not even any military benefits anymore?"

THREE

MERCY

JULIA WAS GETTING a lot of attention that she didn't care for.

After their shaky victory at the airport several days back, they'd sent some of the tankers that they'd captured from *Nuevas Fronteras* off with the Marine detachment. Then Julia, Lee, and Abe had dusted out with Captain Terrence "Tex" Lehy, back to Texas.

There, they'd started to get familiarized with Tex's guerilla-style campaign. While Lee and Abe healed up from their various wounds, Julia decided to start making herself useful and going with Tex's squads on their raids.

It seemed like there weren't many females in any of Tex's squads. Which was understandable, given that they were almost entirely military, most of them from combat MOSs.

They would've been happy to see Julia even if she was plain. But she wasn't. She was naturally pretty, so even though her tawny hair hadn't been washed in a week, and her face had dirt on it, she still got looks.

In fact, they spent as much time watching her as they did the long, empty stretch of highway that led out of Texas.

Julia was acutely aware that only *groups* of women had a civilizing influence on men. A lone woman was just something to chase down and screw. She didn't think it would come to that, but men starved of women could be unpredictable. So she kept as much of the squad in front of her at all times, frequently checked her six, and didn't let her rifle leave her grasp.

They were positioned near a solitary overpass on a long, straight section of the I-35 corridor, about a mile from the Oklahoma border.

There were two squads total. One on either side of the interstate, hiding just inside the clumps of forest that stood in the unpaved sections of the interchange.

Somewhere on the highway that ran across the overpass, far enough to be out of sight, a tractor-trailer waited.

Julia sat with her back against a tree, about twenty feet in from the edge of the woods. The air was very still, and getting hot. Inside the shade, it was bearable, but humid.

From her vantage, she could see all ten members of the squad, of which she was number eleven. Eight of them lay prone at the very edge of the trees. One of them had an M249. Another had a tripod-mounted M2.

The squad leader and his radioman sat back, closer to Julia.

Sergeant Menendez was a good-humored guy of about twenty-five, with short, scraggly facial hair. While his gaze still lingered a bit long every time he looked at Julia, it seemed like he considered it his responsibility to be the gentleman of the group, and gave a good faith effort to make Julia feel comfortable.

The other guys would peek over their shoulders, as though making sure she was still there, and then they would huddle and mumble and chuckle to each other at whatever ribald joke they'd made.

"So," Menendez said, conversationally. "What's the United Eastern States like?"

Julia frowned at him. "How do you mean?"

Menendez eyed her up and down, then shrugged and looked away. "Like…you guys got enough food to eat? You got a lot of civilians? Is life pretty normal, or is it pretty militaristic? Like, for us, it's like active duty all the time, you know? Always with the squad. Always doin' ops. Always outside the wire." He looked at her again. "You guys have a wire? Isn't that right? Fortifications and shit?"

Julia nodded. "We have places we call Safe Zones. They're secured with fences and high voltage. Keeps the primals out. Mostly."

"Primals is teepios, right?"

"Right."

"Fuck those bastards." Menendez shook his head. "Who'da thought, you know?"

"Yeah," Julia replied. "Who'da thought."

"Sounds nice," Menendez sniffed. "Makes me wanna visit."

"How's that?"

He shrugged. "Like I said. Been a long time since I've been around civilians, you know? Long time since I could just walk around without my rifle and shit. Y'all probably have a lot of pretty girls like yourself."

Julia smiled in spite of herself. "Y'all sound like you need some R&R."

"You have no idea."

Julia watched him for a moment, then looked away. For a flash the conversation made her think of Lee, and a topic that he'd been bringing up since they'd left Fort Bragg. It usually started with something like, "Once we're done here, and we get back to Bragg..."

Lee wanted out. That was the long and short of it. And Julia couldn't blame him. She wanted out too. They'd all been running ragged for years. No stops. There simply wasn't time to stop. But they were going to burn out hard if something didn't change.

Besides that fact, as Lee often pointed out, Fort Bragg had relied on Lee's team and Carl's team for the vast majority of their dirty work. If things continued to heat up between the United Eastern States and Acting President Briggs in Greeley, Colorado—not to mention this oil cartel—then they would need more than two small teams to handle their business.

And Lee was going to train them.

Once they got back.

Julia responded as little as possible to this line of conversation that Lee brought up. She didn't want to encourage it. Because she was the type of person that didn't like to get her hopes up, and history had shown her that hoping for things was a great way to get disappointed.

But she also recognized that maybe Lee needed that hope. Maybe he needed something to look forward to.

In any case, she was worried about him. His attitude had changed in subtle but alarming ways. Ever since they'd lost Tomlin and Nate.

He was harder inside.

Quicker to anger.

Quicker to violence.

About the only time she saw him genuinely smile anymore was when he was talking about these plans for the future. How he was going to start a training cadre, and it was going to have Abe and Julia in it, and they were going to be able to stop running operations non-stop, and actually, for the first time since the collapse of the old world, *breathe*.

It was a wonderful daydream. But Julia didn't like to harbor it for long.

Lying on a forest floor somewhere in Texas, preparing to ambush a convoy of tanker trucks, it felt like such things were too far in the future to be real.

But maybe one day...

The radioman lounging next to Menendez perked up and leaned forward, listening to his radio. Then he tapped Menendez on the shoulder. "Willie's got route clearance rolling through now. One mike out."

"Roger," Menendez nodded. He keyed his own comms, transmitting to this squad, and the squad across the way. "Bigfoot Actual to my homies in the barrio, standby for route clearance to come through." He flashed a wide smile at her as he released his PTT. "I just say that shit to piss off all these racist-ass gringos I gotta work with."

The radioman shook his head. "Can't believe I gotta answer to a fuckin' beaner."

Menendez chuckled as he got to his feet. "What's the world comin' to, right?"

Julia picked her helmet up from the ground next to her and buckled it onto her head. The nerves hit her, sudden and hard, and her fingers trembled with the chinstrap. For the third or fourth time that day, she wondered why the hell she'd volunteered for this.

Because this is your job.
Keep people alive.

Menendez hunched down towards his soldiers, but then stopped and looked back at Julia, putting his own helmet on as he did. "Stay back there until we need you, okay?"

Julia nodded in response and decided to slip around to the back of the thick pine she was leaning against. It wasn't a lot of cover, but it was better than nothing. She went prone behind it. Her heavy medical pack sat on her back and felt almost comforting there.

Menendez and his radioman shuffled over to the front line. Peered down the road.

"Eyes on," Menendez said, looking south. "Everyone standby."

The radioman spoke again: "Willie's got the convoy in sight now. Five tankers."

From behind her tree, Julia watched Menendez go prone behind his machine gunner with the M2. The radioman laid down next to him, almost hip-to-hip.

No one spoke anymore. Everyone was still and tense.

Somewhere in the woods near them a bird chirped and beat its wings through the branches.

Julia focused on her breathing. Steadying her pounding heart. She thought about wounds. And where everything was in her bag. She imagined Menendez with a hole in his chest, and where her chest seals were. Then she imagined him with a blown artery, and visualized herself applying tourniquets, or hemostats, as was needed. She imagined him with his brains hanging out of his skull, and her triaging him and making the call that he couldn't be saved, and moving on to the next person that needed her.

These visualizations didn't amp her up. They brought out the cold clinician in her. They turned human beings into broken machines. It helped her stay calm.

The sound of engines reached her. Faint at first, and then growing.

Another twenty seconds.

The roar of the engines surrounded her.

Out on the interstate, two MATVs roared past.

She saw them in a flash, through the trees ahead of her, and then they were gone, and the noise of their engines faded.

That was the route clearance. They paved the way about a mile or so ahead of the actual convoy, probing the route for ambushes.

It was a good tactic. Unless the people ambushing knew that there was route clearance, and let them pass by so that the real targets could come along.

"Bigfoot Actual to Mikey," Menendez transmitted. "Start rolling now. Everyone else, standby. You know what to do."

Julia stayed flat on her belly. She felt the hollow queasiness overtake her. The same as it always was when she was waiting to see how much she would have to fight death, and whether or not death would come to *her*.

Just as the sound of the two route clearance MATVs faded almost to nothing, a new roar of engines began to build. This one deeper. Throatier.

Everyone waited.

The climbing noise of the approaching convoy seemed to fill the air around them, although she knew it came from her left—from the south. And then, just as she caught the first flash of a semi-truck through the trees, she heard a horrendous lumbering, crashing noise, coming from her right.

She could only see a small portion of the road beyond the overpass, but she saw the tractor-trailer that had been waiting up on the highway, now hitting the road from where it had rolled down the embankment. It collided in a spray of dirt and grass, lurched, tilted, and slammed onto its side like a felled leviathan, blocking the interstate.

There came the screech of brakes.

And then the thunder of guns.

Everyone started shooting at once. Both squads, on either side of the interstate, directing their rounds downwards in a withering crossfire. The small arms targeted the cabs of the trucks, while the bigger machine guns roared and targeted the engine blocks.

Julia watched as Menendez huddled over his M2 machine gunner and directed his fire. The first burst of five rounds hit the lead tanker truck and ripped its engine compartment to shreds, disabling it. Then Menendez slapped the machine gunner's shoulder, and the M2 shifted to the next truck in the line.

On the other side of the interstate, an identical collection of small arms and machine guns mirrored the movements, except they targeted the rearmost tanker and moved up.

The tankers shed soldiers, doing what they were trained to do—assault through an ambush. But Julia didn't see a single one of them get farther than putting their feet on concrete before they were destroyed in a flurry of gunshots.

The guns rolled for what seemed like a long time to Julia.

After what felt like twice the shooting that was necessary to accomplish complete destruction of every enemy combatant on the interstate, she became aware of Menendez's voice shouting and transmitting: "Check fire! Check fire!"

The gunfire ceased.

Julia's ears rang. The nuance of sound was gone. She couldn't register the wind in the trees, or the shuffle of the leaves underneath her body. Just a dull ringing, and the sound of voices calling out.

"You good?"

"We're good!"

"Anybody hit?"

"We're solid."

"Bigfoot Actual, sitrep. Any casualties?"

There did not appear to be any casualties.

Julia felt a wash of relief, but her stomach still remained hollow and achy.

Menendez stood up now. "Squad Two, secure the convoy. Gunners, get on that barricade in case those two MATVs come back."

From the trees on the other side of the interstate, several soldiers emerged and swarmed down the embankment to the roadway. The soldiers in the woods on Julia's side stayed where they were, providing coverage if there happened to be any more live combatants.

The machine gunners with the M249s ran for the tractor-trailer that had been laid out across the road as a barricade. The gunners on the M2s received help from their squad mates, and lugged the heavy machine guns down to support the M249s.

Menendez paced back and forth behind his men. Watching as his other squad took the convoy and swept it. "Fuck yeah," he mumbled to himself, repeatedly. Then he stopped to listen to something on his squad comms and threw a thumbs-up. "It's clear. All clear. Let's move." He turned to his radioman. "Tell Willie to get the wreckers rolling. Let's grab what we can and get outta here."

Julia hauled herself to her feet and crossed over to the edge of the woods, as the soldiers descended on the roadway.

Menendez flashed her a smile, and motioned with his head, and then began to follow his soldiers down. Julia went after him.

About halfway down, Julia watched one of Menendez's men approach a downed soldier. He stripped the rifle out of the man's hands, and then began to harvest everything else he could from the soldier—the helmet, the plate carrier.

In the midst of this, the soldier came alive with a sudden, half-delirious yelp, and started scrabbling with Menendez's guy.

Julia's heart lurched into her throat.

There was a brief struggle, cut through by a few incoherent shouts, and then Menendez's guy jumped back, raised his rifle, and put three rounds into the wounded soldier, putting him down.

They both wore the same uniform.

Menendez didn't hurry his pace, but strode along, watching as it happened.

They're enemy combatants, Julia told herself, trying to quell the feeling of wrongness. *Uniforms don't matter. These are the enemy.*

Her stomach was unconvinced.

Out in the open, the sunlight was sweltering. Julia felt sweat trickle out from under her helmet, and she ripped it off her head and mopped her brow.

Menendez happened to glance back at her, and his brows knit with concern. "You alright? You look a little pale."

Julia nodded hastily. "It's just hot."

They reached the shoulder of the interstate. Julia straddled the guardrail and thumped clumsily over. Her feet felt heavy. Her medical pack, her armor, her rifle, it seemed to have gained weight in the last few minutes. Or she'd gotten weaker.

Down the road to the south, the sun glinted off a windshield.

She squinted into the distance. Saw the wreckers coming.

Someone shouted: "Got a live one!"

Julia started running before she thought about it.

"Julia!" Menendez hollered. "Wait!"

Julia ignored him.

She crossed the roadway. Ran between two tanker trucks, still smoking and stinking of exhaust and burning fluids. She rounded the front of a truck and saw three of Menendez's soldiers down the line, looking up into one of the cabs. One of the soldiers had his rifle up, but the others didn't seem to think it necessary.

Julia wasn't thinking about what she was doing. She just needed to do *something.*

She reached the cab of the truck. The three soldiers around it took a step back, not sure whether they should stop Julia or not.

Julia had expected there to be a soldier in the cab.

What she found was a dark-haired woman in civilian clothing.

The woman was slumped in the seat, but still breathing, eyes open and filled with terror. Her chest heaved, her mouth open and trickling blood. Her entire torso was covered in it, down to the jeans she wore.

Julia put a hand up in front of the single soldier that still had his rifle trained on the woman behind the wheel of the truck. "Stop! Chill out!"

The soldier looked as uncertain as his buddies, but dipped the muzzle of his rifle.

Julia swung up onto the steps of the cab.

The woman inside took a sharp breath and drew back from Julia, scared.

Julia touched her on the shoulder. "It's okay. I'm gonna help you."

"Julia," Menendez's voice behind her. "What are you doing?"

Julia didn't respond. The woman behind the wheel still looked scared, but she didn't resist Julia as she put her arms around the woman and pulled her out of her seat. No one moved to help Julia.

The woman groaned in agony as Julia pulled her out of the cab. It was difficult because the cab was so high off the ground, but Julia grit her teeth and managed it. In the face of a job to do, or a life to save, her strength and energy had come back to her limbs.

The wounded woman's feet thumped gracelessly down out of the truck.

Julia hauled her to the shoulder of the road and laid her down on the dusty, gravelly blacktop. She put her helmet on the ground next to the woman, then slung her medical pack off her back. It was obvious the woman was shot in the chest. Julia was already picturing it. She would need an occlusive dressing. Some gauze to wipe away the blood.

She started to unzip the main compartment of the pack.

"Hey!" Menendez moved in a flash and snatched up the medical pack, pulling it out of Julia's reach. "The fuck you think you're doing?"

Julia shot to her feet. "I'm keeping someone from dying! That's my job!"

"Your job's to keep *my* boys alive, not the enemy."

"She's a civilian!"

"The fuck she is," Menendez spat. "I don't give a shit what clothes she's wearing. She's driving a truck for Briggs. That makes her an enemy combatant."

Julia was nose-to-nose with Menendez now, her pulse pounding in her head. She was peripherally aware that she was on thin ice. She didn't know Menendez enough to push him. She didn't know what he was capable of. Was she willing to put her life on the line to save this stranger?

Menendez jabbed a finger at Julia's medical bag. "You think we got infinity medical supplies? Every bandage you use is one less that could save one of my boys. You save this bitch, you doom one of my friends."

"What am I supposed to do? Let her die?"

"Don't worry about that. We'll take care of it."

"You gonna kill her?"

All semblance of good-humor had long since disappeared from Menendez's face. He leaned into Julia, his lips almost touching her cheek as he spoke, and it was only out of sheer stubbornness that Julia didn't back away from him.

"Whaddaya want, huh?" he hissed. "You ain't gonna waste the supplies to save her. We ain't takin' her back with us. You wanna just leave her out here? Huh? Leave her in the hot sun to die, slow and painful? Leave her for the fuckin' teepios to find?"

Sweat trickled into Julia's eyes. She blinked it away.

On the ground, the woman moaned.

Julia looked at her.

The woman's eyelids fluttered. She was on the verge of losing consciousness. And then what? Julia was going to...do what? Patch the holes. Pump her full of IV fluid to get the blood pressure back up. And then what?

Operate? Put her shredded lungs back together?

Julia would try to do that for one of her team. But for a stranger? A stranger that was most likely going to die anyways?

And for a flash, she saw it as Menendez saw it. Because no one was making medical supplies anymore. She saw it through the eyes of the cold clinician in her head, and she saw this woman, not as a fellow human being, but as a tally of medical equipment that Julia would never get back.

Two chest seals.

An IV.

A dozen bandages.

Pain medication.

A round of antibiotics.

Sutures.

Scalpels.

None of which could be replaced.

The caregiver in her rebelled. But the heartless math couldn't be argued with.

"You're not doin' her any favors," Menendez said, then drew back far enough to look Julia in the eyes. "Quick and painless is the best thing she can hope for."

Julia flushed. She hated that she was embarrassed by her actions—hated to be ashamed of being human—but there it was. Her eyes hit the dirt, and then she dragged them back up. Over to the woman.

The woman's eyes were closed. Her head lolled to one side. Blood dribbled from the corner of her mouth and into her hair.

Her ruined chest hitched, like her heart was trying to restart itself.

And then...nothing.

The sound of diesel engines grew around them. The big wreckers had arrived.

The soldiers gave the woman one last careless glance, and then shrugged to each other, deciding that there were more important things to be done. They moved off to help the wreckers hook up to the tankers.

Julia's eyes stayed on the woman.

She registered the fact that Menendez had moved on, too.

The woman was dead. There was no more concern that Julia might waste valuable medical supplies on her.

Was Briggs sending civilians? Or was Menendez right? Was the woman just another soldier that had chosen to wear civvies to blend in? To confuse the enemy? To confuse Tex and his squads?

Julia's head swirled. It was getting difficult to see the truth.

It was getting difficult to see what was right.

FOUR

TEXAS

FOR LEE HARDEN, being sequestered to a bunker while he waited for his body to heal enough to be operational again was like being locked in a box like veal. Like solitary confinement. Like torture.

Whether or not he was "healed" was a point of debate.

But he had declared himself operational, and the only push back he got was a small downturn of the lips from Julia.

So it was with a sense of fervent—almost pissed off—relief that he strapped his gear to himself for the first time since the operation at the airport in Andalusia, Alabama, and went topside with Abe to see if he could get into trouble.

Which would prove not to be very difficult.

Texas had a unique set of problems that Lee and Abe were about to get acquainted with.

What Lee had gathered so far was that, while Lee had been distributing the supplies from his bunkers to the United Eastern States and trying to rebuild a viable civilian government—the stated mission of Project Hometown—Captain Terrence "Tex" Lehy had gone a different route.

A more...militaristic route.

The freight elevator lifted Lee and Abe from the belly of the bunker, up to the surface.

It was a shock when he caught sight of himself in the reflection of the elevator's stainless steel control panel. He knew he'd lost weight—his chest rig was loose when he'd strapped it on—but Jesus...his face.

The shadows had deepened in the hollows of his cheeks, made even darker by the week of beard growth. He was already tall. If he kept losing muscle mass and fat, he was going to be downright gangly.

But for all of that, Lee felt good. A barrage of antibiotics had cleared the pneumonia out of Lee's lungs, and the bullet hole in his chest had healed up to a puckered scab now.

Abe was also healing up. The wound in his left calf still caused a "hitch in his giddyup," as Tex described it. But Abe was that variety of man that always looked filled out, no matter the severity of the hardships. He had roundish facial features as it was, but even if his face began to go gaunt, you wouldn't be able to see it past the thick black beard he kept.

Glued to Lee's right leg as usual, Deuce stood, his tongue lolling out, and even the dog that seemed to be so serious all the time appeared excited about leaving the bunker. As the elevator reached the top, he wagged his tail a few times and his ears perked forward.

Lee let his hand fall to Deuce's head and gave the dog a scratch behind the ears.

The elevator doors slid open, and warm, dry air gusted in.

They stepped out into an expanse of Texas plains, blinking against the strong sun. The smell of heat and grass and dew hit them, along with the smell of diesel exhaust.

Tex waited for them beside a running Chevy Silverado. He wore a battered pair of jeans and a t-shirt today, but he still had on his plate carrier and his rifle. He smiled at them, his eyes obscured by the Oakley M-frames he cherished.

"How are my two house guests today?" he asked in his Texas drawl.

Lee bumped Tex's fist by way of greeting. "Good. Ready to get out."

"Ready to earn your keep?"

Lee gestured to his own plate carrier and rifle. "We didn't get dressed up for nothing."

Tex nodded. "Well, hopefully it won't be like that. But you never know."

"What are we doing?" Abe asked, smoothing his beard out.

Tex hikcd a thumb over his shoulder to the pickup bed, which was filled with a mix of plastic crates and buckets. Mostly food stuffs, it looked like. "We're running some goodies out to OP Elbert. Little program I like to call 'MREs for TPOs.'"

Lee raised an eyebrow. He was still playing catchup with some of the jargon that Tex and his mostly-military constituents used. He wasn't familiar with "MREs for TPOs," but he understood that they called the primals "teepios," which originated from TPO, which stood for "two-point-oh." As in "Infected: 2.0."

Lee appreciated a good, obscure acronym.

Tex opened the passenger-side door of the truck, and gestured for Lee and Abe to get in the back. "Let's get rolling. I'll explain on the way." He stopped, with one leg in the truck and looked back at Lee and Abe. "Just be forewarned: OP Elbert is one of my civilian groups. And they're squirrelly as fuck. So stay on your toes."

Lee and Abe exchanged a glance.

"Roger that," Lee said, and then climbed in the back. Deuce hopped up to sit on the floorboard between him and Abe.

The pickup took off, not wasting any time. The "roads" were little more than tire trails, and Lee was jostled about violently in the back. The driver was a younger soldier that Lee had seen with Tex before, and he didn't seem to care much for slowing down over potholes.

Tex flicked a hand back and forth. "Lee and Abe, this is Corporal Thompson. Thompson, this is Lee and Abe. Thompson should be a sergeant, I guess. But then again I should be a general, so…"

Thompson didn't give a response to the greeting. Just kept ramming them over the potholes.

Tex turned around in his seat. "By the way, the crew that Julia's with just checked in about fifteen minutes ago. Everything's good." A pause. "I appreciate you letting me dispatch her out there. Good combat medics are something we don't have enough of."

Lee grunted. "You can thank Julia. She pretty much does what she wants."

Tex regarded Lee for a moment with a strange set to his lips. But he never said anything.

Lee hadn't liked Julia running off with Tex's hit squad. But they needed a medic, and she said she'd go, and that was that. Lee wanted to keep his own team together until they got a better sense of things here in Texas. But, so far, there hadn't been much to set off any alarms in Lee's head.

Tex was definitely doing things differently than in the UES. But that didn't mean it was bad. Just different. Ultimately, Lee wanted to get Texas to ally with the UES. They'd be stronger together.

And also, if Lee were being honest with himself, some of his urgency in helping Tex was because the sooner he got the UES and Texas allied, and the sooner they managed to handle the *Nuevas Fronteras* problem, the sooner he and Julia and Abe could go back to Fort Bragg, and Lee could start training the new generation of operators that the UES was desperately going to need.

Not to mention, Lee could finally take a damn break.

Thinking about that was the only thing that seemed to ease the semi-permanent ball of tension that had taken up residence in his chest over the course of the last year.

Lee refocused himself on the task at hand. He nodded at Tex. "So what's 'MREs for TPOs'?"

Tex faced forward again. "It's how we stay alive, my friend. I understand you got fences and whatnot over in the UES. Got a power plant to juice some high voltage wires, keep the teepios from munching on your civvies. But we kind of went a different route around here. More of an 'earn your keep' philosophy."

Lee thought about that. Thought about how the primals had breached Fort Bragg only a few nights ago. Thought about how Abby had been bit. It made his stomach sour. That was the last they'd heard from Fort Bragg, and Lee had opted to keep communications to a minimum until he got a better sense of Texas.

As Tex explained, he had gone a different route with things. At first, it'd been standard Project Hometown: he'd begun to gather everyone at Fort Hood, trying to set up an interim government. But after finding out that Greeley was on the hunt for Coordinators that weren't toeing the line with President Briggs, he decided that a more guerilla-style approach suited Texas better.

They'd dispersed. Around a thousand former soldiers, airmen, and Texas National Guardsmen. And another thousand civilians that were able to keep up. The Texas Coalition consisted of ten outposts, spread out around the northern half of Texas and into the panhandle.

Their philosophy was "Small, light, mobile."

So far, it had worked. They'd stayed alive and combat effective, despite the fact that Texas was a triple-decker shit sandwich of war fronts: Greeley's growing influence to the north; the *Nuevas Fronteras* cartel pushing up from the south; and the constant war with the infected, which were everywhere.

"Anyway," Tex kept on. "Keeping our exposure low, we haven't put up barriers or anything. So we just have to stay very heads-up. And we pay for teepios killed. It's a bit of a subjective system. But you show me the bodies, you get food and medicine. Hence 'MREs for TPOs.'"

Lee looked across the cab at Abe. "Kinda makes me wish we'd done something like that in the UES." He thought about the posters that some of the civilians had posted on light poles in Fort Bragg—always depicting Lee as a mindless killer. It still rankled. "We got a lot of idiot civvies that need taking care of."

A frown creased Abe's dark brow, but he didn't say anything.

"Yeah, well," Tex said. "We don't have the luxury of taking care of people that aren't fighting. I'm not saying that we have it harder than y'all or anything. Just saying…the situation is different. We're at war. And a civilian-run government like what you got in the UES would have us all dead in a month. Maybe someday when we've made things safe enough for them, we can let the civvies take control again."

Abe shifted in his seat. It didn't escape Lee that he looked troubled.

Thompson suddenly jammed on the brakes.

The big pickup came skidding to a stop, their own cloud of dust rolling over them.

"Nine o'clock," was all Thompson said, before kicking his door open and dragging his rifle out from between the two front seats.

They were all out of the truck within a few seconds, all four pairs of eyes darting out to their left flank where a copse of trees clung to the top of a hill.

Thompson had his rifle up to his shoulder. "In the mesquite. See 'em?"

"Yup," Tex answered. He hadn't pulled his rifle up. He walked around the front of the truck, and Lee followed. The heat from the running engine gusted up at him.

The trees were three hundred yards out. Scraggly things, with just enough leaf to give shade. Lee didn't see them at first, but when he squinted against the bright sun, he caught the stir of movement in the shadows.

"Want me to peg 'em from here?" Thompson asked.

"How many are there?" Tex wondered.

Lee wished he had his scoped M14, but he'd come out with his lighter M4 today. All this open country around here was better suited to the bigger bullet of the M14.

"Five. Six, maybe," Thompson counted.

Tex stepped out from the tire trail now, into the knee-high prairie grass. He looked relaxed. Kept walking out, slow and steady. "Let's see if they won't come to us."

Abe looked unsure. "Be easier to hit them while they're sitting still."

"We start hitting them now, they might take off. They're smart enough. Until their blood gets up."

"There's four of us," Abe pressed. "We can take most of them out."

Tex didn't answer. Instead he waved one of his tattooed arms over his head and let out a high-pitched yelp.

There was an immediate reaction.

The shapes in the shadows stirred, two of them coming upright and, as though it was somehow pre-planned, one started cutting wide to the right, and one to the left. They were far away, but Lee saw how strange their almost-human shapes were when they went onto all fours and started wolf-trotting through the grass.

"There you go," Tex murmured to himself, and raised his rifle.

Lee hadn't noticed Deuce jump out of the truck, but the dog caught the scent in the air and started barking, right next to Lee's leg. He jolted at the sudden noise and almost kneed the dog out of pure reaction.

Tex looked over his shoulder at Deuce. "Yeah, boy. You keep calling to them."

The other shapes emerged from under the trees now. Four of them. Which made it six in total. The ones in the center spread out, while the ones on the flanks started to curve in.

"How close you wanna let them get?" Lee asked, tracking the one on the right flank, now about two hundred yards out, and closing fast.

He realized that his heart was slamming in his chest.

And he realized it was only half from fear. The other half was savage anticipation. He had the thought, in the middle of it all, that he and that primal at the other end of his rifle, they were probably feeling the same thing. They both sensed the destruction in the wind, like lightning in the air. And they both wanted it.

One wanted to feed its belly.

The other wanted a different type of satisfaction.

Tex's voice was muffled by the stock of the rifle pressed to his cheek. "Let them get close enough that they won't get away if they choose to hightail it."

Lee felt Deuce pressed against his leg. Felt the heat of the dog's body, the flanks heaving as he barked. He didn't bother telling Deuce to quiet down. It wouldn't do any good at this point—when the primals were this close, Deuce couldn't be reasoned with.

Lee kept tracking. That little red dot, dialed down as low as it could be seen in the bright daylight, leading that loping shape by about a foot. He couldn't see much of the primal. Just it's sun-tanned back, slipping through the grasses. Its eyes, locked onto Lee. Like no eyes that should be in a human face.

Breathing.

And tracking.

"Alright, hit 'em."

Lee fired.

Watched pink mist puff out behind the primal. It kept coming. Faster now, like the bullet had only spurred it.

He was peripherally aware of the other gunfire, but he was focused on his target, that surging, burning sensation in him. Primal in its own rights.

Lee fired again. Hit again. And this time the creature seemed to lose its momentum, but then it charged forward again. 5.56mm was a small round. And these were big, dangerous game.

It was closing fast.

Fifty yards.

Heart pounding.

More fear now.

Lee let loose. Three rounds, as fast as he could pull them. Two struck. The third plumed in the dirt behind the primal, but its legs went out from under it and it planted itself in the grasses and didn't get back up.

Lee pivoted. No more breathing. The air was trapped in his lungs now. He bore down on it, teeth clenched.

Another, much closer.

It was full-on towards Lee, racing at him like a bull. He saw its muscles rippling under its browned hide, the claws chewing up dirt, the wide, inhuman mouth hanging open. Lee fired, staring into that mouth, and that's where the rounds went, and knocked the base of its brain out the back of its skull.

It tumbled into the dirt twenty yards from him.

Lee scanned. Left. Right.

No one fired.

Everyone searched for another target, and didn't find one.

Lee let the air out of his lungs when they started to burn. Took in a steady breath. Purged the carbon dioxide out of him.

A tremble worked its way into his limbs. He clutched his rifle harder so it didn't show.

One by one, the four of them lowered their rifles.

The only sound was that of the pickup idling behind them.

Deuce had gone quiet, like he knew that it was over.

"Got 'em all?" Tex asked, his voice over-loud, despite the ringing in Lee's ears.

Lee glanced to his left at Tex. The man's lips trembled.

Thompson spat into the dirt. He let out a swear under his breath. He'd fired a lot. He took a second to swap his magazine out with a fresh one.

"Alright, let's clean 'em up," Tex said. "Thompson and Abe, start over there. Me and Lee'll start over here."

Thompson led Abe off to the left. Lee and Tex went right.

The one that had died within twenty yards of them was dead. No brain left in it to make the muscles move. It was a male. Young. Lee wasn't sure how young. Age was difficult to calculate with them. This one might've been born a primal.

The next they came to was the first one that Lee had shot. The one that wouldn't go down. And it was still kicking. It was older. Streaks of gray in the long, dreadlocked hair. This one had once been a man. But a bacteria had eaten away its frontal lobe three years ago, and it'd done something to it. Sparked off some evolutionary spurt. It wasn't a man anymore.

It pawed at the dirt and murmured, deep in its perforated chest.

Lee listened to it for a moment.

Tex seemed pensive. "What do you think it's saying?"

Lee jerked his head at Tex. For some reason he couldn't put his finger on, the question had caused his stomach to flip-flop. "They don't speak anymore, Tex."

He popped it in the head to put it out of its misery.

That was the most mercy Lee could afford.

They kept walking through the grass. Almost a full minute passed in silence.

Off to their left, Abe finished off another live one.

"I don't know about that," Tex said.

"About what?"

"I think they talk."

"You mean they communicate. Hoots and howls."

"No. I mean they talk." Tex glanced in Lee's direction, and then away. "Consonants. Vowels. Sounds that mean specific things. You know. Words."

Lee stared at the other man, but didn't say anything back.

The next one they found was dead.

That made three.

Tex called out to Thompson: "You got three dead?"

"Yeah."

"We got three. That's all six."

"Let's roll, then."

But Lee looked up the hill into the shadows of those mesquite trees. The thin, scraggly limbs, tracing every which way. The way the shade seemed black when compared to the blazing sun around them.

He looked back to the truck, and saw Deuce, pacing anxious circles around the pickup. The dog hadn't followed them into the grass.

He turned, and started towards the copse of mesquite. "Just gonna take a look in there," Lee said. "Come back me up."

Tex only hesitated for a moment, like he couldn't see the point in it, but he shrugged and started after Lee. He shot a glance over at Thompson and Abe and nodded towards the copse at the top of the hill. Thompson and Abe started toward it as well.

Lee listened as he approached the trees. He moved steadily through the grass, his feet rustling through the dry thatch. He held his rifle at a low ready. Looked out over top of his sights, into the shadows that grew before him. The thought that he might be acting strange didn't occur to him.

He stopped at the very edge of the trees. The sun was high enough at that moment that the shadows didn't stretch out very far. Once you were in the shadows, you were in the trees.

Standing close to them, some of the darkness had dissipated. He could see into it now. The shade and the carpet of leaves kept the ground mulched and clear. There was some brush grown up, but not much. And it had a trampled appearance.

He had a flash of memory.

Deer hunting with his father when he was young.

Going through a field of waist-high grasses, and finding the collection of small depressions where warm bodies had curled in upon themselves all night. He remembered his dad looking it over with a knowing eye and gesturing to it.

"This is a bedding area," his dad had said. "You can see where they slept."

The trampled brush in the shade of the mesquite had the same look to it.

Lee stepped into the thicket, and Tex followed.

There were some boulders. The scraggly mesquite had grown up around them, and through the cracks. It was behind one of these boulders that Lee found it.

It yowled at him when he cleared the back of the rock and saw it. The noise sparked a surge of adrenaline that set his heart thudding in his chest again and he brought his rifle up to his cheek. The little red dot on his optic hovering there on a small, skinny chest.

It couldn't have been more than two feet tall if it had stood up. But it was crouched down, and backed up into a corner created by the hollow of a rock and a trunk of mesquite. Where pudgy, toddler's fingers should have been, the fingers were elongated, and clutched reflexively in the moldering leaves and dirt. Where baby fat should have been, there was only skin stretched taut across abnormally developed cords of muscle. Where a child's face might have existed in another world, a gaping mouth slavered and spat and snapped at the air. Wild eyes, with not a drop of humanity in them.

Within ten yards, you had to account for sight over bore, which was about two inches. So Lee put the dot on the top of the juvenile's head, right where a dim hairline was sprouting, and fired one round through its brain.

The thing slumped in place. One hand made a last scratch at the dirt. But that was it.

The other three padded up quickly behind him to see what he'd fired at.

"Damn," Tex breathed, after a moment. "Lookit that."

"You ever dealt with juveniles before?" Lee asked him.

"Yeah. But I never seen one that young."

"Couple weeks ago we bagged a juvenile," Lee said. "Brought it back to our doctor in Bragg for an autopsy." Lee recalled the information he'd received from his last satphone contact with Fort Bragg. "It was female. Bit bigger than this one. Doc said she was menstruating already." Lee gestured at the small, deceased form. "Another year, this one would be hunting. And mating."

"That fast, huh?"

Lee nodded. "We don't know for sure, but we're guessing that at two years they're dangerous. And procreating. Maybe full grown by three years."

Thompson made an unhappy noise. "That's not encouraging."

"All the more reason to hunt them out," Tex said. "Come on. We're expected in OP Elbert."

FIVE

PEER PRESSURE

SAM RYDER WAS NOT AN IDIOT.

Before the end of the world, he'd been a smart kid. His father had hammered him on math and science, believing—no, *insisting*—that Sam was going to be a doctor one day. Only straight A's for the kid that had once been known as Sameer Balawi.

Through the end of the world, Sam had become more than book smart. He'd become savvy.

Smart and savvy.

Not an idiot at all.

But if there was one thing that could lay utter waste to any young man's smarts and savvy, it was sex—or at least the never-ending, never-reached promise of it. The female form like a curl of smoke in the back of your mind, befuddling your thoughts, always so close, and yet far away.

Like a Will-o'-the-Wisp, leading you deeper and deeper into the bog of your own stupidity.

Not being an idiot by nature, Sam had discovered that he wasn't looking at his relationship with Charlie very objectively. Objectivity usually didn't occur until an hour or so after their meetings, at which point he would frown and consider everything that happened in the stark, cold light of *not being horny*.

There was a common thread to their meetings, Sam had discovered, though it hurt his young man's ego to admit it—because every young man wants to believe that the girl he loves is just as eager to jump his bones as he is hers.

The common thread was this: Charlie had a lot of questions, and not a lot of lovin'.

When she mined his head for gossip, her eyes shone bright and focused.

When they necked afterward, she became limp and disinterested, but she let Sam do his thing, until of course he tried to reach into her pants, at which point she said she didn't want to go that far, and, almost with relief, used that as an excuse to terminate their time together.

At first, Sam told himself he was just being a little bitch about it, because he wasn't getting what he wanted. He was manufacturing some big conflict, when in fact it was just that Charlie had the decency to put a stop to him when he wasn't controlling himself.

Gradually, over several nights of pensive guard shifts spent stalking the high voltage fences around Fort Bragg, Sam had realized there could be only one real explanation for Charlie's behavior.

She was more interested in asking him questions than getting physical.

So, this time around, he played the game her way.

This all made him feel like an insecure and manipulative boyfriend trope, but then he couldn't quite get rid of the warning bells in his head that had been chiming—very quietly—ever since he'd come to this realization.

They met by the Community Center, which was normal. Then they walked along paths, while they talked. Or, more correctly: she asked him questions and he answered them.

It was interesting. In the light of his new understanding, she didn't seem to want to be there with him at all. It became obvious to him that her smiles never reached her eyes, and her saccharine words weren't sincere. These observations hit him like body blows from a heavyweight boxer.

He'd kind of been hoping he *was* the insecure boyfriend, and that it was all in his head.

With a little more clarity, he also noted that she asked a lot of questions about Lee.

What was Lee doing?

Who was Lee with?

Where was Lee right at that moment?

"Why're you so concerned with Lee?" Sam couldn't help asking.

Charlie looked briefly surprised. But then she smiled at him and said, "You know how it is, Sam. He's the hero around here. *Everyone* wants to know what he's doing."

Sam held eye contact with her longer than was necessary, and he knew that her smile was fake. Time and time again she'd dazzled him with that smile and he'd been fooled by it. But now it was like that optical illusion where the drawing is both a beautiful young woman, and a haggard old lady— once you've seen the trick, it can't be unseen.

They made some perfunctory small talk.

They stopped in a quiet section of woods where they traditionally did some of their making out. Charlie seemed to be steeling herself. This didn't escape Sam—once again, he couldn't unsee it. And, frankly, it hurt.

"Well," he said, looking away from her. "I better head on."

She looked surprised again. And…relieved.

"Oh?" she asked, which was a safe way to answer. Neither encouraging him to stay, nor pushing him away.

"Yeah," he mumbled, feeling his heart sink. "I got guard duty tonight. Need to get some sleep. Been running a little ragged."

Charlie nodded. "Okay then. Don't let me stop you. You need your sleep."

He nodded back. Forced a smile.

She gave him a little goodbye wave, and then started off through the woods.

Sam turned and headed back the way he'd come.

About twenty yards down the path, he ducked behind a thick pine and he waited for a moment. Until the sound of her footsteps could barely be heard. Then he peeked out from behind the tree, and barely caught the flash of the tan overalls she wore for work, disappearing into the trees.

He stepped out and quietly followed.

***

Charlie went through the woods in the usual direction until she could no longer hear Sam's footsteps, and then she cut through the woods towards the customary meeting spot.

These woods had a lot of customary spots. Charlie thought of them as checkpoints. Checkpoint One was meeting Sam at the Community Center. Checkpoint Two was the spot that she usually let him clumsily make out with her until she finally put a stop to it. Then he went his way, and she went hers, and the last stop she would make would be Checkpoint Three, here in the middle of the woods, off the path, where Claire Staley would be waiting for her.

Claire wore her usual work attire. She was Angela's secretary, so it was generally something in the realm of business casual. Angela liked to wear jeans to work, so Claire had figured it was okay for her to do the same, though she would don a gray women's blazer to make her look more professional. And it covered the .38 snub nose she kept tucked in her waistband.

Charlie also wore work attire, but since she worked with farm animals, it was always the same pair of tan Carhartts.

Claire had her hands in her jacket pockets. Her intense green eyes marked Charlie's face with interest. "What? No making out this time?"

Charlie frowned. "How…?"

"Usually your lips are all flushed and plump." Claire smirked. "Made a clean getaway this time?"

Charlie touched her lips absently. "Yeah. He said he needed to get some sleep."

Claire seemed to consider this seriously. "You think he's losing interest in you?"

Charlie fidgeted. She didn't want Sam, but somehow the prospect of him not wanting *her* was irritating. "I don't know," she admitted.

"Well." Claire considered the trees around them. "Perhaps it's time to seal the deal."

"What?" Charlie gaped. "You mean have sex with him?"

Claire shrugged one, noncommittal shoulder. "Men are easy marks, Charlie. It might behoove you to get a little more serious about what you're doing here."

"I thought you said I didn't need to do that."

"That was then. This is now." Claire sighed. "It's just business, Charlie. Don't get all wound up. Think of it like a well: You have to keep the pump primed. Sometimes that just takes a little more effort."

"I'm not having sex with him."

"Then maybe your usefulness has run its course."

Charlie was wholly offended. "Hey! I've done good work!"

"You have. I'm not saying you haven't." Claire's eyebrows cinched down. "But if you let Sam lose interest in you, then we lose a very valuable potential asset. And then what do I have for you to do? Not a whole lot, Charlie. Sam is your job right now. It's your job to keep the information flowing."

Charlie pouted. Crossed her arms.

Claire rolled her eyes and seemed to let it go. "What did he have for you today?"

"Not much," Charlie admitted.

"Does he know where Lee is?"

"No."

"Does he know what Lee's doing?"

"I don't think he knows shit."

"Does he not know, or is he no longer willing to tell you?"

Charlie glared.

Claire grew stern. "It's a serious question, Charlie. Remember what I told you?"

"That I need to grow up?" Charlie snapped.

"Yeah," Claire nodded. "This isn't about your girlish pride or the sanctity of your pussy." Claire jabbed a finger in the air. "This is about *information*. This is about *war*. And I'm not going to lose an edge—I'm not going to lose an insider in Angela's house—because you're too damn high and mighty to put out."

"Why don't *you* fuck him then?"

Claire seemed to genuinely consider it. She put her hands back in her pockets. Looked away into the woods again. "I've done plenty to get what I need. I'd do that too, if it was necessary. Do you want to continue to be useful to the cause, Charlie?"

"Yes," Charlie answered, without hesitation.

Claire smiled, and it seemed genuine. "I believe you. And maybe you're right. Maybe he was just tired today. Maybe you just keep doing what you're doing and see what happens. But I need to know that you'll do whatever you need to do to keep the information flowing."

"Fine," Charlie said, sullenly. "I'll keep it in mind."

Claire reached out and touched Charlie on the shoulder. "History is going to remember what we did, Charlie. They're going to remember what we sacrificed to make this country whole again."

***

Sam watched from fifty yards away, crouched low at the base of a tree.

A line of ants marched through the flaky chunks of pine bark, but Sam didn't see them.

All he saw was Charlie and Claire.

He couldn't hear what they said. Only the murmur of their voices, and a few odd words here and there. Charlie seemed pissed. Claire kept looking around, as though she didn't want anyone to know that she and Charlie were meeting.

After a brief but heated exchange, the two young women parted ways, and then it was just Sam in those woods, and he sat there on his knees for a while, thinking.

Charlie and Claire.

Claire and Charlie.

Charlie, asking so many questions.

Then meeting with Claire.

Claire, at the house out beyond the wire with a bunch of drunk teenagers.

Claire, showing up in Angela's office while there were primals loose in Fort Bragg. She showed up to help, but what had she done? She'd hovered near to Marie while Marie had a quiet conversation with Lee on the satphone. She'd taken the satphone back down to the Watch Commander afterwards.

He remembered all of this, but it still felt disjointed in his mind. The connection between all of these memories wasn't there.

Or maybe he just didn't want to admit to himself what was really going on.

After about ten minutes, he rose up from his position, and left the woods, telling himself, *They're just friends. Charlie and Claire. Girlfriends. Swapping gossip.*

Except they hadn't looked very friendly to him.

And whatever they were swapping looked much more serious than gossip.

***

Sam swung by The Barn because there wasn't anywhere else to go, and he didn't feel like sleeping just yet.

The Barn was a big building they used as a home base for all the active troops in Bragg, including the guards, of which Sam was one. This was where his roll call was. This was where they housed the vehicles, and handed out the weapons from the armory, and generally kept all their day-to-day military admin stuff for keeping the Fort Bragg Safe Zone *relatively safe.*

There was a stir over by the First Sergeant's office. He wasn't in, but there was a cluster of young soldiers outside of his door, looking at something on the corkboard like high school students checking their posted test scores.

A lot of the "soldiers" weren't original US military. They ranged in age from fifteen to twenty, and a lot of them had signed up after the Fort Bragg Safe Zone had been established, just like Sam had. There was always a need for young men to do stupid, dangerous shit because young men don't believe they can die.

Sam was well aware of his mortality. But he'd signed up like everyone else because…that was the thing to do.

Peer pressure and all that.

They'd all received an abbreviated form of Basic Training, and an even more abbreviated form of Infantry AIT. The Old Heads (the ones that were actual soldiers before the world went to shit) scoffed and turned up their noses at all these young "half-boots," but Sam had still thought the training was pretty hard.

In reality, although abbreviated, the training had been harsher than was typical back in the day. None of the Old Heads would admit this, but the drill instructors that had run the thing—and still did augmentative classes every so often—disliked the half-boots, and made sure to take it out on them in training. And there was much less overview than there used to be, and almost zero backlash if some young half-boot got rolled down a flight of stairs in his footlocker for being a fat, lazy shit that couldn't make the run time.

The civilian populace didn't waste energy getting up in arms about it like they used to when getting up in arms about things was the national pastime. Nowadays they all figured the world was harsher than it had been, so it only stood to reason that the military training should be harsher too.

Sam had never received the footlocker treatment—he was good at PT, and he followed orders and mostly kept his mouth shut—but he remembered a few guys that had. They'd gone silently to the medical center to have their broken arms casted, and then they recycled through to the next class. Now they laughed about the time they took a trip downstairs in the "thinking box."

Sam nudged his way into the scrum of young men, some in ACUs, some in MultiCam. He found a familiar face and parked himself there.

"What's this?" Sam asked.

Private Gomez nodded towards the corkboard, where Sam now saw a clipboard had been placed, and the half-boots (and a few Old Heads) were taking turns going up to it and scribbling something on it with the pen that hung from the clipboard on a piece of string.

"Sign-up sheet," Gomez said.

"For what?"

"For huntin' primals, bro." Gomez smiled. "Since we got fuel now, they're reinstating the hunt-and-kill ops. Apparently they've been out tagging these motherfuckers with a tracker or something. Gonna track 'em down and snuff 'em out."

"Oh."

They shuffled forward a few paces, the crowd forming itself into something of a line.

"Are you signing up?" Sam asked.

"Fuck yeah, I'm signing up," Gomez said.

"You know any details about it?"

"Yeah." Gomez shot Sam an insolent look. "Gonna kill primals. What else you need to know about it?"

Sam shrugged.

The line continued to move forward.

Sam guessed he was in line now.

If the sign-up sheet had come out two weeks ago, before Sam had started to think that maybe his relationship with Charlie was more one-sided than she let on, he probably would have taken a pass.

But now he felt like he needed to do something dangerous. Very suddenly, the idea of not seeing Charlie again seemed more like a relief than anything else. And going off to do something life-threatening felt like it had an added element of "screw you" to it, that, in that particular moment, felt right to him.

Like he might prove something.

And then he thought of Abby, sitting in a hospital room, still waiting to see if the white blood cells in her body were going to start raging, still waiting to see if that bite from the primal was going to infect her. And he thought of Sergeant Hauer, being dragged underneath a car, screaming as he was eaten alive...

And then it felt like he was *supposed* to do this.

Gomez scrawled his name on the sign-up sheet.

Sam had already made up his mind at that point, but even if he hadn't, with everyone watching, he would've done it anyway. Peer pressure and all that.

SIX

PALE HORSE

HE STOOD AT THE TOP of the refinery and looked northward.

Beneath his feet, machinery rattled and rumbled, and crude oil was turned into fuel. A substance that was more valuable than gold had ever been in any distant time. It was liquid power. And it belonged to him.

The sea was at his back, five miles distant. Just a tiny glimmer of sunlight on water. But it was not the sea that held his destiny. It was everything that stretched out before him to the north.

An endless Promised Land magnitudes larger than the patch of desert the Jews had fought for.

His own people had wandered in a desert of sorts, for far longer than forty years. And now Mateo Ibarra Espinoza had breached the defenses of the Canaanites, and brought his people across the border to finally take what was owed to them.

He didn't indulge in melodrama, but the comparison made him smile nonetheless. He enjoyed it when history proved itself to be a wheel. It gave him a sense of control. It made the future less nebulous, because if he wanted to know the future, all he needed to do was look into the past.

The southwind blew at Mateo's back, whipping his loose-fitting *guayabera* and causing strands of his long black hair to tickle his face. The wind smelled of Louisiana salt marshes. But it also smelled of Mateo's home state of Nuevo Leon. These two places were not so different.

"I like having the sea at my back," Mateo said, loud enough to be heard over the buffeting wind. He spoke English, because the man standing on the platform with him was an American, and that was all he understood.

Mateo turned with a faint smile, allowing the wind to clear the hair out of his face. "It reminds me of Hernan Cortez."

The American on the platform with him was a decent-sized man of maybe forty years. His light brown hair was going gray, and there were streaks of white in his very macho, horseshoe mustache. A mustache that seemed incongruous on a face with so much fear in it.

The man would not even make eye contact with Mateo. He stared off into the distance, like a soldier at parade rest. Perhaps out of some misguided sense of respect.

There was no one else on the platform with them.

Mateo had come up in an organization run by tough guys who were only tough when they were surrounded by their bodyguards. This had always struck Mateo as ludicrous. He was either on the path of destiny, in which case, no one could stop him, or he was against destiny, and someone stronger than him would kill him and take the reigns.

Mateo spoke as he approached the man, the heels of his fine leather boots clicking on the concrete deck of the platform. "When Cortez arrived in the New World with his conquistadors, he burned the boats so that it was clear to his men that there was no turning back. The only way was forward. And then six hundred men conquered an empire."

He now stood within arm's reach of the other man, and he stopped there. "That's why I like the sea at my back." He gestured out to the north. "All of that is for us. We can conquer it, but only if we recognize that there is no turning back."

The man in front of him gave a shaky nod.

Sweat glistened at his hairline.

Mateo quirked an eyebrow. "Joseph, do you think I'm going to kill you?"

A tremble ran through the other man's features. His mouth opened, and worked like a fish out of water.

Mateo was aware that Joseph was bigger and stronger than him. And yet, Joseph was terrified, and Mateo was at peace. Mateo found this fascinating.

"If I were to take ahold of you and try to throw you off this platform, would you fight back?"

Finally, Joseph's nervous eyes flicked down to Mateo's calm gaze. Mateo could see the man trying to figure out whether this was a trick question or not.

It wasn't. Mateo was simply curious.

Mateo smiled to break the tension. "Relax, Joseph. You're acting like a *puta*."

Joseph tittered, and a shaky smile flitted across his mouth for a moment.

Mateo clasped his hands in front of him. "You ever read Sun Tzu?"

Joseph shook his head. "No."

Mateo shrugged. "Don't bother. It's mostly bullshit. But there was a good lesson on command that I remember. Sun Tzu was displaying his prowess as a general to the emperor, and he said he could make the emperor's geishas march like soldiers. So he told the geishas how to march. But when he ordered them to do it, they just laughed at him. Sun Tzu did not take offense. He told the emperor, 'If the orders are not clear, then it is the fault of the general if they are not obeyed.' Then he had his soldiers demonstrate to the geishas exactly how to march, and asked the geishas if they now understood exactly what they were supposed to do. They said that they understood, so he ordered them to march. Again they laughed. Sun Tzu then told the emperor, 'If the orders are clear, and still not obeyed, then the soldiers must be executed.'" Mateo laughed.

Joseph blanched at the mention of execution.

"I believe the emperor stopped Sun Tzu before he could behead the geishas. Or something like that." Mateo waved it off. "My point is this: I ordered you to oversee the transfer of fuel to President Briggs in Colorado. And what happened to that convoy?"

Joseph swallowed. "The convoy was ambushed. Sir."

Mateo nodded. "And we lost all the fuel, didn't we?"

"Yes, sir."

"Yes." Mateo sighed. "Perhaps my orders were not specific enough. So perhaps the responsibility lies on my shoulders as commander. Do you think that is the case?"

Joseph gaped. Again fearing a trick question.

Mateo's eyes flashed with irritation. "Have the *cajones* to answer the question, Joseph. If it was my fault, then tell me so. Otherwise it was your fault and you must be executed."

Joseph blinked. "Your orders weren't clear. Sir."

Mateo took a deep breath. Pressed it out of his lungs. Nodded again. "You are right. Thank you. It is not enough for me to suppose that my soldiers will somehow intuit exactly what I want for them. That is bad leadership. So I'm going to give you new orders."

He stepped up close to Joseph, so that he could lower his voice and still be heard over the wind whipping across the platform. "You are going to organize a new convoy. President Briggs still needs his fuel, and he still has value to me as an ally. I want another twenty-one thousand gallons sent—fourteen thousand of jet fuel, and seven thousand of diesel. And I want you to personally make sure that this convoy reaches Greeley, Colorado, no matter what. Do you understand the orders that I'm giving you?"

"Yes, sir," Joseph said without hesitation.

Mateo thought a more intelligent man might've asked some clarifying questions, given the stakes involved. But Joseph was eager for the meeting to be over, and Mateo could understand that.

Mateo favored his man with a smile. Held up a finger. "So if the fuel does not get to Greeley for whatever reason, and turned over into the hands of President Briggs, then you understand that I will take your wife and your daughter and your son and I will force you to watch as I burn them alive? And then I will burn you alive, as well?"

Joseph's entire body shook.

Mateo watched him, and couldn't help feeling a sense of disdain for the man. He reconsidered throwing him off the platform anyways, and almost did it. But some of his best lieutenants had been formed by allowing them a second chance. They worked very hard when they finally understood and accepted what was at stake.

Their backs were to the sea.

The only way was forward.

Perhaps Joseph would make a good lieutenant yet.

"I understand," Joseph said, finally.

"Good." Mateo reached up to Joseph, and the man flinched as Mateo's hand took him by the side of the head...and gave him a gentle pat. "See that it gets done."

***

Mateo remained on the platform after Joseph had left.

He stood against the railing, staring out at the land that fate was going to deliver into his hands. But he didn't see it. In his mind's eye, he saw the convoy, and he saw where they had been ambushed, and he saw who it was that had ambushed them.

Captain Terrance Lehy. Mateo was sure of that.

Mateo understood that Captain Lehy had been one of these "Coordinators," one of the soldiers that the United States government had left behind with access to bunkers full of supplies, and a mission to rebuild American society if it were to fall.

Which it had. As all empires eventually fall.

Mateo had spent his life waiting for it, a barbarian at the gates of Rome, waiting for the disease of weakness to soften his target. All of Mateo's life had led to this point, right here, standing on a refinery platform and looking out over the territory that he had claimed for himself.

Captain Lehy had been a thorn in his side since day one.

He'd disrupted their operations, fighting a guerilla war all across Texas, and making every mile a hard-fought one. Mateo had grudging respect for Captain Lehy, and he did not underestimate the man.

But now two instances had been brought to light that revealed something about Captain Lehy. Something that, at the surface, seemed to make him a more daunting adversary, but, upon further inspection, could also be a weakness that Mateo might exploit.

The previous week, Mateo had been informed of an imminent raid on a fuel cache in Alabama—one of the states that *Nuevas Fronteras* owned only by a thread. Mateo had dispatched a large contingent of his men to thwart the commandos from the United Eastern States that were carrying out the raid on his fuel cache.

Only a handful of the men he'd dispatched had made it back.

Somehow, miraculously, Captain Lehy had appeared with a tank and delivered a catastrophic counter attack.

But…perhaps it wasn't so miraculous.

Today, Captain Lehy had executed another raid. This time on a convoy that no one but *Nuevas Fronteras* and Greeley should have known about.

Which meant that Captain Lehy was either incredibly lucky…

Or someone was feeding him information.

Mateo pondered this for a while. The wind in his ears created a white noise that made it easy for him to think. And after a time, he came to his decision. And Mateo never second-guessed his decisions.

Once it was made, he descended the stairs from the platform, and entered the offices of the refinery where his headquarters now sat. He found his second-in-command at a table in an old break room with a vending machine that had long since been emptied.

Joaquin Lazcano Leyva was playing *conquian* with two other lieutenants. He laid his cards down immediately when Mateo entered the room, knowing that Mateo wanted him for something.

Mateo motioned him out of the room, and he followed. When they were in the hall outside, Mateo put his arm around Joaquin's shoulder with brotherly affection, and spoke in Spanish. "I have something I need you to do."

***

Carl arrived in Fort Bragg midmorning.

They rolled in through the main gates. The guard towers bristled with weaponry. The fences shimmered with high voltage wires. Dust plumed up behind the convoy of vehicles: One white Ford F-150 that looked like it'd been through the ringer, followed by four tanker trunks, and a Humvee taking up the rear.

The gates shut quickly behind them, barring the predatory world outside.

Carl was in the front passenger's seat of the F-150. The sun glinted into his face. He squinted against it. His mouth was downturned at the corners.

He was still not fully healed. Doubted his busted ribs would be good to go for several weeks yet, especially after the stress he'd put them through at the airport. Unconsciously, he found his right arm constantly cinching into his right side, to protect the damage there.

He'd also taken a bullet to the leg. Luckily, just a hole in the meat. Hurt like hell, but he'd been shot before. He could manage.

Despite getting shot up, the operation at the airport in Alabama had been a success, and a portion of the spoils of the raid were riding into Fort Bragg with him. They'd captured twelve tankers in all. Four stayed in the Butler Safe Zone in Georgia. Four came back to Fort Bragg with Carl.

The other four went with Lee, Abe, and Julia, into Texas.

The 28,000 gallons of fuel that Carl brought back with him would get the farming operations started again. They'd be able to secure all thirty fields with high voltage wire, and then they'd be able to plant, and harvest what they planted.

That was all fine and dandy.

But farming wasn't what Carl was here for.

Carl was here for blood.

Someone in the Fort Bragg Safe Zone had sold them down the river.

Someone had been talking with Greeley, Colorado.

Whoever that leak was, they had cost the lives of some of Carl's friends.

And Carl was not a man that had many friends to begin with.

Passing over those streets, into the center of the Safe Zone, Carl looked out and he saw filth. Oh, it looked nice enough. These neighborhood streets where people lived in safety, with food to eat, and electric lighting, and running water. All these cozy civilians.

But he saw treachery lurking in them like infection in a limb.

He meant to cut it out.

How many of these people were Lincolnists? How many of them sided with Elsie Foster? How many of them wanted to watch the Fort Bragg Safe Zone fall apart, and the entire United Eastern States crumble, and President Briggs from Greeley, Colorado come riding in on a white charger?

It'd be hard to root them all out.

Carl was about to turn on the lights, and he knew the cockroaches would scatter.

"Drop me at the Support Center," Carl said.

Mitch, in the driver's seat, nodded.

In the back, Rudy, Morrow, and Logan—Carl's team—remained as silent as they had the whole way back.

The white pickup separated from the convoy, and plunged straight into the heart of Fort Bragg. And Carl thought that the color of the pickup was fitting for him.

Some people around here might be waiting for a hero on a white charger.

But they were going to have to accept death on a pale horse instead.

***

Angela was expecting him.

She'd heard him coming through the command-net radio that sat on her desk, but besides that—and perhaps what had filled her with a sense of unease—she kept a civilian-band radio on her desk as well. It was there to monitor emergencies, but as the convoy bearing Carl Gilliard passed through Fort Bragg, she heard various transmissions, civilian-to-civilian. Some of them in awe. Some of them hostile.

Eventually she'd shut the civilian radio off, unable to take the combination of bitter speculation and hero worship.

Now she watched from the window of her office, as the dirty, white pickup rolled up to the front of the Soldier Support Center. It looked worse than it had when it had left Fort Bragg the week before. The front brush guard was dented. The windshield cracked. Sprays of mud and dirt coated the sides in ochre.

The passenger door opened.

Master Sergeant Carl Gilliard stepped out.

His bald head looked sunburned. He wore combat pants and shirt. The shirt untucked, and unzipped down to the center of his chest, revealing a white strip of bandaging underneath. He wore only a sidearm. He looked tired as hell, and beat up. He with his right arm hovering protectively at his side, and his left leg stiff and unwieldy.

But then Carl closed his pickup door and he turned, and he looked right up at Angela.

And she saw that he had hellfire burning in his eyes.

Angela nodded down to him. And he nodded up at her.

The pickup drove off, and Carl walked into the front doors of the Support Center.

Angela turned away from the window. Her hands hung at her sides. She took a big breath and steeled herself for the conversation to come.

Angela wasn't sure who had occupied her office before the end of society, but it was spacious, so they must have been somewhat important. The far side of the office, near the door, was big enough for a rug and two chairs. Her side of the office, near the window, held her desk. On the desk was a plaque, and it said President Angela Houston.

A title she still couldn't get used to.

It hung on her like an adult's clothes on a girl playing dress-up.

She sat down behind her desk. Then decided that seemed too casual and stood up again. She ran a hand over the top of her curly blonde hair. She kept it in a plain pony tail, but it had always been unruly—moreso now that she didn't have a cache of beauty products to tame it with. She felt no flyaways, though. So she had that going for her.

Did natural-born leaders just have an instinct for how to appear when someone came in the room? Or was she putting too much thought into this? At the end of the day, she was the elected leader of the United Eastern States. And as ridiculous as that was to her, that meant she had the authority to put the leash on Carl. It didn't matter how she presented herself.

Confidence. You need to just have confidence.

There was a knock at the door.

Claire Staley opened it and looked in at Angela. "Master Sergeant Gilliard, ma'am."

Angela nodded, and Claire stepped back from the doorway, and Carl stepped in.

The door closed behind him.

He limped to the front of her desk. Eyes up. Head back. He stopped about a pace off of Angela's desk.

Angela looked at him with genuine concern. "Jesus, Carl. What happened to you?"

"Nothing that won't heal."

She gestured to one of the chairs across from her. "Please, sit."

"I've been sitting for five hours. I'd just as soon work the stiffness out, if you don't mind."

Angela smiled graciously. "I don't mind at all."

Still, she saw a shimmer of sweat breaking out on Carl's forehead.

Angela decided to walk around to Carl's side of the desk. She didn't want to appear like she was hiding behind it. "You need some water or anything? Have you had anything to eat?"

Carl nodded. "I have. I'm fine."

"Alright." Angela tapped her fingertips on the desk. "Look. Carl. I know you don't like beating around the bush and I'm sure you want to get right to the point..."

"That'd be ideal."

A breath. "But I'm going to tell you that I'm glad you and your boys are back. And I'm sorry for your losses. *Our* losses. I didn't know Tomlin and

Blake and Nate like you did. But we're all reeling here."

It sounded like something a politician would say, and she immediately hated it.

She wasn't lying. She *was* reeling. But she'd spent so much time over the last two days deadening herself to everything that had happened, all the shit that had been wrought, that now when she spoke of it her voice had a far-off and impersonal tone to it.

"How is Abby?" Carl asked, ignoring her condolences.

Yet another thing that Angela had been trying to deaden herself to. Except that you can't deaden yourself to your own kid. A mother's brain simply doesn't work like that.

"She's..." Angela felt a tremor move across her face. "...I think she's going to be okay."

"That's good." Carl frowned. "Didn't she get bitten? I'm not trying to pry, Angela. But it has some consequence to everybody."

Angela nodded. "She was bitten in the leg. By a primal."

"And she didn't get infected?"

"No." Angela swallowed. "Or...or it hasn't presented yet."

"It's been two days. It would have if it was going to."

Angela knew that that was as close to comforting as Carl Gilliard would ever be. "Thank you. We have a lot of hope."

"Any idea how the primals got in?"

"It wasn't the Lincolnists," Angela said, maybe a little too quickly. "They got in through the drain pipe near MacFayden Pond."

"I'm aware of that pipe. We padlocked it years ago."

"Well...someone cut the padlock."

"And who do you think that would be?"

Angela took a deep breath through her nose. "Carl, I'm glad you're back. We need you here. We need you to continue your investigation into the Lincolnists. We need to solve this problem so we can be civilized around here again." She held up a finger. "But we're going to do it the right way."

Carl quirked an eyebrow, his cold, gray eyes evaluating her. "What way is that?"

"Legally."

"There's no such thing, ma'am. No such thing as due process anymore. There's just common law. Things that we all agree to as a society. Such as not trying to assassinate the elected leader. Such as not letting primals in the wire just to cause chaos."

Angela knew that Carl was going to be like this. She'd prepared herself for it. But she still felt a surge of anger. And a measure of fear that went along with it.

"Well," she said. "Maybe we should start thinking about laying down some laws."

"Ms. Houston," Carl lowered his head. "Now would be the wrong time to put shackles on me."

"No one's putting shackles on you."

"Restraint is not the answer. We tried restraint. And the Lincolnists have only used it against us. We tried to give them the benefit of the doubt. And they turned around and tried to kill you."

Angela felt her pulse elevating. "If we handle this too harshly, we run the risk of creating a bigger rift in our community. I don't want a civil war."

"I think you already have one."

Angela's face flushed. "You want to speak plainly, let's speak plainly. Cards on the table. I'm not asking you to be restrained. I'm telling you. You *will* act like there is still a goddamned constitution. You *will* treat these people like they still have rights."

"Alright," Carl said. "Cards on the table. This isn't a civil issue, Angela. This is war. There's a leak in Fort Bragg, and they are somehow getting information to Greeley, Colorado. That information led to the deaths of Tomlin, Nate, and Blake. Whoever is leaking that information is in bed with the Lincolnists. And that means the Lincolnists are in bed with President Briggs. They want to see you dead, and they want to see the UES burn. That makes them spies of an enemy. And that means they don't have rights."

Angela had to clasp her hands together to keep them from trembling. She wasn't scared of Carl. She knew that he would never harm her. But she was scared of what he might do. And infuriated by the pushback she was getting.

Time to try a different tack.

"Do you know why Abe Darabie deserted from President Briggs?" she asked. Forcing her tone to be level.

Carl didn't answer. He just watched her with his icy gaze.

"President Briggs was starving people in Greeley for dissenting. If they disagreed with him, they didn't get any food. And when he realized that Abe knew about it, you know what he said? He told Abe that in order to rebuild a civilized society, they couldn't be democratic. In order to make the country safe enough to harbor democracy again, they had to be a dictatorship."

Angela jabbed a finger in a general westward direction. "That is the enemy. That is what he is doing to his people. That is why we seceded in the first damn place. I'm not going to copy his methods, Carl. I'm not going to be a dictator. Fighting fire with fire just leaves everything burned."

Carl considered this for a moment. His eyes strayed from Angela's and looked out the window. Looked out at the view of Fort Bragg. The view of everything they were trying to build.

"Do you know where that phrase comes from?" Carl asked. "Fighting fire with fire?"

Angela didn't.

"Settlers would do controlled burns of the grasslands around them when a grassfire started up nearby. They'd carefully burn the flammable materials around them, so that when the grassfire reached them it wouldn't engulf everything they'd worked so hard to build."

Carl took in a long, heavy breath. Dragged his eyes back to Angela. "You're in charge, ma'am. I'm not going to buck your leadership. If you want restraint, I'll do my level best. I just want to be sure that you know there's a fire coming. And if we don't do everything we can to stop it, it will consume us."

"We're going to do everything we can, Carl." Angela softened. "I don't want to micromanage you. And I'm sure you don't want to be micromanaged. Will you give me your word that you will treat these people like they still have rights?"

Carl seemed tired. But she still saw that hatred in his eyes, and it worried her.

But he nodded. "You have my word, ma'am."

SEVEN

MORALS

You could've driven through Elbert and not known you'd been through the center of a town.

Thompson pulled the pickup into a dusty parking lot beside a tumble-down structure with an ancient rusted sign that declared it "Elbert Farm Store." With the exception of a few houses, a Quonset hut, and some grain silos, that was it.

"Welcome to Elbert," Tex said as they rolled to a halt. "Only town that grew in population since the plague."

"Yeah?" Lee squinted out into the bright, flat environment. He saw a single, battered farm truck, tucked back in some overgrown brush. The houses looked dark and unused. The only sign of human habitation came from the Quonset hut: a thin trail of gray smoke that lifted into the sky.

Tex kicked his door open. "Population was thirty back in the day. Now it's fifty."

"Quite a metropolis," Abe murmured as he stepped out.

Lee followed. They all closed their doors behind them.

In the hour that it had taken them to drive here, the temperature had risen. The sun was near its highest point, and the terrain around them seemed mostly sand that reflected the sharp sunlight, with some patches of green here and there.

The wind gusted along the street, stirring up man-sized dust devils.

Between gusts, Lee smelled the faint scent of cooking meat. "Aren't you worried about that smell drawing in primals—teepios?"

Tex didn't appear interested in moving. He stood at the front of the vehicle with his hands clasped on the buttstock of his slung rifle. He turned his head, and Lee saw his own reflection in the scratched-up surface of Tex's sunglasses.

"Well," Tex said. "It'd only give them more food to earn from us."

After a long moment waiting in the sun, the sound of a door opening reached Lee's ears.

Out of the Quonset hut came three men. One was a large, bearded man, with wild, curly hair. The two that trailed him looked like they might be his sons. They shared the same wild hair and the same broad faces, though their beards were not as prodigious as the man in the lead.

One of them dragged what looked like a large feed sack behind him.

Tex spoke quietly as they approached. "Just...like I said...be on your toes."

Lee had already given the three men a quick once-over for weapons. The two younger ones both had a rifle slung on their backs—one a deer rifle, and the other an AR. The big man in the lead had a black, semi-auto pistol on his hip. The pistol sat in an unsecured, neoprene holster that flopped around as the man walked.

There might be exceptions to the rule, but a man with a floppy neoprene holster was probably not a quick-draw expert.

"Captain Lehy," the big man said, as he reached them. He held out a massive paw, and Tex reached forward and gave it a single shake.

"Arnold," Tex said. "How's business?"

Arnold gave a large grin. "Oh, we're keepin' our heads above water. Speaking of, we could use some. Been drier than a popcorn fart."

"Your well not pumpin' anymore?" Tex inquired.

"Oh," Arnold waved him off. "She's pumpin' most of the time. I'm just bitchin'. Don't like the well water if I can help it—too much iron in the water. Gimme goddamn kidney stones. Prefer the rain catches, but we ain't had none." Arnold surveyed Lee and Abe with a suspicious glint. "Got some new hands, I see."

Tex didn't seem to want to introduce them, and that was fine by Lee. It didn't seem like Tex trusted these people much, and if that was the case, Lee didn't either. It would be simpler to remain strangers.

"Well," Tex cleared his throat. "Whatcha got for us, Arnold?"

Arnold let his eyes linger on Lee. As though to test Lee's mettle. Testing to see who would look away first. A version of chicken favored by men and boys with things to prove.

Lee held his gaze, unperturbed. Arnold was the type of large man that was used to elbowing his way through life. Getting what he wanted based purely on his size. The end of society had probably only reinforced this behavior.

Arnold was the type of guy that thought he could take anyone.

Lee smiled pleasantly at him, thinking, *It's never too late to learn something new, old boy.*

A frown creased Arnold's brow, and he looked away from Lee. He motioned for the younger guy with the feed sack. The young man stepped forward and placed the sack on the ground, between Arnold and Tex.

Lee became aware of the smell of decay. A few flies made anxious circles around the sack.

Tex sucked his teeth. "Arnold. We talked about this."

Arnold pushed the sack with the toe of a boot. "Them's eleven heads in there. You can count 'em."

"I don't wanna count 'em," Tex snapped. "It's supposed to be *bodies*."

"Eleven bodies is hard to haul."

"Bullshit," Tex growled. "Where are they?"

Arnold made a face. "I dunno. Out wherever we shot 'em."

Lee watched the exchange carefully. Out of his peripheral vision, he saw Tex getting agitated. But he was focused on Arnold and the two younger men behind him, and how their fingers kept creeping towards their weapons.

Tex stepped forward, pointing a finger. "So if I walked back to whatever you got cookin' in that smokefire, what am I gonna find, huh?"

Arnold's jaw worked. The fingers on his gun hand twitched. "You ain't goin in there. You got no right."

"It's just some antelope," one of the younger men said, but he didn't even sound convinced of himself.

Lee was focused on hands, but in the back of his mind, he put two and two together, and the realization made a weed of violence bloom up in him, invasive. He wanted to hurt these men. Because...because they were vile.

Tex's lips were pulled back tight, showing his bottom teeth. "Bodies, Arnold. Fucking bodies. You show me them bodies, and you get the supplies. But not before." And Tex leaned forward. "And by the way, this is your last chance."

Arnold glared. "Or what?"

"Or I'm done with you."

"You see them heads. That's eleven teepios kilt. I've got a right to them supplies, and you're gonna give 'em over." Arnold took a step forward.

Arnold might've gotten away with his tone, but combined with the step forward, and his hand twitching towards his sidearm, Lee decided that a line had been crossed.

Lee took one step to his right, so that all three of the OP Elbert men were fully visible to him, and swept his rifle up.

Everyone tensed. Hands touched weapons, but no one really made a move.

Lee had them dead to rights and they knew it.

He had both eyes open. His left held eye contact with Arnold. Through his right, he saw the reticle hovering over Arnold's unruly hairline. "You got a twitchy right hand. It twitches again, I might twitch myself."

Arnold's jaw muscles pulsed. His eyes zig-zagged from Lee to Tex, wondering if Captain Lehy was going to call Lee off. But Tex just stood there. Waiting to see how things played out.

Lee's heart beat steady. Something like gratification flooded his veins.

Through his eyes, he willed Arnold—*Do it. Move.*

He *wanted* the shooting to start.

"I got a rifleman," Arnold stammered. "He's aimin' for you now."

"Good for him," Lee said. "All that tainted meat. He's probably got the shakes. You trust his aim? I wouldn't. Maybe that's why your own hand is so damn twitchy."

"Tex," Arnold said, his voice pitching up, worried at what he saw staring back at him. "What're you doin'?"

Tex snorted. "Me? I ain't doin' shit." He leaned forward. "We're through, Arnold. You hear me? I gave you a second chance last time. That's all you'll ever get outta me."

Arnold was sweating hard, his nostrils flaring. "Well. What's that mean for us?"

"What's that mean for you?" Tex scoffed. "I don't know, Arnold. I guess that's up to you. But you won't see my face anymore. You're not a part of us if you can't follow my goddamned orders. So we're gonna walk away. And you're gonna walk away. And that's that."

Jump, motherfucker, Lee thought.

Arnold's lower lip quivered. "You're not gonna...send anyone else? To take us out?"

Tex shook his head. "Now, what would be the point in that?"

Arnold didn't seem to have a reply.

Tex reached out and touched Lee's shoulder. "Alright now."

Lee ground his teeth together. Hanging on the moment for a second longer.

Eagerness turned to stale frustration.

Shit.

Lee didn't lower his weapon, but he did come out of the sights. He was confident that, from this distance, he could snap-shoot all three of them before any of them could get a weapon out.

Arnold and his two men didn't move. Lee's rifle was still very much addressed in their direction.

Tex, Thompson, Abe, and Lee, backed all the way to the truck, not moving fast. Slow and easy. They didn't want to look like they were beating a retreat. There was careful calculation to that—not just dick measuring. Human beings were always most aggressive when their opponent appeared to be retreating. Arnold and his boys were not likely to be an exception. They'd lived up to Tex's warning about their squirreliness, and it was obvious they wanted the contents of the truck bad.

Maybe bad enough to get in a gunfight.

At the truck, Lee waited until all three of his companions had entered the truck and gotten into their seats. Then he sidled up into his own seat, keeping his rifle out the open window so Arnold and his ilk knew to keep still.

"Fucking animals," Tex breathed.

Thompson put the truck in gear, and they drove off in the direction that they'd come from, still at the same slow speed, so as not to appear to be retreating.

It wasn't until they were up to sixty miles-per-hour and they could no longer see Arnold, that

Abe let out a loud swear. "You kiddin' me with this shit?"

Tex looked into the back. Then shook his head, his lips pressed together in disappointment. "Un-fucking-believable, huh?"

Abe swore several times, then took to wiping his nose. "And I thought that cooking smelled good."

"Well." Tex turned back around. "Now you know what smoked teepio smells like."

Lee felt as disgusted as Abe. The smell of cooking meat had made him hungry. Now the knowledge of what it was they were cooking had robbed any appetite from him and left a queasy black hole behind.

"How long have they been doing that?" Abe asked.

Tex shrugged. "Hell if I know, man. We discovered it last month. I came down on them pretty hard. They're the reason for the new rule: whole body or no deal. I guess they couldn't stand to pass up all that free meat."

Abe made a disgusted noise.

Lee's nose wrinkled. "Any known affects from eating it?"

Tex shrugged. "Well, they don't get infected from it. We know that. But then again, I can't say for sure whether Arnold and his folks have always been batshit crazy rednecks, or whether that meat is doing something to their brains."

Thompson fidgeted in the driver's seat. Seemed concerned about something. "You're not really gonna just let 'em go? We can't have those psychos hanging out in our backyard."

Tex turned his head, and though Lee couldn't see his eyes through his sunglasses, he could tell by the set of his face that he was not happy with Thompson. "Well, maybe now ain't the time to talk about that, huh?"

Thompson seemed to remember himself.

Lee watched as the corporal's eyes shot up to the rearview mirror, connected with Lee's, then went back to the road. Thompson didn't say anything else after that. He seemed to have said enough.

Tex stared at his driver for another few beats, and then, with a tiny shake of his head, he looked out the window at the passing countryside of the Texas plains.

In the back seat, Lee and Abe exchanged an uncertain look.

***

Major John Bellamy was walking a tightrope and he knew it.

Well...figuratively, anyway.

Literally, he was walking on a sidewalk in Greeley, Colorado, heading back to the Hampton Inn & Suites. The hotel had been taken over years ago to house and provide offices to the hundreds of executive military staff based in the Greeley Green Zone, and had thus earned itself the nickname FOB Hampton.

Bellamy had an office up in that hotel.

And President Briggs—*Acting* President Briggs, though no one around here dared breathe that out loud—had taken the penthouse.

But where Bellamy was heading was Colonel Lineberger's office.

Colonel Lineberger was something like President Briggs's secretary of defense. He was in charge of every military element now under the control of President Briggs, including Major Bellamy himself. And Bellamy was on the way to hand him a bold-faced lie.

This was the proverbial tightrope.

His first foray out onto this tightrope had been when he'd agreed to keep in secret contact with Captain Lehy, thereby betraying Briggs. But he'd merely been dabbling on the edges—not really committed to the balancing act he now found himself in.

When he'd provided Tex with the information about Lee needing his help at the *Nuevas Fronteras* fuel cache in Alabama, he'd taken a few, wobbly, baby steps out, and his nerves had started to jangle inside of him. But, ultimately, that had no effect on Greeley, and so it was highly unlikely that anyone from Greeley would start wondering *how* Tex had known to be in Alabama at such a fortuitous time for Lee Harden.

Then Bellamy had provided Tex with the information on the final fuel convoy from *Nuevas Fronteras* to Greeley.

And now that convoy was three hours late.

Now it *did* effect Greeley. Which meant people were going to start wondering how Tex's people knew where and when to be to take down that convoy. And Bellamy was acutely aware that the trail would lead directly back to him.

His recourse now was to act innocent and disturbed by this news, and to obfuscate his trail as much as possible.

But acting was not one of Bellamy's natural talents. He was an operator, not a double-agent. He been trained as a warfighter, not a spy.

Guess you better learn quick.

He entered the front of the hotel. Two soldiers in ACUs were posted guard. They knew him well from his comings and goings, but checked his pass anyways, saluting him and wishing him a good morning.

Bellamy grunted a response and tossed them back a halfhearted salute.

He walked through the lobby and passed the elevators. He took a sidelong glance at his dim reflection on the brass doors. He wore MultiCam— or OCP, if you wanted to get technical. He spied the little golden oak leaf patch on his chest. It made him feel like he wore a costume rather than a uniform.

He took deep breaths, but the nerves still jangled inside his stomach. He'd been having some acid reflux, and he felt it burning at the bottom of his throat. But his hands were steady, and he thought that he *looked* relaxed enough.

He turned into one of the conference rooms that had been repurposed into offices. Mostly cubicle walls like in any open-air office building. But in the corners they'd constructed rooms out of plywood to give the higher ranking officers some privacy. Bellamy had one himself.

Even two years since they'd been built, they still made the entire area smell like a lumber mill.

At the far back corner, Bellamy stopped outside of Colonel Lineberger's office. The door was open. He peered inside, but no one was there.

Shit. Now he had to track the colonel down to lie to him?

"You looking for Lineberger?"

Bellamy turned and found Mr. Daniels standing there with a cup of coffee and a slight smile, which seemed to be his default expression. Like he always knew something that you didn't and found your ignorance amusing.

He was freshly shaven, as always. Golden hair parted neatly on the side, as always.

Daniels's office was directly adjacent to Lineberger's, but Daniels wasn't military. He was the CEO of Cornerstone, a military contracting company that President Briggs had a vested interest in back in the day when he'd been *Senator* Briggs. Daniels and Briggs were close friends, and they had slowly but surely edged out the military in favor of Cornerstone operatives in several key areas of the Greeley Green Zone.

It seemed that Briggs trusted his mercenaries far more than he trusted his military.

Maybe he's not wrong for that.

Bellamy didn't try to hide his lack of enthusiasm for Mr. Daniels. "Yes. I'm looking for the colonel."

Daniels took a sip of coffee. Eyed the empty office. "He's not in right now."

"It appears that way." Civility was sometimes a struggle for Bellamy. "Do you know when he gets back?"

Daniels shrugged. "I can pass on a message if you'd like."

Bellamy shook his head. "No. I was instructed to report directly to him."

Daniels didn't seem to care. He eyed Bellamy with that knowing look of his.

Bellamy was about to disengage and walk away.

"It's about the fuel convoy, huh?"

The acid in Bellamy's stomach churned, rising.

This fucking prick.

"I'm supposed to report to Lineberger."

"Yeah-yeah. Secret squirrel. I get it." Daniels arched an eyebrow. "They're late."

Bellamy didn't answer. It appeared that Daniels already knew.

"What do you think happened to them?"

Bellamy didn't care at all for the way that Daniels had said it. The way he'd said it, it wasn't a question. It was an accusation.

Or was he just being paranoid?

For a brief moment that felt like a glaringly long time, Bellamy found himself mentally stumbling about for what to reply. It seemed that every set of words that flitted through his brain as a possible answer was rife with guilt. Like if he said one goddamned word, it would give him away.

Bellamy felt the small of his back begin to sweat.

"Who told you that?" Bellamy managed it with an authoritative scowl, that felt fake on his face.

Daniels shrugged again. "People talk." He took another sip of coffee. "Anyways. I'll let him know you were looking for him." Daniels's mouth turned up into a smile, but his eyes remained locked on Bellamy in that same accusing way. "See you around, major."

And Daniels walked off.

Bellamy watched him go, his gut roiling.

He knows something.

Or was that just what Daniels wanted him to think? Was he playing games? Or did he actually know something? And who the hell had he heard it from?

All good questions.

What Bellamy knew for sure was that he was out in the middle of that tightrope for sure now. And his balance was getting wobbly.

***

Angela took a midday break.

She needed it.

She'd planned to work straight through. But, as much as she hated to admit it to herself, the disagreement with Carl had...shaken her up. Not because she felt that Carl would ever do anything to hurt *her*. No, it hadn't been him looming over her desk that had given her a feeble feeling in her gut.

But the entire interaction had made her wonder: How much control did she have in this place? Or was it all an illusion? Was she really the puppet that Elsie Foster claimed her to be?

Well...sometimes Elsie claimed that Angela was a puppet. Other times she was the puppet *master*. It depended on whichever narrative fit Elsie's most recent round of attacks.

So, in this troubled state of mind, she thought a visit with her daughter might do her some good. It was a short walk from the Soldier Support Center to the Medical Center across the street.

Walking down from her office with Kurt, her bodyguard, leading the way, her jaw began to ache and only then did she realize that her teeth were clenched. She forced herself to relax.

At the bottom level, Angela stopped and turned to Kurt, before he could open the stairwell door that led to the lobby of the Soldier Support Center. "Kurt, can I ask you a favor?"

"Of course," Kurt said, hand halfway to the doorknob, hesitating.

Angela's eyes flicked over his face. "Can you let me walk by myself?"

He looked at her like she'd asked to remove his balls with scissors. But he didn't say anything, at least for a moment. His mouth compressed down into a piano-wire line, and then twitched a few times.

"Ms. Houston, the gunshot wound in your side isn't even completely healed from the last time they tried to kill you. And you ask me if you can walk by yourself?"

Angela pointed to the pistol which had taken up residence on her hip. A new accompaniment since the assassination attempt. Or...since she got out of the hospital *after* the assassination attempt. "Kurt, I have this. I know how to use it. I'm actually pretty good."

Kurt must have felt like he was losing ground, because horror flashed across his face. "Nine millimeter is not going to do you a lot of good when they peg you in the face from five hundred yards!" He swallowed. Appeared to regret his outburst. "Sorry. But this is a terrible idea, ma'am."

Angela sighed. "Terrible for me or terrible for you?"

"Both."

Angela rested a hand on his shoulder. "I'll be fine, Kurt. I promise."

"You can't make that promise," Kurt growled at her, but she was already pulling the door open.

"Well, I'm gonna make it anyways," she quipped. "Because if they peg me in the face from five hundred yards then at least I won't have to hear about it from you."

Kurt followed her through the door. "I'm extremely uncomfortable with this."

"I know."

"I want the record to show that I advised you against this."

Angela cast a quizzical glance around her. "What record, Kurt? No one's taking a record."

"You know what I meant."

"I need to be alone for a few minutes."

"Why not be alone in your office?"

"Because then you're hovering outside my door. I want to be alone and *walking.*"

"Not safe."

"Duly noted."

Kurt issued something like a groan. Or he might've been cursing her out without moving his mouth. Angela couldn't tell which. But he seemed to have run out of objections to make.

Angela gave him a smile, because he was very sweet, if not a little obsessive. "Thank you, Kurt. If I'm not back in an hour, I'm probably dead on the sidewalk."

"Not funny," he said, dead serious. "Not something to joke about."

But Angela had already gone through the front doors of the Support Center, with a wave over her shoulder.

The sunlight struck her.

The warmth.

The light glinting off of windows.

It took everything she had to maintain her flippant body language, despite the fact that her insides went to soup, and her legs turned into rubber bands. She walked across the parking lot, straight towards the school a few hundred yards away, with her heart pounding.

She moved out of the glare of the light coming off the school's windows, and she saw that they were all closed, that there were no rifle-barrels protruding from them, or from a shadowy figure on the rooftop.

She couldn't even call herself paranoid anymore, because it had happened.

So she told herself they wouldn't try anything at this stage in the game. She told herself that she was armed. She told herself that they'd posted extra guards at the public buildings so that people like the guy that had shot her couldn't set something up like that again.

And she also told herself that, in all likelihood, Kurt was going to follow her at a discreet distance.

And that was fine. Even the *appearance* of being alone felt like she'd been cut free of ropes that had been constricting her chest for days on end.

Even the fear that she felt was better.

She wasn't cut out for this. She couldn't handle all the attention, all the time. When she walked down the street with a bodyguard, she felt like everyone's eyes were on her, judging her, sneering at her. She was set apart. Spotlighted. Observed. Scrutinized. And those that sat in judgement were not impressed.

But...

When she walked alone?

She felt like just another person.

Or at least, it was easier for her to pretend that.

She was relieved to walk through the doors of the hospital. But more than that, she was relieved that she was walking through the doors alone. Without bodyguards, she felt like she could slip in quietly through the door and past the triage station, to the room where her daughter was stationed.

When she opened the door, she found Abby sitting up in bed, with a book in her hand that was probably above her reading level. Marie sat on the chair next to the bed, also with a tattered paperback. They both set the books down as Angela came in the room.

"Mommy!" Abby greeted her. Her excitement level for seeing her mother had skyrocketed with her being sequestered to a hospital room. Angela felt a twinge of guilt for enjoying that.

"Hey, Sweetie," Angela said, moving to the bed and hugging her daughter with both arms. "Whatcha reading?"

"I dunno," Abby admitted. She turned the cover over with a frown. "It's like…some kids…on a train or something. I don't get it."

"Boxcar Kids," Marie said, with a nostalgic smile. "I used to love those as a kid." She looked up at Angela, her sharp eyes evaluating her friend. "Everything okay?"

"Yeah," Angela replied, completely unconvincing. "How about we see if we can't get some lunch for the kiddo. You hungry, Abby?"

"Sure."

Marie rose from her seat, dog-earring her page in her book and laying the book behind her. "You just keep reading that book, Abby. I promise it'll make sense if you keep trying."

Abby looked dubious, but picked up the book again.

Angela and Marie exited the room. In order to get food, they'd first have to find a nurse. There wasn't a hospital cafeteria anymore. They were lucky just to have a few nurses and a couple doctors, and enough medical equipment to keep people alive. For now.

What they were going to do when those supplies started running out was just one more thing that circled the back of Angela's mind, incessantly demanding attention that she couldn't give it. There were more urgent matters at hand.

"You hear Carl's back in town?" Angela asked.

Marie nodded. "I did. Is that what's got you so edgy?"

"Do I seem edgy?"

"Yeah, you do."

"Hm. Well, you're right."

"What happened?" Marie's tone was reserved.

"We had a bit of a disagreement," Angela sighed. Then she related most of what had happened in her office, sanitized and truncated for public consumption.

When Angela finished, they had stopped walking and now stood halfway down a long hall with no doors or windows or offices near them. The hall was empty. They were alone.

Marie looked troubled. "That's not good, Angela."

"What part?"

Marie's gaze hit hers, sharp as a tack. "You don't want to alienate Carl Gilliard. For that matter, you don't want to alienate the military."

Angela felt a little miffed that Marie wasn't taking her side. "If I let them dictate everything to me then I become the puppet that everyone already thinks I am! And this becomes a military dictatorship, and then I'm just the dumb-blonde-bitch-figurehead." Angela snorted. "On the upside, maybe they'll stop trying to kill me."

Marie smiled, but only with half her mouth. Her eyes still looked concerned. "Angela, I'm not saying you did the wrong thing."

Angela's fleeting humor left her. "It kind of feels like you are."

Marie shook her head. "No, I'm just saying…shit. I don't even know what I'm saying. Tread carefully?"

"You think Carl's in the right?" Angela tried not to bristle, and only half-succeeded. "You think we should just turn this into a police state? Lock every suspect up? Waterboard them? Throw them in work camps?"

Marie raised a sardonic eyebrow. "Well…free labor sounds pretty good."

"Stop it."

Marie grew serious again. "Okay. Here's what I'm saying, Angela. You are right for wanting this to be civil. And Carl's right for recognizing that it's not." She held up a hand, because Angela looked like she was going to start arguing again. "And if you were to ask me my opinion—which I'm assuming is the reason you're talking to me right now—then I'd tell you that the right answer probably lies somewhere in the middle."

Angela frowned. "What does that even look like?"

"Do what Carl is telling you to do. But make him be very discreet about it. Then deny everything."

Angela was already shaking her head before Marie finished. "No way. I'm not playing those games." Her voice dropped down to a harsh whisper. "We're at the cusp of a straight-up shooting war with Greeley, Colorado for doing *exactly* what you're talking about doing."

Marie looked unconvinced. "Well, I suppose we see things differently."

"There's no 'way to see things.' There's just the truth."

"You're talking about politics, Angela. It's never that black and white." Marie rubbed her eyebrows. "You're trying to take the moral high ground on an issue that has nothing to do with morals."

Angela crossed her arms, glaring, but not quite clear on what Marie was saying.

Marie continued. "We're not fighting Greeley because of some humanitarian crisis, Angela. You think the average person in Fort Bragg gives a shit how President Briggs is treating his populace a thousand miles away? No. They don't like Briggs. That's it. They don't like Briggs, because Briggs left them to die and then wants to come in after the fact and still act like King Shit, and they think that's a load of horseshit. Which it is. But don't mistake that for some crazy crisis of conscience."

Angela dug her heels in. "I'm not doing it. I think we're better than that. We're going to act civilized, because unless we are civilized and restrained, we sure as hell can't ask anyone else to act that way, can we?"

Marie smiled wanly. "You're not wrong."

Angela snorted and looked away. "But you don't think I'm right."

Marie reached out and put a comforting hand on Angela's shoulder. "I think I would hate to be in your shoes."

It was hard for Angela to stay mad when Marie was always such a comforting figure. She took a few deep breaths to settle herself down. "I apologize. I'm just…"

"Edgy?"

"Yes."

Marie squeezed her shoulder, then let go. "Abby's doing very well. No signs of anything. She had a little bit of a stomachache this morning, but I think it was probably just homesickness. She wants to get out of here. I think they'll release her soon."

Angela nodded. Her own bit of information received, she figured it was her duty to give Marie hers. "I haven't heard from Lee in a few days. I think they're still trying to determine their footing over in Texas. But, the good news is that if there was anything wrong, I think they'd let us know."

Marie nodded, a look of brief concern crossing her features.

Julia was Marie's younger sister. She'd been with them since the beginning. And during all those years of hard fighting, Marie had never gotten completely comfortable with her sister being in harm's way all the time.

When Angela got updates from Lee and the team, she tried to pass on any news about Julia.

It was still strange for Angela. There'd been something between her and Lee, back when they were just two people trying to survive in a place called Camp Ryder. But he'd gone someplace in his heart, and in his mind, and he'd never come back. It seemed like the only person he connected with now was Julia. They had something.

It wasn't jealousy that Angela felt when these thoughts came on. It was just...regret. She wished that she could comprehend the dark places that Lee had gone to. In a way, she wished she could have been darker herself, so that she could have commiserated with him.

But they were too different.

Angela's worldview was as different from Lee's as it was from Carl's, and Angela didn't think she'd ever be the type of person that could understand and appreciate the utilitarian thinking that those guys sometimes showed. How sometimes cold-blooded murder is the best thing for everyone.

Angela couldn't wrap her head around it.

Maybe it was her job to balance out the equation, but sometimes it felt like a lonely side of the scales to stand on.

"Come on," Marie said, breaking the silence, and gesturing down the hall. "Let's find a nurse. I'm sure they've got some grub around here somewhere."

***

Carl was still irritable when he arrived back at The Compound. He was not the type to storm around—or really emote at all—but his team detected his mood, nonetheless.

It was in the cinch of his icy gray eyes.

It was in the flat line of his lips.

And in the gait of his walk as he stalked into the main building of The Compound.

The Compound was a set of large but simple steel structures that had, back in the day, housed the offices of Carl's team, and a few others under the Combat Applications Group.

It was the very same set of buildings that had, once upon a time, been the only occupied ones in Fort Bragg. The same set of buildings where Carl and his team of operatives had captured Abe Darabie, along with the ill-fated Lucas Wright.

Tucked back in the woods, and undisturbed by all the civilian traffic.

The Compound had never stopped being Carl's homebase, though he did keep a desk in the Support Center, in the room that Lee and the team—what was left of them, anyways—had called The Cave. Carl had no desire to go back there. He had no desire to look at his dead friends' belongings.

In the main building, in one of the common rooms that served as the armory and equipment storage for Carl's team, his men were unpacking their things. Mitch and Rudy were hanging up their kit on designated sections of a pegboard that sat on the wall. Logan was cleaning his rifle.

Morrow sat inspecting the damage to a shirt he'd worn during the operation at the airport a few days prior. The shoulder of it had been shredded by spall—not to mention Morrow's actual flesh, but he seemed more concerned with the shirt.

Luckily, his ancient MultiCam ballcap had survived relatively unscathed, and was now perched on his head, Morrow's wild chestnut mane curling out from under it.

There was some light banter that died as Carl walked into the room, but mostly everyone kept doing what they were doing, giving him a glance, and grunting a greeting to him.

Morrow looked perturbed at the condition of his shirt and then glowered in Carl's direction. "I can already tell that it didn't go well."

Carl put his hands on his hips and considered this. "Define 'well.'"

Mitch decided to offer an explanation as he untangled commo wires from his plate carrier. "Angela doesn't want us going around black bagging civilians."

Carl shook his head. "No. She doesn't."

Logan—their youngest member—made a series of disgruntled noises, then set the disassembled upper receiver of his rifle down with a clank. "Un-fucking-believable. They just tried to kill her. *Literally. Just. Tried.*"

Morrow leaned back into his seat. "So what do you want us to be doing, Boss?"

Carl sighed through his nose, thinking. Then: "No change. Do what you were doing before wc got mixed up in Lee's shit. Keep your eye on the Lincolnists. Follow them. Track them. ID them." He looked at each of his team members in turn, to make sure that they made eye contact with him and understood the meaning beneath his words. "There may come a time when we have to…diverge…from official policy. If you got a problem with that, then I need to know now."

Rudy looked back over his shoulder for a moment. He gave a facial shrug that made his Huckleberry Hound jowls even more pronounced, then went back to hanging his gear.

No one said a word.

Carl nodded to them. "Then we just keep on keepin' on. And we hope that the Lincolnists force Angela's hand before she forces ours."

EIGHT

NO WAY OUT

THE HIDEOUT was high in the Texas hill country.

By the time Thompson drove them up to the ramshackle hunting cabin, a squad of Tex's raiders had already arrived, and Julia was with them.

The hunting cabin looked like it had been nice at one point in time. More of a lodge. Tex said these used to be private hunting grounds where rich folks would sit in comfortable stands and peg antelope from three hundred yards.

Now the siding moldered, the roof looked like shit, and several windows were busted out. But there were obvious signs of recent habitation by Tex's men.

They had hideouts like this sprinkled all over North Texas. They preferred a lot of small satellite locations to one big central location. Tex was well aware that President Briggs would eventually get air power again, and Tex didn't want to give him any juicy targets on which to drop bombs.

Thompson drove them around to the back of the cabin, where a few other vehicles were parked under a canopy of mesquite and oak. He sidled the truck between two thick trees, with just enough room for them to open the doors and squeeze out.

The back door opened into a common area where some of Tex's men were already lounging.

The second that Lee saw Julia, he knew something was off.

The common area was a mash of stuffed animal heads, crappy nature paintings, and wood paneling. There was an old leather couch, and a few chairs with fraying upholstery. There was also a collection of sun-bleached camping chairs and rickety folding chairs.

Julia slouched in one of the camping chairs, surrounded by ten of Tex's men. Greetings were passed back and forth between Tex and his crew, but Julia remained silent, and looked meaningfully at Lee from under her eyebrows, like she had something she wanted to say, but was holding it back.

Shit, Lee thought. *What happened now?*

The squad leader, Menendez, had risen and traded a casual back-slap with Tex.

"How'd it go?" Tex asked.

"Good." Menendez smiled. "We hit five tankers. We were able to haul three of them off. Fired the other two. No casualties. For us, anyways."

"Good." Tex nodded, thinking. "Great, actually. Stellar job. Squad Two got the three tankers secured?"

"Took 'em to the quarry."

Tex squeezed his man on the shoulder. "That's why I keep you around, Menendez."

"Stop. I'm blushing."

Lee and Abe sidled casually over to Julia while Tex and Menendez conversed.

Lee nodded to her. "Everything alright?"

"Hunky dory, Lee," Julia replied, not looking at him. Which was as good as saying, *No, it's all fucked up.*

Lee exchanged a quick glance with Abe.

Tex turned his attention on them. He had his M-frames pushed up onto his head, which made him look relaxed. Like maybe he was on his way to hang out on a lake. Except for the body armor and weapons.

"Lee," Tex said. "I got some important people I need to meet with. I'm taking Thompson and Menendez with me. You gonna be okay sticking around here?"

Lee was surprised that Tex didn't ask him to come along, but he nodded. It would work out better anyway—he needed to talk to his team in private. "Yeah. We'll be good." He gestured to Deuce, who sat against his leg now. "Need to let this guy take a few laps around the cabin anyways. He's been cooped up."

Tex smiled. "Right. Well. We'll be back by tonight." A wink. "If all goes well." He waved his pointer finger at everyone else in the room. "The rest of you maniacs be good." He paused, looking over the shoulder of the soldier nearest him, who was cobbling together a cigarette. "You ain't got watch anytime soon, do you?"

The man stopped picking through his cigarette and looked up at Tex. "'Course not. Not until midnight."

Tex seemed satisfied with that answer. He gave one last nod to Lee, and then he, Menendez, and Thompson departed out the back again.

Lee watched the man with the cigarette for a moment. Realized he was picking marijuana seeds out of it. He wasn't surprised. Entertainment in any form you could get it was vital for morale, and there weren't a lot of other options out here. Tex had to be lenient out of necessity, and Lee could appreciate that position.

Lee was curious though. "You find a stash somewhere?"

The soldier looked up, now in the process of rolling. "Pff. I wish. This is just some Mexican ditch weed we found growing wild. Better than nothing. Tex don't mind as long as we don't have a scheduled mission or watch within eight hours." He licked, and pasted. Held it up to Lee. "Want some?"

Lee smiled, but shook his head. "Maybe later."

He wouldn't have any later, either. Maybe if he were back inside a Safe Zone, but there wasn't a chance in hell he was taking anything mind-altering while out here.

He gave Julia and Abe a look. "I'm gonna walk Deuce around a bit outside. Let him get a feel for the area."

Julia stood up. "I'll grab some fresh air with you."

Abe nodded and followed them out.

The three of them stayed quiet as they walked away from the house. Lee scanned all around him, and managed to slip a glance back at the cabin. He was curious if any of Tex's men were watching them.

Was that paranoid?

There was no one visible.

The forest huddled close to the cabin, and within a minute they could barely see the cabin through the trees. Lee started angling to the left. Walking slowly in a fifty yard radius from the cabin. Deuce trotted off and meandered between trees, constantly sniffing the air and expertly rationing two or three drops of urine for every other tree trunk.

"So, what's wrong?" Lee asked, taking another long look at Julia.

Julia considered the question with a scrunched brow. "I dunno. I didn't like how some things went down."

Julia handled herself well, but Lee also knew that being the only female had to take a toll on her. He just wasn't sure how to frame that question without getting her hackles up.

He went with, "You catch any flak from the guys?"

Julia shook her head. "No. Nothing like that. Ogling, which I guess is to be expected, but nothing more." She gave a disconcerted huff of breath. "No. There was a woman. In the convoy."

Lee's mind immediately went to the darkest aspect that could be interpreted from that.

Julia must have noticed him stiffen as they walked. "It wasn't rape," she corrected.

"Okay…"

"She was wounded during the ambush. I tried to treat her. Menendez wouldn't let me. We got into an argument about it. She died. They *let* her die."

The three of them walked in silence for a moment.

"I keep going back and forth," Julia continued. "Wondering who was right. But it felt wrong. I didn't like it."

Abe was the one that spoke up, and Lee appreciated that. Sometimes Lee and Julia could butt heads about things, and Julia tended to react more strongly to Lee than to Abe, so he was glad to have Abe take the heat.

"Jules, they don't exactly have the infrastructure to take prisoners."

"I know." But her expression remained pensive. She pulled to a stop, and Lee and Abe stopped with her. She looked between the two of them. "What are we doing here?"

Lee considered this for a moment, watching Deuce make his rounds. His plate carrier felt heavy on his shoulders and he shifted around, grimacing slightly at the discomfort of the healing gunshot wound to his chest. He'd be glad to get the armor off of him.

"We have a shared enemy," Lee said. "Two shared enemies, actually. Greeley, and *Nuevas Fronteras*. Right now, we've got fuel tankers being sent to the UES, and that's a stopgap that'll last us a little bit. But our original mission remains the same: We need what *Nuevas Fronteras* has. We need the oil rigs. We need the refineries. Without them, the UES doesn't stand a chance in the long run. And right now, I see Tex as our one viable option for taking control of what we need."

"So how much are we going to overlook?" Julia asked.

Lee loosened the cummerbund on his rig and shifted it to alleviate some of the pain. "Frankly, Jules, I'm willing to overlook a lot."

118

Abe tugged gently at his dark beard. "What about OP Elbert?"

Julia raised an eyebrow. "What happened there?"

"We went to deliver supplies," Abe answered her, lowering his voice, like he was concerned someone might overhear them. "Some crazy, backwoods rednecks. They were supposed to show us bodies from all the primals they'd killed, and Tex was gonna give them supplies for it. But they only had the heads." Abe's nose wrinkled and he looked off into the woods. "Apparently they were...using the bodies for meat."

Julia's eyes widened. "Like...to eat?"

Abe nodded.

"Christ."

Lee's face darkened. "I felt that the situation was handled as best as could be expected, Abe."

Abe shrugged. "Yeah. Maybe. Until the part where they started talking about wiping them out."

Lee held up a finger. "*Thompson* started talking about that. Not Tex."

Abe made a face. "Come on, Lee. Tex just didn't want to say it in front of you. Those guys are as good as dead."

"So, what?" Julia looked shocked. "They're just gonna send a kill squad to take them out?"

"No, they didn't say anything like that," Lee snapped.

"You're right." Abe's tone said that Lee wasn't. "They implied it. Heavily."

Lee frowned at him. "And so what if they do? Thompson made the only point that matters here, Abe: They can't have those yahoos roaming around in their backyard." Lee's face felt hot as he grumbled, "I had half a mind to kill them myself."

He'd had more than half a mind.

He'd been damn close to doing it.

But he kept that to himself.

The three of them were quiet for a moment.

A dozen yards from them, Deuce scented the air, then looked back at Lee, as though to see if he was needed for anything. Then he continued on his way.

"Let's put that aside for a minute," Julia said. "It's not about the woman they let die, or whether OP Elbert is gonna get shellacked. Let's talk about the endgame here."

"Fine," Lee nodded. "The endgame, as I see it, is that I trust Tex. He might be going about things differently than I would, but they've had different problems to solve than we have. They're sandwiched between Greeley and *Nuevas Fronteras*. Tex has been fighting two wars practically since the beginning. That doesn't leave a whole lot of leeway for civility, and frankly, I don't blame him."

"He has zero civilian oversight," Julia said.

"And that's a bad thing?" Lee raised his eyebrows. "Imagine how much more successful the UES would be if we didn't have to deal with a bunch of dissenters like the Lincolnists."

Julia pointed to the ground. "Lee, he's Julius Caesar out here. And at some point in time, that's something that's going to have to be dealt with."

Lee looked to Abe, hoping for backup, but Abe shied away from his gaze, and nodded along with Julia. "She's right. This isn't what the Coordinators were supposed to do. They weren't supposed to set up a military regime."

Lee grunted. "I don't think you can call a dozen hideouts in the hills a military regime."

"What he said concerns me."

"About what?"

"About how when things are safe enough, then they'll worry about a civilian government." Abe looked at Lee, with an uncertain squint to his eyes. "Briggs said a very similar thing to me once. How he couldn't afford to let Greeley be too democratic, because it wasn't safe enough yet."

Lee couldn't help but wince at that. Sharing an opinion with Briggs didn't automatically make you wrong. But it wasn't a shining recommendation either.

"We're supposed to be re-establishing society," Abe continued. "He *has* no society. Any civilians that are in his ranks have been militarized. And he's the dictator-general. I agree with Julia. That's a problem."

Lee shook his head. "So maybe that's a problem, Abe. A problem for years down the road. What about right now? What about the problems that we're facing *right now*? You wanna go back to the UES and tell them, 'Hey, that twenty-eight thousand gallons is all we're ever gonna get, so make it last'? We bought ourselves a year. At best."

Abe bobbled his head, not entirely convinced, but not arguing either.

Lee looked at Julia. "You know, the civilians in Fort Bragg accuse *us* of being a kill squad, too. Did you know that?"

Julia nodded. "Yeah, of course I know that. But not everyone thinks that way. It's a small sect of people. If I were to guess, they'd all have ties to Elsie Foster."

"My point is," Lee growled. "We do what we have to, no matter the fact that it's unpalatable to some people. And I think Tex is doing what he has to do. If he played by the same rules we did, he'd be dead by now." Lee was getting hot under the collar and took a breath to cool himself. "He's not a warlord. Not a *dictator-general*. I trust him. And when the time comes, I don't think we'll have to wrestle power away from him."

"You don't know that."

"No, I don't know that. No one *knows* anything. But I can make a reasonable inference based on what I know about Tex. And I say he's not like that." Lee pointed to Abe. "Christ, Abe, you know the guy, too. Are you really worried about this?"

Abe held up both hands. "All I'm saying is that Julia makes a good point. Allies can be tricky. We gotta think about who we're getting into bed with. We gotta think about the long run."

"I am thinking about the long run," Lee said. "I'm thinking about *surviving* the long run. But we gotta fight one battle at a time, guys. Right now, that battle is against *Nuevas Fronteras*."

Julia surprised Lee by being the one to squash it. "You're right, Lee."

He waited for a caveat.

She reached out and touched his arm, looking earnest. "But just keep it mind, Lee. Play your cards close to your chest, and know that your friends today might not be your friends tomorrow."

Lee grimaced. "Sounds like politics."

She offered him a grim smile. "It is. And we all know how good you are with that."

Lee admitted it with a nod. Politics was poison to him. He wanted to confront all his problems head on, he wanted to defeat them in battle. It was a great way to win fights, and a lousy way to play politics.

"You do what you're good at, Lee," she said. "Just don't forget that other people might be playing different games, and have different prizes in mind."

Lee took a deep breath and looked at each of them. "I got only one prize in mind. And that's getting Texas and the UES hooked up so that the three of us can get out of here and back to Bragg."

***

Claire Staley moved through Fort Bragg like it was an alternate plane of existence.

Like she was a bubble of reality floating through an expanse of nothingness.

She sometimes felt very strongly, as she did in that moment, that none of this could possibly be real. That it was all a vivid fever dream, and she would wake up at any moment, back in a wooden cage surrounded by a dozen other females whose sole purpose in life was to be impregnated like breeding sows.

When this thought came to her, it felt like the world was tilting, and only through sheer force of concentration could she stabilize it and keep herself from tumbling off.

She had escaped them.

But she would never *really* be free.

Anger helped. Her body vibrated with it. It clouded pain like an opioid. It reworked the framework of her existence into something simpler.

Life is always simpler when there is an enemy to direct yourself at. It keeps you from thinking too much about yourself.

Her enemy was all around her.

They passed her on the sidewalk. Too stupid or too uncaring to see her for what she was.

These people are not what you sacrificed yourself for.

And oh, how Claire had sacrificed herself.

When she'd first been captured by The Followers of the Rapture, three years ago, she'd resisted them at every step. When they came to the wooden cage with all the other females that they kept as concubines, she would fight them, believing that if she held out long enough, her father—the great Colonel Staley—would eventually rescue her.

What she'd discovered was that he would never save her.

The only ally she had in the world was herself.

And then she had sacrificed a piece of herself. She'd given them a great chunk of her soul, knowing that it would eventually allow her to escape them. She had begun to go willingly with them to their beds. She had begun to actually *hope* she would get pregnant. Because if she could get pregnant, she knew that they would take her out of the cage, and once she was out of the cage, she knew she might find a way to escape.

She had never gotten pregnant, but she had escaped.

And she'd come here, amongst these people, and they told her that she was safe. And for a time, that worked, because for a time she still had an enemy. They would capture people suspected of being a part of The Followers, and Claire would positively identify them, and then they would be executed. And she didn't think she'd ever felt such satisfaction in her life as when she'd looked on the face of their leader, a man named Wiscoe, and knew that she was condemning him to death.

But after that…she'd had nothing.

Now that they were all dead, she'd been left adrift in a world she no longer understood.

And yet the sensation of being among the enemy never left her.

It was Elsie Foster whom Claire had first confided this to. And it was Elsie who had showed her the truth. It was Elsie that had showed her *why* she still felt like she was surrounded by the enemy.

"Are they any different?" Elsie had said, sitting at her kitchen table where she and Claire sometimes talked about the madness of the world.

On the other side of that table, Claire had frowned. "Who?"

"The Followers…" she gestured around them. "…and these people." Elsie smiled and reached across the table and laid her hand on Claire's. "I think that you know, deep down, that they're the same. They're all just warlords, Claire. Power hungry people that have filled the vacuum created in the wake of the fall of the United States. No matter how well the UES dresses themselves up, they're still another illegal fiefdom. Just like Wiscoe's Followers."

Elsie's hand was warm. Soft.

Her fingers stroked gently over top of Claire's.

Her eyes were kind. Loving, even.

"You sacrificed so much," Elsie continued. "Believing that you were going to escape to a better place. Back to true civilization. But then your father threw all of that out the window, didn't he? He could've taken you away. He *should've* taken you to Greeley, back to civilization. But instead, after all that you had given up, you escape here and you find your father bending the knee to *these people*. You find your father submitting to an organization just like the one you'd escaped from."

Elsie looked sad. She shook her head. "Your father betrayed you, Claire. After everything was said and done, after everything you'd lost—your innocence, your humanity—he was never able to protect you. And then he forced you right back in amongst the enemy."

Claire opened her mouth to object, but Elsie's firm, quiet voice overrode her. "You're not wrong for feeling how you feel, Claire. There's nothing wrong with you. You know that, right?"

Claire felt her hand tremble beneath Elsie's. And she felt on the cusp of absolution.

It is difficult for a person to feel like they are losing their mind—that what they are perceiving as reality is *wrong*. And when someone comes to you and tells you that you are not wrong, and provides you with a framework in which your troubles suddenly make sense...

You can't help but love them for it.

Elsie kept stroking her hand. Then her wrist.

It made her feel forgiven. Absolved. Righteous, even.

"I can help you," Elsie had said. "We can help each other."

It was in this tumult of memories that Claire pushed the front door of her house open and found her father waiting for her.

It was unusual enough that she froze in the door when she saw him.

The door opened on the living room, of which there was only a less-than-sanitary looking couch that Claire had yet to touch. But across the living room was the kitchen, and at the small kitchen table, Colonel Staley sat, facing her.

He wore his desert digital uniform. The matte black eagles on his collar. His gray hair neatly combed. He sat straight-backed, with his hands in his lap. He looked like he held something there, but the table blocked Claire's view.

He looked right at her, and he didn't smile, or greet her, and she knew that he had been waiting for her. She often came home for a short break around midday.

Claire realized that her heart was lodged somewhere in her throat. It felt like it was blocking her windpipe, and she had to swallow twice before she seemed able to breathe again. She closed the front door behind her.

"Dad," she managed. Single syllables were safe.

Something terrible crossed over his face when she said this.

He raised one hand from his lap, and gave a very military-father knife hand to the chair opposite him. "Claire. Come sit."

Claire hesitated only for a moment. But even now, the surprise of walking in and finding her father waiting for her—of being snapped out of her dark, strange memories—began to fade.

She'd been pretending for a long time.

She was very good at it.

As her feet got moving, she came back to herself and smiled. "I didn't expect you here," she said. "Did you want some lunch?"

"Claire," Staley said, sharper now, his gray eyebrows beetling. "I want you to sit down."

Claire blinked a few times, as though she couldn't possibly imagine what this was about. "Okaaaayyy," she drew out. She pulled out the chair opposite her father, and then sat in it. "What's wrong?"

She'd successfully swallowed her heart back to where it belonged, but it was still thumping along. She hoped her pulse wasn't visible in her neck. She reached up and casually drew her hair across her throat.

Staley stared at her for another long moment. Wrestling with something in his mind.

She'd never seen him like this before. It scared the shit out of her, but she was determined not to let that show.

She raised her eyebrows, prompting him to speak.

He took a sharp breath, like he'd been stung, and then his hands came out of his lap and he placed something on the table between them.

A satellite phone.

Claire stared at it. Her mind racing.

Staley stared at her.

"A satphone," she said. She dragged her eyes off of it and managed to look confused. "Okay. What gives?"

"Stop." He said it so quietly, and yet so enraged, that Claire's teeth clacked together when her mouth snapped shut.

Father and daughter regarded each other for a long moment.

"No more lies," Staley husked. "No more bullshit. This was taped to the back of your dresser. Hidden. You've only ever called one number on it. The same number that you called on the satphone from the Watch Commander's office the night the primals attacked us."

Claire felt like her brain was full of flies. Buzzing angrily. Every fly a swirling thought that she couldn't catch hold of. She needed to adapt. She needed to stabilize herself. Find a way out.

There was always a way out.

She forced her breathing to remain level. In. Out. Steady.

"Well," she said, after a moment. "What is it you want me to tell you?"

She was buying time. She needed a few seconds to sort things out.

"Who have you been calling?"

"I think you know who I've been calling."

Staley's eyes sparked. His nostril's flared.

Claire decided to push. It was the only move that made sense: Attack. She leaned forward onto the table. "No bullshit, right? That's what you asked for. Now do me a favor and give me the same courtesy. You know who I've been calling."

Staley slammed his hand flat on the table. It made a sound like a gunshot. "What the fuck is the matter with you?"

Claire raised her voice right back. "What's the matter with *me*? What's the matter with *you*? This isn't who you're supposed to be serving! This isn't the United States! The president is in Colorado! And you're sworn to serve *him*! Not some two-bit dictator that's filled a power vacuum! Who the fuck do you think you are?"

"People died, Claire! You gave information to Greeley, and people lost their lives because of it!"

"Yeah, I gave information to Greeley. Because someone has to do the right thing. And it's obvious you don't have the balls to do it, you fucking coward!"

Staley slapped her so hard she tumbled out of her chair.

Her ears were ringing. Her face felt numb at first, and then began to sting like a sunburn. She stared at the cheap linoleum floor. She had one hand on the table and she dragged herself back up.

Staley rocketed out of his chair, tipping it backwards onto the floor. He let out a string of curses, took two paces away, and then thundered back to her. "President Briggs left us to die out here, do you understand that? Do you?"

Claire raised her eyes defiantly. She tasted blood on her lips. But it wasn't the first time she'd been slapped around. "I understand that you're on the wrong side of history, *Dad*. And I won't be a part of it."

Staley looked at his daughter in amazement. "What the hell happened to you?"

Claire had pulled herself back into her chair now. Her hair had fallen over her face. It stuck to her bloody lip. She took a breath and screamed at him. "You never came for me! That's what fucking happened! I was raped and beaten for a fucking *year*, waiting for you to find me! And you never came for me!"

All the strength seemed to come out of the man standing in front of her. His knees buckled and he knelt down in front of her, suddenly looking decades older. No longer a colonel. Just a stricken old man.

He reached out with a shaking hand and grasped Claire's on the table. His hands were cold and callused. He tried to speak, but only issued a shallow groan. His fingers felt like they were clawing needfully at her.

Claire realized that she was crying when thin snot started to pool at the tip of her nose. She sniffed. Grabbed the old man's shoulder, his Marine uniform bunched in her fist. "Who knows about this, Dad? Who else knows?"

"I'm so sorry," he whispered. Weak. "I tried to find you! I tried—"

She shook him. "Who else knows?"

"Lieutenant Derrick," her father croaked. "He saw the calls you made."

"Is that it?" Claire demanded. She had him on the ropes. She couldn't help but feel vindicated. "Does Angela know? Does Carl Gilliard know?"

Staley shook his head. "No, no. No one else."

"We have to go," Claire blurted. "We can get out of here before anyone finds out. Dad. We can leave here. We can go to Greeley. You can take me. President Briggs will still take you back, I know he will. You can take me to Greeley like you should have done years ago!"

But her father kept shaking his head. "No, Claire. We can't do that. We can't. We have to…" he looked around, desperately. Still kneeling before his daughter, begging her forgiveness with his body, though words failed him. He seemed to seize on an idea. "No. We're going to make this right, Claire. We have to make this right. We're going to go to Angela. We're going to explain everything to her."

Adrenaline surged through Claire's body. "No!"

"We'll explain everything to her, and it will be okay. You're going to come clean, Claire. You're going to come clean about what you did. And…and I'll come clean too, for hiding you. I'll talk to Angela. I'll make this right. If you give them what you know about the Lincolnists, they'll let you stay. We can make a deal."

Claire was horrified. Her mouth worked soundlessly.

Her father stared up at her, his eyes pleading. "Please, Claire. We can make a deal. I can convince Angela. I can convince Carl, too." He reached up, and his chilly, rough hands touched her face. "I can protect you. I will. I *will* protect you."

There's no way out.

That's all Claire could think.

She was trapped.

She reached her left arm around her father's neck and she pulled him closer to her. Pulled his head into her chest. Hugged him tightly there. He sobbed into her. The tears came off of her own face and wet the top of his gray head.

No way out.

"I'm sorry, Dad. I'm so, so sorry."

She was operating in a blinding rush of panic now. A cornered animal. With her right hand, she pulled the small snub-nosed .38 from where she kept it under her gray blazer, and she placed this against her father's temple.

"I'm so sorry."

His body stiffened.

She ratcheted her arm down hard on his neck to keep him from escaping.

And then she fired a single round that killed him instantly.

NINE

COVER-UP

HER EARS RANG.

She tried to scream, but she had no breath.

It'd come out of her in a rush, and she couldn't breathe in again.

Her father's body was still and slack in her arms. She felt the warmth of his blood rushing down her midsection. A trail of brain matter lay across her left arm where she'd held him so close. She could taste the gunsmoke.

Everything inside of her felt like it had died. She'd done the unthinkable. She'd committed to a path from which there was no coming back.

But even as she fought to take a breath, and her vision sparkled around the edges, she knew she wouldn't have taken that bullet back.

What else could she have done?

At best, her father had become weak.

At worst, he'd become evil.

She did not want to be the type of person that was capable of killing their own father. But it was just one more thing that she would have to sacrifice. One more part of her that she would lay down, so that the small sliver of good that was left in the world had a chance to survive.

She couldn't take it back.

She *wouldn't* take it back.

Finally, her chest unlocked and air flooded her lungs.

Her head cleared. Just enough for some clarity.

She gasped a few times, the air stagnant and hot in her throat.

She jolted to her feet, and her father's body slumped to the floor, like it was groveling at her feet. She took a few hurried steps back, and for the first time, took a good, hard look at the situation she'd created.

Colonel Staley, one of the top military men in the UES, was now shot through the head in his kitchen. Small bits of his skull were scattered across the kitchen table top. Some of that was on Claire's left arm. When that bullet had pulverized the inside of his cranium, his nose had poured like a spigot. His face was covered in blood from his nose down.

And that blood was on Claire too. Soaking her white shirt, from her belly all the way down to the waistline of her pants.

She realized she was pulling at the blood-sodden shirt in a panic, making small, fearful noises. She was desperate to get the shirt off of her, but she was still wearing the gray suit jacket.

She didn't know she was backpedaling until her back hit the wall of the kitchen. She stopped there, leaning hard against it and trying to recover herself again. Panic and clarity smashed into her in alternating waves.

Stop stop stop stop stop.

She got control of her breathing.

In through the nose. Out through the mouth.

Steady.

Think.

She needed to compartmentalize.

After a year of having filthy, sweat-stinking strangers huff their sour breath into her face and neck as they rammed themselves inside of her, she'd learned a lot about how to compartmentalize.

This was no different.

First off, she'd done what she'd had to do. There was no way around that. This was war. And Colonel Staley, father or not, was on the wrong side of it.

So she put that part of her to rest right then and there. She would not even consider it again.

Second, she was behind enemy lines, and she'd created a murder scene. The most obvious thing to do was to make it look like a suicide. She didn't spend more than a few seconds assessing whether that was the best course of action. She'd shot him in the head. There were no forensic investigators anymore. It would be easy to cover up.

She took a few more breaths, waiting until her heart rate had slowed. A high heart rate could make thinking difficult. She needed to be clear headed.

She crossed the kitchen again, moving now with purpose. She straddled the dead body—she refused to think of it as her father now, it was only a dead body—and she hooked her arms under his and hauled up. It wasn't easy. Claire was not a large woman.

It took nearly a minute of effort to get him into his chair again. With him slouched in the chair, she scooted it so that it was positioned in line with the blood splatter going across the table top.

She'd dropped the .38 revolver on the ground at some point. She scooped it up and stood there holding it for a moment, getting her breath back again, and thinking this through.

She'd shot him on the left side of his head.

But he was right-handed.

Shit.

A small inconsistency. It might raise suspicion, but there was nothing she could do about it now. She shucked her gray blazer off. It was the garment on her body with the least amount of blood on it. She used this to wipe the revolver down. They didn't have forensics, but fingerprints were not hard to raise.

Handling the revolver through the cloth of her jacket, she placed this in Staley's dead left hand. She curled the fingers around it, put the index finger in the trigger, brought it up to the side of the head where the entrance wound was, and then let the arm fall back naturally.

The revolver held in his grip, but just barely.

It hung there by his index finger through the trigger guard.

She thought it looked natural enough.

There. Okay. What next?

A note?

No. It raised more problems than it solved.

So the next thing was what the hell she was going to do with herself.

She grabbed her suit jacket and went to the bathroom.

She took a good look at herself in the mirror.

She looked terrible. Scared and frazzled. But she ignored this. She inspected herself clinically. She searched for evidence.

She started shucking off her clothes. First the blood-soaked white shirt. Then her pants. She piled these into the sink with her suit jacket. Her socks. Even her shoes.

Her belly was pink with the remnants of blood. The only item of clothing that wasn't soaked seemed to be her bra. Even her panties were bloody. She took off the panties and put them in the sink, then decided to get rid of the bra as well.

Naked and trembling, she wet a towel and scrubbed the blood off her skin. Off her belly. Off her thighs. It was even in the thatch of her reddish pubic hair.

She put the towel in the sink, now overflowing with bloody clothing.

Took another hard look at herself in the mirror.

There. In her hair.

She leaned close and looked at it.

A single piece of gristle, or bone, or brain.

She shuddered violently, staring at it. Fought for control of herself, and then plucked it out of her hair, and flicked it into the sink amongst the clothing. Then she scrubbed those fingers on the towel, like they would never be clean again.

She left the bathroom. Naked, she stalked to her bedroom.

She stood in the doorway and stared.

The drawers of the small dresser were pulled out. She had hidden the satphone there, taped to the back wall of the dresser, behind the drawers.

Another wave of anger slammed into her.

How dare he!

It was a third and final betrayal. First, he had not come for her. Second, he had forced her to be a part of a dictatorship just like the one that she'd escaped from. And third, he'd planned to out her to them.

The fact that *he* was her *father* seemed to rise up in her again, like watching the wall of a tsunami approach. But before it could crash into her, she made it disappear.

She could not feel hurt. She could not feel betrayed.

Those feelings only made sense if she acknowledged that he was someone that she loved and trusted, and she refused to let that touch her.

This was war. And he was an enemy. That's all there was to it.

She dressed herself quickly. Jeans and a t-shirt.

Would anyone recall what she'd been wearing for the first half of the day? Would they think it weird that she had changed outfits?

She pulled on socks, and then a pair of old, battered boots that she hadn't worn in a very long time. She found it difficult to lace them. She grew enraged with her clumsy fingers and swore incessantly until she got them knotted.

She replaced the drawers in her dresser. Looked about the room. Found that it looked normal. Before leaving her bedroom, she grabbed a tattered pack—yet another thing she hadn't used in the last few years.

Back in the bathroom, she shoved all the bloody clothing into the pack and closed it. Then she rinsed the ghostly bloodstains out of the sink.

She slung the pack onto her back and went to the kitchen again.

She stared at the scene for a long while, wondering if she'd missed…

Shit!

The satphone!

It was still sitting in the middle of the table.

She snatched it, buried it deep into her backpack and then stood there shaking, terrified by the fact that she'd been about to leave behind such a condemning piece of evidence. Was there anything else that she'd forgotten?

She stood there for a long time, staring at it all, looking at every detail and trying to think if there was anything else. She couldn't believe she'd almost left the satphone.

Are you thinking clear?

Have you thought of everything?

After almost five minutes, she decided that she had.

She went to the back door and looked out. She could see the neighbor's houses. The bit of pine trees that grew up between them. There was no one out, though. The way looked clear.

She left through the back door with her bag of evidence on her back, and made straight for Elsie Foster's.

***

The door to Angela's office was open, and Kurt stood outside of it. Angela was just coming back from her midday break.

When Angela saw that the door was open, and how Kurt stood outside of it, she frowned. She generally kept the door closed when she left, and Kurt's body language was stiff. When his eyes met hers, she felt a small, hollow space appear in her gut.

Something bad happened.

Kurt nodded into Angela's office. "Someone to see you," he said.

Angela kept walking, though it took some effort.

She reached the door and stepped through.

Across from her, seated in one of the chairs in the room, was Nurse Sullivan.

This time, Angela did stop. She stood frozen in place, staring at the woman.

Nurse Sullivan was the one that had taken the lead on Abby's medical care. That was the first and most obvious place that Angela's mind went to. And here Nurse Sullivan sat, with her hands clutched in her lap, looking terrified.

Angela couldn't breathe. Her vision swam. Hot tears flooded her eyes.

Something happened.

Abby...

Sullivan stared, as though she couldn't understand Angela's sudden welling of emotion, as though she were lost in her own problems...and then it seemed to snap into place. She jolted out of her chair and held out a staying hand.

"Angela, it's not that. Abby is fine."

Breath came back into Angela's chest in a sudden gasp.

She felt relief, and then a hot blanket of anger.

"What the *hell*!" she hissed, then reached across and slammed the door to her office shut. "Don't scare me like that, Taylor!"

Sullivan blinked a few times, and then looked down at her feet. "I'm sorry. I should have...I didn't..."

Angela took a few stabilizing breaths.

Sullivan looked up again, and there were tears in her own eyes now.

What the hell is going on here?

"Abby is fine," Sullivan repeated. "She's going to be...she's *going* to be just fine."

***

Carl pushed his way into Angela's office, his eyes taking in the scene.

Angela, hunched over her desk, looking both worried and angry.

A nurse that Carl recognized from the medical center, sitting in one of the chairs, looking nervous.

Carl closed the doors behind him.

Angela's eyes were on him. She'd called him moments before, asking him to come upstairs from his office on the bottom floor where he'd been with Mitch, reviewing everything they knew about the Lincolnists and trying to find a weak link to start picking them apart.

Angela hadn't told him anything. She'd just asked him to get into her office immediately.

"Ma'am," Carl said, taking a few steps from the door, but stopping there, still unsure what he was supposed to be doing.

Angela pushed herself off of her desk. Her lips looked tight. Her eyes piercing. "Carl, this is Taylor Sullivan. She's the nurse that's been working on Abby."

Carl frowned. "Is everything alright?"

What he really wanted to ask was *What's this got to do with me?* but that would be cold, even for him.

Angela crossed her arms. "Well. I don't know. Nurse Sullivan wanted you present in order to talk."

Carl turned his gaze to the woman in the chair. Dressed in scrubs. Black bottoms. Teal top. Her hands wringing in her lap. Taylor met his gaze.

"You're Master Sergeant Gilliard, correct?" she asked.

"I am."

"And you're in charge of the investigation into the Lincolnists?" Taylor's eyes darted. "That's what I heard."

Carl took a few more steps into the room. He put his hands in the pockets of the khaki pants he'd changed into after arriving. He gave a slight nod. "You heard correctly. And if you know something, I'd advise you to let it out. Don't play with fire."

Taylor Sullivan looked at her hands for a moment. Clenched them. And then closed her eyes. Steeling herself. "I can help you," she said. "But before I can tell you anything, I need you and Angela both to make me a guarantee."

Carl and Angela exchanged a glance.

Angela still appeared very perturbed.

But Carl smelled blood in the water now. The Lincolnists were a tight group. They'd interviewed and interrogated as much as Angela would allow them, while still keeping with traditional *due process*. Nobody would say shit. They all claimed they were peaceful, and they didn't know anything about the violence.

Perhaps the weak link that he'd been searching for was sitting right in front of him.

Was Nurse Sullivan a Lincolnist?

Anything was possible. Carl knew to keep an open mind. A good investigator doesn't jump to conclusions.

"Well," Carl began. "That depends on what you can offer us. And what you want in return."

Taylor gave him a tight little shake of her head, her eyes coming open again. "No. I won't say anything until I have your guarantee."

Angela stirred at her desk. "You mean to say you'll hide information from us?"

Taylor looked terrified. "No. I mean…" she took a shaky breath. "You don't understand. I have to. It's about…It's about my son. I have to have your guarantee. Or I won't…I can't…say anything."

Angela looked like she was about to light into Taylor, but Carl held up a hand. *Let me handle this.* Angela reeled herself back in and crossed her arms, eyes narrowing at Taylor.

Carl considered the situation in front of him, and then stepped forward. He chose the chair across from Taylor, and sat down on the edge of it, leaning forward on his elbows.

"Alright," he said. "Let's start with what you want from us. What is it that you want me and Angela to guarantee you?"

Taylor blinked several times, and Carl realized there was the glistening of tears in her eyes. "Total immunity for me and my son. And protection."

Carl lifted a single eyebrow. "We'll address what you need total immunity from in a moment. For now, how about you tell me what you mean by protection. Who do you need protection from, and how do you think we're going to accomplish that?"

Taylor's face became blank. Like she hadn't quite puzzled all of that out in her mind yet, and was surprised that Carl didn't know what she meant. "Uh...I guess I mean...that you need to hide us. From Elsie Foster. From the Lincolnists." Her eyes flicked back and forth from Carl to Angela several times. "Don't you have a place where we can go? Where you can keep us safe from them?"

Carl considered this for a moment. There was The Complex. It wouldn't be ideal to house civilians there, but it was a viable option to work as a safehouse, if need be.

Carl gave Angela a small nod, and then gave the same nod to Taylor. "Yes. We have a place that might work to keep you and your son safe."

Taylor looked relieved.

"Now, let's address what you mean by immunity."

The look of relief fled from Taylor's face. She swallowed hard. "I mean that no matter what I say, no matter what I tell you guys, you have to promise that you won't hold it against me and my son. That's the guarantee that I need from you."

Out of the corner of his eye, Carl saw Angela gearing up to squash this. But Carl saw a way in, a weak link, the sole opportunity that he'd been granted to rip these Lincolnists apart. Angela might not like making deals with the devil, but if she wanted traditional due process, then she'd just have to swallow that and allow Carl to work with a willing informant, no matter what the informant and her son were guilty of.

"What do we get out of it?" Carl asked, before Angela could say anything.

Taylor looked frozen. Stuck. "I'm not sure I can say...I shouldn't say anything. Not until I have your guarantee—"

"No." Carl shook his head. "That's not how it works, Taylor. You want us to make a deal, then you need to tell us what we get out of it."

Taylor frowned. "And if I don't?"

"Then I'll just arrest you," Carl said. "I think I've got plenty at this point to believe that you're a Lincolnist, based on what you've told me."

"I'm not!"

"Then you better start telling us what it is that you're going to give us." Carl's voice stopped being friendly. "This isn't the time to mess around, Ms. Sullivan. And I'm not the one to mess around with. You started this game, now it's time to play ball."

Taylor's jaw worked silently for a few seconds. "Fine." Her eyes flew back and forth again. "It's Elsie Foster. I can give you Elsie Foster."

***

"Don't torpedo this," Carl growled from across the desk.

Taylor Sullivan was now outside the office, watched by Kurt. Mitch and Logan were on their way up to retrieve her, and Rudy and Morrow were prepping to drive out to the Sullivan house, get Ben Sullivan—her son—and secure them at The Complex.

But Angela didn't like it.

Carl wasn't trying to intimidate Angela, but he was passionate about the subject at hand, and leaned across her desk, glowering at her for her resistance.

"The kid's a rapist!" Angela hissed, not wanting to be heard through the office door. "No, not a *kid*. Let's call it like it is, Carl. He's a goddamned *man*, and he raped one of the girls! That's not something you get a free pass on!"

Carl was not a man prone to losing his temper, but he would've liked to hurl everything off of Angela's desk in that moment, just to get her attention. But, as always, Carl controlled himself.

He pushed himself upright again. Took a breath. "Angela, you want me to take these people down through *legal means*. Due process. All that horseshit. Well, this is it. This is how we get in. You wanted proof? Now you've got it. You can't throw that away."

"What if people find out that we're harboring a rapist?"

"We won't tell them. And I don't think the Sullivan's will either."

"But Elsie Foster will!" Angela smacked the desktop. "She has proof! She'll come out with it if we make a move!"

Carl nodded. "Then we'll work quietly, and quickly. Before they have a chance to react. Let me secure the Sullivans, we'll debrief the Benjamin kid, and we'll take down everyone we need to take down before they can start muddying the waters."

Angela raked a hand through her hair. "It's not *right*."

Carl hadn't wanted to bring up the trump card here, but he had no other option. "Angela, they were trying to poison your daughter."

Angela stared at him like he'd smacked her.

The two of them remained silent for a long moment.

Carl could see Angela struggling with this. She wanted to do the civilized thing—that was her big hang-up. She wanted them all to be so civilized. But they weren't dealing with civilized people. They were dealing with people that would infect a young girl with plague-tainted tissue, just to get at her mother.

For a flash, Carl saw the same hatred in Angela's eyes that he felt in his own soul.

The desire to throw civility to the wind and scorch the earth.

"Let me do my job," Carl pressed. "I can dismantle them before they even know what's going on. All I need is for you to let me do it. Let me off the leash, Angela. Let me handle this. You've got the proof you've been waiting for."

Angela crossed her arms over her chest. Put one hand over her mouth. Looked off at nothing in particular. Her eyes showed the faintest glimmer of moisture, but all of the emotion had been stricken from her face. Save for the hint of tears in her eyes, she looked cold and dead.

Finally, her blue eyes met his gray ones.

Across the small span of desktop, and vastly different life experiences, they shared a moment of grim determination.

"Let's get one thing straight," Angela said quietly. "This Sullivan man-child piece of shit. I won't go back on my word to Taylor. But you put the fear of God into him, Carl. I want him to understand in no uncertain terms, that if he ever makes another slip, if he even so much as swipes an extra can of beans from a ration box, then him and his mother are both done here. I'll kick their asses out of this Safe Zone so fast, the primals will be picking their bones clean before they can say the word 'immunity.' Is that understood?"

Carl nodded. "Perfectly."

Angela leaned forward. "Do this quick and quiet, Carl. Before Elsie can catch wind of it."

"Enough said." Carl spun on his heels, not wanting to wait another moment. The leash had been removed. It was time to do work.

When he opened the door to Angela's office, he stopped, staring at the scene outside.

Kurt was there, standing next to Taylor Sullivan.

But someone else was present as well.

Claire Staley stood across from them, staring at Taylor, while Taylor stared at the ground.

For a brief moment, Carl was concerned about discretion, and the security of the operation, but when Claire turned to look at him, he saw that there might be other problems at hand.

Claire's face was pale, and her sharp, green eyes were bloodshot and puffy, like she'd been crying.

Carl didn't know what else to do, so he stood aside, holding the door for Claire.

Claire stepped into the room and looked at Angela. Her mouth worked silently for a second or two. Fresh tears sprang into her eyes.

"It's my father," she choked out. "I think he committed suicide."

TEN

TARGETS

When Tex got back to the hideout, Lee could immediately see that he was excited.

The second that the big pickup truck rolled to a stop beneath the canopy of mesquite, the front passenger door opened and Tex slid out. He had a spring in his step as he walked towards the house, trailing Corporal Thompson. He wasn't exactly smiling, but the corners of his mouth were quirked up.

Lee watched him from the window in the common area that looked into the back of the property. He glanced to his right, to where Julia and Abe sat in quiet conversation with two members of Tex's crew, playing an inscrutable card game they called euchre. Deuce lay a pace away from Lee, his head on his paws, watching Lee carefully like he might spring up at any moment. Deuce was never relaxed around this many strangers.

Tex entered the back door and flowed into the living room, bringing with him a rush of activity.

"We got word," he announced to everyone in the room. He spied Lee as he pushed his Oakleys up onto his head and motioned Lee over. "Come join us in the war room."

The "war room" turned out to be the dining room, situated just off the living room. It had a table that was large enough for everyone to huddle over. There was enough seating, but everyone chose to stand.

Tex placed his rifle on the table and started shucking off his armor. "Just got back from a meeting with several of our satellite groups, as well as some new allies." He looked at Lee and Abe. "Y'all remember Cheech and Tully?"

"No shit?" Lee's eyebrows went up. "You've been in contact with them?"

Cheech and Tully were both Coordinators. Oklahoma and New Mexico, respectively.

Cheech was not his actual name. It was Trzetrzelewska, but nobody could pronounce it. When they'd met at Project Hometown selection, he'd introduced himself as "Captain *cheh-cheh-LEV-ska*," which he quickly followed with a knowing smile and "just call me Cheech."

Tully was just Captain Tully.

Tex nodded. "They've been busy. Cheech in particular. He's got Greeley breathing down his neck, but he's managed to keep a low profile. From what I can tell from our source in Greeley, Briggs still doesn't know whether Cheech and Tully are *non-viable*, or simply dead. Which will work to our advantage."

Lee frowned, and felt old memories washing up on him. "How are they?"

Tex eyed Lee. "Well. They're still alive. But they don't have near the infrastructure you have." Tex favored him with a small smile. "I don't know if you know this, Lee. But amongst our friends from Project Hometown, there's really only two categories: Those that have gone to Briggs, and those that are barely surviving. What you accomplished in North Carolina…well, you're the only one that's done it."

"Texas seems to be doing okay," Lee pointed out.

Tex snorted. "Us? We're just a bunch of guerillas in the hills, my friend. And right now we're sandwiched between two very big threats—three, if you count the teepios. But that brings me back to Oklahoma and New Mexico. I've been in talks with them for a while, but since they learned that I've got the great Lee Harden in my midst, they're in with both feet. They don't have a lot to commit to the fight, but we know that we've got allies on two sides of us, so that's good. And Cheech can offer a buffer between us and Colorado. Against ground mobilization, anyways…"

As Tex spoke, Lee glanced to his right, looking to get a gauge on Julia's reaction to what she was hearing. But when his eyes fell on her, he saw her lips were tight, and she was staring daggers across the table. For a second, Lee thought this rancor was directed at Tex, which seemed odd, but when he followed her gaze he saw one of Tex's troops on the far end of the table, smiling back at Julia.

It was a young guy with sunburned skin, and Lee didn't know his name. But Lee saw that his right hand was deep in the pocket of his pants, moving slowly back and forth over his crotch as he looked at Julia. He parted his lips, and his pink tongue flashed around inside.

Lee's first instinct was to call the guy out. But the second he considered it, he could almost hear Julia's angry voice: "If I wanted to make a scene, *I* would have made the scene!"

So Lee kept his mouth shut.

In the background, Tex's voice.

And somewhere under Lee's skin, right along his spine, a cold, steel thread drew tight. He didn't feel enraged. It wasn't hot and unthinking. It was a chilly sort of scientific curiosity that wondered *how long could this guy keep his erection if I cut him open and spilled his guts on his feet?*

"Lee."

Lee blinked and looked at Tex.

Tex's eyebrows were up. "You with me, brother?"

Lee gave him a perfunctory smile. "Yeah. I'm with you. Just...thinking."

"So? Can you get your Marines over here?"

Lee hadn't been tracking what Tex was saying. That was out of character for him, but then again, maybe he felt a little out of character lately. Regardless, it didn't change Lee's mental calculations. "I don't know," he said.

Tex looked like he was trying hard not to appear crestfallen. "Okay...what's the problem?"

Someone off to the side let out a weird little titter.

Lee glanced over and saw that it was Jackoff himself.

The guy still had his hand in his pocket, but he wasn't rubbing himself anymore. He'd turned his smile on Lee now. "I thought this guy was supposed to be in charge of...like...the military or something."

Lee stared at him. Pictured that look of amusement changing to shock as he felt his intestines pile up at his feet...

Tex made a noise in the back of his throat. Something between a groan and a throat clear. "Thank you, Pikes. As usual, you add so much to the conversation. Don't you have watch tonight? Shouldn't you be catching up on sleep?"

A few of the soldiers around Pikes gave him derisive snickers, and one of them prodded his shoulder the way you would to get an annoying child to go back to their toys and leave the adults alone.

Pikes just kept smiling that idiot smile of his. "Yeah, alright."

He turned with one last lecherous gaze at Julia, and departed from the table, hand still in his pocket.

Tex watched him go with irritation scribbled across his features. Then he turned his gaze to Lee. "What's up?"

"First off," Lee said. "I don't control the military. We have an elected civilian that makes the decisions. Commander and chief shit."

Tex nodded. "Sure. But she pretty much does what you tell her to, right?"

Lee shook his head. "Not necessarily. And we don't want to plan around an assumption." Lee took a breath. "The second thing is that the Marines are currently stationed in Georgia, waiting for orders. Which means they've got three states of hostile territory to cross."

"The I-20 corridor is mostly clear," Tex pointed out. "Could have them here within a day."

Lee folded his arms across his chest. "What are we talking about here, Tex? You trying to retake Texas?"

His fellow Coordinator shook his head. "Eventually, yes. But not right now. Right now, we need the same thing we've always needed: A big target. Something that will weaken *Nuevas Fronteras* and Greeley at the same time. Ideally, it would also strengthen us."

"So a fuel depot?" Abe offered. "Again?"

"Nah," Tex replied. "We need something bigger. Something like one of their refineries. Or a transfer station. Something that damages their production capability."

Abe and Lee exchanged a look. Lee nodded to encourage Abe to go on. Lee didn't always want to be the nay-sayer.

Abe looked to Tex. "Listen. Even if we could time it perfectly and get all the Marines from Georgia to Texas safely and when we need them, there's still a big issue here."

"What's that?"

"You want a prime target, right?"

"Right."

Abe nodded. "Well, what do you think *Nuevas Fronteras* is gonna think when they see a contingent of Marines hightailing it towards Texas? And they *will* see it. That's the problem. Even if they cross those three states without getting ambushed, they're guaranteed to get noticed. And once they're noticed, *Nuevas Fronteras* is gonna go on high alert and double down on any strategically valuable locations they have. Which means any attack we have planned is going to be exponentially harder."

Lee listened, and nodded his head.

Tex frowned but didn't disagree. It was simple enough that Tex should have seen it, but at the same time, Lee could appreciate that sometimes positive momentum could blind you to the weak points in a plan. You needed someone to play devil's advocate and deliberately poke holes to see the weak points.

"Alright," Tex rubbed his mouth. "I won't argue that point. Element of surprise. That's our biggest advantage. And we shit it out the window if they see all those Marines coming."

Abe nodded.

"Where are we getting this target?" Lee inquired.

"I'm scheduled to talk to our guy in Greeley tomorrow afternoon. I'll let him know we're ready to make a move. He'll probe around for something juicy, and pass it on."

Lee was aware that their "guy in Greeley" was Major John Bellamy. Tex had confided that to him, but for purposes of opsec, they referred to him in general terms. Tex didn't expect any of his guys to be in Briggs's pocket, but you could never be too careful.

Lee chose his words carefully, because he was aware that he'd poked away at Tex's plan in front of his men, and he didn't want to appear like he was undermining Tex's authority. "That's why I'm *hesitant* to call the Marines in *right now*. But...if I can make a suggestion?"

Tex leaned back and gave Lee a *go ahead* wave.

"You work your magic with your guy in Greeley," Lee said. "Get the target. Once we have a plan, we start moving on it. Send one tanker of diesel from the convoy earlier today over to the Marines in Georgia. I'll have them bolster up an even bigger force out of Fort Bragg. When we're ready to make the hit on the target, we can start them moving in our direction. We'll hopefully have the target hit before *Nuevas Fronteras* gets word of the Marines coming, and then once they're here, we can use them to bolster our defenses against a counter-attack. Which we're going to need. Because both Greeley and *Nuevas Fronteras* are going to be pissed if we pull this off." Lee held up his hands. "Your guys—your call. I'm simply offering my advice."

Tex eyed him, but Lee couldn't tell what he was thinking. He could tell that he was being gauged, but other than that, Tex kept a pretty good poker face.

Finally, he nodded. "Well, like you said: Why don't we get the target first and go from there?"

***

The two-engine Cessna landed at the airport in Greeley, Colorado at about midday.

The Greeley-Webb County Airport had recently been annexed into the official Greeley Green Zone, which meant that all the military birds—mostly helicopters—that had been clustered in a large shopping mall parking lot, now had a little elbow room.

The Cessna, however, was an unwelcome guest.

It had not responded to any transmissions, and it was not on any official schedule.

As its tires chirped on the tarmac and the flaps slowed it down, a pair of pickup trucks with an ample amount of soldiers in the bed and on the running boards, tore after it.

The Cessna buzzed to a stop about halfway down the airfield. The props still spun, but whoever was in the pilot's seat had at least noticed the pickup trucks approaching and wasn't taxiing away from them.

A soldier on a bullhorn shouted commands that may or may not have been audible to the pilot.

The two pickups came roaring to a stop, about twenty yards off the right wing.

"You are not authorized to use this airfield!" the soldier with the bullhorn repeated for the third time. "Shut down the engines! Exit the plane with your hands over your head! If you do not comply, we will fire on you!"

The soldiers pointed their rifles, ready and more than willing to demolish the little Cessna at the slightest provocation. Airport security was one of the more boring assignments. Everyone was starving for some entertainment, and shredding a small aircraft seemed like just the thing to scour their doldrums away.

The soldier with the bullhorn waited, glaring at the Cessna, and right about the time when he took a breath to blare out a final warning, he heard a car horn behind him.

He turned to look.

Two black SUVs were hauling up to them. They both bore a red delta symbol on their front doors.

Cornerstone.

The two Cornerstone vehicles went around the left side of the pickups and stopped, creating a barricade between the soldiers and the Cessna.

The passenger door of the lead SUV opened and Mr. Daniels, the CEO for Cornerstone, stepped out. He smiled and waved at them. Over the sound of the Cessna's dying engines (the pilot had complied and shut them off) Daniels called to the soldier with the bullhorn.

"We got this! Thank you!"

Another Cornerstone operative, a burly merc with a devilishly pointed beard, trotted up to the side of the pickup. He wore black sunglasses that completely hid his eyes, and he had a bare-bones chest-rig with a nametape that read MCNAIR. He was aggressively chewing gum.

The soldier with the bullhorn instantly hated everything about him.

"This plane is here on Cornerstone's request," the merc named McNair stated between gum-chomps. "It's a private matter. Thank you for your diligence. You can stand down."

The sergeant felt the usual fire in his gut that he felt when he and his men were ordered around by Cornerstone operatives. But this had become commonplace, and though it chapped his ass, Cornerstone had pretty much been given carte blanche to operate as they saw fit within the Greeley Green Zone.

The why of the matter was above the sergeant's paygrade.

That paygrade being a military ration card for two thousand calories a day, plus 1800 for his wife, and 700 each for his two kids. And in this day and age, you didn't mess around with that. Getting into pissing contests with Mr. Daniels's minions was a quick way to get your ration card suspended. Literally taking food out of your family's mouth.

The sergeant lowered his bullhorn and keyed his radio. "All units, stand down. Pull back. Cornerstone's got this one."

He could imagine the general grumbles, but the soldiers did as they were told, mounted back onto the pickup trucks, and then retreated to a safe and unassuming distance.

At the side of the Cessna, Daniels and two of his operatives waited while the cabin door and the built in stairs descended.

A dark-haired man emerged, wearing khakis and a loose-fitting yellow shirt.

The man descended the stairs and took a glance over his shoulder to see the pickup trucks that had accosted his plane, now approximately three hundred yards away.

Daniels smiled and extended his hand.

The man in the yellow shirt took the hand and gave it a casual shake.

"Mr. Leyva," Daniels said. "I apologize for the ruckus. I figured it would be safer to handle this out here than to notify them ahead of time, based on the information you gave me when you called."

Joaquin Leyva gave a smirk. "Not a problem," he said in accented but clear English.

Daniels led Joaquin back to the lead SUV, and the two of them climbed in the back.

Only one operative accompanied them, the man with the pointed beard taking the driver's seat. The beard seemed to shimmer and shiver with the flexing of his jaw muscles as he continued to gnaw at the gum in his mouth.

When they were secure inside the vehicle, Daniels pointed to the driver. "McNair is one of my most trusted operatives. You can speak freely here, Mr. Leyva."

The SUV began to move, accelerating away from the Cessna and back towards the gates of the airfield.

Joaquin leaned into the center of the SUV, looking out the windshield at the sprawl of the Greeley Green Zone that they approached. "So, this is where the power sits now? A bit less impressive than Washington D.C., no?"

Daniels just kept smiling, waiting for him to get to the point.

Joaquin sighed and leaned back. "I'm glad we were able to contact you directly. We believe that there is a leak in your organization."

ELEVEN

PRIMALS

THE ALPHA HEADED INTO THE SETTING SUN. The red and orange glow flashed at him like a signal through the trees. He smelled the tang of the pine all around him, the mustiness of the forest loam.

And of course, he smelled the Easy Prey.

He was not trying to go to any particular place, so he did not run.

But he also needed to make up ground. So he moved along at a strong trot.

He was *probing*.

He circled the place where all the Easy Prey had clustered themselves. The clustering was good for predators, but usually not good for prey. The only thing that kept the Easy Prey safe was their cleverness.

But The Alpha knew that sometimes, their cleverness had *holes*.

Gaps.

He and his pack had fed well a few nights ago, after they had found one of those holes. They'd returned to it, but the Easy Prey had been clever again, and made the hole so that it would not open anymore.

So now The Alpha was probing again, looking for a new hole.

A new weakness.

To his left, he was aware of the constant, dim hum given off by the very thin sticks that would kill you if you touched them. The Alpha could not decide if they were more like very straight sticks, or like very thick strands of spiderweb. He only knew not to touch them.

Another trick of the Easy Prey.

Behind him, he heard the quiet padding of his packmates, and the susurration of their collective breaths as they followed him.

They would need to feed again soon. If they could not find a way to get at all the Easy Prey inside those humming strands, then they would have to go out into the woods and catch some not-so-easy prey. But for now he could keep probing.

He trotted along for another quarter mile before coming to a halt, his sharp eyes picking out movement on the other side of the humming strands. Behind him, his packmates came to a stop as well. Quiet and still.

In the darkening dusk, he saw a figure moving along. Its body was swathed in something that made it hard to pick out amongst the foliage, but the movement was easy enough to see. And the scent...

It came to an abrupt halt, almost directly across from The Alpha.

The Alpha did not try to hide itself. It sat on its haunches, watching.

The Easy Prey squinted through the humming strands, and its eyes widened when they locked onto The Alpha. Its feet did a little shuffle, and the breeze carried a sudden dank whiff of panic-sweat. The smell tickled something deep in The Alpha's brain, and its mouth began to water.

The Easy Prey was only two quick lopes away. If it weren't for the humming strands between them, The Alpha could feed on it now...

But the humming strands were there.

So The Alpha simply sat there, watching it, and the Easy Prey stood there, shaking, and exuding that pungent scent that all prey gave off when they encountered a predator.

The Easy Prey on the other side made some noises with its mouth, and The Alpha knew what the noises were, though he could not remember what they meant. He knew that this was how the Easy Prey communicated, and deep in its vestigial self, knew that it used to communicate the same way.

Now it was just the excited tittering of an animal preparing to die.

The Alpha pulled its attention away from the prey on the other side and gave one last, long look at the humming strands, to see if, perhaps, by some chance, there was a way to take this prey down. But he saw no way past the humming strands.

The Alpha lost interest, knowing he couldn't get through.

He chuffed, and then continued along the perimeter of the humming strands.

Probing for weaknesses.

***

Sam hadn't heard from anyone about his name being on the sign up list, and he assumed that it was still too early for them to have made their selections from the available volunteers.

That all changed when he arrived at The Barn for his third shift guard duty.

As he entered the large hangar, he became aware of a bustle of activity down at the far end, where two pickup trucks and a gun truck Humvee sat, and a collection of soldiers in full battle rattle lounged about, as soldiers tend to do when they are waiting for someone in charge to finish getting their shit together.

He didn't give it much more than a glance. There was always something going on that he was not privy to, and he'd learned long ago not to get curious about things, because when you asked about them, you were typically given *the look*, and told to mind your own business, often in terms far less civil.

He was making his way to the armorer to be issued his M4 for tonight's long walk around whatever section of the perimeter he was supposed to patrol this evening, when the first sergeant scuttled out of his office with a clipboard in his hand.

"Private Ryder!" It was First Sergeant Hamrick, who was no great fan of "half-boots" in general, and Sam in particular.

Sam rocked to a halt, evaluated the distance between him and Hamrick, and decided that he should sprint closer before offering his salute.

Hamrick didn't look up from his clipboard as Sam did this. His brow was beetled over his dark eyes, his bristly black hair looking like he was beginning to sweat, thought it was a fairly cool night out.

Without looking up, Hamrick moved his hand in what Sam understood to be a return salute, and he muttered something that Sam interpreted as "at ease."

When Sam put his arm down, Hamrick turned the clipboard and shoved it uncomfortably close to his face.

"That your fucking scrawl right there?" Hamrick's blunt-ended index finger was hooked around the clipboard and pointing to slot number 23, where Sam recognized his own handwriting.

"Yes, sir."

"Well, fuckin' congrats. Thought you'da written in Arabic or some shit." Hamrick's eyes finally came up to Sam's. "Does your mommy know that you signed up for this shit?"

"No, sir." *And she's not my mother,* Sam thought, but wisely kept that to himself.

Hamrick retracted the clipboard. "Am I gonna get in trouble by sending you out?"

"No, sir."

"So if you get your ass chewed off by a primal, President Houston isn't gonna want to chew my ass off for letting you go out?"

Sam's stomach did a little flip flop. "No, sir."

"Great." Hamrick tucked the clipboard under one arm, and used the other to form the most rigid knife-hand ever seen, which he used to point to Sam's head. "Get a lid." The knife-hand moved to his chest. "Get some flak." The knife-hand pivoted out to the two pickups and the guntruck on the far end of The Barn. "Report to Corporal Billings."

Sam blinked a few times. "Yes, sir. Do I need a rifle, sir?"

Hamrick looked at him like a pile of white dog shit on a pristine lawn. "Oh my Christ. Well, you're going outside the wire, you dumbshit, so yes. But you're on the turret." Hamrick frowned. "You do know how to work the M2, don't you?"

Sam swallowed. No one wanted to be in the turret. The turret was open. They all wanted the suppressive firepower of the M2, but no one wanted to hang out where a primal could leap up from behind and drag you out.

But, yes, Sam had been trained on the M2.

Very briefly.

They hadn't even been allowed to fire it.

The whole lesson on the M2 had consisted of thirty minutes of nomenclature, how to load it, how to charge it, how to aim it, and how to press both thumbs to the butterfly trigger. Then they'd all been given one opportunity to pull the monstrous charging handle back and click the trigger on an empty chamber.

Viola. You're trained.

"Yes, sir," Sam managed. "I've been trained on it."

"My confidence in you is nearly overwhelming," Hamrick remarked, and then he turned back to his office and tossed over his shoulder. "Don't die!"

And that was that.

Five minutes later Sam had a helmet strapped to his head that was a size too large, and an old woodland camouflage OTV "flak jacket" strapped to his chest that smelled of someone else's stress sweat.

He hustled over to the guntruck, his eyes fixated on the big machine gun on the turret, his stomach turning over, first excited, and then fearful.

He thought of Charlie, and how she'd feel if she found out he'd gone out and died, and the thought was strangely satisfying, considering the fact that it was predicated on his death.

As though he'd be present to watch her feel bad.

Nope, he told himself. *When you're dead you're dead.*

"You the half-boot?" A hand came out of nowhere and planted itself on Sam's armored chest, stopping him.

He looked over. He'd been halted by a fair-haired soldier with a scowl across his young face, a helmet under his arm, corporal's stripes, and a nametape that said BILLINGS.

"You Corporal Billings?" Sam asked, and immediately regretted it for the idiot question it was.

Billings's scowl turned almost disappointed. "First off, you half-boot fuck, I asked you a goddamned question. Second off, do you have fucking eyeballs and do they fucking see my nametape, and can you fucking read English?"

"Yes, sir."

Billings dropped his hands and looked even more distraught. "Yes, to what?"

Sam inwardly kicked himself as he stood there, feeling ten years old in front of this guy, and getting pissed, both at himself and Corporal Billings. He was acting exactly how they expected him to act—green and stupid.

But Sam had plenty of experience under his belt. He wasn't an idiot. He knew how to handle himself.

Sam drew himself up, and let a flash of irritation take his face and squash the nervousness that had resided there before. "Yes to all of it, sir. I have eyes, they can see, and I can read English, and also speak it, as you can see."

Billings looked partially mollified to see that the half-boot at least had a spine. "Alright, don't be a fucking sassy pants. And stop calling me 'sir,' I'm a fucking corporal." He stepped back and gestured to a few of the soldiers lounging around the guntruck, and one guy that was clearly *not* a soldier, and looked about as out-of-place as Sam felt.

Billings did rapid-fire introductions and finished with, "This is our new gunner. He's a half-boot, and I think he's a hadji, but we won't hold that against him, will we?"

"I dunno." The guy that had been introduced as Jones gave Sam a speculative look. "Say something American, like…like 'get some, motherfucker!'"

Sam glanced at Billings to see if this was actually required. Billings seemed to be watching him expectantly. Sam shifted his weight. "Uh…get some, motherfucker."

Jones winced. "I mean…you don't sound like a hadji, but it's not great. Can you do like a deep south accent when you say it? Do that. Do a deep south accent."

There was a series of concurring nods from Billings and the third soldier, Chris. The one that wasn't a soldier—Allen, Sam thought—merely watched with a dazed expression.

Sam felt a slight burn of humiliation. But he knew he was the new guy, and the new guy always had to prove himself, and at least they weren't throwing him down stairs in a footlocker.

Sam hadn't been born in the United States, but he'd lived here all his life. Despite that, he'd never picked up the various versions of southern that were represented in North Carolina, and he spoke without an accent.

He had to think of Mr. Keith, the grizzled old man that had originally given him the little .22 caliber rifle, way back when he was still a scared kid in Camp Ryder, and he did his best to mimic Mr. Keith's mumbly southern dialect.

"Git sum, muhfuckerr!"

He expelled it with enough gusto that Jones gave him an approving look. "Okay. Not bad. You can ride in my truck."

Billings let out a long-suffering sigh. "Alright. What's your name, half-boot?"

"Sam Ryder."

"Ryder, you know what we're doing?"

"Going to hunt primals?"

"More or less." Billings gestured to Allen, the non-soldier. "He's like a game tracker or some shit. We tagged a primal. Now we're gonna see where it went. According to the GPS, it looks like it's over near the Cross Creek Mall in Fayetteville. You familiar?"

Sam nodded. Fayetteville used to be synonymous with Fort Bragg, but the Safe Zone didn't include it. Fayetteville hadn't done well after the collapse of society, and during the first year of Fort Bragg being a Safe Zone, they'd picked the remains clean. It was now just a gutted-out ghost town with nothing left to give, and Sam didn't think anyone had been there in over a year.

"Alright." Billings pulled Sam around to the open backend of the guntruck and pulled out what looked like a large green ammo can. He opened it and extracted a PVS-14 Monocular Night Vision Device, which he handed to Sam. "That's our spare set. It's squirrelly sometimes, but that's all you got right now. You know how to hook it up?"

Sam nodded again, and clumsily began to attach it to the mount on his helmet with unpracticed fingers. Billings watched him with something like pity, but let him puzzle his way through it. When Sam thought he had it on correctly, he held his hands out and looked to Billings for approval.

The corporal eyed it to make sure it was properly attached, and then gave Sam a wan smile and a pat on the shoulder. "Alright. You'll do fine, Ryder." He twirled his finger in the air, signaling to the other soldiers at the pickups. "We're oscar-mike, gents."

***

Lieutenant Derrick felt troubled.

They tried to keep things quiet, but the Safe Zone was like a small town, and word spread fast.

Colonel Staley was dead.

He'd committed suicide in his home.

One of Derrick's neighbors had come over to his house, right as Derrick was rolling out of bed and preparing for his third shift duty as watch commander. Derrick had answered the door in his "Ranger Panties," rubbing the sleep out of his eyes and scowling as he wondered why someone was banging on his door when they knew he was a third shifter.

The neighbor had spilled the beans in a state of overexcitement, and then stood there, like an emotional vulture, waiting to see Derrick's reaction to the news.

Derrick's reaction had been disbelief.

He said, "Thanks for telling me," and closed the door on his neighbor's expectant face.

He'd gotten dressed in his ACUs, moving slow, in a state of shock.

Suicide?

That didn't sound like Colonel Staley at all. But people said you could never really tell when someone had reached the end of their rope.

And that got Derrick thinking about what had caused Staley to get to that point.

And that got Derrick thinking about the satphone.

Someone had used that satphone to call an unknown number, right smack dab in the middle of everyone trying to figure out who the hell was leaking information to Greeley, Colorado. And the last person to have that satphone had been Staley's daughter, Claire.

Claire. Who worked for President Houston.

Derrick was still frowning as he looked himself over in the mirror and made sure his uniform was up to snuff.

Derrick was a man who took pride in the confidence of his superior officers. He'd gone to Colonel Staley directly with what he'd found, not wanting to go behind the man's back and betray him.

Staley had told him that he would handle it, and not to speak to anyone else about it.

So Derrick hadn't.

The picture of discretion, he'd deliberately forgotten about it.

Until now.

Now, his mind was rife with misgivings. Had he done the right thing by keeping silent about it? Of course he had. His superior officer had asked him for silence.

But was he really thinking what he was thinking?

Claire...

Derrick didn't want to be a panic hound or a rumor monger. But on the other side of that, this was about a potentially huge leak in Fort Bragg. And no one knew about the satphone except Colonel Staley and him.

And now Colonel Staley was dead.

Looking at himself in the mirror, Derrick came to the only conclusion that he supposed a good soldier *should* come to. He'd sworn to be quiet to protect Colonel Staley. Now the man was dead, which meant that silence needed to be broken.

He simply couldn't sit on it anymore.

He had thirty minutes before he needed to report to the watch commander's post. He had time to go by Carl Gilliard's office and tell him what he knew about the satphone. Because *someone* needed to know. And at that point, Derrick would have done his due diligence, and it would be someone else's problem.

Resolute, he walked to the front of his residence, and was nearly to the door when someone knocked on it from the other side.

Derrick felt a flood of irritation.

Another neighbor, come to blab about the bad news and see if Derrick got emotional.

He swung the door open, frowning.

A man in a black sweatshirt with the hood pulled up over his head levelled a shotgun at his chest. There was a single, bright bloom of fire from the muzzle, and Derrick felt a massive lead fist punch him in the chest, lifting him briefly off his feet, and then slamming him onto the floor on his back.

His heart was pulverized instantly.

His last fading thought as he stared at the ceiling of his house was that it was strange that he hadn't even heard the shotgun blast, but how he heard the very clear sound of the man's footsteps running away...

TWELVE

INTERROGATIONS

CARL STEPPED OUT of his office in The Compound, leaving Taylor Sullivan alone to wring her hands.

He closed the door behind him, and looked bleakly at the legal pad in his hand. His notes were sparse, because the information was sparse.

Giving Sullivan her due, they had Elsie Foster dead to rights. She'd coerced Sullivan into trying to infect Abby with tissue taken from the primal that Doc Trent had autopsied. To nurse Sullivan's credit, she hadn't even got to the point where she'd harvested the tissue from the primal to do the job.

But Carl didn't want to move on Elsie out of a knee-jerk reaction. If he locked her up, all her little compatriots were going to go to ground. And Carl wanted to wipe them out in one fell swoop.

Problem was, Sullivan had no clue who Elsie's associates were. Carl had grilled her for an hour, going over the same damn shit, and ultimately gotten the same answers: Elsie had always met with

Sullivan alone. There was no third party. No one else around when they met.

The one potential thread he had to pursue here was in reference to her son.

Her *rapist* son.

Ben Sullivan had been caught at a party date raping some girl, using drugs that he'd stolen from his mother's nursing kit. The pure negligence of Sullivan leaving those things accessible rankled Carl, but he could no more punish her for that than he could punish Ben for being a rapist.

Angela and Carl had guaranteed complete immunity to them in exchange for Elsie.

So as much as Carl wanted to beat the hell out of the kid, he wasn't going to do it. But he was going to ask him a few pertinent questions that might reveal more of Elsie's crew. After all, *someone* had been at the party to take compromising pictures of Ben.

Carl went two doors down, to another office that was no longer used, accept to now contain Ben Sullivan. They weren't purpose-built for interrogation rooms, but they would have to suffice. The Compound was the safest place for them right now.

Carl opened the office door and slid in, giving the young man inside a long, cold look.

Ben Sullivan jerked when Carl opened the door, like he'd been caught doing something wrong. Guilty conscience, Carl supposed. The office was mostly empty. Ben was standing over by a bookshelf that contained a few three-ring binders that belonged to its previous occupant.

Ben was a tall, good-looking kid. Carl wondered why he found the need to date rape girls. Maybe he liked the sense of power and control.

Carl closed the office door and pointed to a chair on the visitor's side of the empty metal desk that stood in the room. "Ben. Have a seat."

"Where's my mom? Is she alright?"

Carl tucked the legal pad under his arm and stepped further into the office. He grabbed the chair he'd motioned to and jerked it out so that the seat of it was facing Ben. "Sit," he commanded.

Ben looked like he might start making a deal out of it, but then withered under Carl's icy gaze, and took the seat.

Carl stepped to the desk and sat on the edge of it so that he loomed over the kid. He scanned his legal pad as he spoke. "She's fine. She's a few doors down. She's worried about you. But both of you are safe here. Per the deal that she struck with President Houston and I."

Ben gave a nervous nod. He had the basics down—Mitch had given him the general overview when he'd transported him to this location. A form of "witness protection," one might say.

"I'm Master Sergeant Carl Gilliard. I'd like to talk to you about a few things." Carl let his eyes sneak up and bore into the young man sitting across from him. "And let me remind you that your complete and total cooperation is a prerequisite to you and your mother's continued safety here."

Ben looked worried. "What's that supposed to mean?"

"It means that the only reason I have to protect a rapist is because you have information that I want."

Ben's face paled, and then flushed at the cheeks. His mouth started to work up a denial.

Carl held up a hand to stop him. "Ben, don't start this off on the wrong foot. Remember: Complete and total cooperation. That means honesty. As long as you're honest with me, the slate's wiped clean. You'll never be punished for what happened."

Ben appeared to be going through some mental gymnastics, trying to deal with this.

Carl let him squirm for a moment before continuing. "Somehow, Elsie Foster, the leader of the Lincolnists, came into possession of some photographs that showed you...doing things you shouldn't have been doing. Elsie used those photographs to try to coerce your mother into killing someone. Your mother came clean to us about this, in exchange for our promise of protection over you and her."

"What were the photographs?" Ben demanded. "I want to see them."

"We don't have them."

Ben looked triumphant. "Then how do you know they're even real?"

"Your mother saw them. She knows it was you. A mother recognizes her son."

Ben shrunk into his chair. His face flushed.

"I'm not interested in the photographs, or what you were doing in them," Carl went on. "What I am interested in is *who* took the photographs. Because whoever took the photographs is likely tied to Elsie Foster."

Ben shook his head. "I don't know."

"Alright." Carl shrugged. "Let's start with the party then. Whose house was it at?"

"It wasn't at anybody's house."

"Was it one of the unoccupied houses in the Safe Zone?"

Ben avoided eye contact. "It wasn't in the Safe Zone."

Carl frowned. "You guys went *outside* the Safe Zone? To have a party?"

Ben considered the ramifications of admitting to this, but then seemed to recall Carl's warning for complete cooperation. "Look. It wasn't my idea, okay? I thought it was stupid to go outside the wire. But...but that's what we did."

"How'd you get outside the Safe Zone?"

"The culvert," Ben mumbled. "The one where the primals got through."

Carl stared at the young man, making a few unpleasant connections in his head. "Christ. So that was how they got in. You guys left the goddamned door open for them."

"No! We didn't leave it open! I swear. It was closed and locked last time I saw it."

"Locked with what? They found a padlock down there, but it was old."

Ben looked sheepish. "A...uh...carabiner."

"It was locked with a carabiner?"

Ben nodded.

Carl rubbed his face. So...that answered the mystery of how the primals had gotten inside the wire, and who had unlocked the drain gate in the first place. And wasn't it just goddamned typical that it would be teenagers, off to do stupid teenager shit without a care in the world for the consequences.

"Alright," Carl rallied himself. "That's getting off topic. So there was a party. Who was at this party?"

"A lot of people."

"Any adults?"

"No. Not really."

"Not really? What's that mean?"

Ben huffed. "Well, like, *I'm* an adult, right? I mean, I know I'm only seventeen, but I'm old enough to join y'all's army. So, like, I'm an adult."

God help me. "Okay. Anyone older than that? Any *real* adults there?"

"No."

"Okay. Who *was* there?"

"You want me to name all of them?"

"If that's what it takes."

Ben fidgeted, looking flustered. "Uh...well...Charlie was there. The girl that hangs out with Sam Ryder." Ben seemed to seize on something that he felt put him on the high ground. "Yeah, Sam was there, too. You know? Angela's son? Adopted son, or whatever..."

Carl's eyes narrowed. "Sam was there?"

Ben nodded eagerly. "Yeah. Yeah, he was there. Maybe *he* took the pictures."

Carl stared at Ben for a long moment, wondering if this was bullshit, but he didn't think that it was. He pursued several trains of thought to a few basic conclusions, none of which were very good for Sam Ryder.

"Okay. Who else?"

Ben flopped around in frustration. "I don't know, man. Just...a lot of people. I don't even remember everyone that was there."

"Who put it on? There must have been someone that invited you out. Someone who appeared to be running the party, or had set it up."

Ben rubbed his brow and looked at the ceiling. "Well...yeah. There was the chick that...man, we were all just trying to have a good time, but she would always start talking about freedom and the old United States, and whether or not anyone at the party felt like the UES was illegitimate—a bunch of shit like that. It was annoying. No one cared. Everyone was just trying to cut loose for a little bit."

Now we're getting somewhere.

Carl tried not to appear too eager. "And who was that?"

"Hell, I can't even remember her name. But she's around, you know? I think she works for President Houston. Or something. Maybe she just works at the Support Center. I dunno." Ben seemed to alight on some nugget of recognizance. He held up a finger. "Her dad's the general, though."

Carl tilted his head. "The general?"

"Yeah. For the Marines, I guess."

There was no one in Fort Bragg that held the rank of general—Marine, or otherwise.

"You mean Colonel Staley?" Carl probed, feeling his pulse quicken.

Ben nodded. "Right. Yeah. Colonel. The guy in charge of all the Marines. That's her father. I remember that, because I always thought it was weird that she would talk about that shit when her father's...you know...one of you guys."

Carl felt a tingling in his fingers. Heat on the back of his neck. "Okay. Staley. You remember her first name?"

He didn't want to lead Ben into an accusation. It needed to come out of Ben's mouth, not Carl's.

"Staley. Right." Ben nodded. "Crystal Staley."

Carl's mind pursued new trains of thought now, and he suddenly became acutely aware that his window of opportunity to snatch up the Lincolnists had suddenly shrunk down to nothing.

The kid had said Crystal, which was close, and he'd also been clear that it was Colonel Staley's daughter. Carl decided he needed to go ahead and cut a corner to fill in some blanks.

"You mean Claire."

Ben had the enlightened expression of someone who has just remembered something. He snapped his fingers and pointed to Carl. "Yes. That's it. Claire Staley."

Carl's mind had already gone down this rabbit hole, but now, upon having the name confirmed, he pictured it more clearly, and it made his heart sink.

Claire. In Angela's office, just hours ago.

There to report that her father had committed suicide.

And who had Claire observed in Angela's office?

Taylor Sullivan.

Everything came together suddenly in Carl's mind.

He rocketed off the desk and rushed to the door, barking behind him, "Don't move from this spot."

***

As the last bit of color bled out of the sky, Claire Staley walked quickly through a strip of woods in the Fort Bragg Safe Zone.

Things were starting to unravel. The careful tapestry that she'd woven for the last two years in this place was starting to pull apart, and she needed to stop the damage before shit got out of control.

Urgency pulled at her feet like an aggressive dog on a leash. It was only through concerted, controlled breathing that she kept the rising panic at bay and kept her feet moving normally.

Running would only draw attention.

She'd been stuck with Carl Gilliard and Angela Houston, answering their questions and trying to keep her pounding pulse from being noticeable. She wept, and the tears were genuine, because she hadn't *wanted* to do what she'd done. The circumstances had simply forced her hand.

Angela was pitying.

Carl was suspicious.

He hid it well enough, but Claire wasn't blind. One liar is good at spotting another.

As she went through the story that she and Elsie had come up with, careful to answer as much truthfully as she possibly could, and leave the untruths non-specific, her mind had been locked onto a single image.

Taylor Sullivan, standing there in Angela's office.

Something had happened. Something had been said.

Some of Carl's men had arrived and whisked Sullivan away without a word.

Then Carl had left to pursue some other duty, and been replaced by one of his men—Mitch—who then conferred quietly with Angela outside her office while Claire sat inside of it. All the while she was left alone she wracked her brain, trying to think how quickly she could get the hell out of there and warn Elsie.

If Taylor had talked, then it was only a matter of time before Carl and his goons went to snatch up Elsie. And then everything that they worked for was going to be undone.

She'd gotten free of Angela's office only twenty minutes ago. They'd talked about where Claire was going to stay, and Angela offered to let her stay in her house, but Claire had said that she needed to walk. She needed to clear her head.

It was the best she could come up with.

Time was short. Risks had to be taken.

Angela didn't seem to think it suspicious that Claire needed to take a walk.

Mitch didn't seem so sure, but he was less suspicious than Carl had been.

She'd checked her surroundings multiple times as she'd walked, and she'd done it as discreetly as possible, wanting to know if Carl's suspicions were strong enough that he or someone else might be tailing her to see where she went.

But she didn't catch sight of a tail.

She'd ducked into the woods, and was now cutting across to the back of Elsie Foster's residence, in the northwestern corner of the Safe Zone.

She stopped at the edge of the woods and stared at the back of all the little tract houses that used to house military families. The lights were starting to come on as the darkness spread across the sky. The light at the back door of Elsie's house was on. Which meant the coast was clear.

Supposedly.

Claire had not lasted this long by being trusting.

She took a long moment to check the other houses that bordered the street beyond, and she tried hard to get a glimpse of the street itself, to see if there was anyone out, any vehicles in the road that might indicate that Carl and his men had already been there.

But all was still and quiet.

Claire crossed the small backyard at a jog. She didn't want to be out in the open longer than she needed to be, and she was aware that, if Carl had gotten the full implications from Sullivan, he might already have operatives watching the house.

At the backdoor, Claire knocked, then stood there, burning and itching to hide. But she listened. When she heard the soft footsteps approach the backdoor, she whispered: "Elsie! It's me!"

The shades on the back of the door drew back an inch, and one of Elsie Foster's eyes peered out at Claire.

Relief flooded her.

They hadn't taken her yet.

Elsie unlatched the door and pulled it open.

Claire slipped in, and the second the door shut behind her, she grabbed Elsie by the shoulders and said, "Sullivan talked. You need to get the out of here, Elsie. They're coming for you."

***

Carl sped through Fort Bragg.

Mitch was already in his armor, driving the pickup truck and swearing under his breath as they punched heedlessly through the darkened streets. "I had her. I fucking *had her.*"

"You didn't know," was all Carl could say.

In the back, Rudy, Morrow, and Logan were strapping up. Carl had time to grab his rifle and his radio, but nothing else.

He keyed the radio. "Gilliard to command."

He twisted and looked in the back while he waited for them to answer.

Rudy, Morrow, and Logan were buckling the straps of their helmets and calmly checking their gear. Carl had no armor, but he also had no time. He would just have to operate accordingly.

"This is command," the radio mumbled. "Go ahead, Sergeant Gilliard."

Carl frowned at the radio, not recognizing the voice. "Where's Lieutenant Derrick?" he transmitted.

"Lieutenant Derrick hasn't arrived on post yet. This is Corporal Townsend."

Carl swore under his breath, then keyed the radio again. "Corporal, are you alone in the Watch Commander's office?"

"Yes, sir."

"I want you to transmit to any active patrols you can get word out to. Number one, me and my team are hitting a target residence, located at..." Carl consulted the scrawl he'd penned onto his wrist. "...One-Two-Five London Drive. Number two, I want you to tell the patrols to be on the lookout for Elsie Foster and Claire Staley. If either are seen, they are to be detained immediately. Green light on use of force. How copy?"

The corporal came back, sounding unsure of himself. "Solid copy."

Carl waited for him to ask whose authority the green light was under, but the corporal didn't ask.

Instead, Carl said, "Nothing further. Out." He placed the radio in the cup holder of the truck and looked at his team as they turned north onto Chute Street and hauled past the former North Post Main

Exchange. Chute Street would become London Drive in another block.

"Mitch, park us short of one-two-five. If we take fire on approach, we'll pull back and set up a perimeter as best we can. I'll take A-side from the truck, you guys move through the woods to take B, C, and D. Otherwise, we hit it quietly as possible, snatch Elsie and whoever is in that place with her, and get her out. If there's too many people, we'll hold them tight and call for additional. Everyone clear?"

They all nodded and mumbled various affirmatives.

Carl turned back to look out the windshield, thinking, *Should've just snatched her ass when we had the chance...*

They crossed over Butner Road, barely slowing down to clear the intersection.

Elsie's house was the second one on the right.

Mitch killed the headlights and coasted them to a quick stop in front of the first house.

"No lights in the house," Carl observed, with a sinking feeling in his gut as he threw his door open and let it close as gently as his urgency would allow. He took his radio with him and stuck it in his back pocket.

They formed up into a loose stack as they approached the front of the house, moving diagonally across the weedy lawn. Carl took up the rear, right behind Mitch and Logan. Rudy took point, and Morrow hovered close by to breach.

Their rifles scanned over windows. Doors. Corners. But there wasn't a peep from the house.

"I'll cover the back," Carl whispered, and split off around the side of the house to cover the back door. Everything was still and dark. He took the corner, then backed off a few paces, keeping himself under cover but peering around the house to see the back door.

The porch light was on. That might be a good sign.

If that bitch came out the back door, he'd give her exactly one chance to hit the dirt before he waylaid her. And if she was armed...

The crash of the front door being kicked in shattered the quiet.

Weaponlights bloomed on the interior of the house, sweeping past windows.

Carl held his rifle on the back door, waiting.

He heard the muffled movements of his team inside, but no gunshots. No shouts. No running feet. He kept waiting for the sound of loud commands as they took Elsie to the ground and zip-cuffed her hands. The longer the silence stretched, the more Carl's heart sank.

For two minutes he stood there on the corner of the house, feeling worse and worse.

And then Mitch's voice, as disconsolate as it could be over the radio in his back pocket: "Carl, the place is empty. She's gone."

THIRTEEN

INTELLIGENCE

THE LANDSCAPE FLEW BY SAM in an alien green.

The cool night air buffeted in his ears. The weather was still in that strange limbo of spring where the days could be summery, and the nights downright chilly. His hands became cold as they clutched the handles of the M2. There was just the roar of the wind, and the engines, and the strange sight of everything in night vision green through his right eye, and black through his left.

The drivers wore NVGs as well, so there were no lights. Not even the dull red glow of brake lights or running lights. They were blacked out as they navigated the pitted and pot holed and washed out sections of forgotten and unused American highway, leading towards the Cross Creek Mall.

Sam's ass was beginning to hurt and he shifted around frequently. The "seat" of the turret was nothing more than a wide nylon strap that went across the circular opening. He kept trying to adjust his weight, his feet looking for a new point of purchase, which they would generally find, accidentally, on the top of the radio between the two front seats.

For the third time, Corporal Billings shoved Sam's boots off the radio. "Ryder, I'm fuckin' serious. Next time I'm gonna chop your goddamned foot off."

Flustered, Sam ducked his head down, projecting his voice into the vehicle through the turret hole. "Sorry, corporal. This strap…"

"Well, don't sit on the fucking strap then. Stand up."

Sam stood up. The strap now hovered around his lower back. He wasn't tall, so he had to crane his neck to see up over the M2. On the plus side, it was easier to swivel the turret now.

"You don't wanna use that strap anyways," Jones called cheerily from down below. "Shuts off your circulation. It'll give you dead legs. Then you can't run from the primals."

"Alright," Billings called in his usual parental tone. "We're two mikes out. Allen, what's the position?"

Sam went back to staring out at the alien landscape. Green in one eye. Black in the other. But he imagined the nervous wildlife officer consulting the screen of the GPS unit that was leading them into Fayetteville.

"Uh," came Allen's quieter voice. "No change. Maybe three hundred yards east of Skibo Road. Right on the northern edge of the mall."

"Is it *inside* the mall?" Billings asked.

Allen didn't immediately answer. Sam pictured him frowning and giving an unconfident shrug. "Waypoint's accurate up to ten meters. So if it's inside, it's not far in."

There was some general grumbling that Sam couldn't make out.

"I think it took it off," Chris, the driver, weighed in.

"Yeah?" Billings sighed. "That what you think?"

Jones made a raspberry noise. "They ain't that smart."

"They got into the Safe Zone," Chris said, defensively. "They're smart enough."

"So they found an opening. That was our fault, not having that shit welded shut. It's not like they cracked a safe or anything."

"We shall see," Billings advised, sagely.

"Maybe they fuckin' ate him," Jones said.

No one responded, which Jones took to mean he should expound on this new theory.

"You know? If they're so goddamned smart, Chris, maybe they saw that one fuck was wearin' a transmitter and they killed him and ate him for being a rat."

Chris sounded indignant. "So, they're not smart enough to take off the fucking collar, but all of the sudden they're gonna start patting each other down for wires like the mob?"

"Yeah, man."

"You're an asshole, Jones."

"Yeah, I know."

"Alright," Billings refereed again. "One mike out. Let's pretend to be soldiers. Eyes peeled. No surprises."

No one said anything else. There was general shuffling around as the occupants of the Humvee addressed themselves to their open windows, the muzzles of their rifles sticking out.

They'd taken Bragg Boulevard out of the Safe Zone and were turning onto Swain Street, which would connect them to Skibo Road. All around them was the defunct remains of a city that had given it a good go three years ago, but had ultimately been ravaged, and its corpse picked over by two years of scavenging.

Dark buildings began to cluster closer on either side of them. Wreckage in the form of abandoned and burned-out vehicles clustered the sides of the road. Jersey barriers with old concertina wire wilting from the tops of them. Large swaths of the road had been overtaken by the never-ending spread of nature, spreading out from what had once been grassy medians that now held two-year old saplings and scrub brush.

Sam glanced over his shoulder and saw the two pickup trucks following them.

Chris slowed to take the turn onto Skibo, but didn't stop. The tires chirped as he swung around a Volvo that stuck out into the road. Sam hung onto the M2 as the centrifugal force tugged him through the turn, and he stared at the Volvo. Every door was open. The interior was shredded. The exterior pocked with bullet holes.

The road obstructions thickened, and the convoy of three vehicles had to slow to twenty miles an hour as they cut a serpentine course through it all.

Sam found he had a hard time focusing with both eyes open, so he squinted his left and focused on the night vision scene provided by his right. He scanned carefully, the ball bearings rumbling as he swiveled the gun to face right, then left.

They made the overpass that crossed the All American Freeway. Below them, stretching to the north and south, the freeway was a landscape of forgotten wreckage.

Sam had begun to hate cities, right around the time when they'd become the most dangerous places to be, when the hordes of infected clustered in them, numbering in the thousands. Even now, though the hordes had died through the attrition of starvation, exposure, and Marine artillery, Sam still felt acid roil in his gut as they delved deeper into Fayetteville.

"There's Cross Creek," Billings announced. "Take this first entrance. Right here."

The mall loomed up to Sam's left. The fronts of the department stores seemed to rise up like monoliths in the darkness, their unlit signs a sad monument to life before. More like tombstones now, than advertisements.

Chris turned them right, and slowed to a crawl, approaching the massive buildings, the parking lots vast and empty.

"Where we goin', Allen?" Billings asked.

"Uh...straight ahead there. Right between the department store and the auto center."

They drove straight forward, through a pair of jersey barriers that might've been a checkpoint in their former life.

The place where they appeared to be heading was a dark corner nestled in the V shape created by the department store to the left, and a car care center to their right. Through his night vision, Sam saw Corporal Billing's infrared laser lance out and scour a shaky path across the building fronts and linger in a whorl right there at the entrance to the mall.

"Shit," Jones murmured from below, his voice more audible without the wind blowing in Sam's ears. "We're not going in there, are we?"

"I don't think it's inside," Allen said as they drew closer. "I think it's right there in front of us."

They were about a hundred yards from the entrance now, moving forward at an idle.

Sam stared hard into the mall's entrance but saw nothing there.

"I don't see no primals," Jones remarked.

"I told you," Chris said, vindicated. "Fucker took it off."

"Alright," Billings said. "Swing us around right here so we can hightail it quick. We're gonna dismount."

Chris drove them just into the V of the buildings, then swung them around in a wide arc and stopped, the right side of the Humvee facing the entrance to the mall, the tires turned hard left towards their exit.

The two pickup trucks moved in behind them.

Sam swiveled the turret, scanning along the department store, and then the entrance, and then the car care center. His cheek began to ache from squinting his left eye.

Doors opened and closed in rapid succession. They were gentle about it but the noise still seemed loud to Sam, even with the thrumming engines of the three trucks in the background. Billings, Jones, and Allen dismounted, joined by two soldiers each from the two pickups. Chris stayed in the driver's seat, as did the drivers of the pickups. The last two soldiers took up positions on the opposite side of the line of trucks to cover their exit.

Sam heard quiet voices, but couldn't tell what they were saying.

Billings and his group of six approached the belly of the V, the soldiers scanning outwards, their IR lasers swooping and arcing across the building faces, invisible to the naked eye. Allen huddled in the middle of their small formation, looking at the glowing readout of his GPS receiver.

"You alright up there, half-boot?"

Sam turned his head and saw one of the soldiers from the pickups looking up at him. Beneath his NVGs, his mouth was split into a snarky grin. Sam gave him a thumbs up.

The soldier pointed out towards their exit. "How about you help us cover the exit, then?"

Sam swung the turret around. Out towards the abandoned parking lots with their overgrown natural areas and clumps of weeds starting to push up from between cracks in the concrete. A gentle breeze blew, stirring everything, causing a disconcerting amount of movement.

Sam's eyes tried to dart around, but he couldn't see much with the narrow field of view provided by his NVGs. He had to pan his head around to get the whole scene. Every time the wind stirred something his heart inched a tad higher into his throat.

He didn't like having his back to the mall, but he kept telling himself, *watch your lane.*

He heard shuffling around inside the Humvee. Chris's voice hissed up at him. "Fuck, Ryder, why you lookin' out there?"

Nerves let a bump of frustration through Sam's placid demeanor. "They just told me to look out here!"

"Fuck that," Chris snapped. "Watch the roofline."

"Motherfucker." Sam jerked the turret around, getting angrier, which he found was nicer than being scared, so he clung to it. Facing back towards the entrance, he saw Billings and his guys down in the dark hole at the belly of the V, looking at something on the ground.

That's the transponder, Sam realized.

His eyes fixed on Billings's figure. The corporal bent down and took something off the ground and held it up at eye-level. Sam couldn't see the details of it, but he knew what it was. Chris had been right. The primals were smart enough to take the damn thing off.

Smart enough?

Or had it been like a dog that doesn't want a collar on his neck?

Surely it had just made the primal uncomfortable to have a foreign object strapped to it.

Surely they didn't understand what it was.

Watch your lane.

Sam tilted his M2 up.

Brought his narrow, green-filled gaze up to the roofline of the department store.

A flash of movement at the right-hand corner of his vision.

He snapped his head to the car care center.

Something moved out of view as he focused on it.

"Hey," Sam's voice came out higher than he would have liked. "I think there's movement."

"What?" Chris sounded exasperated. "You gettin' jumpy up there, half-boot?"

"I swear…" Sam stared hard at the top of the roof. Nothing else moved.

"Just chill out and confirm what you saw," Chris intoned from below.

Sam felt a tickle in his subconscious. Maybe he'd seen something at the left corner of his vision, or maybe it was some sixth sense that told him to look left.

He swung to the department store roof.

A figure hung, halfway over the line of the roof, like a spider about to descend.

"Oh shit!" Sam gasped, then belted out: "Contact! Contact!"

As he yelled, the soldiers at the entrance to the mall all snapped around.

And so did the head of the figure.

Fifty yards from Sam, it stared him dead in the face, its eyes wide and shimmering like silver coins in a flash of light, its mouth open, teeth bared.

Sam's thumbs wrenched down on the butterfly trigger.

The M2 blasted out two rounds and then *clunked*—jammed.

Sam tried to yell a curse, but all that came out was something like a painful groan, as he stared out across the muzzle of the machine gun, saw the two big rounds punch the brick, and then watched as dozens of primals began to pour over the top of the roof, gripping to the crevices in the bricks with inhuman strength, leaping across to a metal awning over the entrance, and vaulting to the ground…

"Get that fuckin' fiddy up!" Chris screamed at him.

Billings and his squad sprinted for the vehicles, firing blindly behind them as they ran, their shots wild, striking more brick and concrete than flesh.

The primals poured towards them like ants out of a disturbed mound.

Sam had never seen that many primals in one place before...

"You fuckin' half-boot motherfucker!"

Sam snapped out of it. Leapt forward. Grabbed the charging handle of the M2 and hauled back with his entire body weight. The gun spat out the jammed round, then *clunked* forward on a fresh one. Sam swiveled the fifty around and down, seeing that the lead primals were only paces behind Billings—and gaining—and he fired.

The machine gun chugged, thrashing in Sam's grip like a beast. The tracer rounds plunged through the air and ripped bodies that were no more than thirty yards away. The soldiers running for the vehicles ducked their heads, but didn't stop.

Sam screamed as he swept the pumping tracer fire back and forth through the encroaching crowd of primals, and they began to scream back at him, to howl as they were torn apart.

But they didn't stop coming.

Sam's eyesight had shrunk to two-degree tunnel vision, and all he saw was the mass of bodies flowing towards him, leaping towards him, their jaws hanging open, slavering, their misshapen limbs clawing up the ground, tearing through the distance between them...

All the air had left Sam's lungs, and he didn't seem to be able to draw a new breath.

Car doors slammed.

Engines roared.

Sam lurched in the turret, pulling the M2 off aim as the Humvee jumped forward.

The sound of its pounding reports ceased, as his thumbs slipped off the trigger.

He heard Billings screaming, "Go! Go! Go!"

Rifle fire crackled in Sam's dim ears.

Sam righted himself, sucked in air, and wrenched the M2 around again, just in time to see a shape hurtling through the air at him. It struck the side of the Humvee and swatted the barrel of the machine gun so hard that it wrenched out of Sam's grip and spun it—

The barrel smacked Sam in the helmet.

The creature bellowed, and all he saw was the mouth gaping towards him, the two hands like claws reaching.

Sam yanked his legs up, and let his body drop. He fell through the turret and tumbled into the mix of limbs and rifle fire that filled the interior of the Humvee.

"The roof!" he screamed.

Jones shoved Sam hard, crushing him into something like a fetal position, his body on top of Sam's, almost laying on top of him as he pointed his rifle towards the opening in the roof of the Humvee.

The primal thrust its torso through, snapping and growling.

Jones fired a burst on automatic. In the enclosed space, the rifle sounded louder than the M2 had. The primal's face disintegrated in the volley of projectiles and went limp, spilling gouts of blood across Sam's head and chest.

Jones rolled off of Sam and hauled him up, shouting, "Get back on the fiddy!"

Sam didn't hesitate. He sprung up, and despite the panic that he felt coursing through him as he touched the still-twitching body of the primal, he thrust upward with a cry of effort, pushing the primal's torso out of the turret hole.

He scrambled up to his feet, shoved the body with everything he had, and it tumbled off the hood of the Humvee.

Night wind thrashed around Sam's face, but he couldn't hear it.

He seized a hold of the M2 again and swung it around to point at their rear.

The vehicles hauled towards the exit, but behind them and all around them, the crowd of primals chased them with superhuman speed, managing somehow to stay with the fleeing trucks.

Sam brought the machine gun around and fired again, guiding his shots by the light of the tracers, rather than the sights of the gun.

The two pickup trucks did the smartest thing and charged forward, hugging the backend of the Humvee's bumper to give Sam more room to shoot.

The three vehicles hit Skibo Road in a scramble of screeching tires, right about the same moment that the machine gun went dry. Sam thought that it had jammed again and he ripped the charging handle again and tried to fire more, but it was done.

Had he already fired a hundred rounds?

"I'm empty!" he yelled, at about the same point that he realized that they were gaining distance on the primals now. The primals were fast, but not forty-five miles an hour fast.

"We're clear!" Billings shouted from below. "Is everyone alright?"

Sam didn't hear the rest of it.

He stood in the turret, gasping for air, and watching the green shapes of the primals, growing smaller with distance. As they reached the edge of the parking lot, they seemed to realize as one that they would not catch these prey, and they pulled up and stood there on two feet, watching them get away.

Snippets of the shouting below started to make it through to Sam's brain.

"What the fuck was that?"

"I've never seen that many primals before!"

"How many were there?"

"Did you see how they came over the walls like that?"

"It's like they were waiting for us!"

Mottled green darkness all around.

The wind of their acceleration buffeting him.

Sam kept thinking those last words to himself, over and over.

It's like they were waiting for us.

It's like they were waiting for us…

FOURTEEN

JULIA

By MIDNIGHT, Julia could no longer hold it.

Through an irritated half-sleep, she'd tried to ignore the growing pressure in her bladder, hoping that it was one of those times when she could just hold it until dawn broke. In the last few years, with so many field operations under her belt, she'd become an expert at holding it.

It wasn't a big deal for guys who could simply turn around, unzip, and direct their piss where it was best. But Julia had to take her pants all the way down and squat, which made her very vulnerable, and it wasn't something she wanted to do in the dark when she was half awake.

None of the guys had ever complained about having to cover her back while she took a nighttime piss, but she loathed having to wake them up and ask. And she was determined not to do so now.

But she wasn't going to last until morning.

They'd been given one of the four bedrooms in the hunting cabin. It held two, bare twin mattresses on rickety pine bedframes, but compared to how they usually slept in the field, this was luxury.

Julia and Lee shared one of the mattresses, and Abe snored softly on the other.

Lee's back was to her at the moment, which was good. She wouldn't need to disentangle herself.

She began the slow process of rolling away from Lee and rising up to a sitting position. She slipped out of the poncho liner that she used as a blanket and set her socked feet on the ground. Deuce, who lay next to the bed, lifted his head and watched her with silent curiosity.

When she reached for her boots, the pine bedframe gave a treacherous creak.

Lee jerked and came up on an elbow, his hand going under his backpack that he was using as a pillow, reaching for the Glock he kept there most nights.

"What's wrong?" he whispered.

Julia felt a wash of irritation directed at the bedframe. "Nothing. Go back to sleep."

"You need a piss?"

Julia grabbed her boots and slipped them on her feet. "I'll be fine. They've got people on watch. Go back to sleep."

Lee hesitated. Then melted back down. "Stay close to the cabin," he advised.

Abe snorted and shuffled around in his bed. His breathing stayed steady. He was a heavy sleeper.

"I will," Julia said, standing up gently to prevent another noise from the bedframe.

She eyed the two men with a rueful smirk.

They'd become her family. Though she sometimes joked that Abe was her "field brother" and Lee her "field husband," they'd become more than just field-expedient relationships. They'd become everything to her. To each other.

Because everyone else is dead.

The thought struck the smirk from her mouth.

She grabbed her rifle from where it sat underneath the side of the bed, and padded out of the room, rolling her feet along the outside of her boots so that the heels wouldn't clump.

Before she closed the bedroom door behind her, she took a peek back and saw that Lee had rolled back over, and Abe was snoring again.

Good.

She descended the wooden staircase with care, trying to avoid creaks, and failing. How annoying nature was when it called in the middle of the night.

At the bottom of the staircase was the front door of the cabin, but it was barricaded by a strip of what looked like weathered barn wood, tacked into the frame. The back door was the only entrance she'd seen used, so she moved in that direction.

In the living room where Tex's squad had congregated earlier, only two soldiers slept, one on the old couch, and the other on the floor. They didn't stir as she moved past them, though one of them let out a soft fart and a grunt.

To her relief, the back door opened without squeaks, and she slipped outside into the cool night air. A half-moon was up, and it gave plenty of light for her to see by. She scanned along the woods, saw the dark shapes of the vehicles parked under the trees.

She wasn't sure where Tex's guys kept watch, but she wasn't venturing out into the woods. Besides the possibility of primals, Texas had plenty of other unpleasant creatures that concerned her. Specifically snakes. And tarantulas. And scorpions.

No, she'd stick close to the cabin, as Lee had advised.

She went around the side of the house, found a corner where the log walls met the brick chimney, and she figured it was as good a place as any. She gave another look around her, saw nothing concerning—at least that she could make out by moonlight. She set her rifle against the brick of the fireplace, pulled her pants down to mid-thigh, and squatted.

She breathed a sigh of relief. The sound of urine splashing the ground mingled with the steady, rhythmic chirping of crickets.

She felt like she peed for five minutes straight.

No way she would've lasted through the night.

At least she'd been able to get it done without disturbing anyone.

She stood up and began to pull her pants up.

She registered the rush of footfalls just a half-second before she was slammed in the back.

Her first thought was *Primals!* Then her head struck the brick fireplace, and things became fuzzy.

She was still conscious. She groped for her rifle as she felt the weight starting to ride her down to the ground.

She hit the dirt on her belly. An arm reached out and swiped the rifle away from her in one movement, sending it clattering five feet out of her reach.

Not a primal's arm.

Oh, shit.

She felt her pants yanked down farther, past her knees, and the reality hit her harder than the physical tackle had. She tried to writhe, to spin, to roll, but a hand clamped onto the back of her neck and pressed her face into the dirt, and a body put all of its weight on her back. She tried to yell, but it only came out in a muffled groan, and she tasted dirt in her mouth.

Hot breath struck her ear.

"Ssh! Ssh!" a voice hissed at her. "Don't fight. I'll be quick. I promise."

Fear mixed with instant rage.

She clenched her teeth, and felt the grit of dirt between them.

She felt a fist between her legs, someone trying to guide themselves into her.

She took a big, dusty breath and bucked backward with her hips, knowing in an instant that, yes, it would make it easier for him to get at her, but also that it pitched his weight forward, and put him off-balance.

The second she felt his balance teeter, she rolled with everything she had, felt her hips come out from under the crushing weight. There was scuffling limbs and whispered curses, and then she was on her back, staring up at a stranger's face, obscured by darkness.

He tried to straddle her again.

She brought her knee up hard, but it glanced off his thigh.

"Fucking bitch! Stop fighting!"

She thrust her arm up, grabbing his neck, sinking her fingers into the skin on either side of his larynx, trying like hell to rip his throat out. He gagged, jerked backwards, then reared a fist back and the next thing she felt was her nose breaking, and stars colliding in her vision.

She thought she blacked out.

She panicked, thinking that she couldn't defend herself if she had blacked out...

She couldn't feel the weight of him anymore.

Her sparkling vision cleared enough for her to perceive two shapes in the moonlight. She scrambled backwards, running into the brick wall and hauling herself up, pulling her pants up at the same time so she could get her legs moving.

The first figure started coming at her again and she managed to get her pants high enough that she was able to send out a single solid kick that landed in the man's belly and sent a gust of air out of his lungs.

The second figure was just a flash of shadow.

Two arms snaked under her attacker's armpits, then thrust up, the hands interlocking behind her attacker's head so that his arms jutted out at an awkward and useless angle. His body writhed, his feet kicking, but whoever had ahold of him from behind kept him standing and exposed.

Julia didn't think. She moved. She saw the man's half-erection, still hanging out of his pants, and she lunged forward in a fury, her arm coming up like a softball pitch. She slammed her hand into the man's crotch and wrenched her fingers hard down on his genitals, and she felt one of his testis pop like a grape.

The man's eyes went wide, and his body seemed to implode, trying to curl around the pain.

Forced into a standing position, the moonlight hit his face, and Julia registered that it was the man from the meeting earlier. The one who'd been jerking himself in his pants.

Pikes.

The figure behind her attacker heaved, and sent the man flying into the side of the log cabin in a tumble of limbs.

It only took Julia a bare second to realize that the other figure was Lee. And in that fractional moment, he snatched his pistol out of his waistband and brought it up.

"Lee!" Julia shouted at him, not sure why.

The man on the ground moaned and wrapped himself in a fetal position, like a dying bug.

Lee didn't say anything. His face was emotionless, but the moonlight hit his eyes at a strange angle and made them look wild. "You want me to pop him?" Lee's voice ground out, quiet to the point that Julia could barely hear it over her own pulse pounding in her head.

Yes.

Julia almost said it.

But a moment's hesitation gave enough time for reason to reassert itself into the situation.

And she registered the sound of shouts from inside the cabin, and the rumble of several feet running. The sound of the backdoor slamming open. A light struck them from out in the woods, wavering and shaking. The weaponlight from one of the sentries, running towards them.

"Stop!" the sentry shouted. "Drop that weapon!"

Lee turned his face to Julia. Still and cold. Half in stark white light, half in blackness. "Do you want me to kill him? Or do you want to do it?"

He wanted an answer from her.

"Don't," Julia said.

If he shot the guy on the ground, the sentry would shoot him. Julia knew it. Lee had to know it too, and maybe he just didn't care.

From around the back of the house a cluster of figures appeared at a sprint.

Sergeant Menendez was in the lead, trailing a few of his troops, and Tex was in the rear.

They all rushed to a stop in front of Lee and Julia and the man on the ground.

They were all shouting, and Julia couldn't pick out what any of them were saying.

Tex's voice hissed, making it somehow clearer than everyone else's yelling. "Shut up! Shut up! Everyone shut the fuck up!" He shouldered his way to the front of his soldiers, all in various states of dress. All pointing their rifles at Lee.

Still looking at Julia, Lee pulled his fingers away from the trigger guard and grip so that his pistol rested in the crook of his thumb, and he raised it so it pointed at the sky.

It was abruptly silent.

Tex put his hand on Lee's shoulder, but didn't reach for Lee's weapon. "The fuck is this?" he demanded in a harsh whisper. "What the fuck is going on?"

Lee hadn't taken his eyes off of Julia. And he didn't respond.

Julia became aware that her right eye was swelling. She tasted blood on her lips and wiped it with the back of her wrist. A hundred thoughts collided in her head, action and consequence, all of them muddled by a swirl of anger and fear and violation.

Tex seemed to register that Lee was looking at Julia, and his eyes landed on her as well, then went down and took in her pants hanging off of her, then back up to her bloodied nose, and her swollen eye.

The man on the ground let out a low groan and spoke in a high-pitched mewl: "She fuckin' popped my nuts!"

A wash of embarrassment hit Julia and she grappled her pants back up onto her hips, her fingers shaking so that she couldn't get them buttoned again. She knew that she shouldn't feel shame. But that didn't stop it from coming over her in a burning wave that made her want to sit down, made her eyes sting like they were about to tear up. And all of that just fed her anger even more.

I should've let Lee kill him!
I should've killed him myself!
Say something!

She coughed to hide a sudden sob, and hated herself, and hated the man on the ground, and even hated Lee.

"Someone better start fucking talking!" Tex commanded.

Julia couldn't make sense of herself. She just wanted the situation to dissolve. Like it had never happened. Or she wanted to deliver the facts in a calm and collected way, like she always imagined that she would if she ever found herself in this situation.

"Jules," Lee prompted.

Julia jerked. Her spine went erect. Her shoulders drew back. She nodded towards the man on the ground, and she shielded herself behind a façade of hardness. "Your boy can't keep his dick in his pants. That's all."

More silence. A lot of glancing around from the men present. Julia saw the theories rolling around in their heads, she saw the disbelief, the suspicion, the falseness, the rejection, and she had to fight to keep from screaming at them.

Tex frowned at her. He shifted his weight. "What…what are you saying?"

Lee stirred, his face screwing up under a sudden surge of violence, and then it was calm again. "First of all," he grated. "Jules, are you okay? Are you injured?"

The man on the ground moaned. "*I'm* fucking injured! I need a fucking doctor!"

Lee's eyes didn't come away from Julia's, but he spoke to Tex. "You shut that motherfucker up, or I'll kill him and deal with the consequences. You understand me?"

Tex blinked, trying to compute. Flustered, he turned to the man on the ground. "Pikes, shut your fucking mouth for two goddamned seconds." He turned back to Julia. "I need you to tell me what happened. Because it doesn't look good."

"It doesn't look good?" Julia's eye flared wide. The muscles in her legs started jumping like her knees were going to give out on her. "It doesn't *look good*? How the fuck does it look besides that he tried to rape me and got his balls crushed for it?" She took a step forward, like she might start swinging on Tex and was stopped only by Lee's hand on her chest. Julia felt herself losing control and couldn't bring herself back again. "What's it look like to you? What do *you* think happened? You think I seduced him? You think I was out here giving him a blow job and decided to pop his nuts instead? You think this is *my* fault somehow?"

216

Tex looked caught. "That's not what I'm saying."

One of the other soldiers mumbled, "This is bullshit."

"Julia," Lee raised his voice. "Are you okay?"

Julia slapped Lee's hand away from her. "I'm fucking fine, Lee. I'm goddamned right as rain."

"Don't get mad at me," Lee snarled at her. "I'm on your side."

"Is this true, Lee?" Tex demanded.

Julia's face tingled with heat. "What're you asking him for? You don't believe me?"

Tex's lips curled up. "I don't fucking *know* you."

Lee spun towards Tex, but another body interjected itself between them. Julia hadn't seen Abe approach, had no idea how much he'd seen or heard, but for some unknown reason she felt a melting relief at his presence.

He put a gentle elbow against Tex, and a hand against Lee, and spoke in a quiet, calm voice. "Alright, everyone chill out. Y'all're out here yelling and attracting primals. Let's move this shit show inside." As though he was supremely confident that his words had calmed everyone, he slipped from between Lee and Tex and scooped a hand up around Julia's shoulders and started guiding her around the others. "Come on, let's have a look at your face."

Julia found herself leaning on Abe. The rest of the world melted into a confusion of whispered voices and shuffling steps, and she had to move her feet to keep up with Abe as he ushered her around everyone, keeping his body between her and them.

He stayed with her all the way into the cabin and back up the stairs to the bedroom with the two twin mattresses, and Julia followed him numbly. It wasn't until he had closed the bedroom door behind them and Julia sat on the edge of the bed with her arms wrapped around her, that she let any of it out.

***

"Menendez," Tex snapped as they all bustled back into the cabin. "Post extra lookouts until daylight."

Sergeant Menendez nodded. "Got it."

The other soldiers tramped inside and stood about, unsure of what to do with themselves at this juncture. Two of them hauled their injured teammate—Pikes—to a separate room. He moaned and whimpered the whole way, and Lee watched him go, thinking, *I should've killed him. There was no reason to stop. I should've splattered his brains.*

"Everybody else," Tex continued, still sounding irritated. "Stand down. Go back to sleep. Stare at the wall. I don't care. But chill out and stay quiet." He turned to Lee. "I need to speak to you. Privately."

Tex stalked off, and Lee followed.

In the background of his anger, there was the thought that *You're trying to make an alliance with these people—don't throw that away.*

And yet he found himself willing to do exactly that.

For what? Not for Julia. Killing him wouldn't do anything for her. Killing Pikes would only make Lee feel better. But it would hamstring his mission here in Texas.

Lee gulped a big breath of air and held it. Then let it out slow.

What's your mission?

Unite the UES and Texas.

It's difficult to see the big picture when you want to brutalize another human being. And yet Lee had lived in conflict and violence for so long that he was capable of doing just that.

Big picture: The UES and Texas needed each other. They had too many common enemies to survive without an alliance.

Lee didn't want to put his relationship with Julia on a balancing scale with the survival of the United Eastern States...and yet here he was.

Tex led him into a spacious laundry closet and swiped the sliding doors shut behind him.

Lee was the first to speak. "What the fuck, Tex?"

Tex's eyes blazed, but he kept his voice low. "What the fuck *me*?" he jabbed a finger out behind them. "I'm not the one that brought my girlfriend into a crew of killers. What the fuck did you think was gonna happen?"

Lee's fingers tensed and he felt heat rising up his neck. "I didn't see you complaining when you found out she was a medic."

Tex ignored the assertion. "Surely she knew this could happen?"

Lee leaned in close. "Are you really not holding your man responsible?"

"Yes, I'm fucking holding him responsible! He's a fuck-ass and he always has been. And now he's got a crushed testicle. Meanwhile your girl is perfectly fine."

"Fine?"

"Did he get his dick in?"

It was only by monumental effort that Lee didn't smash Tex's face in right then. Sure, Lee still wasn't a hundred percent, and after he had his face smashed in, Tex would return the favor with interest, but for a moment Lee forgot all the ramifications of what he was trying to accomplish.

"He tried to rape her," Lee hissed.

"But he didn't, did he?"

Lee was silent. Burning.

Tex seemed to rally himself. He took a deep breath and let it out, and spoke in a whisper. "All I'm saying is that your girl is physically fine—minus the black eye and the busted nose—and my guy is out of commish. I call that square."

"I don't."

"I think that's your emotions talking." Tex raked his fingers through his short hair. "What do you want me to do? Execute him?"

Yes. That was exactly what Lee wanted. Better yet, he wanted Tex to let *Lee* execute him.

And yet...

For the moment, Pikes's crew was mad that their guy had been injured. But that would cool.

If Pikes became a martyr, their feelings towards Lee and Abe and Julia would only become more strained.

Lee didn't respond to Tex's question, because he couldn't bring himself to admit that, in a way, Tex was right. As disgusting as that made Lee feel, he wasn't going to torpedo the whole operation against *Nuevas Fronteras* over this.

The two of them sat in silence for nearly a minute, gathering themselves.

When Tex spoke again, his tone was more level. "What happened?"

"You should've let Julia talk," Lee said. "I didn't see how it started. Just how it ended."

Tex looked at the tile floor under their feet. "Lee, you know as well as I do that that shit wouldn't have flown. The guys were worried about Pikes. They didn't want to hear anything about Julia. If we started having a public hearing about this shit, it was going to go downhill quick. You know how these guys are. Pikes is an idiot—I'm not denying that—but he's one of our brothers. All these guys are brothers. They've been fighting and keeping each other alive for years before your crew came along. They aren't going to want to hear the facts of the matter. Not until they cool off. I know you thought I did the wrong thing there, and maybe I did—maybe I did wrong by Julia—but you also know I was right to get everybody separated and cooling off."

Lee didn't respond to that. He didn't *want* to respond. He didn't want to feel like he'd betrayed Julia.

"She got up to go take a piss," Lee said, his low voice suddenly tired. "She usually has one of us watch her back. She said she'd be fine because you had sentries. She was only worried about primals— teepios. I felt weird about it, so I waited a few minutes and followed her outside. I didn't want her to see that I followed her, because she gets mad at me if she thinks I'm handling her with kid gloves. By the time I went outside, I heard them struggling. I ran around the corner. Saw Pikes on top of her. Saw her pants were pulled down. I jumped in, pulled him off of her. Then she crushed his balls, and the rest you saw."

Tex looked Lee over. Processing.

"You must've really wanted to kill him," he said.

Lee's eyes hit Tex's. "Still do."

"I guess I owe you one for not."

Lee's eyes narrowed. "What am I supposed to tell Julia?"

Tex took another deep breath and leaned back onto the old dryer. "We're in a bit of a pickle, huh?"

"If that's what you want to call it."

"You have to back up your people. And I have to back up mine."

"Do you want this to work?"

Tex thought about it for a moment, and Lee wished that he'd been quicker to answer. But he did eventually nod. "Yeah, Lee. I think we need to help each other."

"How about your guys?"

"What about them?"

"Are they going to work with us now?"

Again, Tex took longer to consider than Lee would have liked. But again, he nodded. "Yeah. I tell them what went down, I think they'll call it a wash. They want to back up their boy, but they're smart enough to know he made a shitty decision and got his shit crushed for it."

"Alright." Lee shifted. "So what do I tell Julia?"

Tex shook his head. "You know her better than I do, Lee. Is she going to go apeshit about this, or will she be cool?"

Lee wanted to believe that she'd do what was necessary to keep the mission going. But this was one of those things that men only understood academically. The ugly truth was that he couldn't really put himself in her shoes. It was a delicate and spiny issue that Lee was unprepared to tackle.

"I don't know," Lee finally admitted. "But Tex…you know me. You know I don't say stupid shit. I'm not making a threat here. I'm just telling you ahead of time: If Pikes steps on the wrong side of me or any of my team again, I'm gonna kill him."

That last sentence hung there for a moment.

Tex appeared to be measuring the appropriate reaction to that. And eventually he just nodded. "Well. Thanks for letting me know, I guess."

A sharp knock rattled the laundry closet door.

Lee's heart sank, thinking that new problems had arisen.

Tex spat a quiet curse and flung the door open. "What?"

Sergeant Menendez stood there, and immediately Lee knew this wasn't about Julia and Pikes. Menendez's dark features weren't angry and suspicious. They were alarmed.

"Tex," Menendez spoke rapidly, giving Lee a sidelong glance. "OP Casa's on the line. They got hit, and they're gettin' their shit pushed in. They're asking for help exfilling."

Tex was already moving before Menendez had stopped talking. He looked over his shoulder as he stalked out of the laundry closet. "Say whatever you need to say to her Lee. We're gonna need a medic."

***

When Lee opened the door to the bedroom, he found Julia dressed, pulling her armor on. Abe was at his bedside, doing the same. He looked over his shoulder as Lee stopped in the door with a frown on his face.

Abe gave him a pointed glance towards Julia.

Julia was focused on her task, to the deliberate exclusion of Lee.

"Julia…" Lee started, knowing he was on unsteady footing.

She looked up at him. Her one good eye seemed flat and gray. Her swollen left eye was turning purple. The only expression on her face was the slight downturn at the corners of her mouth.

"We heard, Lee," she said. "I'll be ready in less than a minute."

She was shut off. Closed down.

No longer open for business.

Lee wondered where he'd made the misstep, or if he even had, or if Julia was simply coping with it in the only way she knew how. It left a big, open hole that gaped between them, unfulfilled and unacknowledged.

"So, you're aware?" was all Lee could think of to say.

She nodded as she pulled her medical pack off the floor and slung it onto her back. "I heard Menendez tell Tex there was a problem with one of their outposts. And they're gonna need a medic."

Shit. What else had she heard?

He registered suddenly that the laundry closet was below this bedroom.

Lee took a step towards her. "Listen…"

Her eyes flashed. "Lee, do you not think I have my priorities straight?"

He didn't know how to take that.

Julia shook her head at him. "You don't think I know that there are bigger things at stake?"

Lee looked away. "No...I just..."

Julia put a hand on his chest. "Lee. I'm fine. It's not like I haven't had a busted face before. I'm fine, and I can operate. We need to do this. For the UES." She jerked her head over her shoulder to where Lee's gear sat next to the bed. "And you need to get dressed."

FIFTEEN

CADDO

FIVE MINUTES LATER, they tore through the early-morning darkness in Tex's pickup. The clock on the dash said 4:00 a.m., and Lee thought that felt about right, judging by the tremble of fatigue and tension in his gut.

Lee, Abe, and Julia were crammed into the back, their armor and weapons making them rub against each other in what would normally be ample passenger space. Out of necessity, Deuce was in the truck bed, looking half-worried and half-excited as he tried to brace his body against the wall of the truck bed to keep from sliding around the more aggressive curves. Thompson drove, and Tex rode shotgun with his rifle in one hand and a satphone in the other.

They'd lost contact with their outpost shortly before hitting the road. Tex waited for them to call back with any extra details, but both he and Lee knew that wasn't likely.

"They have any idea who hit them?" Lee asked.

"I'd guess *Nuevas Fronteras*, but they couldn't confirm," Tex said, turning in his seat to look into the back. The headlights of the other three vehicles trailing behind them splashed over Tex's worried face. "Whoever it is, they hit hard about thirty minutes ago. Our boys are pulling out of OP La Casa, trying to head for one of my bunkers as a rally point. We need to cut off their pursuit—give them enough time to break contact and get to ground."

"How far out?" Abe asked.

"About thirty mikes," Tex replied.

Julia had her medical pack between her knees and her face was all business as she went through the contents with rapid, practiced fingers, prepping what she thought she might need. "You have any details on casualties?"

"Negative." Tex shook his head. "I'll try to get that if we can make contact again."

The tension in the air was like a stifling blanket when you're already hot and out of breath. And yet everyone was ignoring it.

Lee leaned forward. "How far between OP La Casa and the bunker?"

"Roughly five miles. Hilly terrain."

"Your boys on foot or do they have vehicles?"

"They have *some* vehicles, but not enough. If they did what they're supposed to do, vehicles will help stage a base of fire in the high ground and cover the retreat of the guys on foot."

Lee nodded along to this, forcing his tired brain to work in the mode that he needed it to. It was almost a relief, after what had happened at the cabin.

Exhausted though he may be, and dire as the situation sounded, at least this was familiar footing.

"Are we heading to that high ground?" Lee asked.

"That's the plan. We'll see how it shapes out when we get there."

"What intel do we have on the enemy?"

"Limited," Tex said. "But there's enough of a force that they pushed fifty of my troops out of their fortifications. Breckenridge is my guy on the ground and he said they hit them with some big guns— fifties, he thought. I'm assuming vehicle-mounted."

"Shit." Lee frowned. "Any reason *Nuevas Fronteras* would be interested in your position at OP La Casa?"

"La Casa's our southernmost outpost. The closest thing for *Nuevas Fronteras* to reach out and touch. My best guess is a reprisal for hitting their convoy."

"Were any of the tankers stashed there?"

"No, we have them secured farther north."

"You got on the line with any of your other outposts?"

Concern creased Tex's brow. "You think this could be a feint?"

"It won't hurt to check."

"I don't want to tie up the line," Tex said, waggling his satphone in the air.

Lee dove into his pack and pulled out their own satphone, handing it over to Tex. "Use mine. Hit up your other outposts. Let them know what's going on and get them on standby just in case."

For the next ten minutes of hurtling through the dark countryside, Tex called every outpost along their southern border, plus the one where they'd hidden the stolen fuel tankers. The best that Lee could decipher from hearing half the conversations, it sounded like all was quiet elsewhere.

That didn't mean that the attack on OP La Casa wasn't a distraction from something larger. But Lee began to wrack his brain, trying to figure out what the endgame of this was. If it even was *Nuevas Fronteras*, what were they hoping to accomplish here?

No sooner had Tex hung up Lee's satphone for the last time, than his own began to chirp a cheerily discordant tune. Tex opened the line and switched it to speakerphone, holding it over the center console so they could all hear.

"This is Captain Lehy. Go."

Gunfire erupted over the speaker.

"Tex!" the voice on the other end was raised and strained, but not panicked. "You got an ETA?"

"Less than twenty out," Tex said. "Where do you need us?"

"That depends on what you got."

"Four vehicles. Squad of twenty."

"You got heavy guns?"

"I got two fiddies."

"Roger 'at. I need 'em in the first line of hills north of Caddo." A brief pause as the speaker— Breckenridge, Lee assumed—fired off a volley of shots. Then there was the clatter and heavy breathing of running and repeated swearing.

Everyone in the truck sat tense and silent, listening.

Breckenridge came back: "We're getting light contact right now, tailing us through Caddo. I think it's recon. I got eyes in the hills and they've ID'd what looks like a larger force of technicals moving up seven-seventeen in pursuit. That's the force that pushed us out of La Casa. If we can pin 'em in the flats around Caddo, we can get enough time to get to the bunker and activate the bunker defenses. How copy?"

Tex had his eyes closed as though picturing the landscape from a map he had committed to memory. "Solid copy. Get your ass in those hills and take that high ground. Any ID on who's coming after you?"

"No fucking clue. The technicals look like *Nuevas Fronteras*, so that's my best guess."

"What do you have on foot with you, and what do you have in the hills already?"

"I got a dozen guys that took the vehicles up into the hills. I got another two dozen on foot with me."

Lee looked at Tex. "Can they mount a defense in Caddo to buy us time to get there?"

Tex opened his eyes. "Standby, Breck." Then, to Lee, he shook his head. "Caddo's not much bigger than Elbert. Just houses. They won't be able to hold them there." Tex's eyes flicked to Julia, but he spoke to the satphone. "Breck, what's your casualty situation looking like?"

"I lost ten getting out of La Casa. Packed a half-dozen wounded into the truck beds. I don't know how they're doing."

"Alright, Breck, I got a good doc enroute to your boys in the hills. Stay on the line with me."

To the background chatter of gunfire and distant shouts coming through the satphone, Tex began to coordinate, using their squad comms. Abe took charge of syncing their own squad comms to Tex's, while Lee stayed glued to Tex and the satphone, listening for the ever-changing shift in real-time information.

A quarter of an hour evaporated in a flurry of developments that Lee could barely keep track of.

The fighting through Caddo reached a lull. Breckenridge's men on the hillside no longer had visual contact with the larger force pursuing them northward. There was a brief respite in the gunfire and the possibility that the pursuit had ended.

Then it started up again. No less than ten technicals identified, plunging into Caddo from the south and east. A rough estimate of twenty attackers on foot. Then fifty. Then maybe a dozen. The numbers kept shifting back and forth.

Breckenridge's base of fire from the hills north of Caddo sported only two light machine guns. At first it looked like they were going to barrage the technicals enough to push them back, but then the technicals returned fire with their own light machine guns and forced Breckenridge's gunners to the far side of the hill to take cover.

By the time they were able to creep back up onto the ridge and get eyes on Caddo, the flats were swarming with attackers, and Breckenridge and a small fire team of five men were pinned in a ranch house at the base of the hills.

And then Tex and his convoy made its approach.

"Breck, we're coming in now across Roger's Lake, tell your boys not to fire, you copy?"

"Roger, relaying now. Tex, I need you to get some fucking guns on that hill so we can get out of here."

Breckenridge's voice still had not reached the point of panic, but there was a discernible note of anxiety to it now that hadn't been there before.

Lee understood. He'd been pinned down himself, and very recently. It was not a good feeling.

"I'm working on it," Tex replied. "You gotta stay alive for ten more minutes, Breck. Ten minutes."

The first inkling that Lee had of the hills came when the giant, black humps of them suddenly rose up from the flat landscape and blotted out the deep navy sky. Thompson was still driving at breakneck speeds—hadn't let up since they'd left the cabin. The roads were dirt, and narrow, and pitted, so that the truck rumbled violently over them and Lee felt the backend loosening and skidding when they took turns.

A narrow road appeared to their right, nothing more than twin ruts created by tires. Thompson swerved onto it, and the road tilted upward, and then they were roaring up into the hills.

Abe rolled down his window, and Lee did the same, and through the buffeting of the cool night air, they heard the rattle of machine gun fire, closer and closer.

"Julia," Tex said. "I'm dropping you up top to work on the wounded. Lee and Abe, I want you with me."

"Where are we going?"

"We're going down the hill to get Breck out of that house."

Lee glanced at Julia, feeling his stomach sink at the prospect of dropping her alone. Julia seemed to know without words what Lee's concern was, and she met his gaze and gave him a small nod of assurance. She knew what her job was. She didn't care.

Or at least she *acted* like she didn't.

"Alright," Lee nodded. "We're with you."

A glimmer of taillights ahead of them drew Lee's eyes. The details of the hilltop were concealed by the darkness. In the flash of their own headlights, and the strobing of nearby machine gun fire, Lee saw the scraggly trunks and branches of scrubby trees.

They pulled to a stop in a wash of dust that chased over them. A dozen yards ahead, in a small, flat area run through with a flurry of tire tracks, a small, red pickup with an M240 bolted to it edged back and forth while the gunner on the back yelled at the driver and let out bursts of fire.

They were trying to position themselves so that the gunner had a line of sight on the small town below them, but the truck itself was hidden as much as possible by the horizon line of the hill.

On the "safe" side of the hill, a collection of chemlights danced back and forth in the darkness. Some of them were red, some of them were green. It was a triage station—green if you were injured; red if you were about to die.

Julia had already fixated on them.

The second that Tex's pickup truck rocked to a stop, she elbowed Abe out of the way. He opened his door and slid out and Julia squeezed around him and headed to the wounded without another word to Lee or anyone else in the pickup.

Lee flew out of the pickup truck and into the sounds of battle that he knew so well. The chatter of machine guns punched at his eardrums, the shouted communications, the snap of incoming rounds over their heads, and the terrible, warbling moan of ricochets, smacking the stony earth around them and scattering off into the night in every direction.

Lee hunched, though they were on the far side of the hill from the incoming fire. He heard the bullets thrash through tree branches over his head, but he didn't think any of them could strike him.

Deuce scrambled his front paws onto the top of the truck bed, making to jump out.

"No!" Lee commanded. "You stay!"

There was too much going on. Lee would not be able to keep track of the dog in all of this.

Deuce whimpered and moaned about it, but stayed put.

Abe, Lee, and Tex converged at the front of the pickup truck, where a soldier ran to meet them.

"Where's Breck?" Tex demanded as soon as the soldier was close enough to hear him.

The soldier's face looked young in the blaze of light from the truck's headlights. He seemed urgent, but calm. He shook his head. "Breck's pinned down, sir. He's got three wounded and not enough hands to move 'em. They're stuck in a ranch house, right at the base of the hill."

"Shit. What about everyone else?"

"Everyone else has already come up over the top and is on their way to the bunker."

Tex turned and caught the eyes of his soldiers from the other trucks in his convoy that were gathering around him. "If you don't have a gun on your truck, hit the trails and pick up any of our boys that are on foot. Get everyone you can to the bunker. If you got a gun, get in position and lay some hate down on that town. Breck and five others are pinned down. I'm gonna ID what building he's in and we're gonna get him out of there."

Tex didn't wait for affirmation. He turned and looked at Lee and Abe, and they were with him, ready and willing, so he turned to the soldier that had given him the sitrep and nodded to the other side of the hill. "You got comms with Breck? He's not answering the satphone."

The soldier nodded, then touched a PTT hooked to his chest rig. "Williams to Breckenridge. How copy?" Williams listened for a moment, then nodded to Tex. "I got him."

"Tell him to answer his fucking satphone."

Williams relayed the message. Listened. "He said it got dropped and now it won't turn on."

"Dammit." Tex put a hand on Williams's shoulder. "You're gonna have to be my radioman then. You got a good spot to overlook Caddo?"

Williams nodded. "Come with me. Stay low."

Williams headed off into the darkness, with Tex, Lee, and Abe following in a line. The closer they got to the crest of the hill, the lower they crept, until they were crawling on all fours, and then on their bellies.

The gunfire from below became more audible. The snap and crackle of bullets whipping through the trees above them became more pronounced. Closer.

A handful of large projectiles struck a tree trunk just above Lee's prone body. He felt splinters of wood stinging the back of his head and neck and he pressed his face into the dirt with a quiet curse.

The tracer fire moved on.

His heart beating hard, not only from exertion, but from the closeness of the fire, Lee pulled his head up and saw that he trailed Tex by a few yards now. He gulped air and clawed forward faster, tasting the dust of the sandy ground on his tongue.

Tex came to a stop.

Lee looked back and saw Abe slithering into position nearly on top of him.

They were now in a shallow depression—almost a foxhole. Between them and the whining bullets coming at them was a large, circular chunk of earth. Lee realized it was a root ball. One of the trees had fallen over, creating the depression that they were now sitting in, and the root ball that now provided them with cover.

Williams had squirmed up so that his back was to the root ball. He hiked a thumb behind him. "Straight down that way is Caddo."

There was enough cover that Lee was able to sidle up onto his knees. "Can Breck identify the house that he's in?"

Williams relayed the question and waited, flinching once or twice as a round smacked the root ball and sent clumps of dirt skittering over their heads.

In the midst of this, Lee became aware of a howl, and for a slender second, his heart jumped into his throat, thinking, *primals!*

But right about that time, his brain went back ten years and connected that sound to something *else* that Lee was horribly familiar with. The howl terminated in a crashing boom, and a sudden flash of menacing orange light that lit all of their faces for a moment.

Lee snapped his head around, in time to see the fireball disappear into the blackness of night, leaving behind an afterimage in his eyes.

"Motherfucker," was all that Lee commented. He didn't need to say anything else. They all knew what an RPG looked and sounded like.

Tex looked pissed. He keyed his own comms. "Menendez! ID who the fuck just shot that shit at us and splatter his ass!"

Lee heard Menendez grunt out a reply over his own earpiece.

Williams leaned forward, smacking Tex on the chest to get his attention. "Breck says he's gonna strobe a window with his weaponlight."

As one, Tex, Abe, and Lee all sidled up to the big root ball and stuck just enough of their heads over it that they could see down into the inky blackness below them. Lee couldn't tell the difference between the hillside and the tiny town that lay in the flats. There were headlights below him—the technicals that had been reported—and that gave him a sense of distance, but he couldn't see any of the structures or the shape of the land that was spread out in front of him.

A string of tracer fire jumped out from one of the technicals, crawling towards them through the night, like a multi-jointed worm, and then whipping over their heads and to the left.

An answering string of tracers lanced out from Tex's boys on the hilltop and Lee watched the rounds spark and smash the vehicle that had delivered the previous volley.

Tracers work both ways, as the adage goes.

"Alright," Tex called out. "Tell him to send it."

The three of them waited in tense silence, staring down into the blackness below, flinching despite themselves as they watched the tracers hurtle back and forth, and feared the invisible non-tracers that struck around them.

The land was pitch black, and the sky was navy blue with sparkling stars.

And then, down at the very bottom of their field of view, and all the way to the left, nearly blocked by the curvature of the hillside, they saw the window of a house light up and strobe.

"Okay," Tex said, as they all pulled their heads back into cover. "Tell him we got a visual. Tell him we need five minutes, but we're gonna get him out of there."

In the span of the next five minutes, another three RPGs impacted the top of the hill.

The four men found themselves prone again, slithering their way downhill through the trees.

They'd all wanted to take the truck.

But they'd all admitted it was too big a target.

Breck had one other soldier besides himself, and then three wounded. Between Williams, Tex, Lee, and Abe, they figured they could get everyone up the hill.

They could also get their asses shot up, both in the coming and going, but the other alternative was to abandon the wounded men, and not a single one of them was willing to do that. The option hadn't even been voiced.

The only thing they had going for them was that Breck hadn't fired a shot from the house where he hid. The attackers in Caddo were not focusing on Breck's hideout, too concerned with the machine gun fire they were getting from the top of the hill.

Which left the eastern side of the hill ignored.

And it was down this side of the hill that Lee snaked his way.

They moved diagonal to the chattering of the enemy fire, so that it was to their right as they crawled. After a few minutes, they managed to put a horizon of hillside between them and the town of Caddo. They stood and picked up the pace, plunging down the hillside in great galloping strides.

The moon shown brighter on this side of the hill, and Lee was able to make out where to put his feet as the four of them descended. It took them less than a minute to reach the bottom.

Lee took a position about a pace off of a thick tree trunk. He went to one knee, propping his rifle on the other and taking a moment to catch his breath. He scanned, saw the edge of the house where Breck hid. Everything else around them was flatness. Pastureland that stretched like an alien landscape in the moonlight.

Another RPG ripped through the air and detonated low on the hillside.

·Lee squinted out to what he could see of Caddo beyond the side of the hill. The technicals had taken up positions, using the existing structures as cover. But they weren't pushing the hill. They'd bogged down.

Lee heard Tex's whisper from the shadowy woods beside him: "Tell him we're coming in. Right now. Eastern side of the building." A pause. "Moving!"

Lee pulled his rifle tighter into his shoulder and sighted out into the flatness beyond the target house where all was still. "Move!"

There was the shuffle and tramp of feet.

Williams and Tex sprinted past, hugging the curvature of the hillside as they approached the target house. Williams took the eastern corner, addressing the pastureland that Lee was now scanning. Tex took the right, scanning deeper into Caddo.

Lee and Abe didn't wait for commands. The second they saw Williams and Tex settle into coverage, they pushed out of their spots and ran the last fifty yards to the side of the house.

As they stumbled to a stop outside the target house, the back door swung open. A stocky soldier with a radio headset and no helmet, flattened himself against the door and motioned for them to get inside.

The four newcomers tumbled into the house and the man that Lee assumed to be Breckenridge wasted no time. He gave Tex a hearty slap on the back as he pushed him into what looked like a living room. There were no lights—not even chemlights—but the moonglow through a window showed Lee three prone forms, and one other that had taken up a position near the front door.

"How are they?" Tex murmured.

"They need medical attention," Breck answered. He took an additional step into the room so he hovered over the three wounded soldiers on the ground, all of which appeared to be conscious, and struggling with pain, but otherwise composed. "You guys ready to get out of here?"

They mumbled affirmatives. Quiet, but eager.

Tex pointed to Breck and his man covering the front window. "You two take up coverage for us. We'll grab the wounded. We're going around to the eastern side of the hill, and then straight up."

"Hold up," came an urgent grunt.

It came from the man at the front window.

All eyes pivoted to him.

His body tensed and he pulled away from the window with a muttered curse. The whites of his eyes shone out from his face. "Flankers. About fifty yards out and moving around in our direction. Five of them."

"Shit," Tex spat, moving towards the front of the house. He stood close to the other man and leaned out, peeking through the window, then ducking back in. "Looks like we're not the only ones trying to use the lull on this side of the hill."

"We got time to get them out?" Lee asked.

Tex shook his head.

Lee considered their dwindling options. "We gotta hit that squad hard and take them all out. And then we're gonna have to hightail it fast."

The man that had been watching the window peeked out again. "They're taking the roadway on our left side. We'll have a clear shot at them out these windows."

Tex nodded. "If you can pull a trigger, get on a window."

Lee had already registered that the house was standard construction. Vinyl siding. Stick-built. It would provide minimal cover when the bullets started flying. But they didn't have a choice in the matter either. If they let that fire team get around them and onto the hillside, then they were just going to give up the high ground position on them. They had to hit them before they reached the hillside.

Lee and Abe broke for the back door, while Tex and his remaining fighters took up the windows of the living room.

Lee edged out the backdoor. He knew that the thin walls of the house weren't going to stop any incoming rounds, but it still didn't feel good to be so exposed. He crouched low, and Abe took up a position over top of him, both of them hugging the side of the house.

Lee inched closer to the corner. Tex's voice whispered over the comms in his ear: "Everyone wait for my first shot. Lee and Abe, take the front runners. We'll take the rest."

Lee clicked his comms to indicate they understood.

At the corner of the house, Lee looked out into the open area to their east. The sky was beginning to lighten with the first hints of dawn. About thirty yards to the east of the house was a dirt road that looked like it circumvented the hill. It was on this road that Lee spotted the line of men, moving in a file.

His first thought upon seeing them was, *These aren't cartel.*

The details were lost in the darkness, but the impression was that these five men were well-equipped. From the outline of their figures, Lee perceived the familiar silhouette of helmet and body armor, and they moved like professionals.

The lead pair scanned efficiently, and it was only at the very last second that Lee saw what looked like NVGs on their heads...

The pointman in their column rocked to a halt, his head turned in Lee's direction.

"Contact!" the pointman shouted.

Lee fired.

The pointman jerked as though hit, but kept his aim and spat out a string of automatic fire. The first round buzzed by Lee's face, but he was already lurching backward into cover. Abe fired over him, the team on the road fired back, Tex's team inside the house opened up, and everything devolved into a cacophony of crackling rifle fire and whining near-misses and dull smacks of jacketed lead on the side of the house.

Already crouched, and with Abe firing over him, Lee couldn't rise to change levels, so he did the only thing he could do. He slipped into a prone position and rolled his head and rifle out of cover.

A flurry of rounds impacted the corner of the house at the level that Lee's face had been moments before, obliterating an aluminum downspout with a sound like steel drums being shredded, and wood and vinyl particles peppered Lee's skin.

He got the barest impression of his dim red dot touching the silhouette of one of the targets, and he fired again, three rounds in rapid succession and watched the man spin, caught in the shoulder, and then slump as the final round found something vital to penetrate.

Lee rolled back into cover with a grunt of effort. A round shattered against the rocky ground in front of them and Lee felt sharp stings all across his face. He let out a small cry and blinked rapidly. Instant relief that both of his eyes still worked.

Another fusillade of rifle reports issued from the house, and the response from the fire team they'd ambushed became sporadic, then just a single rifle. Then nothing.

Tex yelled from inside. It took a moment for Lee's ringing ears to register what he was saying.

"Lee! Abe! We gotta move!"

Lee felt Abe's hand on the collar of his armor, hauling him up. He thrust himself into a standing position and then they both tumbled back into the house.

The interior stank of spent propellant. It hung thick in the air as they barged back into the living room area, shafts of moonlight making it glow.

Tex and his three able-bodied soldiers were already grabbing hold of the wounded, picking them up off the ground. One looked like he'd joined them at the window. He was now slumped against the sill, the drywall near his head broken open by incoming rounds, and his own blood and brain matter dripping down his ruined face.

In that moment, all that Lee could perceive was a sense of relief that they would have one less body to weigh them down on their way back up the hill.

The plan that Tex had outlined before went out the window. Now it looked like Lee and Abe were going to be hands-free, so it would fall to them to cover the others as they carried the wounded. No one argued about it. They were all forward momentum now.

Tex and Williams each had the arm of a soldier with a wounded and tourniqueted leg. The wounded man's face was blank and pale and sweaty with impending shock. Breckenridge and his other man supported the last wounded soldier.

No one said a word about the one that was now slumped against the wall.

Lee did a quick mental check of himself and his ammunition as he and Abe stalked to the backdoor. He was bleeding from bits of bullet jacketing that had caught the right side of his face, but other than that he was whole.

At the back door, Tex called up: "We got all of them, I think."

"Roger," Lee replied.

But that didn't answer the question of who the hell they were.

Lee took the door first, punching through and retaking the corner of the house, this time standing. He scanned out to the road. In the moonlight, he could see three humps lying in the road. The last two might have died in the brush on the other side.

The line of people exited the house behind Lee.

The last man out gave Lee a slap on the shoulder to let him know they were clear.

Then they ran for the hills, all the while with Lee wondering who that squad had been, and where they'd come from.

***

Lee's half-healed lungs burned like red pepper was stuck in them. The urge to cough was strong, but he resisted, knowing it was only going to take more air away from him, and probably make his chest feel worse.

He was at the lead of the column, and Abe was taking up the rear, Tex and his men between them, struggling up the hillside in a slurry of curses and huffing breath.

Lee was just beginning to feel the slope level out—thought he could see one of Tex's trucks through the trees—when he rocked to a stiff halt, one arm raised.

Everyone else stopped behind him, the sound of their feet in the leaves silenced, and only their gasping breath audible now.

Lee pivoted to his left, towards the town of Caddo, and where the back-and-forth stream of tracers had been a near constant. He glared into the woods, registering that he was still hearing the pound of machine guns, but that something was different.

"They're not shooting at us," Lee husked.

Tex, gulping air next to him and supporting a wounded man, struggled to see why that was a problem. "Maybe they've had enough."

"No, they're still shooting," Lee said. He peered down the slope into the darkness of the town below them, and he could still see the twinkling of muzzle flashes down there. But he could hear something else.

The screaming of men.

"Shit," Lee muttered, then turned and shoved Tex up the hill. "Primals! Teepios! They're getting hit by teepios!"

Lee didn't need to explain his urgency. This wasn't a stroke of luck: The primals didn't discriminate, and they were just as likely to shift their attention in your direction at some random sensory input—a shift in the wind that brought your scent to them, or the shuffling of your feet that somehow carried to their ears.

The two wounded and the men that were hauling them up the hill started to lurch their way up the last fifty yards, all pretense of stealth now thrown to the wind.

"Abe!" Lee called, looking through the darkness for him, and finding his friend already in a cover position about ten yards from Lee. Abe's dark eyes glimmered in the pale dawn light now coming through the trees. He made eye contact with Lee and nodded.

No further speaking was necessary.

Abe held coverage down the slope. Lee turned and ran back about five strides, then posted on a tree. When Abe heard Lee stop moving, he started. The two continued to bound in this manner, always keeping one gun trained down the hill.

They had less than a second of warning when it happened.

Lee was just posting on a tree, his own feet falling silent, and in that small moment, he heard the thud of something galloping toward them.

His eyes came up over his rifle just in time to see a gray shape hurtle out of a thicket of low brush, crashing through it and launching itself through the air in an inhuman leap.

"Abe!" Lee yelled.

Abe ducked, firing a burst on automatic that clattered through the branches, and one or two of the rounds caught the primal, but didn't stop it.

The primal hit the tree that Abe was shoving off of, and spun around it with an eerie rapidity, swiping out with its long-fingered hands and catching ahold of Abe's elbow just as Abe jumped backward.

Lee had no choice.

The creature was right on Abe, but Abe was off-balance.

Lee was already in his sights as Abe started to go down.

Lee aimed high, hoping to catch vital organs and punch the spine out of the primal. He fired, registered that his first two shots splintered into the tree behind the primal, adjusted lower, and caught the primal in the hump of its back as it gnashed at Abe's face.

The creature jerked and twisted like it'd been bit in the back, let out a yelp, and rolled off of Abe, its wide, predatory eyes fixing now on Lee. Abe crabbed backward, one hand in the dirt and leaves, one hand holding his rifle like a pistol, and fired another burst that carried his rifle far off the mark, but the first three rounds found their mark and ripped the creature's face to shreds at point blank.

Abe twisted, shouted at Lee, just as Lee heard another scramble of limbs to his right.

He dropped his shoulder.

Something hit him, but glanced off, then went rolling past him through the dirt—a missed tackle. On one knee, Lee righted his weapon and fired five rounds straight down the primal's mouth as it scrabbled through the leaves at him, all five projectiles punching through its head, through its body, and exiting somewhere out the backend of its torso, dropping it instantly.

The second that Lee perceived it was no longer a threat, he swung around to cover his right flank again, searching for another target, but all he saw was the dim shape of gray trees.

"You alright?" Abe gasped as he sprinted up to Lee.

"Are you?"

"I'm fine."

Lee's hands and knees shook. "Let's go."

Below them, in the town of Caddo, the machine gun fire became sporadic. The screams of men were silenced now. Shouts of command split the air. Were their attackers still dealing with the primals or were they going to return their attention to the hilltop?

Lee and Abe ran, their legs tightening as they did, the lactic acid taking its toll, making each stride shorter and less powerful, but the slope was leveling out now, and when Lee looked forward again, he saw the trucks waiting for them, only twenty yards ahead.

They stumbled into the clearing and Lee saw Tex in the bed of one of the pickup trucks, urging them on, while behind him, the other trucks turned around in clouds of dust and hightailed it off the hilltop, making quick use of the cessation in enemy fire.

Abe hit the truck bed first in a clatter of gear and vaulted himself inside, somersaulting into the backend.

Lee spun and took one last look at the woods that surrounded them, saw no immediate threats, and pulled himself up into the bed. Tex grabbed him by the shoulder as he did and hauled him in, sending Lee sprawling over top of a wounded man who swore at him.

And then the truck was moving, tearing out of there, putting distance between them and the threats below.

SIXTEEN

LINCOLNISTS

IN THE DARKNESS of the early morning hours, a radio transmission was sent out in Fort Bragg. It originated from the northwestern corner of the Fort Bragg Safe Zone, and it was sent out on channel 13 of a standard civilian FRS.

The transmission had no voice. It was the click of a transmit button, three times in succession, followed by a three second pause, at which point the sequence repeated. It was repeated five times, and then was silent.

In a single-family dwelling, not far from the place where the transmission had originated, a man awoke, hearing the *ksh-ksh-ksh* of the handheld radio that sat in its charging cradle next to his bed. He didn't move. He lay on his side, with his head still on his pillow, but his eyes open, staring at the dark bedroom that he shared with his wife.

He listened to the sequence of "clicks."

He listened to the silence that followed.

His wife had come awake as well.

She said nothing.

He rolled into a sitting position and reached down and took the radio off its cradle, his heart ramping up from its resting rate. He repeated the sequence of clicks. Three clicks, followed by a pause. Repeated five times.

Then he stood up and started to get dressed.

"I'll get ready," his wife said.

Ten minutes after that, this sequence had bounced from one end of the Fort Bragg Safe Zone to the other, reaching nine other single family households. The people in these houses then used their handhelds as a repeater to send the transmission on to the next.

As the sky began to gray, these people left their houses, on their way to report to their work stations for the day. As they walked through Fort Bragg, each of them held a piece of white chalk in their hand, which they used to swipe a mark on every telephone pole they passed.

As the first rays of sunlight broke across the eastern horizon, the rest of Fort Bragg began to wake and leave their houses to report to their places of work for the day. Most people took no notice of the small white mark on the telephone poles. But many did.

Those that noticed it, stopped in their tracks, then turned around and went back to the houses they had come from. They all smiled and told their neighbors or house-mates that they'd forgotten something they needed. They went to their bedrooms, and from under beds and in the top shelves of closets, they all drew out large duffel bags of various shapes and colors, slung these over their shoulders, and headed out again, but this time not to their places of work.

They began to gather at the nine single-family homes that the transmission had reached. They arrived in singles, and sometimes pairs. Sometimes ten to a house, sometimes eight. But they arrived discreetly, and locked the doors behind them. In quiet, nervous huddles, they began to unpack the contents of their duffel bags.

Across Fort Bragg, foremen and forewomen waited for tardy workers to arrive. The woman in charge of the chickens was missing five people. The man in charge of the stockyards was missing six. A planting crew that was designated to leave the wire and plant corn in Field 15 was missing three.

At a large vegetable patch that had a literal ton of cabbage that needed to be harvested, the foreman went to one of his best and most punctual workers, who happened to be the man that had first been awakened by the transmission. A man whose house now contained ten people that did not live there.

"Hey," the foreman called to the good worker as he frowned at the clipboard that held the day's roster. "You seen the Bakers?"

The good worker had a white, plastic laundry basket in one hand, and a sharp knife in the other. He smiled, in a somewhat confused manner, and shook his head. "No, I haven't seen them."

The foreman's frown deepened. "Frank? Tilly? Price? You see any of them?"

The good worker laughed. "To be honest, this early in the morning I wouldn't notice a bear walking through the streets. Sorry, boss."

The foreman grumbled under his breath. "Alright then. 'Preciate it."

The good worker took his basket and his knife, and walked out into the dew-covered fields and began to harvest cabbage.

The vegetable fields were grown on a large chunk of golf course that sat in the middle of Fort Bragg. The foreman's "office" was an old grounds maintenance shed near the eighteenth green. It had a direct line to the Soldier Support Center, which, despite the name, pretty much supported—and coordinated—all of Fort Bragg, both military and civilian.

For safety reasons, all foremen were required to report "conspicuous absences," which was defined as two or more people missing from work without explanation. This particular foreman figured it was a way for the powers that be to make sure everyone was putting in the sweat equity to make sure the Safe Zone ran smoothly.

But he supposed it could be for the stated reason: to ensure that outbreaks of any sort didn't go unnoticed.

He called in the names of the missing people. The Bakers were a couple, so that meant he was down five workers today. He hung up the trench phone with the Soldier Support Center, irritated, and grabbed a basket and a knife.

Looked like he was going to have to put in some sweat equity himself.

He thought nothing else of it, aside from the fact that the five people missing today better have damn good excuses whenever he saw them again. It was harvest, and these cabbages didn't pick themselves.

In fact, none of the five foremen and forewomen thought anything of their weak rosters on that particular morning. But they all called their conspicuous absences in, as they were required to do.

Corporal Townsend at the Support Center, however, did notice it.

Not at first. At first, he jotted down the names without a second thought. As he received the second call in, and added another eight names to the list, he wondered if there was a spring flu going around, and, being a bit of a hypochondriac, wondered if he felt ill himself.

By the time he'd put the phone down for the fifth time and had a total of forty names, Corporal Townsend was in a near panic. The body of his boss, Lieutenant Derrick, was barely cold after a brutal and senseless murder, and now forty-plus people were not reporting to work. He had the deep-seeded suspicion that these two occurrences were somehow linked, but he had no idea how to link them.

So he did the only thing he could think of to do.

He called someone who had more authority than him.

Master Sergeant Carl Gilliard was quick to answer his radio: "Go ahead, command."

"Sir," Corporal Townsend stared at the list of papers, as the phone on his desk started to ring yet again. "We got a problem."

***

In a single-family residence in the northwestern corner of the Fort Bragg Safe Zone—the very same residence where the transmission of clicks had originated—Elsie Foster sat in a living room made dim by the drawn shades and closed blinds on the windows.

Elsie was seated on a couch, hunched forward, with her elbows on her knees, her hands clenched together. Her knees bouncing. On the small coffee table in front of her, a plate held a single piece of coarse bread, homemade from the hard red wheat they grew.

It had a single bite out of it. Save for that bite, Elsie hadn't eaten in almost twenty-four hours, but the nerves roiling through her made her nauseas.

Standing beside the couch was her only companion in that house: Claire Staley.

Claire held one of the FRS civilian radios in one hand, and in the other she held the satphone that she'd secreted away in her backpack when she'd fled the house she'd once shared with her father.

"Everyone's in position," Claire stated.

"Except the captains," Elsie pointed out.

"They'll be there as soon as they get out of work."

Elsie looked up at Claire. "Gilliard's going to go to their houses," she said, referring to all the people that *hadn't* shown up to their work that morning. Those people were now stationed in the houses of the captains. "He'll investigate the absences."

Claire nodded. "Probably. But he won't find them. And he has no reason to go to the captains' houses."

The captains had been the ones that *did* show up to work that morning. They would not be on the list of houses for Gilliard and his goons to investigate.

Elsie cupped her hands over her mouth. Her fingers felt like ice. After a moment, she pulled them away, and rubbed them together to try to get some blood flowing in them. "There's a lot of ways this could go wrong."

Claire nodded. "You're right. But you can't anticipate every way it might go wrong. All we can do is what we have to do. We'll make adjustments as needed."

Elsie's eyebrows twitched up. A grim smile touched her lips. "You're always so calm, Claire. I admire that."

Claire stared down at the leader of the Lincolnists. The leader of the *resistance*. "We're doing the right thing, Elsie."

Elsie nodded. "I know that. I've never doubted it for a second."

Claire held out the satphone. "Make the call."

Elsie took the satphone and cradled it in her hands like it was capable of starting a nuclear war. And perhaps she wasn't so wrong. It wasn't going to be nuclear, but it was going to be a war. And it was going to start with her. It was going to start with dialing a number.

Elsie nodded again, and then dialed the number. The only number that that satphone had ever dialed.

Elsie Foster contacted Greeley, Colorado.

***

Angela stood with her arm around Abby in the emergency room of the medical center.

Abby was hale and hearty, and ready to go home. She was smiling and happy. The bite from the

257

primal hadn't infected her. And she didn't know how close she'd come to being deliberately infected by Nurse Sullivan.

Angela hadn't told her.

Another nurse—not Sullivan—stood in front of them, giving them some discharge instructions to care for the healing bite wound. Angela nodded along, and held eye contact with the nurse, but she didn't hear much of what was said.

Her brain was trapped in an invasive loop. It had enslaved her thoughts, and chained them to this treadmill. She saw Abby, frothing at the mouth, strapped to a hospital bed, gone mad with infection. And who was going to make the call to put Abby out of her misery? Could Angela?

She knew that she shouldn't even be thinking about that shit right then—what was the point? Abby was safe. It hadn't happened. They had dodged that bullet.

But it had been close.

And that closeness terrified her.

What would she have done?

The very thought of having to make that call—or even just turning her back while somebody else did—robbed Angela of every bit of courage she possessed, and though she stood there, with a half-smile on her lips, nodding to the nurse, inside, she felt like every hard thing in her had been melted like wax.

She had been through a lot. She had changed a lot.

Somehow, someway, she had made it through the end of the world without losing her only child.

And for a while, perhaps, she'd fooled herself into believing that those days were over.

But they weren't.

They were never going to be over.

They were all in danger, all the time.

Fucking Elsie Foster...

Angela pictured the woman's face and never in her life, in all the hellish times she'd been through over the last few years, had she felt so removed from any semblance of human empathy. She had killed before, in anger and out of necessity, and for the protection of her child. But this was different somehow.

All of what she'd done before had been purely animal. Maternal instinct.

This had left that territory now. It had gone into some dark land that Angela was unaware even existed inside of her.

She could make Elsie suffer.

She could make that woman scream and never feel a stir in her soul beyond satisfaction.

And as Angela knew this, and accepted it, some of the things that had melted inside of her turned hard again.

"Mom," Abby's voice poked in.

Angela blinked. Looked at her daughter. "What?"

Abby glanced at Angela's hand that gripped her shoulder, the fingers pressed into her flesh. "That hurts."

Angela released her grip on Abby's shoulder. Her fingers left little indents in the cloth of Abby's shirt. She smoothed them out, then patted Abby's shoulder. "Sorry, Honey." She swallowed, then looked at the nurse with a frown. "Is that everything?"

The nurse gave her a queer look, but then forced a wooden smile and nodded. "Yes, ma'am. That's everything."

Angela tried to return the smile, but it only flittered across her face and was gone. She turned around, guiding Abby with her, towards the doors of the emergency room where Kurt Barsch stood, waiting.

"All ready, ma'am?"

Angela nodded. "Yes. Let's go."

Kurt went first through the sliding doors, his sharp eyes tracking over everything in sight, searching for anything that could be a threat. As he walked, he keyed his comms. "Diamondback's on the move."

As they walked out into sunshine, Angela's mind flashed back. The imagery was nearly identical: walking out into daylight, an SUV pulling around to pick her up, her bodyguard walking in front of her.

She felt a knot form in her stomach, and as her heart started ramping up, she glanced up at the school building, expecting once again to see the twinkle of a riflescope in sunlight, or the puff of a muzzle flash...

But of course, just like last time, there was nothing there to be concerned—

Kurt stiffened. Grabbed her shoulder.

Angela's mind went into a blank, buzzing space of panic, thinking, *it's happening again!*

A white pickup truck, speeding into the lot.

Kurt pushed her towards their waiting SUV, his rifle starting to come up towards the fast-approaching pickup.

Again? She almost couldn't believe it. *They're going to try to kill me again?*

Angela grabbed Abby and started shoving her for the SUV, all concern for herself supplanted by the fact that her daughter was present.

Kurt abruptly halted. Appeared to hear something over his comms, and then swore under his breath. They had reached the SUV, but he wasn't opening the door.

"What's going on?" Angela demanded, her voice husky.

"Sorry, ma'am," Kurt said, annoyed. "Didn't mean to alarm you. It's fine."

The pickup came into the roundabout that fed the entrance to the Medical Center, and before it had even rocked to a stop, the door opened, and Carl Gilliard stepped out.

Angela swore. Her heart still knocking.

For a second she thought about releasing some of that tension onto Carl—bitching him out for rolling up on them like that, but Carl's face put an end to that train of thought.

"Angela," Carl said, stalking up, still with a pronounced limp. "We have a situation that needs your immediate attention."

Angela took a breath to settle herself. Quelled the feelings of fear, and the irritation that they'd even been sparked in her. She looked at Kurt. "Can you take Abby back to the house, please? I'll go with Sergeant Gilliard."

Kurt looked perturbed, as he always did when there was a change of plans. He liked things to move along the pre-arranged rails. Any divergence from them was a source of danger in his mind.

"What's going on, Mom?" Abby asked, as Kurt opened the back door for her.

Angela gave her daughter's hand a squeeze. She looked at her daughter's worried face, and she wanted to say that everything was going to be fine, but was it?

She kept saying that. And she kept making herself a liar.

"I don't know, Honey. Go with Kurt. I'll send Marie over."

A flash of a frown went across Abby's face, but she let Kurt guide her into the back of the SUV.

Carl waited, his stern face showing signs of impatience.

Kurt closed the back door, then looked over the hood of the SUV to the truck, where he saw Mitch in the driver's seat, Logan, Rudy, and Morrow in the back. All were strapped up with armor and rifles. This seemed to placate Kurt.

"Diamondback one to command," Kurt transmitted over his comms. Waited for the return, which Angela couldn't hear. "Diamondback Actual will be with Master Sergeant Gilliard, moving to..." he arched his eyebrows at Carl.

"Support Center," Carl grunted.

"To the Support Center," Kurt finished his transmission, then gave Carl a curt little nod, and relinquished his duties.

Formalities taken care of, Carl gestured for the truck. "After you, ma'am."

Angela got into the back of the truck. Carl closed her door after her, suspicious eyes scanning over everything, just as Kurt's had. He was far more dour than Kurt, but took the responsibilities of keeping Angela safe just as seriously.

The SUV bearing her daughter roared out of the Medical Center parking lot, and the pickup truck followed after, turning towards the Support Center while the SUV turned towards Angela's neighborhood.

Angela wiped her palms across her thighs as they started moving. "What's happening now?"

"Nearly a hundred people have failed to report for their assigned duties this morning."

Angela stared at the back of Carl's head, trying to make the connection and failing. "Okay..."

"Elsie Foster is missing. So's Claire Staley. Lieutenant Derrick was found dead in his house." This was all recap—Angela had already been briefed on these developments. But Carl wasn't done. "Eight of the missing ninety-five people are on our watchlist of suspected Lincolnists."

This time, Angela made the connection. "Shit!"

Carl nodded. "The Lincolnists are making their move."

SEVENTEEN

DOORS

JOHN BELLAMY'S PLYWOOD BOX of an office was three boxes down from Captain Perry Griffin. Between them sat some administrative positions—lieutenants mostly—that Bellamy didn't even bother to learn the names of anymore, because they cycled through so rapidly. Bellamy had paid enough attention to the lieutenants to deduce that whatever they did was of no grand importance. They were paper-pushers in camouflage uniforms. So he ignored them.

Captain Perry Griffin, however, was a fellow Coordinator.

Unlike Bellamy, Griffin had drank Briggs's proverbial Kool-Aid.

Perry Griffin was the point-of-contact for their element in Fort Bragg. The element was codenamed FLY, as in "fly on the wall." Griffin did his due diligence in keeping FLY secret, as he was supposed to, but in months past he'd let a few things slip to Bellamy.

Bellamy had determined that FLY was a woman who worked very close to Angela Houston, the elected leader of the United Eastern States. He'd also determined that there had been some recent developments happening over there.

What bothered Bellamy was that sometime in the last few days, Griffin had become more secretive than usual.

As the sole POC, Griffin was entitled to this secrecy. On paper, at least, he was supposed to report to Lineberger and Briggs with information from FLY. For the purposes of operational security, he was not *supposed* to let Bellamy in on anything.

But it didn't escape Bellamy that in the past Griffin had been pretty loose about his opsec, and that recently, he'd tightened up.

Guilty of treason as he was, Bellamy found this new development disturbing.

He tried to tell himself that it was just because something important was happening, and so Griffin was taking things more seriously. But in the back of his head he began to wonder. He began to analyze the way that Griffin looked at him. Began to wonder if Griffin knew something.

And if Griffin knew something, who else knew?

In his plywood office, Bellamy popped a chalky antacid into his mouth and crunched it, frowning. He'd had to do a bit of bartering with a scavenger in the Yellow Zone for the bottle of TUMS. He could've requisitioned it from the PX at FOB Hampton, but then he would have had to tell someone about his acid reflux, and he didn't want anyone to know that he was feeling more stressed than usual. Word got around.

He washed the antacid down with the dregs of his coffee.

He'd been drinking a lot of coffee lately—or at least what passed for coffee these days.

It gave him an opportunity to walk past Griffin's office.

Bellamy stood with his Styrofoam cup still in hand, and exited his office. He closed his office door behind him, always aware of the fact that he had an unregistered satphone in the bottom of his desk.

The bubble of light, office conversation lilted through the air from the cubicles erected all through the conference room outside.

As he drew closer to Griffin's office, he heard the man's voice speaking from inside, in quiet, urgent tones.

Drawing abreast of the office, he saw Griffin with a satphone to his ear. He was walking to his open office door, and as Bellamy walked past, Griffin's eyes came up, held his for a brief moment, and then Griffin swung his door shut.

Shit.

Bellamy felt his gut roil again.

Just that bare moment of eye contact had spoken volumes.

Something was up.

Bellamy continued on his way, his mind running in a dozen different directions.

Was he being paranoid? It was difficult to make the distinction between paranoia and reasonable suspicion when it was your ass on the line. But it sure as hell felt like Griffin was hiding something from Bellamy.

Like he didn't trust him.

Shit, shit, shit.

Bellamy needed an out. He thought about it for the hundredth time in the past few days. Maybe it was paranoia, but it couldn't hurt to have a contingency plan in place to get his ass out of this place if things went sour.

He'd already begun socking away some food and water. Some items for barter. Some things that might help him get out of the Green Zone. The problem remained that he was stranded in Colorado, and he had a lot of territory to cross to get to people that would be friendly.

He had been toying with the idea of making contact with some of the "coyotes" in the Yellow Zone—people who made a living by locating the loved ones of Greeley residents and bringing them back to Colorado. The practice was a concern for the higher ups in Greeley, but as of yet, they hadn't taken any action on it.

Bellamy's major concern was that these coyotes were just mercenaries. If they recognized Bellamy, or felt that they could get a better price for turning him in than Bellamy could pay them for getting him out, then they wouldn't bat an eye to betray him.

Bellamy found himself standing in front of the coffee maker.

Someone had taken the last of the coffee and not reset it to brew.

As with everything else these days, coffee was a finite resource. The coffee table was stocked with enough for five pots. Once it was gone, there was no more coffee for that day. And the coffee that was provided had already degraded to a mix of decaf and regular.

Pretty soon they'd be re-using the previous day's grounds, or adding burnt bread crumbs.

Bellamy grumbled another curse and turned around, intending to return his well-used coffee cup to his office.

Griffin exited his office. He closed the door behind him, much as Bellamy had done, and began marching across the conference room with purpose in his steps.

He didn't look around. Didn't see Bellamy watching him.

He let Griffin get most of the way across the conference room before he started to follow him.

This conference room was connected to the adjacent one by a single door on the far side. The next conference room over was the one where Lineberger had his office, and Bellamy felt confident that was where Griffin was heading.

Bellamy let Griffin get to the door between the two conference rooms before he pushed himself off of the table that held the coffee maker, and followed after him.

Griffin remained fixated on his task—he kept his eyes forward, and kept up a brisk pace.

Whatever had just happened, whoever it had been on the satphone with Griffin, it looked like it was urgent.

As Bellamy followed, half his mind was trying to puzzle out what had happened, while the other half was screaming at him that he might give himself away by showing this much interest…

But he kept following. Whatever news it was, Bellamy needed to figure it out—it could be important to Tex—and that was Bellamy's job right now. Besides, he also reported on a regular basis to

Lineberger, so it wasn't going to seem amiss for him to appear outside of the colonel's office.

By the time he made it to Lineberger's office, the door was closed, and he could hear quiet conversation beyond the plywood walls. Griffin and Lineberger were both speaking quickly, but keeping their voices down.

Bellamy glanced around him, but no one else seemed to be paying much attention to the fact that he stood there. He chose a spot nearby that didn't look like he was hovering so close to the door as to be eavesdropping—just waiting for the colonel to be available so Bellamy could make his report.

Shit. What was Bellamy going to say?

What was his reason for being outside the colonel's door?

He started to rack his brains for a reasonable answer, but before he could settle on one, the conversation inside the office came to an abrupt halt, and a second later, the door opened up.

Griffin emerged, looking as focused as he had when he'd been on the satphone. He caught sight of Bellamy standing off to the side, and he stiffened.

"John," Griffin said, his eyes narrowing.

"Perry," Bellamy returned, trying on an ill-fitted smile. "You look particularly tense today. Everything alright?"

Griffin mirrored the smile, and it was just as awkward on his mouth as it was on Bellamy's. "Just busy. Lot of pans in the fire. You know how it is."

"You know it," Bellamy chuckled, and then, in a sudden flash of inspiration, went with, "Hey, if you get a little time off, I still got a few cans of Coors Original in my room. Bet it's been a long time since you had a legit beer. You should come by. Tie one off."

Griffin nodded. "Yeah. That sounds great."

They split apart.

Neither one convinced of the other.

"Major," Colonel Lineberger growled from inside the office. "Did you need something?"

Bellamy swung himself into the open doorway, still trying to appear casual. "Yes, sir. Was just planning on making contact with our allies down south this afternoon and confirm the re-shipment of fuel." His excuse came to his tongue almost without forethought. "I was curious if we had any intel on the routes into Colorado. You know—which ones would be safer for the convoy at this point. Try to avoid any more drama."

Lineberger listened to this with an enigmatic expression on his face. Bellamy couldn't tell whether the excuse had flown or crashed. So he stood there, still trying to smile and look casual.

Perhaps ill-conceived, or perhaps an inspired gamble, Bellamy jacked a thumb behind him. "Perry seems edgy today. Everything okay? Anything I should know about?"

Colonel Lineberger then surprised Bellamy by cracking a smile. "Well, you know Perry. He's a little tense as it is. But yes, there's some stuff going down." Lineberger gestured to the open door. "Close the door. I'll bring you into the loop."

***

Elsie Foster disconnected the satphone, and for a moment, her gaze lingered on the blind-drawn windows.

Claire watched her, trying to discern the gist of the message that they'd just received from their contact in Greeley. As Claire watched, Elsie's lips tensed, and her face hardened into the expression of determination for which she was known. As though just like that all the uncertainty had been banished and she was now, once again, completely sure of herself.

"They say they want some proof of our capabilities. We need to determine a target," Elsie said. "Somewhere inside the Safe Zone. Something that will do damage to Angela. Something that will make it easy for them to come in and help us take over."

Claire bit her lip. "Shit. Elsie. That sounds like they're using us."

Elsie nodded. "They *are* using us. And you shouldn't be surprised. We're the ones that need help. But they have a team they're ready to deploy close by to us. Within striking range of Fort Bragg. But they're not going to hit until we cripple the defenses."

Claire covered her mouth and nose with both hands and took a deep breath. Her hands smelled musty. After a moment's thought, she pulled them away from her face. "I've got an idea, but we'll need to coordinate with the captains."

***

"House-to-house," Carl stated. "That's the only way."

It was only him and Angela, standing in her office, the desk separating them.

Carl hunched over the desk, his fists propping him up. Angela stood back, her arms crossed over her shoulder. She stared at the master sergeant across from her, at the bitter lines of his face. A thin vein had started to show under his right eye.

"You mean start kicking in doors?" Angela said, and found her voice devoid of emotion. She felt that she was stewing in a mental fallout zone. Everything was too big for her. And in her failure to grasp its enormity, she found herself detached and calm.

Was this how real leaders made their hard decisions?

Was it just a matter of dissociation?

She wouldn't know.

She was a fraud.

Regardless of her lack of tone, Carl seemed to sense push-back, and he wasn't wrong—indiscriminate house-to-house raids went counter to everything Angela wanted to believe about their burgeoning society.

"Angela, this is what has to be done. The Lincolnists are mobilizing." He started to slap a hand down into his open palm to punctuate each point as he made it. "If they're mobilizing, that means they want to fight us. We can't wait for them to choose the place and time of the fight. We have to cripple them as soon as possible. But that requires that we know where they are. And there is no way to route them out in a timely manner without going house-to-house through Fort Bragg, and flushing them out."

"You can't just go through Fort Bragg, kicking in everyone's doors."

"We don't have to kick in everyone's doors. Just the people that won't let us in."

"Carl, this is not a dictatorship! You are not the gestapo!" Angela raised her hands up and clutched the air in front of her face, trying to claw adequate words into existence. "We're...we're *civilized*!"

"You get too civilized and you get overrun by barbarians," Carl growled. "Ask any number of other civilized people. You want to survive and preserve your ideals? Well, then you have to get rough sometimes. You have to do dirty shit. That's the way it is, Angela."

Angela never presumed to be an amazing leader. But she also didn't like being talked down to. Her eyebrows cinched into a glare at Carl. "How much of this is because it's the right thing to do? And how much of it is because you just want to kill them all for betraying you and Tomlin?"

Carl's bottom lip pulled back in an almost spasmodic move, exposing his lower teeth for a flash. A wince. The prodding of an unhealed wound. "It doesn't matter if it's right or wrong, Angela. It's the *only* thing to do."

Angela shook her head fiercely. "I don't believe that."

"Then enlighten me as to our other options."

"You have your men go in an orderly fashion to the houses of the people that didn't show up to work today. You knock on doors. You ask questions. Civilly."

"You're treating a matter of warfare like a police action," Carl snapped.

"That's because it's not war!" Angela took a moment to breathe and reign herself in. "These people are our neighbors. And there hasn't been any overtly violent act. Yet."

Carl looked shocked at this assertion. "No overtly...?" He leaned in. "What about the fucker that tried to kill you, Angela? What about Lieutenant Derrick, dead on his goddamn doorstep? Holy shit. What about Elsie Foster trying to get Sullivan to *infect your daughter*? Those feel awfully overt to me!"

Angela felt like she was suddenly split right down the middle.

The feeling that she'd had as she held onto Abby, thinking of what Elsie Foster had been willing to do just to get at Angela, and how Angela wouldn't feel anything but good about beating that woman to death with her own hands...

And then the feeling, like she'd helped create this tottering house of cards. And that house of cards was the UES, and in it was sheltered the belief that they were good again, they were beyond the dirty, pathetic, scrabbling in the dirt and blood and savagery of the years that followed the collapse of the world's societies.

She didn't want that house of cards to fall, but it was so fragile.

Those two sides of her, warring.

The savage, and the civilized.

Angela took a shaky breath and rolled her shoulders back so she felt erect and in control. She looked Carl in the eye. "No house-to-house raids. It's an option, Carl. And I respect your professional opinion. But we're going to hold onto the hope for a peaceful option as long as we can. If it becomes obvious that there won't be a peaceful option, then we will do it your way."

Carl, feeling something in the air change between them, drew back from the desk, and it didn't escape Angela that his nose curled for a moment, like he found her distasteful.

Angela had never felt so alone in her life.

She wished that Lee were in the room at that moment, even though she thought that he would probably agree with Carl. It didn't matter. Right now it was just Angela, one tiny island, and not a friendly face in sight, and she felt lost.

She was just acting like she had her shit together.

Like she was the president of this place.

Like she was firm in her resolutions.

But she was perched on a razor's edge. Barely hanging on.

With some apparent effort, Carl smoothed the sneer from his face, and gave Angela a nod. "We will continue to make contact with the houses that did not report for their work details and hopefully we will come up with something that we can use." He looked like he was about to say something else, but then decided not to.

It didn't matter.

Angela was able to read it in his eyes.

Hopefully it won't be too little, too late.

EIGHTEEN

TRIAGE

TEX'S BUNKER, north of the town of Caddo, was a madhouse.

Lee had stood topside amid the camouflage of a small radio tower used to disguise the entrance to the bunker, while the wounded and the soldiers carrying them hit the lift and were taken underground, and the sun came up over the tree-lined hills.

His face began to ache from the bits of copper bullet jacketing that had peppered it earlier, but he knew that was only cosmetic damage, and others had serious wounds.

No primal bites, though.

The only two primals that had attacked up the hill had been the two that Lee and Abe had put down.

It was only once they'd reached the bunker that Lee realized Deuce had not been in the truck bed with him when they'd escaped the hilltop. His stomach dropped, and he began coursing through the flashes of memory, trying to remember if he'd seen the dog during the firefight.

Had he run off when he'd scented the primals on the hilltop?

Had he been shot?

His brain went through all of this several times before he registered that he hadn't seen Julia either. With every pickup truck full of escaping and wounded soldiers, his hopes rose and then fell. No sign of Julia.

She'd been on the hill when Tex had told everyone to hightail it.

She would have arrived first.

She would be underground, tending to the wounded.

Perhaps Deuce would be with her.

That's what he told himself, and every time he did, it quelled the nausea gripping his stomach for a handful of seconds, but then it would come back.

Finally, they were down to stragglers, and Lee found an open spot to park himself in the lift, and took it.

In the cold confines of the steel freight elevator, there were two soldiers with minor wounds who handled their situations with a grim sense of humor, asking if this meant they got extra rations. Their buddies supporting them laughed dutifully and kept things light.

When Lee made it to the inside of the bunker, twenty minutes after arriving topside, the doors opened and a tsunami of noise rushed at him.

The jokes of the soldiers in the lift were drowned out by someone screaming, and at least three other soldiers shouting things back and forth to each other, trying to be heard over everyone else that was trying to be heard.

The soldiers in the lift with him edged forward, and Lee let them shoulder him out of the way. One wounded soldier limped along, supported by his buddy, a hole in the top of his boot, and dark red staining the tan leather. The other soldier clutched his arm to his chest and exited.

Lee slipped through the doors, trying to catch sight of either Abe or Julia, or even Tex, but the main level of the bunker was a mish-mash of bustling bodies. Lee had never been in an Emergency Room after a major disaster, but he imagined this is what it looked like.

The lift opened on a long hall, off of which were several doors. Lee was familiar with the layout of the bunker, because it was a template from which every Project Hometown bunker was created.

On the edges of the hall, the less-wounded stood or sat against the walls. Others that were worse off were being carted by comrades, by hand or in makeshift litters, and they were being stopped and inspected by a cluster of what looked like three other soldiers that were either combat medics or, perhaps, just Combat Life Saver-certified.

The soldiers pleaded their cases, and the interim medics triaged them, everyone speaking very loudly.

But no sign of Julia or Abe.

As though materialized out of thin air, Lee became aware of a face in front of him. It wasn't until Lee looked down and saw the lips moving that he realized his ears were still ringing, and he wasn't catching much of what was being said.

He blinked a few times to refocus. "What?"

The soldier in front of him—a man with a two-day growth of beard and a streak of blood across his brow like war paint—looked exasperated. "I said, is there anyone else topside? Tex wants to activate the security."

Lee frowned, abruptly irritated. "I don't fucking know. Tell him to check the fucking cameras." Lee shouldered past the man, and into the bustle of the hallway.

The doors to either side of the hallway hung open. The rooms were filled with supplies, but in the center of them, wherever space could be had, there was a wounded person being cared for.

In the armory room, a soldier lay on a stack of ammunition boxes in place of a gurney. He was conscious, leaning up, and staring back at Lee. The pants on his left thigh had been cut away all the way to his groin, and a tourniquet was cinched tight into his flesh, just above a bundle of bloody bandages at mid-thigh.

"Hey man," the soldier said, his eyes worried. "You gonna help me?"

Lee passed on. There wasn't much he could do for the man, and he had neither the time nor the energy to express useless condolences. He needed to put his eyes on his people. He needed to make sure that Julia and Abe had arrived back in one piece.

At the very end of the hall, he looked in on the room where foodstuffs were stored, and found Julia hunched over the abdomen of a body, her hands gloved, and wrist-deep in the man's gut.

Lee felt the tension in his body release. His knees gave a twitch like they might go out.

The swelling around her eye had gone down some, and she must have seen him out of her periphery, because her head snapped up, stray strands of hair across her face. "Hey!" she snapped. "Lee! Get in here!"

Lee stepped into the room, letting out a pent-up breath. "You okay?"

"Yeah, yeah. Drop the rifle and armor. Gimme a hand."

Lee unslung his rifle and propped it up in the corner of the room, then shucked his sweaty armor off and tumbled it next to his rifle. His chest felt better for having been relieved of the constant pressure.

As he approached the body of the man, laying on a stainless steel table, his eyes went first to Julia's hands, which were inserted into what looked like an incision that she'd made. She pressed them into the man's guts, deep enough that Lee thought her fingers were touching the back wall of the abdominal cavity.

Then Lee's eyes went up to the man's face, registered the pale, waxy skin, and the fact that the man was unconscious—either by shock, or by anesthetic, Lee didn't know—and only then did Lee realize that it was Pikes.

The man that had tried to rape Julia, only hours before.

"Motherfucker..." Lee gaped.

"We got a problem," Julia husked.

"No shit."

Julia looked at him. "I got my finger on the bleeding. I need you to grab that hemostat. There. The one on his chest. I don't wanna move or I'm gonna lose it."

Lee stared at her for a moment, wondering if this was a perverse joke of some sort.

"Lee!" she raised her voice. "The hemostat!"

She was serious about this. She was actually worried about saving the man's life.

Lee snapped up the hemostat and handed it to Julia.

She shook her head. "I need you to do it. I can't move my hands. I'll guide you in."

"Should I glove up?"

"He's already got open bowels in here. Your dirty hands aren't gonna make a difference. Put it in there."

"Okay." Lee pressed up against the table, leaning over Pikes's inert form. "Where?"

"Right on top of my left hand. The space between my index and middle finger. Okay? Slide it down in there. Do exactly what I tell you to do."

Lee placed the closed end of the hemostat against the blue nitrile of Julia's gloves and began sliding it into Pikes's body, slow. He felt Julia's fingers moving against it as it disappeared into the bloody mess. She probed it. Getting a feel for where it was.

"Keep going. Slowly. Okay stop." She took a quick breath. "Now open them. Just a bit."

Lee opened them. Felt one of Julia's fingers pushing the hemostat where she wanted it.

"Little further," she said. "There. Stop. Okay. You're right on the artery. Clamp it down."

Lee clamped the hemostat.

There was a moment of silence.

Lee looked at Julia, but her eyes were unfocused, fixed on the far side of the room. She was visualizing the interior of Pikes's abdomen.

"Okay. I think you got it. I'm not feeling the pulse anymore." Her eyes became focused again, locked onto Lee's. "Let go of the hemostat. Grab those bandages there. I'm going to pull my finger off the artery, and you're going to mop some of this blood up and we're going to see if it fills up again."

"Alright."

Lee grabbed the wad of bandages she'd indicated, and when she nodded to him, he pressed them into the wound between her hands. The blood soaked through the bandage as he sopped it up, and he felt it, warm on his fingertips. He adjusted, then blotted some more, then removed the bandages.

They stood for another twenty seconds in silence, staring at the opening. Lee saw the pale jumble of Pikes's small intestine bulging around Julia's hands. There was still blood, but it wasn't pulsing or welling rapidly. Lee detected a faint fecal smell, and he wasn't sure if it was coming from inside the man's perforated bowels, or because Pikes had shit his pants.

"I think we're okay," Julia said, and then withdrew her hands. She watched it for another moment, and when the blood didn't well up, she nodded to herself. "I think we got it." Then her eyes went to Lee again. "We got a problem."

"What?"

"Bullet hit him in the hip. Rebounded into his abdomen. It's still in there. It perforated his bowels in I don't know how many places." She blew her hair out of her face, only to have it fall back again. She used her wrist to swipe it away, leaving a pale streak of blood on her forehead. "You recognize him?"

"Yeah. Pikes. From last night."

Julia nodded. Her eyes registered panic. "Lee, I don't think I can save him." She thrust a bloody hand at the man. "The bullet's still in him, and he's gonna go septic, I can almost guarantee you that." She shook her head, her eyes wide. "I can't perform perforated bowel surgery, Lee! I don't have the equipment for that!"

Lee's brow cinched down in confusion. "Julia, you can't save everyone…"

"You don't fucking get it!" she snapped. "They're gonna think I didn't save him on purpose!"

Lee took her shoulders. "Jules, it doesn't matter."

"Of course it fucking matters!"

"Then they can do the goddamned surgery themselves!" Lee glanced at the body. "Fucker's already lived eight hours longer than he should've. Fuck him. Look at me." He lowered his voice. "Do the best you can. Stop the bleeding. Get the bullet out. Mop up what you can. Or triage him as a total loss and move on to someone you *can* save."

Julia's face was blank. "I can't save him."

"Then move on, Jules. If anyone's got a problem with that, you can tell 'em what you told me. I'll have your back on it."

Julia breathed. Swallowed. Seemed to be testing herself to see if she could do what Lee advised. And then, after some thought, a very small nod.

She was okay.

They were *both* okay.

They'd made it one step closer to getting out.

Something in the back of his mind spurred him.

Another spike of worry hit him.

Deuce.

He looked at Julia, and was about to ask her, but then he hesitated. She had enough on her plate.

He didn't want to worry her any more than she already was. And if Deuce had been in this bunker…

Shit. Lee felt his stomach rolling again. Let out a slew of curses that never made it past his lips because he didn't want to concern Julia.

Deuce would have come to him. He would have smelled Lee or heard him when he entered the bunker, and he would have run to him, because he hated to be around this many strangers.

He wasn't here.

A dozen different possibilities for where Deuce might be ran through Lee's head, but there was only one reality to it: Deuce was not *here*.

Movement at the door.

Lee turned, found Abe standing there. This time Lee felt his relief mixed with agitation. "Where did you run off to?" he demanded.

"I was helping one of the wounded guys," Abe said, but he seemed too distracted to be defensive at Lee's tone. "Tex needs us. In the control center. Now."

***

The control center was positioned at the front of the bunker, near the doors to the lift. It was a small room that contained a bank of monitors and system panels that controlled everything inside and outside the bunker.

It was here that they found Tex and Menendez.

The two of them were huddled over a satphone in Tex's hands, and they glanced up when Lee and Abe hustled in. Tex made a definitive motion towards the satphone, and no one spoke.

Someone was already speaking.

It was a voice that rattled around in Lee's head like a pinball for a moment before he was able to place how he recognized it.

"Is that John Bellamy?" Lee whispered to Abe.

Abe nodded, and they stepped closer to Tex and Menendez's huddle.

Lee swung the door closed behind him to cut off any eavesdroppers.

Bellamy was talking: "...don't know how long I've got. I might not be a viable option for you guys much longer."

"Roger that," Tex said. "Hey, Lee and Abe just joined us. You're on speaker."

There was a moment of silence that sounded to Lee like surprise.

"That really Mr. Immortal himself?"

With considerable effort, Lee pushed his worries about Deuce out of his mind—for now. He smiled, more for Tex and Abe's benefit, and responded to Bellamy. "I don't *feel* very immortal."

"You have no idea how many times they've tried to kill you."

"Actually, I've got a pretty fair idea."

"And Abe," Bellamy said. "I didn't think I'd ever talk to you again."

"Same here, man," Abe said, smiling down at the satphone. "Good to hear from you again. Even better to hear that you're on our side."

"Listen, guys," Bellamy's voice became guarded. "I can't stay on long. I'm in a quiet section of Greeley right now, but the shorter I keep this the safer I'll be. And like I was just telling Tex...things are getting a little tight around here."

Tex nodded. "Go ahead, John. We're listening."

"Right. So these fuckers you guys are dealing with down there, these *Nuevas Fronteras* characters..."

"We're familiar," Tex grumbled.

"...You know that I'm the POC for them here in Greeley."

"Right."

"Well, I just got half-chewed out because they went over my head and talked to Colonel Lineberger. According to Lineberger, the cartel is in a fucking panic, requesting that Greeley send them troops to help secure a power plant that they think you're getting too close to."

Tex frowned. "John, I don't know if you're aware, but they just hit one of our outposts. Pushed us completely out of the area. We're currently taking refuge in one of my bunkers. I gotta say, they didn't seem like they were too worried when they pushed us back here."

"Okay," Bellamy sounded like he was piecing something together. "That makes sense. Lineberger said that they'd mentioned something about a big move against you guys. Problem is, they took pretty bad casualties on it. They're weak, and they don't think they can hold the power plant."

Staring at the satphone, Lee realized his heart had started to thump. "John, is there any chance that Greeley already has troops on the ground with the cartel?"

Bellamy was quiet for a beat. "No. I feel like I would've known about that. Why are you asking?"

"We had contact with a squad of guys yesterday," Lee said, frowning. "They weren't cartel.

They seemed like military. They had the equipment and the night vision and the tactics, anyways."

"I dunno, Lee," Bellamy said. "But from what I've seen dealing with this cartel, I wouldn't be surprised if they had some military working for them. Cartels traditionally have a lot of Central American military personnel in their ranks." There was a pause, and Bellamy continued, sounding disgruntled. "Not to mention the fact that I had to turn over a bunch of bunkers into their control. A lot of that military equipment you saw might've come out of a Project Hometown bunker."

Lee rubbed his face pensively, but didn't say anything else.

"The power plant," Tex said, circling back around. "Are you advising this as a target?"

"Well, I'm relaying what I heard. I can't tell you to take it...but..."

Tex clenched his eyes closed. "Do you have any further intel on it? How well it's defended? And which one are we talking about?"

"Shit, Tex, it's all through context. Nothing definitive, and I didn't want to ask too many questions and seem weird. All I know is that *Nuevas Fronteras* is pretty convinced that you guys could take it down if you made a move, and they're desperate for our help. Lineberger mentioned it was located somewhere near Comanche? Or that might be the name of the plant?"

Tex nodded, making a link in his mind. "Okay. I know the one they're talking about."

"And, guys," Bellamy continued. "I think Lineberger is gonna commit some Cornerstone operatives to help them secure it, but I gather that's still twenty-or-so hours out."

"Fuck." Tex rubbed his face. Finally opened his eyes. "John, that's a small window, man."

"I know it is. But—and Lee, I'm lookin' at you, buddy—this might be your ticket to mobilizing the UES."

Tex's expression was still pained. "John, you're talking a twenty hour window, which shrinks to twelve if we want to play it safe. That's twelve hours to put together a major operation against unknown odds. And I don't know if I said it, but they banged us up pretty good last night. Everyone's been fighting for the last eight hours straight. Nobody slept. We got our arms full with wounded."

There was a definite note of disappointment in Bellamy's voice when he spoke again. "I understand, Tex. I do. And you're the one that has to call the shots down there. All I can do is pass on the bits and pieces I find out about. I guess I'm just...Tex, this might be the last piece of intel I can get you."

"Is it looking that bad there?"

"Shit, I don't know. I recognize that it might be paranoia on my part. But if I wait until the hammer falls on my head, it's gonna be too late, you know?"

"Alright. Well, listen. I can't guarantee you that we'll make a move on this thing. I guess you'll find out through the grapevine if we do. In the meantime, keep yourself safe, and if you gotta jet outta there, don't think twice. Do you have a plan in place?"

"Yeah, something like that. I'm working on it."

"Well, finish it. Like you said, if the hammer's dropping, it's already too late."

"Roger that. Hey, I gotta go."

Nothing else was said.

The line clicked dead.

They all stared at the satphone for another few seconds until Tex closed it and collapsed the antenna.

Lee crossed his arms over his chest and took a heavy breath. "Shit. I can't tell whether this is good news or bad news."

"Good news that we got the intel," Menendez pointed out. "Bad news that we can't take advantage of it."

Tex looked at his sergeant earnestly. "Is that your real opinion? You think we can't foot it right now?"

Menendez looked surprised. "Hell...I thought that was *your* opinion."

Tex grimaced. "I don't know what my opinion is."

Lee scratched at the stubble on his face then winced as his fingers touched a piece of bullet shrapnel. "Keep it simple, Tex. Run the numbers. If the numbers make sense, we roll with it. If they don't make sense, we hold back."

Tex huffed out a sigh and leaned back against the desk that held all the computerized bunker control systems. "Alright. I have yet to get an exact headcount for our most recent disaster..."

"We got sixty-seven people in this bunker right now," Menendez interrupted. "Including us. Eight of them are completely out of commish—no way they can fight. There's another twenty with minor booboos that we can give 'em some Ibuprofen and tell 'em to buck up. There's another twelve that are somewhere in between—I was waiting to hear from the docs—but I wouldn't count on them." His recount of the figures done, Menendez glanced from Tex, to Lee, to Abe. "That leaves us with twenty-seven fighters. Maybe forty-seven, if we count the probables."

Tex smiled. "That's why I keep you around, Menendez. You're like my personal assistant."

"What about Oklahoma?" Lee asked.

Tex pursed his lips, musing. "You think they can get down here in time?"

Lee shrugged. "I suppose we'd need to ask them that." Lee thought of another question. "How close is this power plant?"

"Close," Tex said. "Which makes sense why they pushed us out of Caddo. We were right in their backyard. Though, I don't think they actually have possession of that power plant. I feel like we would have caught wind of them moving in."

"Maybe that was the push on Caddo," Lee pointed out. "Maybe that was them moving in."

"Then it turned into more of a fight than they were expecting," Tex postulated. "And now they don't know if they can hold the power plant."

Menendez looked troubled. "You think they really want the power plant? What the hell are they gonna do with it?"

"Well, we know they're using power plants elsewhere," Abe said, stroking his bushy black beard. "There's no way they could've gotten the refineries running without a power plant. Which means they have some nuclear engineers. Or…" Abe shrugged. "Whatever you need to get a power plant running."

Lee nodded along with him. "We got one running up in the UES."

"No shit?" Menendez looked impressed. "Well, damn. So, they want the power plant for what?"

"Push more pumping stations?" Abe suggested.

Lee nodded again. "That would be my guess. I'd go one step further and suggest that this is how they plan on pumping oil to Greeley. Which explains why Lineberger would commit troops to it."

Something sparkled in Tex's eyes. "So taking this power plant is going to starve Greeley of oil."

"For now," Lee said. "Which might give us the opportunity to get the UES involved, like John pointed out."

Tex leaned forward on his elbows, staring at the floor. "Alright. If we decide to do this—and I'm not saying we are—but if we do, I can probably get Oklahoma to send us...twenty? I'm just guessing here."

Menendez squinted shrewdly. "But will they be here on time?"

"Well, that I can't say."

"Can you contact them?" Lee asked. "From here?"

Tex waggled the satphone that was still in his hands. "Yup."

Lee nodded, thoughtfully. "Tex, I can't tell you what to do. But if I were you, I'd see if the timeline works out. And if it did, I'd take that place down. Starve Greeley. Starve *Nuevas Fronteras* of Greeley's support. And give the UES time to get down here with some troops."

Lee paused, to see if there was anything anyone else needed to say. When no one spoke up, he finally let it out, trying to sound level about it. "Has anyone seen Deuce?"

All eyes turned to him. Blank expressions. Then, regret.

Everyone shook their heads.

No one had seen him since the firefight on the hill.

NINETEEN

PILLOW TALK

THINGS SEEMED TO BE getting out of control in Fort Bragg.

This was less of something that was apparent, and more of a general *feeling* that Sam had in the low parts of his gut.

It was like that person that you know so well, you can tell from the miniscule movements of their face if they are happy or sad or angry.

It was the same way with Fort Bragg.

Sam had been around these people every day for years. This little society of theirs, it had something of its own unique, collective personality.

And there was something wrong with it right now.

Sam stood at the kitchen sink, which had a window that looked out over the neighborhood streets. It was getting into the late morning hours now, and given Sam's third-shift excitement the previous night, he should've been sleeping.

He'd awoken to what sounded like someone speaking on a bullhorn.

By the time he'd shuffled downstairs and rubbed the sleep out of his eyes and peered out the kitchen window, nothing was happening.

The streets were empty.

But still.

There was something wrong with this place.

Sam pushed himself away from the sink and the window and stood in the middle of the kitchen, considering himself. He was dressed in his underwear and the tan t-shirt he wore under his uniform. He'd been too tired to shower and change last night.

After they'd returned from the mall, they'd been sequestered into the roll call room at The Barn. First Sergeant Hamrick came to retrieve them one at a time, with an incredulous scowl on his face. In private, he'd made each of them recount what had happened, then told them not to talk about it until he said it was okay.

They weren't supposed to talk about it back in the roll call room either, but they did.

Mostly, they theorized.

But they also questioned Allen-The-Wildlife-Guy on what he thought.

Allen tried to suppress these questions—he was afraid of reprisals from Hamrick—but after he'd been badgered for perhaps the tenth time, he got mad and let it out.

"I don't know, alright?" he'd whispered at them. His eyes scanned the room, flashing with defensive anger. "I'm not a goddamned scientist, or—or—or an expert or anything."

He seemed about to leave it at that, but everyone was now staring at him, knowing that he'd broken silence, knowing that if they just provided the verbal vacuum, perhaps Allen would feel compelled to fill it.

Allen looked at the floor, thinking. "You know how you know if you got a rat problem?" he mumbled, almost to himself.

No one answered. They waited. Watched.

"You start finding a lot of snakes," Allen said. He looked up, and for some reason, his eyes landed on Sam's and held there. "That's just how nature works. If a certain animal has a natural predator, then when a lot of those animals gather together, there will be a lot of the predators in the same place. The predators have to eat. They know they have to go where the biggest food supply is." He looked away from Sam. Back to the floor. "When you see predators, you know that the prey is nearby. And vice-a-versa: If you see a lot of prey, you can bet there are a lot of predators."

Sam remained mute to this. But beside him, Jones fidgeted and leaned forward in his seat.

"So..." Jones squinted at Allen. "We're the fucking prey, right? Is that what you're saying? You're saying that them fuckers is all gathered out there because we're gathered in here. Is that right?"

Allen shrugged, unsure of himself again. "I guess. I dunno. I'm not an expert. It's just...that's what makes sense to me."

Jones leaned back, looking disturbed. "Well. Shit."

Sam and the rest of the soldiers that had made the run into Fayetteville weren't released until six o'clock in the morning. Sam had trundled himself home on foot, used his key to open the front door, snuck upstairs, and fallen into bed the second he got his outer uniform off.

"You alright there?" a voice shot into his thoughts.

Sam jerked, like a static shock, and looked around.

Marie stood in the kitchen with her eyebrows up, looking concerned with Sam. He hadn't even heard her walk in. She'd be here to watch Abby.

"Yeah," Sam said, though he still felt the overwhelming *offness* of the world around him. "Hey, did you hear someone on a loudspeaker?"

Marie hesitated for a moment, then seemed to decide that she didn't need to be secretive with Sam—he worked for the UES, after all. "Yes. I'm not quite sure what's going down, but I've seen some troops rolling around, going to some houses."

"All the houses?"

"No, just a few of them. Not sure what the loudspeaker was about. That came from down the street." Marie leaned to peer out the kitchen window. "I think they're gone now."

For the first time, Sam seemed to come to the realization that he was in his underwear in front of Marie. His first instinct was to try to hide himself, which was quickly covered by a more adult thought that figured he should just play it cool.

He started making for the upstairs. "I'm gonna head in," he said. "In case they need me."

"Did you get enough sleep?" Marie called after him.

Sam grunted something in the ballpark of an affirmative and escaped upstairs.

Five minutes later he was in uniform again, walking down the sidewalk.

Even with relatively few people about—most everyone would still be at their work places—it only took a moment for Sam's eyes to fall on a familiar face.

Charlie stalked toward him on the opposite side of the street, and the second his eyes found her, she raised a hand in greeting.

"Sam!" She quickened her pace and hustled across the street.

There was something in the way she'd been walking when he'd first seen her.

It felt almost like she'd come out of nowhere.

Almost like she'd been waiting for him around the corner of one of these houses.

"Hey Charlie," Sam said, as she trotted up.

He kept his greeting subdued, but Charlie seemed to be happy to see him.

A few days ago, Sam would have taken the excitement in her eyes at face value. Now he wondered. Was this the genuine article, or was this another show? Was this just how she got him to open up to her?

Was she pumping him for information?

At first, when he'd come to these realizations, it had seemed more like she might just be a bit of a gossip hound. After seeing her meet up with Claire, though, things had taken on a more conniving caste.

Charlie walked along beside him in silence for a moment, all the while Sam's eyes going here and there, but never locking into Charlie's like they usually did.

"Is everything okay?" Charlie asked.

"Yeah," Sam grunted. "Why?"

"You seem a little...off lately."

"Off?"

"Yeah, you know." She smiled. He caught the flash of her teeth out of the corner of his eye, and—damn himself—he looked. Felt a weak little part of him stir. "Like you're not all that happy to see me."

Sam forced a smile. Somehow, through some feminine sorcery, she'd managed to now make *him* feel guilty. Maybe it had all really been in his head. Was he pushing her away? Was he being an idiot? Was he going to regret this?

"I've just been tired lately," he said, figuring that covered a gamut of bad behaviors.

They walked in silence for a moment.

Charlie seemed to be mulling things over.

Or...strategizing?

Somewhere in the distance, the sound of another voice on loudspeaker reached them. They both looked in the direction that the sound had appeared to come from, but they could see nothing except the houses and the occasional stand of stubborn pine trees.

"What's going on around here?" Charlie asked. "Have you heard anything?"

And that's all it took to rankle him. He stopped dead in his tracks and turned on Charlie, his dark face made darker by the furrow of his brows and the firm set of his mouth.

"What is this?" he said, his voice low, but his words sharp. "What're you doing?"

Charlie looked surprised. "What do you mean?"

Anger flashed through his clouded features. "I mean, do you actually like me, Charlie? 'Cause from where I'm standing, it doesn't really seem like it. Seems like you show up when you wanna pump me for information. Doesn't seem like you're all that into having an actual relationship."

Sam watched her face like trying to read an opponent at a high-stakes poker match.

And what he saw was very odd.

Things blipped across Charlie's face, like she was a shape-shifter trying on every face she knew how to make. First shocked, then sad, then angry, then indignant. They cycled across her face, like they were all pegs on a spinning wheel, and then suddenly they stopped.

Her face bore the expression of someone who had many regrets.

She felt bad.

She had made a mistake.

That's what the face said.

She reached forward and she put her hand around the back of his neck and she pulled herself up, and she pulled him down, and her mouth met his and her lips were open and he felt and tasted her slick warm tongue press into his mouth. She moved her body against him like she'd never moved it before.

When she pulled away from him, her eyes were warm and smoky.

"Let me show you how much you mean to me."

***

It didn't take him long.

Charlie knew that it wouldn't.

When they were finished, there was a small portion of her that felt dirty, but she also felt an electric thrill. Because she'd done what needed to be done. She'd done it for the cause, and she'd gotten what she'd wanted.

Sam had talked to her.

Pillow talk, one might say, though there weren't any pillows—they'd hidden away in a nearby stand of pines. She couldn't have taken him back to a house, so she made do with what she had available, and Sam wasn't complaining.

If Claire could see me now, Charlie thought as she hustled along.

She felt…victorious.

Nearly bursting, because she *had* something.

She wasn't sure if it was going to be useful to the Lincolnists, but it was *something*. And Elsie would know—and Claire too, for that matter—that Charlie wasn't a child. She could hold her own. And she was serious. They would have to admit that now.

She crossed one of the main streets that ran through Fort Bragg, and went into the cluster of houses on the other side. She didn't know a lot, but she knew that she was looking for house number 506.

She kept up a good clip along the sidewalk. She had to restrain herself from running. She didn't want to draw attention.

She passed six houses, and on the seventh, found the number she was looking for.

So. This was her captain's house.

She gave the neighborhood a quick glance to make sure she wasn't being watched, and then dipped in between the houses, and went to the back of 506. The shades were drawn in the windows. She thought she heard the mumble of conversation and movement through the door.

She knocked on the door—three, slow raps. The faint noise from inside went silent.

She stood out on the back stoop, hoping this wasn't drawing even more attention—all this coming and going from the back door.

"Who is it?" a voice said.

"Cherokee." Charlie used the password and prayed it was still correct.

There was a long pause that gave Charlie time to wonder what would happen if she'd given the wrong password.

The door swung open, and Charlie slipped in.

She knew her captain only in passing. They didn't make a habit of being together much, but everyone had an assigned captain—a person to meet up with when things went down. Peter Kerns was hers. She looked around and found many faces in that house, and she recognized some of them, but none of them were Peter Kerns.

The person who had answered the door was a squat man with a suspicious face that peered at her like he still wasn't quite sure she should be inside, despite having the password.

"Where's Peter?" Charlie demanded.

The man squinted at her, like he was trying to gauge her trustworthiness.

"It's Charlie, right?" a man's voice said, from behind her.

Charlie spun and found Peter Kerns standing in the doorway to the kitchen where everyone was gathered. She couldn't wait anymore. The second she locked onto his face, she spilled it out.

"We need to get word to Elsie," Charlie sputtered out. "There's a massive colony of primals, right over in Fayetteville. Fort Bragg command knows about it and is keeping it quiet. We can use this against them."

TWENTY

RECON

ITS NAME WAS COMANCHE PEAK NUCLEAR POWER PLANT.

And, like every other nuclear power plant, it was built to be a fortress.

Three-quarters of a mile north of the power plant, across the greenish waters of Squaw Creek Reservoir—the lake that the power plant used to cool its reactors—a peninsula jutted out from the shore.

On this peninsula, there was a bushy crop of trees, and then a short, steep, sandy beach. Small waves stirred by the wind slopped along the shoreline. A piece of driftwood bobbed in the shallows, as though to a rhythm no one else could hear.

In the copse of trees, Lee Harden lay on his belly, his rifle tucked up tight to him. The leaves and pine needles of the forest floor were bunched up around him and over him, and his head and shoulders and most of his rifle was covered by a mesh-like shroud, in which Lee had stuck various twigs and leaves that he'd found near his hide.

The "sniper shroud" belonged to Tex, who lay beside Lee, similarly camouflaged.

The two of them looked south, across the flat, open water, to the power plant on the other side.

Lee let out a long, soft grumble of misgivings. "I don't like this."

Beside him, Tex squinted through a spotting scope, which had better magnification than the scope on Lee's rifle, but the single glaring fault that it couldn't kill things.

"Yeah," Tex mumbled. "They're in there."

"I've got enough visual to see people, but not specifics," Lee noted. "What kind of details are you picking up? Are these *Nuevas Fronteras*?"

"Yeah, most of them are wearing their cartel flag on their shoulder."

Lee glanced sideways and saw that Tex was smirking. "Alright, smartass. You know what I meant."

"Well." Tex seemed to consider it. "I'm not seeing any military. But I am seeing a lot of guns. If I could be so racist as to identify them by apparent ethnicity, I would, but it seems to be a pretty even mix of whites, blacks, and Hispanics."

"They conscript from the local populations," Lee pointed out.

"Yeah. I'm aware. So, I can't tell you that they're definitely *Nuevas Fronteras*. But given the intel we received, and what we're seeing, I'd say it's pretty consistent."

"Consistent is good enough for me."

"So you wanna hit it?"

"Now, I didn't say that," Lee mumbled, pulling himself away from his scope to give his eyes a rest. "It's still a pretty massive cluster. They've got walls. Electric fences. Guard towers. They're on a peninsula with almost no way to get at them. And they probably outnumber us." Lee glanced at Tex. "Do they outnumber us?"

Tex rested his chin on his fist and squinted across the water with his naked eye. "Don't really have a hard count. It seemed like seven or eight guys. From this angle. I think we can safely assume that they've got about triple that number, stationed around the power plant. We'll say thirty to be safe."

"So the numbers are pretty close." Lee's face screwed up like he was tasting something that had spoiled. "I dunno, man. What do you think?"

Tex lifted his eyebrows. "I think we have something they don't have."

"What's that?"

"A tank."

Lee nodded to admit the point.

Tex rolled to face Lee. "There's nothing they got over there that's going to stop an Abrams. We send that fucker right up the gut, we open up their defenses."

"Yeah. They'll just need to be cautious about what they're shooting if you guys want a working reactor after we're done."

"Restraint is not typically a tanker's strong suit, but I think I can convince them."

Lee's earpiece crackled to life and a familiar voice came over the line. "Abe to Lee."

Lee and Tex exchanged a quick glance. Tex listened in on his own earpiece.

"Go ahead, Abe," Lee prompted.

Abe spoke quietly, as they all were. It was unlikely that sound was going to carry that far. But then again, open water could be tricky, and it never hurt to be cautious. "Me and Menendez are at the boathouse. Looks clear. I've got my eye on eight canoes that look to be in pretty good condition. Also, several other boats around the docks that look promising."

"Roger that," Lee said over the line. Then, just to Tex, he shook his head. "Fucking canoes."

Tex smiled and winked. "Imagine how legendary that will be."

The comms opened again. "Tex, this is Bigfoot Actual," Menendez transmitted. "Just letting you know, I got word from the bunker: Our boys from O-K just arrived."

Tex looked thoughtful. "I copy. Any word on numbers?"

"Yeah. Thirty."

Tex shot a pleased look at Lee. "Looks like the numbers are swinging our way."

Lee nodded, and tried to look confident, despite the fact that he didn't feel it. Perhaps it was just the fact that Deuce was MIA that was making Lee feel "off."

Whenever this came to him, he told himself that the stupid dog had run off because he was a skittish little bitch, and there wasn't a damn thing that Lee could have done about that.

Getting angry about it felt better than letting it touch him.

Dumb fucking mutt should've stayed when I told him to stay.

Emotions properly stunted, Lee decided he couldn't let a missing dog turn him off from a viable plan. You had to bet big to win big, right? And this was big. This was game-changing.

No risk, no reward.

If they did this right, they might have the groundwork laid for a strong alliance between the UES and Texas. Which meant that Lee and Julia and Abe could call it "mission accomplished."

"Alright," Lee grunted, squirming out of his sniper hide. "Let's go stare at some maps."

***

By the time they got back to the bunker, the sun had crested, and began its descent. The shadows got longer, and to the south, a broad bank of threatening clouds glowed yellow, their underbellies a dark charcoal.

"Looks like rain," Tex observed, as they entered the bunker and descended.

The bunker was twice as crowded as before, but half as chaotic.

The wounded had been treated and were quiet now. Either medicated, or too exhausted to moan about it.

But with the addition of the thirty soldiers from Oklahoma, it was getting close to standing room only. However, as any good soldier knows: Don't stand when you can sit. They were packed in on either side of the main hall, their backs against the wall, their packs between their legs, talking and joking with one another.

As Lee, Tex, Abe, and Menendez stepped out of the elevator, the eyes of everyone along the hall shifted in their direction. And it didn't escape Lee that a lot of them were looking at him, and then muttering something to their buddies.

The ripple of hushed comments almost caused Lee to stop, mid-stride.

What *did* cause him to stop in mid-stride, and then take a half-step back, was a grizzly bear of a man who loomed up in front of him, eyes wide and bright, giant arms reaching for him.

Lee's own hands came up as though to ward off blows, and then latched themselves onto the man's thick wrists, as recognition dawned on him.

"Whoa, easy there, tiger!" the man rumbled, like a diesel truck turning over.

"Cheech?" Lee gaped.

Captain Trzetrzelewska grinned, his teeth stark white amid a short but very dense beard.

Cheech had always stayed clean shaven—claimed he didn't need an "operator beard" to make him look tough. Which was a good point. He was 6'5" and sizeable in every other dimension as well.

But the beard had rendered him unrecognizable for a moment.

"I can tell you like it," Cheech observed, and yanked Lee into a bone-crushing embrace.

"Easy, Cheech," Abe said. "Poor bastard's still healing from a chest wound."

Cheech released Lee with a back slap that hurt more than the hug, and held Lee at his considerable arm's length. "No shit? So it's true? They just can't manage to kill you, huh?"

Lee found himself smiling. "Well, it's not for lack of trying, I promise."

"Damn, son," Cheech breathed. "It's good to see you again." He looked at Abe. "And you too, you hadji fuck."

Abe grinned and accepted the impending embrace with a grunt. "Fucking Polack."

When he was finished with Abe, he turned to Tex and Menendez giving them a more average greeting. "You two I see all the time. Tully couldn't make it. He's got his own fires burning on his northern borders."

Tex nodded and gestured deeper into the bunker. "We'll manage without him. If you guys wanna find a spot that's not crammed full of grunts, I'll get the maps, and we'll get this shit show on the road."

Cheech nodded, and regarded Lee with an element of reservation that he hadn't shown before. "So we're not overly enthusiastic about this op, huh?"

Tex slipped around them, heading towards the command center which would have hard copies of satellite imagery of certain points of interest around Texas, nuclear power plants being one of those places.

Lee nodded, feeling the uneasiness come over him again. "Are you ever enthusiastic about assaulting a hard fortification?"

Menendez led them down the hall, looking through doors, searching for a place that they could use to strategize. The soldiers on the ground pulled their boots out of the way. More interested mumbles as Lee passed.

It embarrassed him. But he supposed it was a good thing.

Maybe it would bolster everyone's confidence.

They found a room with only a handful of soldiers in it. It was the food stores. Nice and roomy. And the crates of freeze dried foods made ample seating and table space for the perusal of maps.

Menendez kicked the soldiers out and took over the room.

As they settled in, Lee moved out of their way, then slipped out, mumbling, "Give me a second. I'll be right back."

He pushed through the crowded hall again, and found Julia three rooms down in what constituted a sick bay in the bunker. He knew what room she was in before he got there.

Outside of the room, there were two clusters of soldiers. Heads bowed. Shoulders shaking. Murmuring things to each other. Unabashed that they were surrounded by their comrades. They didn't begrudge their comrades their lack of grief. And their comrades didn't begrudge them for showing it.

Everyone else down the hall just acted like it wasn't happening.

The men in the clusters kept their voices down, like they were in a library.

Lee had been in these situations before, both from the outside, and from the inside. It felt voyeuristic to watch others when it was happening to them, so you pretended it wasn't happening at all. And you felt exposed when it was happening to you, like you'd been stripped naked in front of an audience, and the best thing you could do was block out the fact that others were around.

Deal with it as quietly as you could.

And when you were able, stop emoting.

When you were able, stuff it all down.

You didn't want to affect the other people's morale.

Inside the room, there were several wounded men, IV lines still in, red stains growing on their bandages. There were also three black bags, stacked up near the door, but not blocking it.

It was for these that the men outside held their quiet conferences of grief.

Julia stood, hunched over a table. For a moment, Lee thought she was operating on the man that lay there, but then he realized she was simply staring off into nowhere.

Lee knocked on the open door.

Julia turned her head, like she already knew that it was him standing there. Her eyes looked tired. Spent. He could tell in an instant that she didn't have anything left.

And yet they were still going to hit this objective, weren't they?

And how many casualties were they going to take?

It was hard to put a number on it, but Lee knew one thing for certain: Someone was going to die.

Maybe even him.

But that's not the sort of thing you dwell on when it's an imminent reality. That's something you think about once you're safe again, so you can lie awake at night with your heart pounding in your chest and stare at the black ceiling, thinking of all the ways you *almost* died, and sometimes how your friends *did*.

Lee chucked a thumb over his shoulder. "We're gonna discuss the op. If you're at a stopping point, I'd like to have you there. Can you break free?"

For a flash, Julia's expression read like she didn't know who Lee was, or even *what* he was. He could've been green with three heads, based on her expression.

Then she blinked a few times and was there again. She nodded.

"Yeah." Her voice was a quiet crackle. "Sure. I can break free."

As she strode out of the room, past the body bags, he heard her mumble, "Not like they're going anywhere."

Maybe this was too much.

Maybe she should just stay in the bunker and deal with the wounded.

Surely there were other people that could fill the medic role.

But before Lee could make a decision, they stood in the doorway of the food-storage-turned-briefing-room. And Julia walked through.

***

Tex laid out two maps, and then planted his fists on the crate of freeze-dried vegetables that had become the table, and hunched over them.

Lee, Abe, Julia, Menendez, and Cheech all peered down at them.

The maps were both about two feet square. Laminated satellite imagery. The first map showed a big-picture view of Squaw Creek Reservoir and the roads around it that led into the peninsula on which sat their objective.

The next map was a detail view of Comanche Peak Nuclear Power Station itself.

"Earlier this morning," Tex began. "We got intel from our guy in Greeley about *Nuevas Fronteras* owning this power station." He looked up at Cheech. "If you haven't got the full story yet, we had a bit of a dust-up with them over the course of last night. Which is why everyone's got full luggage racks under their eyes right now."

Dim, tired smirks accompanied this.

Cheech nodded. "I'd heard some of the details. But always best from the horse's mouth."

Tex pushed off of the crate and folded his arms across his chest. "Intel said that *Nuevas Fronteras* got a little banged up after our altercation last night, and was concerned about us hitting the power station, as it was not very well defended." Tex dipped his head in Lee's direction. "Me and Lee put eyes on, just a few hours ago. It does appear to be occupied, and from what we can tell, the occupiers are consistent with *Nuevas Fronteras* personnel we've encountered in the past."

Cheech loomed over the table. "Numbers?"

"Twenty, if we're lucky," Lee said. "Thirty if we're not."

Cheech smiled. "So thirty."

Lee nodded. "Yeah. Let's say thirty."

The big man glanced between Tex and Lee. "I mean…barring some ridiculousness that you guys haven't told us about, me and my guys are in. But I gotta ask: What are we getting out of this, besides pissing off *Nuevas Fronteras*?"

Tex gestured for Lee to explain.

"While it's nice to piss them off," Lee said. "We're getting two things out of it." He held up two fingers and ticked them off. "First, if we can take this out of their hands, we're going to interrupt *Nuevas Fronteras* turning on the pumps straight to Greeley. If we can interrupt that flow of oil, we can put the brakes on the relationship that they're building, maybe even sour it a bit. As we understand it, it's already something of a tense relationship, pretty much exclusively based on convenience and what they can offer each other. Without this power plant, the cartel won't be able to pump oil to Colorado, and without the oil, Greeley won't have any reason to continue to supply the cartel with equipment. So that's number one.

"Number two, the UES has a nuclear engineer. That's how we got the lights turned on over in our neck of the woods. If we can separate *Nuevas Fronteras* and Greeley, and buy ourselves a little bit of breathing room here in Texas, we can send for that engineer and get the power station running *for us*. And if we can accomplish that, I think we can get the UES into the fight here. We just need to create a good opening."

Cheech nodded along. "So we interrupt the love affair between the cartel and Briggs. Then we siphon the resources off to North Carolina. The UES gets involved and teams up with us. We take over the Gulf Coast states, kick the cartel's ass, then turn around and kick Greeley's ass. Divide and conquer." He gave the map an approving look. "I like it. It's optimistic, but I like it."

Abe reached up and squeezed Cheech's shoulder. "Well, you know us. Buncha perennial optimists."

"Of course," Cheech rumbled. "So, how do we implement this majestic *coup de grace*?"

Tex and Lee exchanged a bemused look. "Well," Tex said. "I detect a bit of sarcasm. But I'm sure you'll take it more seriously when I tell you that it involves canoes."

"Excellent," Cheech said. "Summer camp and assaulting a fixed objective—my two favorite childhood activities, now combined into one."

Julia shifted between Lee and Cheech. She bore that expression on her face that she'd given Lee, just before deciding to come sit in on the briefing, except now she gave it to Cheech. Like she couldn't figure out what form of life he was.

It made Lee's gut twist up.

This was not Julia.

She was not the type to look down on other people for using humor to alleviate the stress of impending death. She understood it. And she took part in it.

It was like she was someone else right now.

Cheech seemed to notice after a beat, but said nothing of it.

They all returned their attention to the maps, the air of humor feeling brittle now.

Lee cleared his throat and discreetly touched Julia's lower back, just a gentle connection—*I'm here. Stay with me.*

Tex put his hands on the table and leaned over the maps again. "We need to hit it tonight. Late. There's a storm coming in. I'm hoping it'll dump some rain. That'll help us get close to the objective and limit the defender's visibility." He pointed to the single road that came into the peninsula on which the power plant sat. "This is going to be our first assault point. It's a shitty move, like ramming your running back straight into the defensive line. So that's where we're putting our tank. The tank is going to move in with three light armored Humvees. It should easily be able to smash 'n' bash through any of the defenses on the road in."

Tex traced his finger along the road to where it terminated in the sprawling fortifications of the power plant. "Which brings us to the plant itself. This

317

thick tan line you see surrounding it is a concrete wall, we're estimating about ten feet thick and ten feet high. On the other side of the wall, there's electrified fences—we don't know if the current is running right now or not. There's a few entrances into the power plant itself, but they're all designed to be terrible choke points and they're covered by defensive positions."

He gestured to several tall, white squares. The shadows they gave made it obvious what they were. "Guard towers. They're all over the place. And yes, they are manned. What looks like precision rifles and some machine guns."

Cheech whistled. "Quite the shit show."

"Yes," Tex agreed. "But the upside is that, I guess due to the lack of manpower, their defenses are almost exclusively tied to these guard towers, and a few defensive points, kind of like pill boxes. All of which are excellent targets for an HE round from an Abrams."

Tex pointed to a spot on the thick, concrete wall that surrounded the power plant. Here, they saw what appeared to be an opening wide enough for a vehicle to pass through. "Realistically, this is our only way into the plant. So, we're going to use our Abrams as a battering ram to slam through the defenses, flatten the guard towers and suppress any other pill boxes. Which will open the door for ground forces to move into the compound."

Menendez flicked a finger up in the air. "Question. As the leader of the ground pounders, what do you want us to do once we're inside? I mean, obviously we need to secure it. But…what do you want to do with the people? Do we have to be worried about any civilians? I mean, they were planning on turning the power on, right? Are we concerned about engineers running around?"

Tex responded by looking at Lee and raising an eyebrow.

"No," Lee said.

Menendez looked confused. "No?"

"No, we're not concerned about engineers," Lee clarified. "We don't have any intelligence to suggest that there are civilians inside the power plant. So we treat everyone like a combatant."

Cheech's brow furrowed, but he didn't say anything.

Menendez nodded, once. "But, if people are unarmed or they surrender..."

Julia made a chuffing noise. "Let's be honest here. We're gonna take casualties. I think everyone at this table knows that. Every casualty is two guys down, carrying that casualty to a triage point." She shook her head. "You try to add in prisoners? Taking the time to secure them? Escort them? Guard them?" She folded her arms, her eyes blazing. "No. Uh-uh. That's just gonna cause more casualties on our side."

She stopped talking, but Lee almost heard it, like a faint echo, the rest of Julia's thought: *And I can't handle much more of this.*

"Julia's right," Lee said. "We can't do it. If you're inside that compound, and you're not one of us, then you're shit outta luck."

Tex gave Lee an approving nod and turned to Menendez. "It's not how we typically do things. But necessity dictates. And I happen to agree. ROE is kill everything."

Menendez took a deep breath through his nose, and when he exhaled he looked like he'd made his peace with it. "Alright then. Certainly makes things easy."

"Bringing it back around to the ground forces," Cheech said. "I'm assuming my guys are in that group. And something tells me that this is where it gets interesting." Cheech squinted, as though he was nervous about the answer. "How are the ground forces getting onto the peninsula?"

Tex moved his finger to the big swath of open water between Squaw Creek Park and the power plant. He tapped it twice. "Well, that's where the boats come in."

TWENTY-ONE

THE HOUSEWIFE

INSIDE THE FORT BRAGG SAFE ZONE, near the western boundary, there sat a two hundred acre chunk of pine forest. Near the center of this pine forest, surrounded by chain link fencing topped with barbed wire, was a power substation.

At the access gate of the chain link fence sat a barricade erected out of sandbags.

Behind the sandbags, Private Gomez sat on an upturned bucket, shoulders slumped, head back, mouth open, groaning in abject misery.

"Fuuuuuuuuuuuuuuuuck," was his beleaguered groan.

He sat as though unconscious for a moment and then straightened up, sucking at some saliva that had started to edge toward the open corner of his mouth.

"I'm so…bored…"

His partner for the evening's guard duty was some big, slow motherfucker named Riley. Why was he stuck here, doing this? He'd signed up for primal-hunting operations, just like Sam. Shit, he'd put his name on the list *ahead* of Sam. And yet Sam was off having fun, and here Gomez was, with goddamn Slowsville Riley, who was currently seated on the wall of sandbags, eating a bit of cold meat that didn't smell good.

At Gomez's complaint, Riley nodded out into the forest. "Just watch the wildlife, man."

Gomez looked at him like he was crazy. "Just watch the fucking...? I look like fucking Dora the Explorer to you?"

"Dora the Explorer?"

"Yeah. You know, the little bitch that rescued the animals and shit."

"That was Diego."

Gomez blew a raspberry and looked away, mumbling under his breath, but still loud enough to be heard. "You would know about kids shows, you retarded-ass motherfucker..."

Riley frowned at him. "I'm not retarded."

Gomez evaluated Riley to see how close he was to getting in a fight.

"I'm just bustin' your balls man," Gomez relented. "I know you're not a retard."

"Whatever, man."

Gomez went back to staring at the sky.

The substation was important. He understood that. It was the main hub of all the electricity that not only made life livable in the Safe Zone, but kept the high voltage wires running. Which is kind of what made it the Safe Zone to begin with. Without the substation, there was no Fort Bragg Safe Zone.

Gomez's main problem, was that *he* was having to guard it. And guarding it was sedentary. And sedentary was boring. There is nothing in the world so boring as stationary guard duty. Is there another activity on earth so boring that it has inspired men to put hot sauce in their eyes just to stay awake?

At least the scenery changed when you were walking the perimeter. Here it was just an unending nightmare of pine tree after pine tree sameness. The *same* pine trees. In the *same* spots.

Maybe Gomez wanted to see *other* pine trees.

As it turned out, Gomez would never see any other pine trees.

He felt something hit him hard in the face, and for a moment he thought he'd been struck by some aggressive flying insect, but sometime around when the sound of the rifle report washed over him, and the time that he realized his jaw was missing, he knew that he'd been shot.

He tried to duck down, but the shot that had ripped his jaw off was just the first.

A flurry of them followed the first one, and they crashed into the sandbags, and Riley was screaming, and Gomez thought he was screaming too, he tasted blood, and he felt sand peppering his mouth...

Then one caught him in the eye and it was lights out.

***

Elsie Foster waited in the living room of the house that had become her last stand in the world. Do or die, win or lose, it would all happen as she stood on this patch of stained carpet, surrounded by these people.

Tonight, Fort Bragg would be free again. Or she would be dead.

Around her were several of her captains, and of course, Claire Staley.

There was also the girl. Some asset that Claire had been working. She had a boy's name. Elsie was having a hard time remembering it right now. But Peter Kerns had brought her to Elsie's hideout, and she'd had information to give.

The intelligence had provided Elsie with not only a target that would cripple Angela, but a terrible dilemma to put her into. A dilemma that would prove her to be the incapable housewife that she was.

In the house where Elsie stood, everyone was quiet. They were all waiting to hear from the radio that sat on the table in front of Elsie. This room that they all stood in, it had become mission control, and they were waiting to hear from their operatives on the ground.

Elsie brought her hands together. Steepled her index fingers. Placed them to her lips.

The radio clicked.

One click.

Two.

Three.

Pause.

And then again.

One, two, three.

The pattern repeated, twice more.

Elsie felt a bloom of relief rise up from the concrete slab of her chest. She let loose all her breath that she'd been holding, and looked to Claire. "They're in. They have the power substation."

Claire nodded. "Clock's ticking. You need to talk to the command center before they send anybody out there to investigate."

Elsie turned to the table and snatched up the radio. She held it in her hand for a moment. Hefted it, as though it alone related the weight of the moment. Then she switched it to channel eleven—the channel for civilians to call in emergencies to the Fort Bragg command center.

She pressed transmit.

"Fort Bragg Safe Zone," she began, articulating each word carefully. Almost savoring them. "Command center, this is Elsie Foster, on behalf of the Lincolnists, and all the citizens here in Fort Bragg. We have taken control of the power substation that supplies all electricity for the Safe Zone...and for the perimeter fences."

Elsie turned and looked at the young girl that stood beside Peter Kerns, gawking up at Elsie as though this were some stage and Elsie were a celebrity. "We have come to learn that there is a large colony of primals very near to this location, and that packs of primals from this colony have been observed, probing our perimeter on a regular basis—a fact which you have failed to tell the people. Understand me clearly on this point: If you attempt to retake the power substation, we will destroy it. Then whatever happens is in God's hands. If you attempt to take me out, or any of my people, then we will destroy it. If any of my people currently holding the substation see a single one of your soldiers, they know to destroy it.

"Everything else I have to say, I will say to Angela Houston directly. I pray for the sake of everyone in Fort Bragg that she can do at least one good thing for this population of people, and cooperate with us."

Elsie released the transmit button.

Then she shoved it onto the table, as though it had grown uncomfortably hot.

Beside the radio sat Claire's satellite phone. It was a risk to use it when they also might have to coordinate with Greeley, but Elsie wasn't going to use the radio frequencies, or any communication device provided by Angela or her goons. When they talked, it was going to be on Elsie's terms, and with Elsie's equipment.

And if Greeley called back?

Well...Elsie guessed she'd just put Angela on hold.

Elsie picked up the satphone and dialed the Support Center.

It was time to start a revolution.

***

Angela sat frozen at her desk in the Soldier Support Center.

Staring at the civilian band radio in its cradle, on her desk.

Ten minutes later, and she would've been home. She still had the last item of the day clutched in her hand—a handwritten spreadsheet of projected corn yields for this year.

Staring at the black surface of the little radio that sat at the corner of her desk so that she, the good president Angela Houston of the United Eastern States, could keep tabs on anything bad that might be happening to the people that had elected her to this office, she began to feel a sensation rising up...or maybe it was descending down on her...

It was not a completely foreign sensation.

She'd felt it before.

And, as she sat there staring, she realized that it was neither rising up, nor descending down. It was spreading out from the very center of her. From some spiritual point of origin deep in the epicenter of every human being.

The feeling that coursed through every fiber of her being was like hot gasses expelled from a volcano that's just cracked its crater open. Ages of compressed energy. The first sign that the peaceful mountain might not be what it seemed on the surface.

The spreadsheet of projected corn yields made a rattling sound as it quivered in the air. She looked at it, almost confused, until she realized that the hand that clutched it was beginning to tremble.

There was nothing else being said on the emergency channel of that radio, and yet a voice cawed repetitively in her brain like an angered crow.

I pray for the sake of everyone in Fort Bragg that she can do at least one good thing for this population of people, and cooperate with us.

...at least one good thing for this population...

...at least one good thing...

...at least one...

Angela's ears hummed. She couldn't tell if it was the blood that thrashed out of the chambers of her heart at a rate that suggested she'd just sprinted up a flight of stairs, or if the burning sensation she felt creeping up the back of her neck simply came with an auditory hallucination.

The door to the office flew open and Corporal Townsend from the command center burst in, flush-faced and breathing hard, because he *had* just sprinted up a flight of stairs. He held one of the civilian radios in one hand, and a satphone in the other.

The satphone rang.

Townsend stumbled to a stop in front of her desk and thrust the satphone at her. "Sergeant Gilliard says he heard, and he's on the way, and not to agree to anything until he gets here!"

Angela looked at the ringing satphone. She imagined gripping it so hard that it shattered into a thousand pieces, and that somehow, that kinetic force would travel through the telephone signal to Elsie's Foster's skull...

This was so very strange to Angela, and yet it wasn't the first time she'd felt it.

She'd felt it before, as she'd stood in the Emergency Room with her daughter, as Abby was being discharged. After Elsie had tried to poison Abby. Had tried to kill her.

My daughter.

My one child.

The one thing in the world that means anything.

Thinking these words only stirred up the quaking things inside of her even worse.

How else was she supposed to feel when speaking to the person who had tried to kill her only child? The child that she had managed to keep alive through the collapse of civilization. The child that had been carried from the end of the old world, to the beginning of the new one. And right when she thought things were civilized again, she realized that they weren't, because there was someone out there who was willing to kill a child—*her child*—just to get to her.

The spreadsheet was now a half-crumpled ball in her trembling right fist.

She dropped it like a piece of trash.

Took the satphone and pressed the answer button. Brought it to her ear, and as she stared across her desk at nothing in particular, she heard the sound of breath on the other end of the line, and she had never in her life desired so fervently to extinguish that from another living thing's chest.

The only word Angela was capable of speaking came out as almost a whisper: "What."

Weak.

Housewife.

Unfit.

...at least one good thing...

The phone line susurrated with Elsie Foster's respiration—gentle, calm—and she spoke evenly. "Angela. Thank you for answering so promptly."

Elsie paused for a moment, perhaps for dramatic effect.

In any other time and place, perhaps Angela would have been able to see through the fog that was now shrouding her mental space, and perhaps divine her opponent's strategy. But in that pause, Angela only thought,

Weak.

Housewife.

Unfit.

She thought of another person that had tried to hurt her daughter. A person named Jerry. Angela had shoved a tire pressure gauge into his throat.

And yet, for all of the ferocity she had felt in that moment, it was not the same as what she felt now.

That had been pure survival instinct.

This...

This was different somehow.

Different because this had metastasized out of years of trying to do the right thing, of trying to keep everyone safe, of trying to be a good person, and a good mother, and a good leader, and nevertheless, having everyone question her motives, her competency, and her basic intelligence.

That can wear a deep groove in someone's brain.

It can wear that groove straight down to the bone.

After everything she'd done—the peace with neighboring communities, turning the lights back on, coordinating the growing and distribution of food, keeping everyone safe, letting them live their lives in some semblance of what it used to look like before everything went to shit...

After all of that, she was still seen as

Weak.

Housewife.

Unfit.

From the speaker of the satphone, Elsie's voice continued, confident and collected: "Were you aware of the fact that there is a colony of primals just outside the fences here at Fort Bragg? Were you aware that there had been an increase in sightings of packs of primals over the course of the last few months? Were you aware that your military men knew about this and have speculated that there's an increase in primal activity because we're the prey, and there's a lot of us sitting here like cattle in a stockyard? Were you made aware of *any* of this?"

Angela found it difficult to focus.

Her vision had throbbed down to a pinpoint. She could only see a little swath of the wall of her office, opposite her desk. She could only feel the pressure in her fingertips as she held the satellite phone in a death grip.

She was *trying* to listen and pay attention. But she felt like her thoughts had broken a restraining chain somewhere in her head and were now running off in wild directions, ignoring her calls to focus.

She kept picturing that tire pressure gauge in Jerry's throat.

She kept picturing Elsie Foster's head shattering.

She kept hearing

Weak.

Housewife.

Unfit.

AT LEAST ONE GOOD THING

"Angela," Elsie prompted with a falsely-pleasant tone. "Are you still there?"

"Yes," she managed.

"I take it that you weren't aware of any of that. I'm sure your military cronies who are gathering around you right now will confirm it for you. But it's beside the point. The point is, the threat is there. And the only thing that is keeping you from that threat is the high voltage fencing. And we now possess the power substation that controls the electricity in the Safe Zone. Do you understand what I'm getting at here?"

The tone of her voice.

Like Angela lacked the basic intelligence to comprehend language.

For a moment, Angela was genuinely confused. "Who is it that you think I am, Elsie?"

A moment's hesitation implied that Elsie was taken aback by the question. She sighed over the line, and she started to speak, but Angela talked over her. Her voice was quiet. Mystified. Earnest.

"I know what you must think. I've heard what they say about me. You think that I'm just a housewife that stumbled into this position somehow. You think that I'm weak and unfit for the office that I hold. And you know what? Maybe I'm not the best at it. I never claimed to be. I never campaigned for this. I never asked for it. But what confuses me, Elsie, is where your hatred comes from? You're talking to me right now over a satellite phone that you stole from *us*, while hiding in a house that *we* provided you, secure in the knowledge that you won't be brutalized or raped or eaten alive because of all of the things that *we've* built."

Elsie made a soft, scoffing noise. "I think you're getting off point—"

Angela's lips trembled as she interrupted. "The only reason you're still alive is because I let you stay that way. I've had every chance. Every opportunity to have you taken out. And I didn't. I let you live. And you tried to kill me for it. You tried to kill *my daughter*!"

Elsie Foster's voice became an indignant hiss. "Don't forget that my finger's on the trigger here, Angela! You might want to proceed with some caution, and some intelligence, if you can muster it!"

Everything coalesced in the fog. Like gravity pulling a nebula together to form rock.

What had been misty and searing suddenly flashed into cold granite.

Angela rocketed up out of her chair. "Caution is over," she said, her voice low and dangerous. "I was cautious before. That's the only reason you're still alive. I was told once that loose ends always come back to bite you in the ass, and I didn't listen to that advice, but I intend to correct that now."

Elsie raised her voice, abandoning the pretext of calm. "Interrupt me again and we'll shut the power down!"

"You're going to burn the only bargaining chip you have?" Angela snapped. "You go right ahead! You have demands? I won't hear them. You want my cooperation? You won't get it." Angela clutched the satphone's mic close to her mouth, like it was Elsie's ear that she was hissing into. "Whatever you thought you were going to get from me, you miscalculated, and now you're going to spend the last few hours of your sad existence on the run, in the darkness, hounded by primals and every goddamned soldier in this place. I have no pity for the violent death you're about to experience. You're already dead to me."

Angela disconnected the satphone and slammed it down on the desk, and the blood rushed to her head like a tidal wave and the breath that she'd expelled with each rage-filled word ran out and her vision swam.

She took a sharp breath and braced herself on the desk to keep her feet under her.

Across the desk, Corporal Townsend gaped.

At the door to the office, Carl Gilliard stood, his lips a thin line, his eyes wide.

Angela stared at him, defiant. "I didn't fucking agree to anything!" she barked. Took another breath and thrust herself upright off of the desk. "Carl, I want you initiate the Blackout Plan, and then I want you to take however many soldiers you need and I want you to find Elsie Foster, no matter what it takes. I don't give a shit! You find her and you put her down!"

And that was the moment when the power went out in the Fort Bragg Safe Zone.

TWENTY-TWO

FIRE AND LIGHT

WALKING BACK THROUGH THE DARKNESS, *on their last night in the Butler Safe Zone, Lee felt the warmth of the fire draining off of his clothes like blood from his body.*

By the faint light of the fire behind him, he saw his own elongated shadow, bobbing along. Ahead of him, only by the bare bit of moonlight they had, he saw Julia, and ahead of her, Tomlin and Nate. Everyone heading to their beds, where they were bunked in a few offices of the Sheriff's Station that Ed had provided them.

Quick footfalls behind him made Lee glance over, but he could tell by the breathing that it was Abe. How well did you have to know someone to be able to ID them by their breathing? It required many nights sleeping side by side, and long silences as you crept through woods, or sat in a car watching the landscape of a ruined nation pass you by.

"Y'all just gonna leave me behind?" Abe grouched.

"You 'fraid of the dark?" Lee smiled.

"I feel that I am reasonably circumspect about the dark."

"No shit," Lee agreed, his eyes glancing about into the shadows.

The Butler Safe Zone had high voltage wires around it just like Fort Bragg—that's what made it a Safe Zone—but there was always the sense that you were only slightly removed from the primeval hazards outside the gates.

No one liked being alone in the dark.

Lee and his team, perhaps, had more reason to fear it than most.

Abe made a motion ahead, and looked at Lee.

"What?" Lee asked.

"You and Jules okay?" Abe questioned, keeping his voice down so that Julia couldn't hear them.

"Of course. Why?"

Abe shrugged. "Seem a little distant, that's all."

Lee waved it off. "You know how it is in the field, Abe. That's all."

Lee and Julia had an unspoken agreement. Everyone knew that Lee and Julia had a relationship, but they tried to let them have their privacy about it. And Lee and Julia reinforced this by keeping things as professional as possible when in the field. They rolled their beds out next to each other, but that was pretty much it.

At the end of the day, they had a job to do, and they realized that the job would be easier if they didn't see each other in the light of their relationship, but as teammates.

There would be time enough for their personal relationship when they were back in the Fort Bragg Safe Zone.

Abe was silent on the matter for a few strides. And then: "Well, we are still technically in a Safe Zone, so...is it really the field?"

"Questionable."

"Just sayin'. You know. If you guys want some privacy..."

Lee smiled, but didn't answer Abe.

"Well, anyways," Abe said. "I'm gonna catch up with Tomlin and set that ratfuck bastard straight."

Abe jogged ahead, and Lee knew exactly what Abe was doing, and he appreciated it. In years past, he would have felt a little embarrassed, but there weren't many secrets around here, and no real way to keep them even if you had them.

Lee quickened his pace and caught up with Julia. He knew enough not to give it too much thought. It would be what it would be, and he wasn't going to apply pressure in any particular direction. If he got the greenlight, then fantastic. If not, that was okay too.

Both of them approached each other without expectations, and that seemed to be what made it work.

He did take the opportunity to take her hand, and she took his.

They walked around a building and onto a sidewalk. A block ahead was the Sheriff's Office where they would sleep for the night. Off to the right, a guard station, with a bored-looking twenty-something, staring out into the darkness beyond the high voltage wires.

"Abe's whisper carries a surprisingly long distance," Julia observed.

Lee chuckled. "Well, shit, I guess we're not that sneaky."

"How on earth have you two survived?"

"We have a good medic."

"Flatterer."

"Strategy."

"You know just what to say to a girl," she said, but he could see she was smiling. And it was a good smile. It was a green-light smile.

He smiled now himself.

"Take a detour with me?" she suggested.

"Absolutely."

***

The water was cold. The rain coming down felt even colder.

The days in Texas might've gotten hot, but it hadn't been spring long enough to warm a large body of water like the Squaw Creek Reservoir.

Lee slid through the black waters, keeping his eyes and nose above water. Ahead of him, he could see almost nothing but the faint glow of dim, battery-operated lights, coming from Comanche Peak Nuclear Power Plant. Everything else was black, run through with rain as dark as charcoal.

If he'd stood up, he would've been in knee-deep water. He was in a crawling position, propelling himself along in an alligator crawl over a jumble of head-sized rocks.

To his left, the rocks rose up in an enormous pile. They created a land bridge that extended from a peninsula to the south of the power plant, across the lake to the power plant itself. A single lane, dirt road ran across the top of the rocky land bridge.

What in the hell the land bridge had been used for was a mystery to Lee. But right now it was being used to hide their incursion from the eyes of the guards in the watchtowers.

Lee stopped, his hands and knees braced on the large rocks beneath him, and slowly turned his head to look behind him. He couldn't see the shore that they'd come from. It must be at least a hundred yards behind them by now. The rocky slope of the land bridge was visible for a few yards, and then disappeared into the darkness and rain.

Two heads, barely visible, bobbed in the shallows behind him.

Abe and Tex.

Their painted faces blended with the dark water. Just the hints of the whites of their eyes showed that they were human.

Just the three of them.

Lee turned forward and continued on through the cold waters as the rain washed all around them, making them invisible, and erasing the sound of any splashes they might make.

It was only an hour after dark. Normally they would choose to do an assault in the wee hours of the morning. But sometimes you don't have a choice. And in this case, it was out of their hands. According to the intel from Bellamy, their window of opportunity might be closed if they waited until the early morning. By then, Cornerstone operatives might be on site, and the target would be too dangerous to hit.

A mile or so east of the peninsula on which the power plant sat, an Abrams tank and three up-armored Humvees were waiting.

Out in the waters of Squaw Creek Reservoir, a dozen boats floated in the darkness and obscuring rainfall.

And here on a rocky land bridge, three operators crept through the water, closer to their objective, about to kick off one of the strangest attacks that Lee had ever planned—or even heard of.

It took him another twenty minutes in the chilling water before he saw the first, dark building peering down at him from the gloom. It was not part of the fortified section of the power plant, but an outlying building, long since abandoned. Ivy had begun to creep up the wall that faced them.

Even if it hadn't been abandoned, Lee doubted anyone could have seen them. With just half of their heads above the water, moving through the shallows at the base of the land bridge, they blended in with all the other stones jutting out of the water.

Lee stopped once more and looked behind him, keeping his movements slow. Abe and Tex were still with him.

Lee eased himself into something of a sitting position, nestled in with the boulders. Rising out of the waters, he felt the weight of his gear bear down on him again. In addition to their normal battle gear—armor, rifle, pistol, and a full load of ammunition—they each carried one of the M320 grenade launchers they'd appropriated from Tex's bunker, and ten 40mm grenades each.

They'd stuck to the shallows because they had no floatation devices, and would have otherwise drowned under the weight of their gear.

The upside was that the effort of crawling along with all that gear kept them warm.

Laying with his back to the rocks, Lee pulled a thermal imaging optic from a pouch on his armor—one more piece of weight—and held it up to his left eye. He scanned the building that faced them, and the ground that he could see from his low perspective. It was all shades of dark gray, the structures standing out like ghosts in otherwise pitch black.

No heat signatures.

Lee slipped the thermal optic back into its place, and looked at Abe and Tex. He nodded and pointed up over the top of the land bridge, in the direction of the power plant.

The other two eased out of the water, moving with the same tense stealth that Lee had.

Lee situated his rifle in his arms—his old M4 variant tonight—then checked the action, and switched the sling from two points to one. He waited for the others to settle into place, and then he began to climb his way up the slope of rocks to the top of the land bridge.

It was tough and uncomfortable movement. Sharp angles, and hidden holes, and doing it all so that his gear didn't clatter on anything. It took almost five minutes to reach the top.

The rain started to ease.

Good, because he would be able to see the power plant from here.

Bad, because if the rain let up too much, the watchtowers might catch a glimpse of the improvised flotilla out in the middle of the lake.

Lee needed to pick up the pace.

At the top of the land bridge, Lee lay with his chest on the rocks, looking out at the structures of the power plant. These were more visible, not only because of the slowing rainfall, but because the occupants had lights.

A generator hummed somewhere in there.

Work lights flooded various areas, and several of them were oriented outward.

One rack of work lights pointed right at Lee. He kept from looking straight at it, but even peripherally it would ruin his night vision.

Nothing to be done for it. His night vision would be ruined in a few minutes anyways.

Abe slid up to Lee's left, and Tex to his right. Rifles addressed towards the power plant.

"How's it look?" Abe whispered.

Between the gloom, and the bright work lights in his eyes, Lee couldn't see much detail with the naked eye.

He drew out the thermal optic again, and gave the power plant a slow scan.

Several heat signatures popped.

The work lights, and what was possibly the generator. But also three guards, moving about inside the compound. Lee could see three of the four watchtowers from his current vantage point, and each was occupied by what looked like a single sentry. Only two of those watchtowers were within range of their current position—the other was in the distance, its occupant a small white blob.

"As expected," Lee replied to Abe in a whisper. "Three good targets for us. Well within range. Two watchtowers that cover this southern section, and what I think is the generator that's powering all those lights." Lee passed the thermal imager to Tex. "I'm gonna go for that generator. Tex, can you ID the watchtower that's closest to us, on our right?"

"Yeah, I got it."

Lee took the thermal imager from him, and passed it to Abe. "You got the closest watchtower on the left."

Abe gazed through the optic for a moment, then passed it back. "Alright. I'm good."

"You guys ready?" Lee asked them.

"Ready."

"Good to go."

The three of them slung their rifles around to their backs, and from their backs retrieved the M320 they carried. It was a single shot launcher, and it could be mounted under their rifles, but they'd agreed that it would be easier to handle them as a separate weapon platform. At least for what they had in mind.

They weren't as fancy as Mitch's multi-shot M32, but they would still do the trick.

Lee shucked his first 40mm round from the belt of ten around his waist. Slipped it into the M320's breach, and snapped it shut.

To his left and right, identical sounds indicated that Abe and Tex were also loading up.

Lee reached up and keyed the comms, which had remained dead quiet up to now. "Red Rover and Yacht Club, Fire and Light is in position and ready."

The armored group answered first: "Red Rover, we're good to go when everyone check's ready."

Cheech responded for the flotilla of civilian water craft: "Yacht Club, we're about a thousand meters off the objective, and ready to head in on your mark. Rain's starting to clear, so the sooner the better."

"Fire and Light to Red Rover," Lee transmitted. "Everyone's checked in and ready. It's on you."

"Red Rover copies. We're oscar-mike."

***

Julia had always wanted a pontoon boat.

This desire had grown into a fantasy of hers that started in the eleventh grade, peaked the summer before college, and died down after that. But throughout her adult life, the image of her sunning herself on the floating patio of a pontoon boat still brought a smile to her lips and a wistful feeling to her chest.

Tammy Lundt had had a pontoon boat—or at least her family did. Tammy drove a red Mazda Miata, had platinum blonde hair of the shade that Julia wished hers would be, and had been the popular girl since the first week of ninth grade.

When everyone came back to class in the fall of their junior year in high school, Tammy regaled her friends—which didn't include Julia, but she heard about it anyway—with tales of floating out in the middle of the lake on warm summer days, sunbathing and flirting with boys on water skis.

Thus began Julia's own obsession with the fantasy of the pontoon boat.

She'd half convinced her dad to buy the frame of one for $1200 and fix it up.

But that never happened. And life did. And we move on.

Julia had never been on a pontoon boat in her entire life.

Until tonight.

Julia looked up into the sky and saw only blackness as cold rain speckled her face.

The universe must be a bitter old man with a spiteful sense of humor.

There was no warm, summer sun. There was only a chilly, rainy spring night.

Instead of a bikini, she wore sodden combat fatigues, body armor, rifle, and medical pack. Helmet listing sideways on her head, picking today to decide that it no longer wanted to sit properly.

Instead of cute boys water skiing, she was surrounded by hard men in painted faces, staring ahead through the gloom, at the distant glow from the lights of their objective.

Julia wiped the rain out of her eyes, then adjusted her helmet for the tenth time, swearing at it. Yesterday it had fit her head fine. Now it wobbled toward her right ear. Had she messed with one of the straps? Had the suspension system gotten wonky somehow?

She wanted to take it off and inspect it, but she knew that the second it left her head, the bullets would start flying. So she shoved it back into place and grit her teeth.

Fuck this shit.

And fuck pontoon boats.

There were three of them, and they'd been ripped down to the frames as much as could be managed without tools. Cushions gone. Most of the seating gone. Just two pontoons and a floor between them.

Soldiers on either side, straddling the pontoons with their legs in the water, holding oars that they'd swiped from the canoe and kayak shop at the park on the other side of the lake. With their stolen oars ready, they waited to row like mad for the shore.

There were two other pontoon boats in their "armada," as Cheech called it. On each pontoon boat, a squad of ten huddled, shoulder to shoulder, along with the paddlers on the pontoons, and one guy laying prone up front behind a tripod-mounted M2.

Barely visible in the gloom, about a hundred yards ahead of them, were the ten canoes, each with three soldiers. Two riflemen and one machine gunner, either with an M249 or an M240.

The canoes crept closer to their landing spot on the north shore of the target peninsula, the front rifleman in the boat paddling them gently—not making noise, but enough to keep them drifting forward.

The thought was that the canoes were lower profile and less likely to be seen on their approach. As Red Rover smashed through the barricades of the main road into the power plant, and attacked the main gate, the soldiers in the canoes would land—hopefully not yet under fire, as the tank would be drawing all the agro—and set up a beach head and base of fire.

Lee's Fire and Light team, meanwhile, would start blowing up everything they could on the south side of the peninsula, to further distract the defenders from the north shore.

Then the three squads on the pontoons would land, the tank would obliterate the main gate, and the infantry would storm the power plant.

Easy-peasy-lemon-squeazy.

Right?

For some reason, Julia's heart pumped at a normal, steady rate. Which surprised her. Usually it was elevated before an operation.

But her stomach felt hollow and sick.

Greasy and heavy.

Kneeling beside her, Cheech shifted and eyed her. "You think they'll do a painting of us in the future sometime? Like they did with George Washington Crossing the Delaware?" Cheech nodded and looked out. "Julia and Cheech Crossing the Squaw Creek Reservoir."

Julia tried to think of something funny to say back. She knew he was just trying to lighten her mood. But she came up blank, and all she could offer him was a weak smile that wafted away from her lips with the next cold breeze.

The comms in her ear spoke, and it was Lee's voice.

They were ready. In position.

The tank sounded off.

Then Cheech.

Then Lee told the tank that it could roll when it was ready, and the tank said that it was rolling.

And then the comms were silent again.

For a painful moment, Julia wished she were anywhere else but here.

But here was where she was.

No going back.

Only forward.

She sucked in a deep breath and held it, quelling nausea.

Cheech stood up taller on his knees. "We're on!" he whisper-shouted. "Let's move!"

The paddlers on the pontoons began rowing.

The pontoon boat pulled itself forward, and a moment later, the other two pontoons followed suit, moving steadily towards the northern shore.

In the cold distance, Julia thought she could hear the growl of the Abrams tank.

***

Lee had never used an M320 in combat.

This fact nagged at him.

He'd used the M203, and had had one on his rifle when he'd first come out of his bunker into this world gone to shit. But he'd heard that the M320s were more accurate.

He was going to test that.

He estimated he was about three hundred yards from the generator. He chose the appropriate notch on the simple, flip-up leaf sight, and lay there, waiting.

Shoot, then move.

Quickly.

Then shoot again.

He needed to move enough to stay alive, but he had to balance that with the need to send his ten 40mm grenades into that compound as fast as possible to draw attention from the north shore.

He'd gone over this in his head as many times as one could in the eight hours that this plan had existed. And yet he still felt unprepared.

It's just because we had to execute so fast, he told himself. *Just because we didn't have time for dry-runs or better intel.*

Fuck, I hope Bellamy's info was good.

"Here they come," Abe said, his voice tight.

The rain had weakened to a drizzle now, and in the relative quiet, Lee heard the growl of tracks, and the roar of a turbine engine somewhere in the darkness.

Lee's heart began to bang against the inside of his armor. For a flash, he remembered the cataclysmic feeling of taking a round to the chest, the primal fear that had invaded him as he felt the life slipping out of him and he...

Shit, I died.

Funny, he'd never admitted it until that moment.

"Focus," he whispered to himself. Everyone had their mental battles going into a real battle. It didn't matter how you dealt with it—just that you perform.

The first shot rocked the air. The report from the massive main gun on the tank, and then a fraction of a second later, the explosion, as the northwestern guard tower shattered in a white flash.

Screams and shouts rose from the compound. The shadowy figures that had barely been visible before now came to life as they started scrambling, trying to figure out which direction to run.

"One more shot," Lee called.

The northwestern guard tower listed, the sound of creaking and groaning steel reaching them. It didn't fall, but crumpled to one side and then hung there at an angle, black smoke belching into a black sky.

Machine gun fire erupted from the remaining guard towers, all directed at the tank. Tracers lanced the night air, and then received gales of fire back, coming from the tank's coaxial gun, and the Humvees that followed it.

The sound of bullet strikes, like hammers on steel, back and forth.

The fusillade crashed on, intensifying until it seemed like every gun was firing at its cyclic rate without stopping. It became almost a hum, or a buzz, that made the air warble.

Then the second shot.

The tank's report.

The explosion.

Lee couldn't see where the round had struck, but he saw the flash, and the billow of smoke.

"That's us," Lee grunted, and bore down on all the bad feelings in his stomach, because there was no more time left. Now he had to execute. He had to perform.

The grenade launcher thumped against his shoulder almost before he thought about it. Then two more reports sounded from his right and left.

Lee watched his first round hit as he reached down to his belt for a reload.

The ground about twenty feet behind the generator shattered and bloomed, and a figure that might've been a man flew apart.

Lee had overshot the generator.

He had a second. Maybe two or three, before someone figured out where the grenades were coming from. He needed to get this damn launcher dialed in...

He slammed the fresh round into the breach. Raised it to his eye, using the leaf sight again, but this time using the notch above the previous one. He squinted into the glare from the work light, and fired.

It dropped, slamming down right on the generator.

Or near enough that it didn't matter.

The work lights went out.

Lee pushed himself off the rocks, reloading as he stumbled across the treacherous footing, bounding over Tex's body, even as Tex pulled himself up to change positions.

Lee went prone again on the rocks. His knee struck hard, but he barely felt it. He put another grenade in. Sighted, and let it fly. Accuracy was unnecessary now. His second shot had taken out the generator—the next eight explosions were just to cause havoc.

Fire and Light.

Abe's third round took the southwestern guard tower and ripped the top of it clear off. Something limp and lifeless tumbled out, bouncing off the steel girders on its way down.

Lee ran again. Closer to the power plant now. Edging in.

The southeastern guard tower was all that remained. But then it seemed to realize where the threat was coming from, and a sudden blat of machine gun fire spat out of it, smacking the rocks to Lee's left and tracking toward him fast.

Lee let his legs go out from under him.

He hit the rocks.

Felt the skin come off his left shin.

A round whined through the air just over his head.

Lee swore—at nothing in particular and at everything in general. He slipped another grenade out, popped it in, and waited for a three count.

Three seconds.

Waiting.

Ages.

The machine gun fire started up again, but this time the rounds didn't whine, which meant they weren't close. He heard a clatter of breaking rocks to his left and saw Tex go down with a yelp.

Tex rolled across the jagged rocks and then held up a thumb. "I'm good! I'm good!"

Lee popped up, already visualizing the guard tower, visualizing his sights framing it...

Tracers zipped by, slicing the blackness just to his left.

"Shit!"

He dropped again before they could find him.

A *THUNK* from several yards away.

Abe's launcher, a trail of sparks shooting from the end of it.

BOOM

The round struck low on the southeastern tower, catching somewhere on the stairwell to the top and shearing a series of supports.

The machine gun fire from the tower went silent. It could have been anyone screaming, but Lee thought it was the guy inside, feeling the building beneath him lurch.

"Hit him again!" Abe shouted.

Lee popped up once more and fired, splitting the difference between the tower top and the stairwell and hoping for a hit on either to bring the damn thing down.

The round whiffed, sailing straight past and impacting further into the compound.

Another *THUNK*, this time from Tex, and the guard tower became a metal coffin, bright fire consuming whatever sad bastard was inside, a pressure wave reducing him to jelly.

Lee pulled back into cover behind the slope of rocks, reaching for another grenade. "Bust that fence line!" he shouted to Tex and Abe. "Give it everything you got left!"

The three of them started firing, and moving, and firing, edging closer across the land bridge, their rounds pulverizing the giant fences to ragged threads of metal. Opening a hole. And drawing attention from the infantry hitting the northern shore.

Move and shoot.

Move and shoot.

Shit, Lee thought. *This might actually work!*

TWENTY-THREE

CLEARED HOT

THE LAND BRIDGE connected the power plant to a parcel of forest to the south.

If you continued south, through that bit of forested land, with the lake on either side of it, you'd come to a clearing that cut straight through the forest, and out to the lake. In the center of this clearing was a long-abandoned railroad shunt, that might've, in another life, been used to ferry resources to the power plant.

Now, beside those rusted railroad tracks, two technicals rolled to a stop with their lights off. Their tailgate towards the main land. Their dark headlights towards the lake.

The gunners in the beds swung their machine guns to point north, into the woods, but they didn't fire.

McNair stepped out of the lead technical, gnashing on his chunk of gum.

Through the trees, he couldn't see the firefight at the power plant. But he could hear it. The near-constant chatter of machine guns raging back and forth, and the punctuation marks of what sounded like 40mm grenades thumping and crashing at an aggressive rate.

McNair pointed along the wood line. "Positions," he called. "By pairs. Wait for my mark before engaging."

Out of the technicals, his squad of Cornerstone operatives fanned out, splitting into pairs and positioning themselves along the wood line, with the railroad shunt to their backs. He had ten, including himself and his second, Prince, who stood beside him.

He'd come to Texas with fifteen men, but one of his fire teams had been ambushed and slaughtered the previous day in a little town called Caddo. They'd almost had Lee Harden and Terrence Lehy dead to rights. They'd almost completed their mission.

McNair felt a mingled hatred and despair as he remembered his boys' last radio transmission. They'd ID'd Lee Harden...And then they'd died, screaming and shooting.

And Lee Harden and Terrence Lehy—the two main targets—had escaped up a hillside.

McNair had barely restrained himself from letting the two Apache gunships assigned to him simply wipe that hillside clean.

But his mission was to take Lee out, and provide proof that he was dead. Which meant that McNair needed a picture of Lee Harden with a bullet hole in his face. Not a pile of meat scraps left over from a 30mm strafing run.

And oh, how satisfying it was going to be when he finally took that picture.

He couldn't wait to see Lee's dead face in the cold light of a camera flash.

He couldn't wait to piss on the body.

In Caddo, they'd pulled back, and he'd held off on using the gunships. Then he'd coordinated with Daniels and Lineberger to give misinformation to the leak in Greeley, in order to lure Lee Harden and Terrence Lehy into a trap.

It had worked. They'd taken the bait—hook, line, and sinker.

Now all he had to do was reel them in.

McNair keyed his comms, opening a channel between himself and the two Apache gunships that were in a holding pattern, several miles north. "McNair to Nordic One and Two. We are in position. You're cleared hot. Take out any vehicles they have, and push 'em our way."

***

The pontoon boat thumped into the mud of the northern shore, and the second it rocked to a halt everyone ditched.

The paddlers went over first, shoving their oars onto the flat of the pontoon platform. They splashed into the water, and one of them called back, "Waist deep!" and then started charging through the water and the silt towards the shore line.

Julia shuffled to the left, following the flow of bodies as they dumped themselves off the sides of the pontoon, everyone keenly aware of how exposed they all were at that very moment, and the only thing that seemed to be keeping them from being mowed down was the fact that it didn't seem that the enemy had realized they were there yet.

Out of Julia's peripheral, as she slipped feet-first into the water, she saw the fire and flames and the back-and-forth chaos of tracer fire, and the cries of the men that were dying, and the rattle and clank of the Abrams as it trundled along, destroying everything in front of it like a horseman of doom.

The hectic firefight was reflected in the black water she sunk into. Thick mud grabbed her by the ankles and threatened to not let her go, but someone large—probably Cheech—shoved her by the shoulder and then her feet were unstuck and she waded forward through the murk, towards the hellish destruction ahead of her.

The silhouetted shapes of the soldiers that had been on the pontoon with her were straddling a small cliff of mud that separated the water from the land. Coming up sopping wet, and then sprinting for cover.

Dead ahead were two large, concrete buildings that sat close to the shore and were undefended. The entire assault force stacked up behind these two buildings, the alley between them providing a clear funnel, straight towards the gates of the power plant.

Julia saw the jumble of dark bodies against the pale concrete, all of them clustered on one end or the other. Enterprising young point men taking small peeks around the corner to gauge the progress of the tank.

Julia hit the muddy cliff. It was about three feet tall, which wasn't much, but it crumbled under her hands and knees as she tried to scramble up it, and her weight felt exaggerated by the gear and the soaking clothes.

She managed to get herself up by rolling, then got up on all fours, then got her feet under her, and started running.

She went to the left.

Heavy footfalls beside her.

She glanced and saw Cheech, identifying him in the darkness only by his sheer size.

She hit the wall of the building between two troops, then put her back to the wall and gasped for air. Such a short space to haul across, but the weight and the water and the fear made it harder than it should have been.

Cheech hit the wall near her and started yelling to be heard over the crash of gunfire. "What's it look like?"

The soldier he spoke to looked back at him. "I dunno, sir. I guess it looks good. We're just waiting for the tank to hit that main gate."

Julia gulped a breath and spoke. "Are there any wounded? I'm a medic."

The soldier shook his head. "No, I don't think so. We haven't taken a damn round yet."

Cheech shrugged and smiled. "Well, I prepare for the worst, but I won't complain when it's easy." He started knife-handing select individuals in the crowd of soldiers—Julia figured they were squad leaders. "Gunners keep the corners," he bellowed. "Group by squad. One squad at a time down the alley."

A mess of shuffling occurred as the soldiers began to situate themselves.

A soldier from the other building shouted, "Tank's getting close!"

"Squad leaders!" Cheech yelled. "Hold on the defensive wall until everyone gets across!"

Julia became aware of a thumping noise in her ears.

At first she thought it was her own blood pumping, but it was much too rapid.

Then she thought it was the rumble of the tank, but she could hear the tank and somehow the sounds didn't match up. It was something else. Something that she was starting to feel in her chest, but she couldn't place it...

All at once, something happened.

Like a sudden calm in a storm.

All the soldiers that had been shouting and shuffling, they felt it too. They heard it. They stopped, and they started to look around, but unlike Julia, they seemed to have an inkling of what it was, and their eyes were turned to the sky.

"Everyone get down!" Cheech shouted, the tone of his voice changed.

Soldiers hugged walls.

The thumping became a rattle.

Julia's mind finally categorized the noise where it belonged.

Rotors...

In the lull, Julia heard the tanker over the comms in her ear: "Red Rover, can anyone advise—"

Dragon's fire split the night.

That's what it looked like to Julia, in the split second that she perceived it.

Like two black beasts hovered in the sky over the waters, and they simultaneously let out jets of fire.

Julia's face lit up in the chemical light of burning rocket fuel.

The missiles streaked overhead and impacted.

A rending crash came from the direction of the main battle.

Julia became aware of a pressing, buffeting wind against her face, and she saw it whip the waters of the lake, and the two dark shapes roared over top of them, their chain guns chattering. Julia watched the beach explode in a narrow line that lanced straight up the dirt and smash into the bodies against the wall.

Cheech shouted into the radio: "They have gunships! Two gunships, firing on Red Rover!"

Half a transmission came in after Cheech's: "—down! Red Rover One is down! We lost the tank!"

***

"The fuck was that?" Tex spat as a resounding explosion shook the ground.

The three of them hit cover in a clatter of gear, up against the defensive cement wall, about ten yards from a man-sized opening.

A smattering of radio transmissions answered Tex's question, right at the same time that the roar of helicopter rotors chattered through the air.

Tex and Lee and Abe all exchanged looks born from confusion and sudden, outright fear.

"Those're fuckin' Apaches," Abe identified. "Are they shooting at us?"

"They just took out the Abrams," Tex sounded gobsmacked.

"Whose are they?" Abe demanded.

"It doesn't fucking matter whose they are," Lee snapped. "They're not ours!"

The situation slammed into him with merciless pragmatism. Lee and forty-some-odd soldiers were now trapped on a peninsula. Their objective had turned them to fish in a barrel.

Lee hit several options in his mind, each like a roadblock: *Can the infantry escape? Not in the boats—they'd be sitting ducks. Do we have any anti-aircraft? No. Can we take the power plant and hide inside? Not without the tank.*

"We gotta pull back," Lee spat out, realizing it at the same moment that he said it. "We can't go forward. We gotta go back."

There was no time to argue. They all knew it. Tex held on for another second, his face a grim mask of resistance, but then he nodded.

Lee threw a hand towards the rocks they'd just come off of. "That's our way out. We gotta take the land bridge."

Abe grimaced. "That's four hundred yards of open space."

"It's better than sitting on a fucking boat."

Over the comms, Cheech transmitted. "Those choppers are swinging around! We can't sit here, Lee!"

Lee stabbed the PTT button on his chest rig. "Cheech! Fuck the plan! South! Straight across! Move to the land bridge!"

The thrum of the two gunships sounded like it was dimming, and then it began to get louder again. There was the chirp of tires. The Humvees were trying to make their getaway.

"Lee!" Tex snapped at him. "You seem to be in charge, so what are we doing?"

Lee grabbed Tex and Abe and pointed them back over the land bridge. "This was a trap," he said. "Either Bellamy sold us out or he got sold out himself. Go across the bridge and make sure we don't have hostiles closing off that retreat."

Tex and Abe sprinted away towards the land bridge.

The distinct sound of Hellfire missiles screeched through the air, followed by three solid, chest-thumping explosions. Had that been the Humvees? Had that last pass taken out both of them?

Lee ran north because he couldn't think of anything else to do in that moment, and it had to be better than standing still. Maybe he could help carry some wounded...

The first of the infantry skidded around the corner.

An Apache chain gun burped, and the massive rounds beat the concrete to pieces in a cluster, ripping two of the soldiers to shreds. Lee cried out involuntarily when he saw it, but kept running.

Both gunships roared over top of the fleeing soldiers, low enough that the downdrafts whipped up a mist of water from the wet concrete.

Lee watched their black shapes against the black sky, saw them bank to come around for another pass, and then lost them in the wind and the darkness.

Ahead of him, the few soldiers turned into a flood of them—all forty of them tumbling around the corner at a flat sprint.

"The land bridge!" Lee shouted as the first soldiers reached him, pointing behind him. "Go straight across! Straight across!"

The machine gunners that had set up the bases of fire on the shore line now hit the corner of the thick cement wall and turned, hefting their machine guns if they were smaller, or with the help of a buddy in the case of an M2, and oriented them to the sky while their comrades continued to pull back.

They weren't the best tools against gunships in the dark, but they were the only tools they had for the job.

The two soldiers with the M2 took the corner of the concrete wall, standing. One of the M240s slid prone at their feet, and the other, not having any place else to go, simply planted his feet in the center of the tide of his escaping comrades, like a rock in the middle of a river, and aimed for the sky, waiting for a target to appear out of the darkness.

Lee's eyes tore away from them as he stamped his feet to a stop, cutting left towards the concrete wall to let the retreating men get past him. His eyes coursed over the round domes of helmets and faces and fear, but he didn't see what he was looking for.

Julia.

Cheech came around the corner last—distinguishable by being a head taller than everyone else.

A familiar shape hustled along beside him.

Lee felt relief, mixed with a stab of panic—why had she stayed in the back of the pack?

But Lee knew why.

So she could help any wounded she came across.

The sound of the rotors began to rise again.

Cheech stopped with the machine gunners.

Julia stopped with him.

Lee clawed his way up the wall towards them, yelling at Julia to keep running.

Lee didn't know if Cheech heard him or not, but he seemed to suddenly realize she was there at his side. He turned and shoved her away from him.

She started running again.

Cheech turned back, faced the sky, and raised his rifle.

The machine guns blazed, their muzzles strobing the night sky, each flash catching a thousand raindrops like they were frozen in midair.

Lee saw the hint of the two black shapes in the sky, roaring straight at them.

He had the distinct thought: *This is going to hurt...*

He spun, seizing Julia as she ran into him, and pushed her ahead of him, as though his body might be a barricade to a 30mm projectile.

Ahead of them, the troops were just now reaching the land bridge. They'd be caught on it. Easy pickings for the Apaches, but maybe they could make a dive for the waters...

A black slot in the wall, just ahead of Lee.

The rotors roared behind them, like charging bulls.

Lee fixated on the slot in the wall—a man-sized entrance. Lee knew it would be covered by pill boxes, but he didn't think they were occupied. He had to take the risk. It was better than just letting the Apaches chew him to shreds.

Lee caught up with Julia just as she was about to pass the opening in the wall. He seized her by the arm, dug his heels in as the opening yawned to his right, and hauled her into the space—

—the chain guns thundered—

—an eruption of concrete dust billowed over them—

—the sound of a metoric impact behind him—

—something smacked him in the hip.

He jolted forward, losing his balance, and toppled onto Julia.

He rolled, then scrambled to his feet. He tasted concrete in his mouth. Felt fire in his hip, but he couldn't think about that now. Julia was on the ground, coughing. He must've knocked the wind out of her when they'd landed.

"Come on!" Lee urged, reaching out and grabbing a hold of her arm. "We gotta go!"

He realized she wasn't coughing—they were short, sharp gasps of pain.

He felt an ice pick jab at the bottom of his heart.

"What's wrong?" he went to his knees. "Did you get hit?"

"I dunno," she managed. "I think I'm okay. I think it just grazed me. Shit. What was it?"

"Shrapnel from that round right behind us. I think it bit me too. Can you stand up?"

She nodded, though her mouth still hung open, sucking air, and she looked bewildered. Lee didn't like that expression.

He got her arm again and hauled her up. Her eyes widened and she let out another noise of pain. Lee's own hip flared with the movement, but he was almost certain that it wasn't debilitating.

He propped Julia against the wall, and checked his hip. He couldn't see past all the gear on his torso, but he felt it with his fingertips—a ragged hole at the top of his pants, moist with blood. But it felt like a graze. Whatever piece of nasty metal had hit him had passed right on through.

"I'm okay," Lee said. "Are you okay?"

Julia looked lost. Lee didn't think he'd ever seen her like this. Something was wrong. Was it just the shock of the moment?

But she nodded again. "Yes. Let's go."

Lee took one look to his left—out towards the fleeing soldiers—and knew that wasn't where he was going. A jab of guilt hit him—could he have made a better decision? Was it because of him that all of those soldiers were going to die in strafing runs across the land bridge?

He looked to their right, inside the walled compound. They were exposed to the pill boxes, but they hadn't received any incoming fire. He couldn't see it from his current vantage point, but based on studying the satellite images, he knew there was a sluiceway about a hundred yards from him. The water from the lake was sucked in, used to cool the reactors, and then jetted out the sluiceway back into the lake.

When the reactors were operational, the sluiceway moved like man-made rapids. But now, without the pumps, the water simply sat there.

It was the only way out that Lee could think of.

"Come on," Lee shouldered his rifle with one arm, ignored the fiery pain in his hip, and pulled Julia off the wall with his other hand.

The opening of the man-entrance through the wall stretched out in front of him. He scanned over the fortifications—the pill boxes and the catwalks and the windows that glared down at him in the rainy darkness.

Outside their momentary safety, Lee heard the gunships coming back around again.

The grating sound of men dying.

Julia let out a groan that might've had words somewhere in it, but Lee couldn't tell.

Lee cleared the corner. First right, then left. Then he ducked back in. Julia leaned on the wall, her rifle hanging in her grip.

"You ready?" he asked her.

She looked at him, her eyes still wide, almost confused. "No. I'm sorry. Hold on."

Shit.

The tactical and the personal made a head-on collision in his mind.

They were both exposed.

Twenty-five yards ahead of them, though, there was another structure behind which they could hide.

Lee made a split-second decision. He grabbed Julia's arm again. "Hang on, Jules! We gotta get to cover!"

She grunted something and pulled back against him for a second, but then followed as best she could. Why couldn't she keep up? Why was she dragging her feet like that?

Lee could hardly think passed the imperative of the angles and unknown threat positions that were arrayed out in front of him as he ran for the structure that would give them some momentary cover.

He heard the gunships, coming in again.

Had the rest of the soldiers gotten across the land bridge?

Had Cheech?

Lee hit the corner of the structure. A squat, single story concrete box in the dimensions of a trailer.

He yanked Julia behind it, just as the sound of the gunships rose to a pitch, and the chain guns rattled again, and as the noise died for a third time, Lee heard the sound of carnage, and it felt like ice in his gut.

Lee ripped his attention away and looked at Julia.

She gulped air, staring at Lee.

"What's wrong?" Lee's voice trembled, and he told himself it was from the effort of running.

Julia arched her back, pulling at the bottom corner of her plate carrier. "It's...right in there...something got me right there..."

The bottom of the canvas plate carrier was stained dark.

Lee's heart and stomach tripped over each other.

"You said it was a graze," Lee said. "It's just a graze, right?"

"I dunno," Julia said, her voice tightening. "It keeps feeling worse and worse. I think something's broken..."

"Broken? Like a bone?"

"I don't know..."

"Hold on," Lee said, and pushed his rifle back over his right hip to get it out of the way, and then slipped his hand underneath her plate carrier.

A ragged hole in the fabric. Just like his.

Except that, underneath that fabric, he could feel warm blood pulsing.

And the position of the wound...

This wasn't a graze. This had gone straight into her gut, just beneath the armor plate.

"Okay," Lee said, his voice quieter, less sure than he had intended. "It's okay. I got you." He looked her in the eye. "You took some shrapnel to the stomach, okay? I can feel blood coming out at a steady pulse, but it's not spurting. You don't have an arterial bleed..." he trailed off.

Julia watched him, her eyes frowning now. Like she didn't believe him.

"Should I be telling you this?" he asked.

She nodded. "Do I..." she bared her teeth through a wave of pain, then marshalled herself. "Do I have an exit wound?"

Lee reached around and felt along the small of her back, opposite where the shrapnel had gouged into her. He didn't know whether he was hoping for an exit wound or not. An exit meant it hit more tissue, but at least the piece was out...

He couldn't find another hole.

"I don't..." his hand scrambled over the surface of her back again. "I don't feel anything else."

"Okay. Fuck." Julia sounded like she was puzzling out someone else's predicament. Cold and clinical. Even for herself. "Evaluate the bleed. Do I have time?"

That was a big question to ask.

Lee blinked once, staring at her.

Don't see Julia. See your teammate.

This isn't the woman you love.

This is a wounded buddy.

"Yes," Lee said. "I think you have time."

"How long until we get out of here?" she asked.

"Five minutes? Maybe ten?"

Julia nodded. "Make it five, Lee. I'll help the best I can, but we need to get out of here or we're both gonna die."

"No one's gonna die." Lee had to say it out loud.

Or perhaps that was tempting fate.

He hauled Julia to her feet, pulled her arm under his. "Hook your fingers inside my plate. There. Good. Just keep your feet moving, okay? That's all you gotta do. Just pick up your feet."

She is a wounded buddy.

They moved in a straight line.

Leaving the safety of the concrete structure behind.

Another seventy-five yards of open space lay ahead of them. There were small positions here and there that might provide cover, but Lee wasn't stopping. He was going for the big square hole in the ground that he knew was the start of the sluiceway.

Beyond that hole in the ground, he saw the mangled remains of the fence that they'd hit with the 40mm grenades. It was a secondary exit plan, but then he would be back to going across the land bridge. The sluiceway would keep them low, and hidden in the water.

It wasn't safety, but it was concealment. And that was their best defense at that moment.

As the hole that marked the entrance of the sluiceway approached, Lee realized he had no idea how deep that water was going to be.

And they both wore armor and ammo and rifles.

He thought about taking them off before jumping in.

But they were ten yards from the opening. And the gunships were coming back around again.

There wasn't time.

"Almost there," Lee breathed, then pulled to a stop at the lip of the entrance.

"Fuck. Lee." Julia groaned. "I don't…"

Lee peered over the edge. Black water moved, but it seemed like it might be shallow. Lee wasn't sure why he thought that—maybe he was seeing what he wanted to see.

"Jules, I'm gonna ease you down in there, okay? We gotta move quick."

"Okay."

If it turned out to be too deep, he could haul her back up and try to figure out another plan. If the choppers didn't mow them down first.

Julia managed to sit herself on the edge of the concrete, her feet dangling over the dark water inside the sluiceway and Lee helped her begin easing her way in. She grit her teeth and hissed, but didn't cry out as she had to hang from his hands, twisting her wounded torso.

Her feet hit the water. He kept easing her down, the pain of his own wound in his hip nagging at him, but he refused to even acknowledge it when Julia was worse off than him.

"Can you touch the bottom yet?" Lee asked.

Behind him, the Apaches spit fire and death.

Suspended from Lee's hands, Julia kicked her feet, knee deep in the water. "I can't. I can't touch it yet."

Lee eased himself into a kneeling position, having to take his breaths in sharp chunks, his core locked to stabilize him under load.

Julia was waist deep now.

Her wound in the water.

Then a little more. Almost chest deep.

Lee was hunched over his knees.

"Okay," she said. "I'm standing."

The weight came off his arms. Lee took a deep, relieving breath and then slid over the edge of the concrete and into the water with a clumsy splash. His boots slipped on a layer of scum that clung to the concrete floor of the sluiceway. The water undulated against his chest, but it wasn't flowing.

He regained his footing, then flattened his back against the wall of the sluiceway, and looked to his left, down the long, straight length of it. After about fifty yards, it passed under the ruined wires of the fence, and then it dipped out of sight.

That section wouldn't have any water in it. But at the end of that section, there would be the lake. The portion of the lake that stood, separated from the rest of the reservoir by the land bridge.

If Lee could get them there, they could move through the shallows, back to the peninsula they'd started from, and maybe regroup with the others.

If there were any of them left.

Lee looked back to Julia. "How are you feeling?"

"It hurts," she said, her respiration elevated. "But..." She seemed to re-evaluate what she was going to say, and then shook her head. "Let's go Lee. Come on. Get us out of here."

Just a wounded buddy.

Lee pulled her arm over his shoulders again and the two of them began to move through the chest-deep murk, towards the lake.

TWENTY-FOUR

OBLITERATION

IT HAD BEEN A TRAP.

And the people that had laid it obviously had no intention of letting anyone walk away from it.

Tex crawled through mud and leaves along the forest floor.

The gunships had hit the bridge. Tex couldn't see it anymore—he couldn't see shit except tree trunks and brush and leaves, all around him—but he could still picture the bursting 30mm shells slamming through his men, obliterating their bodies, or shredding them with shrapnel when they impacted nearby.

The land bridge was scattered with broken bodies.

Moaning wounded.

He could still hear them out there. And all through the woods.

The second Tex's retreating forces had entered the woods, a withering barrage of machine gun fire had lanced through the forest. As Lee had suspected, there'd been a force positioned here in these woods to catch those that retreated.

Now, only sporadic gunfire reached Tex's ears.

Small arms fire, taking out stragglers.

There were enemies on foot, combing through the woods, and wiping out the last of Tex's survivors.

A close run by one of the Apaches had sent Tex and Abe in separate directions. Now he had no idea where Abe was, or if he was even still alive. It was possible Abe had been shot up in that run.

What had happened to them?

Tex still couldn't wrap his brain around it, and yet he knew who was responsible.

Fucking Bellamy. You backstabbing piece of shit!

Tex didn't know for sure if this had been orchestrated by Bellamy, or whether he'd been hoodwinked himself. But it didn't matter. Bellamy was still at fault, either way. It was Bellamy's fault that there was a land bridge covered in chunks of Tex's guys...

Tex could feel the noose tightening.

He could feel the end point of his life approaching. He'd kick and scream and spit in the face of death, but no matter what happened, if it was the last goddamn thing that he did, he was going to hear John Bellamy's voice, and Bellamy was going to hear his. And both of them were going to know where the other stood.

Suppressed rifle shots spat throughout the woods, and the barks of unsuppressed rifles answered. Men cried out. Tex's men.

And yet Tex could do nothing for them.

He pulled up to the base of a gnarled oak tree. Leaves piled up around his legs. He looked over his shoulder in both directions, into the dark woods, but he could see nothing. He could only hear the sounds of suppressed gunshots, but they seemed far away.

He swung his small go-bag from his back. Sat it in his lap. He ripped open one of the front compartments and then dove in. He pulled out the satphone.

Another flurry of suppressed gunshots. Nearer than last time.

The noose closing.

Bring it on, motherfuckers. This Texas boy had one more thing to do before he went out.

He pulled the thick antenna up, then dialed the number.

It rang, four times.

A single gunshot, very close by. Someone cried out for Jesus, then groaned and died.

"Tex!" Bellamy's voice on the line. "Is everything okay?"

"Did you do this, you sonofabitch?" Tex hissed into the phone.

There was a pause.

Dread in Bellamy's voice: "Tex. What happened?"

"You killed us," Tex answered, his voice just a breath on the wind.

A twig snapped somewhere nearby.

Tex didn't know whether or not he believed in Bellamy's act of innocence. But he knew that he didn't care either way. He'd delivered his message. And now someone was going to die.

Tex set the satphone on the ground next to him and then rolled out from behind the tree, bringing his rifle up as he did.

***

Bellamy stared at the satphone in his hands.
You killed us.

And then there had been shooting. And screaming.

And then nothing.

His brain buzzed like someone had rammed two electrodes into it. Everything around him was overbright and sharp and seemed to shimmer at the edges.

He'd been close to several explosions during his time in the military—concussions that had rung his bell more than is healthy.

That was how it felt right now.

Everything, all at once, disorienting.

You killed us.

Those were Tex's last words to him. And the full weight of that was still crushing Bellamy flat, and yet he couldn't really feel it. Like you can't feel the pain of a terrible injury at first, but you can still tell that you've been badly damaged.

What had happened?

And who had died?

His brain bounced from question to question, with no answers. All the way back it bounced, until it hit the one question he *did* have the answer to.

Who gave me this intel?

Lineberger.

Shit.

They'd used Bellamy to pass misinformation.

Which meant that they knew about him. For how long was anyone's guess, but at least as long as twenty-four hours ago.

The ringing in his head became the blaring of a mental warning klaxon.

It was only through three very deliberate and forceful breaths that Bellamy cleared the rubble of his former reality away enough to see some daylight.

He had to get the hell out of Greeley.

And he had to leave right that instant.

***

The choppers weren't strafing the woods.

And that meant only one thing to Lee, as he half-floated in the shallows of the lake, along the shore farthest from the land bridge, amongst mud and roots and fallen branches.

It meant that they didn't want to hit their own people.

Julia let out another violent shiver against him.

Lee's back was in the silty mud, his head just above the water. He pulled himself along by clutching the cold, greasy roots of the trees, and the algae-covered branches with one hand. His other was wrapped around Julia's chest, holding her against his body. His rifle was towed through the muck behind him by the sling.

Lake water slipped into his mouth as he maneuvered the two of them under a fallen tree. He spit the water out.

"How you doin', Jules?" Lee whispered.

"I'm fuckin' freezing," she mumbled. The trembling was more constant now. She had less control over it. She started to curl up, trying to curl into Lee for warmth, but the cold water simply sapped it away.

"Just a little longer," Lee told her. "We're almost there, and then I'm gonna start fixing you up."

But he had no idea what the hell he was gonna do.

If there were enemy soldiers in those woods—and why else would the Apaches be circling and not engaging?—then he wouldn't have time or safety to operate on Julia. But something had to happen. He had to do something to start fixing her. She wasn't bleeding arterially, but that didn't mean she couldn't bleed out if he didn't address her wound.

And he needed to get her out of this water! It was too cold. Her body was already struggling against shock. This water was going to make her hypothermic, if it hadn't already.

And what was he going to do if they came for him in the middle of operating on her?

Should he leave her?

No. He couldn't do that.

He didn't care if it was the right tactical decision. He didn't care if that was what survival dictated. He wasn't going to leave Julia's side. Some things were more important than survival.

"Lee," her voice trembled. "I gotta get outta this water."

"I know. I'm getting us there."

"Just get me out of the water."

"I can't let you out of the water yet, Jules," Lee said, straining his way towards a promising-looking bank that had some trees that might give them concealment. "If I stand up now those birds'll see us and take us out."

"It doesn't matter."

"The fuck it doesn't," he snapped.

"I just need to get warm. Then you gotta leave me."

"I'm not..." Lee bared his teeth. "Julia, you need to shut up right now."

She shook against him again, and he realized that it wasn't just the cold—she was holding in sobs.

"I'm sorry," Lee mumbled into her ear. It was ice cold against his lips. "I need you to be positive right now. Okay? Can you do that for me?"

She didn't answer.

Lee made it to the bank. It wasn't great, but it would have to do. He had to get her out of the water. He pressed his back into the mud and sank them deeper, so that their faces were the only thing above the water, and he waited for the Apaches to pass over the woods again, away from him.

The rain had started to drive again, and that was going to help. It was going to decrease the gunships' visibility and obscure the thermal imaging.

One of them roared overhead, shaking the tree branches. But it didn't engage them. It passed on.

Lee hauled himself onto the bank, slipping twice in the mud, but never letting go of Julia. "I got you," he whispered to her. "Let's get you out of the water. Let's get you warmed up."

What are you gonna do about the wound?
Whatever she tells me to do.

It wasn't until she tried to pull herself up that Lee realized how weak she'd become. She tried to get her hands and knees under her, to crawl forward on the leaves, away from the bank, but her arms didn't seem to be able to support her weight, and she pitched forward, rolling onto her side to avoid hitting her face.

"Okay," Lee said. "This is fine. We've got concealment."

Lee straightened, on his knees, and peered through the dark woods all around them, searching for threats. There was the sound of the Apaches, circling. And there was the sound of suppressed gunshots sprinkled throughout the woods.

Those had to be enemy combatants. Lee didn't think any of Tex's guys had come equipped with suppressors.

They're wiping everybody out.

How much time did he have to operate on Julia?

He hunched over her body and pushed her so that she lay on her back. She groaned, but then relaxed with a hiss of pain.

Lee pulled the medical pack from her shoulders and laid it next to her, then ripped open the Velcro straps of her plate carrier and slung the whole thing off of her chest. "Alright, Jules, talk to me, okay? I need you to make sure I'm doing this right."

He could have muddled his way through an abdominal wound without help, but maybe it would keep her engaged. He could sense her consciousness wavering, shock threatening to take her over, and Lee didn't know if he could bring her back from that.

Abdominal wound.

First aide was straightforward: don't pack the wound, but cover it with gauze, a little pressure, and an occlusive dressing to seal it. That would get you to someone who could do the actual surgery.

But they didn't have that, did they?

Lee shook his head, the nagging panic beginning to poke at his brain. A big problem, and no options. He ripped open the pack and started searching for what he needed. "The wound's to your lower abdomen, so I'm gonna put gauze over it, then an occlusive dressing. Is that right?"

A violent tremor took a hold of her, and Lee almost missed the fact that she was shaking her head. Her eyes were clenched closed. Her teeth chattered. It was difficult to tell in the darkness and the rain, but he thought her skin looked shock-white.

"You need…" her voice shook, making her words hard to hear. "You need to…warm me up."

"Okay." Lee's heart gave a lurch of pity, and he ignored it because it threatened to weaken him. *This isn't Julia. This is just a wounded buddy.*

He stripped off his gear. He didn't know how much warmer he could make her—his skin felt chilly. But he could maybe rub some warmth back into her. He'd do his best.

With his gear off, he laid down beside her and pulled her in close. She turned into him, curling again. Her face pressed into his chest. A small hitch in her breathing.

He put his arms around her and rubbed her, trying to work some blood flow and warmth back into her. "It's gonna be okay," he said. "Get warm."

A bad tremble seized her, or a cramp—Lee wasn't sure which. She clutched him tighter. And when it passed after a few seconds, she didn't let go.

"What about the bleeding, Jules? I gotta do something about the bleeding."

He felt her head shake again, side to side. "Just get me warm."

Lee pulled back. "Julia," he said sternly. "I don't know if you're thinking clearly right now. I think I need to do something about the bleeding."

He felt her hand work free of where it was balled up against his chest, and he felt the cold fingers slide up to his neck, his face. Heard them scrape through his thick stubble. She pulled at him, forcing eye-contact. Her face was scribbled over with pain, but the eyes were firm and lucid.

"I'm thinking clearly," she said. "I'm shot in the stomach, Lee. Just like that kid Pikes. Even if there was a good medic around, I wouldn't make it."

Lee felt the approach of something that he had avoided for a very long time. Something he had not allowed to touch him. Something he had hardened himself to. But Julia was spiking right through that hard crust, and underneath that, he didn't think he was strong enough to deal with what came next.

Structures were crumbling in the foundation of his brain.

"No," he said. "Gauze and an occlusive dressing, and then we'll figure it out. We'll get you to safety. And we'll figure it out."

"You stubborn shit."

"Julia, I'm not gonna let you give up like that."

"I'm not…" her voice edged toward anger, but then she stopped, and her hand on his neck became firm. "It could take days for me to die of sepsis. I'll be sick out of my mind. I won't even recognize you. That's how it's going to happen, Lee. Don't fucking tell me otherwise, because you don't know what the fuck you're talking about and I do." Her hand slipped. Fingers curled around the collar of his shirt. "You're going to let me bleed out, Lee. Because that hurts less."

"I'm not gonna let you bleed out," Lee hissed, because his voice had left him.

"Hold onto me and get me warm."

And he did, because he didn't know what else to do except what she told him. Even as he did it, he shook his head in denial. He pulled her in tight, like a bit of driftwood keeping him from sinking into blackness.

Gunships circled like vultures. The rain came down harder. The patter of fat raindrops nearly masked the sound of suppressed gunfire.

What comes next?

What comes next?

He couldn't picture it. Or refused to.

Next was nothing.

Next was obliteration.

Julia stopped shivering.

He rubbed her more vigorously. Like that could give life. Like friction could solve death. He scrambled for words, sensing the terrible thing continuing its approach, bearing down on him. And he thought of dozens of things to say, and yet they all somehow slipped through his mind like water through his fingers. Like a dream that escapes you as soon as you wake.

The thing was coming, and he had nothing to say.

He would never have another chance. And yet he couldn't.

And he hated himself for that.

He hated everything.

He wanted to tell her that she was the only good thing that he had left in the world, but his breath had turned to stone. His throat a collapsed tunnel.

The thing had found him.

And Julia could not hear him anyways.

She was already gone.

TWENTY-FIVE

MCNAIR

IT'D BEEN ALMOST FIVE MINUTES since McNair had heard a gunshot.

He stood, tense, locked, in the darkness of the trees, while rain pattered around him, and two miniature hurricanes circled the chunk of land that had become the center of his trap. One of the gunships went overhead right at that moment, stirring up the tree branches and causing fat droplets to trickle down McNair's collar.

He didn't take his eyes off the woods in front of him.

He wasn't even chewing the hard nugget of gum between his teeth—it made too much noise in his head.

His stomach started to cinch up. So far he'd gotten a single confirmed KIA on a Project Hometown operative they hadn't even expected to be present—some horrific Polish name that McNair couldn't repeat if he tried.

But still, no one had found the body of Lee Harden, or Abe Darabie, or Terrence Lehy.

It was possible that they were sitting in the smoking ruins of the tank or one of the Humvees. Or they could've gotten dashed to mincemeat by a strafing run from the Apaches.

But McNair didn't think that was the case.

Call him paranoid—and he admitted that he was—and perhaps it was simply because no one had identified the remains yet, but he felt like Harden was still out there. That motherfucker was too damn slippery to die in something so banal as a strafing run.

Darabie and Tex too, for that matter. But if McNair had to go back to Greeley with only one photo of a guy with bullet holes in his head, it would be Harden.

It was *going* to be Harden.

Other than not finding the right damn bodies, the trap had been flawless. Minimal casualties for them. The birds had taken out the majority of the hostile forces. Some cartel fucks had to die for that to happen, but McNair wasn't shedding a tear.

The enemy combatants had fled the only direction that they could—across the land bridge, right into these woods, where McNair and his team had been waiting for them. A few passes of machine gun fire from their technicals parked at the edge of the woods, and then they'd gone in on foot to clean up the mess.

Two of his operatives had gone down in a firefight with some of the surviving troops in the woods. But McNair hadn't expected his team to get off scot-free.

Frankly, it was going better than he'd expected.

Except...*no Harden.*

"Anything?" McNair whispered to his left, where Prince stood about five yards away from him in the shadows.

Prince wore his NVGs. McNair didn't want to spoil his natural night vision just yet. Call him old school, but he still felt like he operated better without the bulky four-tube monstrosities.

"Nada," Prince mumbled back.

McNair started moving forward again. The wet leaves and pine needles softening his strides. The background of the helicopters and the rain made him virtually silent.

Funny.

His heart had been steady the entire time. Even when they were about to spring the trap—a point in time when, on any other ambush, McNair would have been at his most tense—he'd maintained an almost Zen-like state of calm.

But the missing Harden was now making his pulse thump harder, and quicker.

McNair wasn't afraid of Harden. Let's just say...he had a healthy respect for dangerous game. He felt that he was having a pretty reasonable physiological reaction to being in the woods with something that was hunting him back. Something that had a pretty good track record of killing others.

He wasn't underestimating Lee Harden—that had killed other people.

Neither was he overestimating him. Dangerous or not, he was on the run, surrounded, possibly wounded, probably low on ammunition, and likely angry at having his plan thwarted.

McNair felt that he had Lee Harden pegged pretty solid.

And that was what was going to allow him to take that fucker down.

In a moment of pique, McNair keyed his comms. "McNair to all units. Gimme a sitrep and pos. Sound off."

They did. One by one, going by two-man teams. McNair still had eight bodies in these woods, including himself and Prince.

They all said that they'd checked every body.

None had seen Harden, or Darabie, or Lehy.

As for their positions, McNair logged them on a mental map of the woods. They'd spread out in a skirmish line. The right side of that line was all the way to the northern bank, near the land bridge.

McNair and Prince were the other side of that skirmish line, all the way to the west.

Which left a small section of woods in the northwestern corner, between McNair and the runoff pond from the power plant's sluiceway.

The forest was framed—open water to the north, east, and west. And a railroad shunt to the south. If anyone had exited the woods, the choppers would have seen them.

McNair transmitted to the Apaches. "Nordic One and Nordic Two. Humor me here. You haven't seen any heat signatures break containment from this forested area, correct?"

"Nordic One, that's negative."

"Nordic Two, yeah, nothing's come out of that forest. But be advised, the canopy's a little thick. Between that and the rain, we're pretty blind to what's going on inside of the woods."

McNair nodded. "Alright, gents," he said to his team. "Let's start moving into that last section and see what we can scare up."

***

He lay there with her.

He was aware of the danger. He was not so far gone for that. But for a while—what felt like a very long time—he just didn't care. He had neither the energy, nor the inclination to care. Self-preservation seemed unimportant.

In the stillness, with her body held to his, no longer able to warm her, no longer able to talk with her, no longer...anything. Though his body didn't move, his mind pitched and rolled like a tiny boat caught on enormous ocean swells.

At the peaks, he would rage.

And then he would drop, and he would mourn, in the only way it seemed he knew how, and that was to sit in stony silence and feel almost nothing, just as a landscape razed by a nuclear blast is almost nothing.

And in the space between the rage and sadness, he wanted to burrow down, beneath the ground, beneath the places where he could be touched, and he wanted to be left alone, and he wanted to remain there in some sort of stasis.

He didn't want to die.

Neither did he want to live.

He just didn't want *this*.

But that's never an option, is it?

Somewhere out there, he heard a voice. It was low. A man's voice. A mumble. But there is something about voices that carries a special weight in the human ear, and even through the rain and the rotors Lee heard it.

No, it's never an option.

They were coming.

And everything else fell away.

The facts came at him single-file.

They were coming for him. That's what this had always been about. When they got there, they were going to kill him. That's what they wanted. They were never going to leave him alone. That much was obvious.

And then it all arrived at a simple choice.

He had two options: Either be done with all of this, and let them take him out…

Or fight.

He was tired of fighting. It seemed like he'd been fighting non-stop his entire life. And was that really who he was? Couldn't he ever try to be something else? Hadn't he earned himself a modicum of peace by now?

No.

Never.

And now they'd done this.

He looked at Julia's face. Her eyes were half open. The rainwater trickled into them. Sliding down. Slipping into her open lips. Her skin was the same temperature as everything else around them. Cold. Unliving. Just an object now.

Peace would have been nice.

It would have been nice with *her*.

Now it seemed like a stale and pointless prospect. Now peace seemed like a useless fantasy. It would never be as good as the small sliver of it that he'd managed to glean in the quiet moments of this ravaged world with her.

Someone on the outside might think that they'd taken away his only reason to fight.

But they hadn't.

They'd taken away his only reason to be at peace.

As he pulled his arms out from around her, and dragged himself to his feet, he left a bit of himself with her.

The good bit.

The human bit.

All that was left was death.

***

"McNair, I got something over here," a transmission sounded.

McNair kept scanning the woods as he eased his way through. "Yeah. What'cha got?"

"I got a dead chick over here," his operative said. "Right next to the runoff pond. But she's got two sets of armor next to her. Good bit of scuffled leaves. Looks like there was someone with her..."

McNair couldn't tell whether his operative had just trailed off. He waited for the man to continue. When he didn't, he frowned and keyed the radio. "I copy, you got a dead female with two sets of armor next to her and it looks like there was someone else there. You got anything else?"

He released the PTT.

Waited.

He looked across at Prince, who looked back at him. He couldn't see the man's expression behind the NVGs he wore, but McNair imagined he looked quizzical.

A series of rapid *pops* perforated the stillness.

Pistol shots.

It only took McNair a fraction of a second to picture why his operative would be firing his pistol and not his rifle: An image shot through his mind of his operative in a hand-to-hand struggle, the bad guy latched onto his rifle, and the operative being forced to draw and fire his secondary weapon...

McNair hit his PTT, but it made a negative *bloop* in his ear.

The sound it made when he tried to transmit while someone else was transmitting...

Then, over the line, he heard heavy breathing and scuffling.

"Shit, he's fighting someone!" McNair jolted forward, and ejected the gum from his mouth before he could choke on it. He almost tried to transmit again, but then remembered that he couldn't while there was an open mic.

***

One operative crumpled.

The other writhed against Lee.

Lee sank into some black place in his mind, where the very audacity of this creature in his grip to dare to fight back was an offense in and of itself. It made him ravenous to tear him apart.

Lee was on his side, on the ground. His left arm was locked under the operative's chin, his right hand clutching the man's PTT in a death grip, transmitting. His legs were wrapped around the man's waist, his right thigh blocking access to the man's sidearm, while Lee fired his own pistol and took down the man's comrade.

The operative managed to get his chin under the cord-like sinews of Lee's forearm.

Lee felt the operative's teeth clamp down, breaking fabric, then breaking skin.

Lee turned what wanted to be a scream of pain into a savage growl into the man's ear. He considered biting the man's ear off, but there wasn't time for that. He brought his own pistol around, his Glock 17 in his right hand.

The operative saw it coming, and tried to ward it off.

Lee slipped past the man's defending arm and jammed the pistol up under the man's helmet, muzzle to temple, and pulled the trigger. The blast was white and red. The body seized, and then was still.

He never let go of the man's PTT.

Lee gasped, searching for a moment of clarity, a return to logic...

He didn't have much time.

He swam over the dead body, still keeping that PTT locked down, because if he let them have the airwaves back, they'd be able to coordinate how to take him down. As long as the dead man's radio kept hogging the airwaves, Lee had reduced them from a team of operatives into a bunch of individuals.

Lee might not be able to kill a squad.

But he could kill several men in a row.

His mind was like a clash of fire and ice. Logic and rage.

The only thing that mattered in that moment was killing them all. It was his singular focus. He was possessed by it.

He huddled behind the dead body. It was no longer a man to Lee. It had become a sandbag. He searched the body for something he might use to lock the PTT down.

Zip cuffs.

Sticking out of the dead man's rear armor carrier. Lee snatched one up, finagled it one-handed, and got it around the PTT module. He ratcheted it down onto the button, hard, keeping it depressed.

Good. He had both hands now.

He took the dead man's rifle and plucked the QD sling attachment from it. When it was free, he rested it on the body's neck. It had an infrared laser aiming device. But for that, Lee would need NVGs.

The dead man wore NVGs. Attached to his helmet.

Communications equipment as well.

Lee unclipped the chin strap from the dead man's head, and inspected the interior. A 9mm bullet was lodged in the top of the helmet, along with a mass of brain tissue. Lee scooped the tissue out and wiped it on the forest floor, then sat the helmet on his head. Buckled the chin strap. Slightly tight, but it would work.

The NVGs were already lowered. Lee had to yank them about to get them positioned for his eyes, but then the world turned to crisp, glowing green. GPNVGs. Four-tubes. Good depth perception. Wide field of view.

The infrared laser at the end of the rifle became visible, shining in the mist and rain. Lee shut it off. He pulled the earcups of the communications headset over his own ears, though all that was transmitted at that moment was his own harsh breathing.

Then he settled behind his sandbag, and he waited.

"I'm here," he whispered, knowing full well they could hear him, since the boom mic was in front of his mouth. "I'm here."

***

There were a lot of things going through McNair's head in that moment.

He was running into an unknown. He wanted to take a moment to puzzle out what felt so wrong to him, but he felt like he was locked into this course of action.

He couldn't leave his guy to fight someone on his own.

But that voice on the radio had sounded strange to him.

Why would anyone say that? What did it have to do with anything?

Was this a trap?

Could McNair stop running and live with himself if it turned out *not* to be a trap? If he stood there while some maniac like Lee Harden gutted or strangled one of his team?

He didn't have the option to sit and consider it.

He had to jump into the fray. The lack of comms rendered him reactionary.

Plunging through the woods now, he'd lowered his NVGs.

Far off to the right, he glimpsed the flash of two infrared laser designators that marked two other members of his team moving in. They were ahead of him by maybe fifty yards, which was close to maximum visibility in this forest.

They'd heard the same thing, and thought the same thing: They had to get there.

This is wrong.

He abruptly knew it, and wanted to tell them to stop, so he could tell the helos to wipe that area of the forest out—nevermind photos of Lee's dead face, McNair would rather his team not die—but he couldn't transmit because the channel was being held open.

"STOP!" he shouted. "DON'T GO IN THERE!"

But the little points of green laser light that marked his teammates continued bobbing through the forest.

And then he heard suppressed gunfire.

***

Lee targeted the first point of light he saw.

He flipped on his own infrared laser at the last second and it stabbed back into the darkness, painting his target. There was a brief moment when Lee saw the man through the brush, and he knew that the man realized what was happening, and he tried to dive for cover, but then Lee stitched him with a three-round burst, from pelvis to shoulder.

The man went down. Lee followed him to the ground, aware that there was a second operative to deal with, but Lee didn't want to leave any of them only wounded. He wanted them all dead.

The first body hit the ground, and tried to roll for cover, but Lee sent a scattering of rounds after his head, and one of those found the exposed face between the chest armor and the helmet, and the body went slack.

Lee transitioned to the left, sighting for the second operative.

Incoming rounds stitched his dead-man-turned-sandbag. He pivoted his body more into cover behind the sandbag's armor, but something got by and bit the back of his leg.

He gritted his teeth and fired on automatic.

The operative dove behind the cover of a tree. Lee couldn't tell if he hit him or not. But it gave him a moment to pull himself tighter into the cover of his sandbag.

Further into the woods, two more points of laser light became visible, and then two more, far off to Lee's left. Five targets, and Lee's protective angles were dwindling. He acknowledge this with a lack of concern. If he died, that wasn't the worst thing, really.

He hugged the dead body in front of him, and switched off his own laser designator, since it only told the man behind the tree where he was aiming. Then he waited, and it might've only been for a second, but he ticked away the fractions of it like they were minutes...

The operative leaned out from behind the tree.

Two rounds incoming, very close to Lee's face.

But the difference was that the operative cared about staying alive, and Lee didn't. So he held his aim while those two bullets slapped his sandbag—one penetrating and skimming a path of open flesh across Lee's shoulder—and then he fired another burst. He saw sparks as his rounds hit the other operative's weapon.

He didn't know what happened to that man. It didn't matter. The man fell back and released his weapon and started writhing on the ground.

Two laser designators ahead of him, maybe fifty yards.

And two more coming in hot to his left, maybe thirty yards.

Lee pivoted his rifle to the more immediate threat and fired again, but felt the bolt lock back.

Dammit.

He grabbed another mag from the pouches on his sandbag's chest rig and swapped them, only peripherally aware of the sticky coat of blood on the back of his leg and on his shoulder.

They were on him.

Fine.

Lee ripped the helmet and NVGs from his head. Pointed the rifle in their general direction and let them have a burst. Then he left the rifle, with the designator still aimed towards them, and rolled over to his own rifle where it lay beside Julia.

He came up on one knee, partially obscured by a copse of brush.

The others were still moving.

It was only that fact that let him see them in the near-blackness.

They were trying to scoot away from the beam of the laser designator on the rifle he'd just left behind, thinking that was where he was aiming.

Lee fired, savagely intent as he watched the rounds strike bodies, and kept shooting them until they were on the ground. He fired until his rifle went empty again, and then he dropped to the ground and slithered back up to his sandbag.

He wasn't sure if he'd gotten both of the threats to his left, but they weren't shooting at him anymore.

He heard someone yelling. An old, battlefield sound that was nearly extinct in the age of squad communications. A commander trying to be heard by his men. Lee couldn't tell what he said, but it reminded him that he'd locked down the airwaves.

He reached over and slipped the zip cuff off of the PTT button, and then he snatched up the helmet again and crammed it down over his own head. It was haphazard, and the NVGs weren't lined up, and only one of the earcups for the communications was over his ear, but he could hear.

He wanted to hear what they were going to say.

It seemed to take them a few seconds to realize that the airwaves weren't blocked anymore.

Then, whoever it was transmitted: "Pull back! Pull back right now! Nordic One and Two! Nordic One and Two! Get in position to blow the northwestern side of these woods! I'll give my mark when we're clear!"

Whoever it was didn't know that there was no one but himself and his buddy to pull back. But he'd piece it together soon enough.

The Apaches roared, and Lee heard them shift around, angling for their shots.

He needed to leave.

He didn't want to.

He hadn't intended to let them have Julia's body.

But with just the half of one of the NVG screens in front of his left eye, he saw the laser designators of the two remaining operatives, and they were running away.

They were sprinting for safety, and it seemed absurdly unfair.

That they should have any place in the world that was safe for them.

Lee had no place left in the world. They'd taken that away.

They didn't get to do that.

They'd created this.

They'd sown the wind, and they were going to reap the storm.

TWENTY-SIX

LIVE OR DIE

MCNAIR RAN as far as he could, but he didn't dare let Lee Harden have too much time. The second he got far enough that he thought he wouldn't get shrapnel up his ass, he keyed his radio and yelled, "Nordic, hit it! Light that fucker up!"

The chain guns rattled, and the sound of their reports reached McNair at almost the same moment as the crash of their impacts, the screech of rockets, the blast of high explosives, and the shattering of trees.

He didn't stop running.

He saw the woods around him strobe and glow, not hot and red like firelight, but cold and white, like flashes of thunder.

The two gunships soaked those woods with ordnance for nearly twenty seconds straight, and all the while McNair and Prince sprinted for the opening in the trees where their technical was parked.

The flashing of exploding ordnance began to fade behind them, the fury tapering out.

McNair saw the opening in the trees ahead. The side of the technicals.

He glanced to his right as he sucked wind and felt the lactic acid building up in his legs as they pumped.

Shit.

He'd left Prince behind.

He slowed his sprint, making sure he didn't plow head-long into a tree, and looked around behind him.

Nothing.

Woods.

Darkness.

Further back, smoke, creeping in low like a fog.

"Prince!" he transmitted. "Where you at, buddy?"

The gunships hovered out beyond sight, like angels of death waiting in the wings. Their guns were silent now, but the woods shook with the rumble of their rotors. Back in the darkness, like pinpoints of starlight, small fires burned.

"Prince!" McNair's heart inched up his throat with each beat. He brought his rifle up to a low-ready, his eyes over the top of the optic, darting back and forth through the darkness. He began to backpedal. "Prince! Give me a holler!"

The fires in the distance twinkled.

No...

Something dark had passed in front of them.

A shadow, slipping from right to left.

McNair slapped his NVGs back over his eyes. The laser designator at the end of his rifle splashed through the woods, tracking the shadowy figure, now no longer a shadow, but a pale wraith, slipping through the trees...

A muzzle flash.

McNair held his breath.

Something walloped him in the chest.

The breath left him in a bark of panic.

He was rocked onto his heels, stumbling. He caught his feet and dove off to the side, behind the only point of cover he had—an emaciated pine tree, no more than a foot wide.

He coughed, cursed, and looked down at his chest.

The round had hit his armor, but as he looked down his chin rubbed against the strap of his helmet and smarted. He touched it and winced, feeling a few puckered slashes in his skin. Damn spall had bit him.

"McNair," one of the gunships transmitted. "You good down there? We don't have visual through the trees."

"Fuck no! He's on me!"

"Can you direct our fire?"

A scattering of gunshots chewed up the side of the tree. One of them split through and sliced his right tricep. McNair yelped, then tucked in, but there just wasn't enough room behind this tree. He had to move.

"McNair, can you direct our fire?"

"NO!" he shouted at them. "He's too close! I'm gonna make a break for the pickup truck and I'll let you know when I get in. You got any ordnance left to roast these woods? You didn't get him last time. You didn't get the motherfucker!"

Some small part of McNair that had been much larger only moments ago, but which had shrunk so dramatically and in such a short amount of time, told him that perhaps he should attempt assaulting back at the man assaulting him.

The best defense is a good offense, after all.

But there's also something about having seven of your friends die in rapid succession, and knowing that they were all at the hands of a single maniac, and that he was coming for you next.

It muddled McNair's thinking.

It didn't feel like there was just a man in the woods that he might shoot it out with.

It felt like something had slipped out of hell, and all McNair wanted to do was get away from it.

He knew he was breathing harder than he should have—*hyperventilating*—but he gulped those shallow breaths in, stacking air on top of air, and then he rolled and blind fired over his shoulder and then straggled to his feet and ran just like you'd expect a man to run when the hounds of hell were after him.

***

Lee watched him go with malice in his eyes.

He was rendered unrecognizable. Soot and blood had mixed to mud and masked his natural flesh, and all humanity had been stricken from his eyes.

His back was scorched, some hair was burned.

His lungs were ragged and he tasted blood.

More shrapnel had found him, tattooed its way up his already-wounded thigh, some in his shoulder and back.

The pain only drove him into darker depths.

He ripped his way from behind the brush that he hid behind, his eyes still locked on the back of the man running from him, and he tore after that man with an animal cry that no part of his normal self would recognize, but his normal self was not present.

He'd finally laid that ragged and war-worn piece of him aside.

The trees cleared.

Ahead was a technical.

The man slammed into it. Ripped the door open.

The gunships circled overhead.

They wouldn't fire, Lee was too close.

The man spun in the seat, his rifle tangled with the steering wheel.

Lee wanted to empty his magazine into the man's face. But no. He couldn't shoot the man. If the gunships saw their man die, they'd open fire on Lee.

The man's eyes were wide, his mouth open.

He abandoned trying to get his rifle around, as Lee loped across the distance between them. The man's hand went down to his side, to his pistol, but Lee speared him, hard, throwing the muzzle of his rifle right into the man's face like he was trying to put a bayonet through his brain.

Lee launched himself inside the cab as the man fell backward in a spurt of blood and teeth. His hand had seized on his pistol, pulling it from its holster as he backpedaled across the bench seat.

Lee abandoned his rifle—too big to use in this space—and he ratcheted both hands down around the man's wrist, keeping that pistol from pointing at him.

The man reacted with shocking speed. The second Lee was latched onto his wrist, he swept one of his legs up, over Lee's head, then straightened it against Lee's neck and chest, locking Lee into an arm bar.

The man's right hand, still trying to draw that pistol. His left hand clapped over Lee's forearms, keeping him there as his legs cinched up tight and he bucked his hips, arching his back so that Lee's arm was being bent backwards against the elbow.

It was going to break.

Lee felt the structure of it straining, the pain spiking.

Lee couldn't hold onto the man's wrist. He held on now only by his forefinger and middle finger. The last tips of those, sliding against sweat and dirt.

The man hauled hard at Lee, pulling with everything he head. A great groan of effort seethed past his bloody lips.

Lee was silent. His breath was coming in sharp, and then hissing out of his teeth. But he made no sound with his voice.

When it happened, it was too rapid for anyone to have known what had gone down in that scrum of grunting movement and grasping fingers.

Lee's fingers slipped.

As they slipped, the pistol rose out of its holster.

Focused on that, the man let the arm bar go.

And it all flowed rapidly from there.

Rather than pull from the man's grip, Lee plunged himself further into it, driving himself into the man's legs, and rolling him up into a ball that was squished against the passenger's side door.

The pistol searched for a spot where it could catch Lee in the brain without also catching the man in the leg.

Lee smashed himself down into the floorboards, because he knew which six inches he needed to gain, and taking this disadvantaged position gave him what he needed.

He was able to thrust his left arm forward just far enough around the man's midsection to grab a hold of the pistol, his palm over the slide.

Lee pressed the gun away from his head.

The gun cracked, deafening.

Lee felt splitting pain in his shoulder.

The slide of the pistol hadn't cycled—Lee's grip had kept it from chambering another round.

Lee released it.

The man aimed for his head again.

Lee didn't care—the gun was dead anyway.

With both arms free again, Lee jammed them under the crook of the man's knees and rammed him upward, rolling him until he was nearly upside down, his feet against the ceiling, and his head smashed up against the door.

The man screamed, looking for an open shot on Lee.

He didn't even realize his gun was dead.

Lee kept him pinned in that little ball with his left arm, and with his right he swept down and grabbed the only weaponry he had left—the knife on his belt. Then he rammed that into the man's lower back, below the armor plates, and the man's screams of effort turned to squeals.

Lee stabbed him again. And again. And then tracked towards his spine, where Lee felt the knife point strike the bone, and he pried at it, struck at it, ripped at it like an animal, until he felt the body go limp with paralysis or death, he didn't know which, and didn't care.

It didn't stop him. Nothing could stop him until he'd burned himself out.

And he went on and on. He screamed now, to fill the silence that the dead man left behind, and he screamed to fill a hole in him that was gouged far deeper than the wounds he was inflicting. He screamed to exhaust himself, to purge the blackness in him that couldn't ever be purged.

When the blood-slicked knife caught on a bone and came out of his grip, he pulled back and began kicking. Pummeling with his feet, his boots spattering mud and blood across the windows. Trying to get at the man's head, for reasons that he would never be able to articulate, beyond the fact that he was not himself in that moment.

He was not anybody, or anything.

He was just angry.

Exhaustion, and the cramping of his legs cooled him very suddenly.

He gasped for breath, and realized as he tried to get more air that he was sobbing, that his face was wet with blood from the man, blood from himself, and tears, and saliva that hung from his lips like a rabid dog.

Like a primal.

You're done.

You're done.

You're done...

The rotorwash outside.

The gunships, still watching.

He couldn't exit the truck. But they hadn't destroyed him yet, so they must not know that their man was dead inside. They'd only seen the two bodies get in, and probably could not differentiate between the scramble of heat signatures inside.

Lee looked out the windshield, spitting, coughing, gasping.

Rain slashed it, muddling his view of the outside world.

But he thought he knew where this truck was parked.

In the clearing through the woods. And at the end of it was the lake.

Trembling, bleeding from a dozen wounds, and just now beginning to feel them gnawing at his nerves, Lee felt for the first time since Julia had passed in his arms, a twinge of survival instinct.

The flesh always wants to live, even when the soul has had enough.

Lee figured it was a coin toss.

He figured he would let fate and the lake decide what to do with him.

He managed to close his bloody fingers around the pickup's shifter, and pulled it into drive. Then he let his foot fall on the accelerator, too exhausted to hold it up, too exhausted to press it down.

He would have to swim to live.

He would have to swim to the opposite bank.

Shrapnel in his back.

Gunshot wound to the shoulder.

A ragged hole in his hip.

And cramping all over from exertion.

The tires thrashed over the uneven ground.

Somewhere in the dim, rain-washed view ahead of him, he thought he saw a great dark expanse opening up for him.

He rolled his window down.

The rain slashed his face.

The sound of gunships, following.

The trees disappeared from around him.

Just black water now.

The lake, and fate, and a small chance.

The truck hit the water like it might strike a smaller car at high speed. The impact slammed Lee into the steering wheel, bludgeoning his brain, and nearly knocking him out.

The water flooded in and poured over him, and the coldness of it brought his mind back from the brink of unconsciousness.

Let it sink.

You have to get deeper, or the gunships will see you...

With his window open, it didn't take long.

Lee let it go, holding onto the steering wheel, riding it like a roller coaster to the bottom of the lake, however deep that was, perhaps deep enough. Or perhaps not. That was in the hands of fate, or the universe, or God, if any of them happened to be watching.

Maybe from the cold water, maybe from nerve damage, he couldn't feel his fingers.

He opened his eyes to the sting of cold water, and saw nothing.

He hadn't prepped his lungs for a big underwater swim either.

Oh well.

He felt around with his numb hands and when he thought he had them hooked into the window of the truck, he pulled, and he felt himself pass into open water, into nothingness, and in the darkness and the weightlessness, it might have been the vacuum of space.

He didn't know which way was up. He tried to decipher it. But when he pointed his head down, it looked just the same as when he pointed his head up, and he could not feel himself floating upwards or down.

I live or die right now.

He began to swim, not knowing if it was towards the surface.

The surface might kill him anyways, but the surface was where the chance lay: On the surface, he would probably get shot; in the deep, he would definitely drown.

He clawed, every stroke seeming like this would be the one where he would break the surface, but it wasn't.

His lungs burned. Began to seize.

He'd rarely addressed himself to a high power, but he did at that moment.

Not to beg for life.

He talked to God and told him, as plain and honest as he'd ever been, *If you save me, I'm going to kill a lot of people. So if you don't believe in that shit, you should probably just let me die.*

The darkness seemed to trap him now.

He wasn't going to break the surface, was he?

Live or die, right now.

Live or die...

TWENTY-SEVEN

FORT BRAGG

THE ALPHA HADN'T EATEN in four days.

It was ravenous. And so was the pack.

It had hunted all day, and into the night, but the prey was scarce. It clawed at the Alpha's mind that even though there were no prey in the woods, the easiest prey was most plentiful, only a short distance from them, just out of reach.

So close, that the wind would often carry their scent to the Alpha's nose.

Hunger and frustration had begun to take its toll.

The Alpha had led his pack back and forth, and back and forth. Into the woods, and then back to the place where the Easy Prey hid behind their clever defenses. And when they were back there, the Alpha would search manically along the thin sticks that hummed dangerously, looking for an opening.

Now, he went back to that again, out of sheer habit.

His irritable pack grumbled and snapped at each other behind him, and he picked up the pace, threading through the well-known woods, his face in the wind, huffing the scent of the Easy Prey, heading straight for them.

When they reached the Easy Prey, the white orb in the night sky sat staring at them through the trees, but it gave them light, even though the Alpha sometimes found it unsettling.

By the light of the orb, the Alpha could see the strands, like thick spider silk.

The Alpha strode up to them, grunting and sniffing.

Beyond the strands, a commotion was raging. The Easy Prey were making a surprising amount of noise. They were perturbed by something. Frightened by something. The Alpha could hear it in their voices, and smell it in their scent.

It excited him.

The Alpha turned a few quick circles, hooting to his packmates as they drew closer, and they got excited too. The hooting turned to barking, the noise from beyond whipping them into a terrible appetite.

When the excitement passed, the pack was quiet, waiting.

And in the quiet, between the bleating of the Easy Prey on the other side, the Alpha tilted its head, looking at the strands, the sticks that hummed dangerously.

Something was off.

They were not humming dangerously.

The Alpha had never actually touched the sticks that hummed. But he'd seen others do it, and they had died, smoking and shrieking. He had learned from that.

Now, decayed and reborn synapses in his brain began to fire again, re-priming themselves.

Cause and effect.

Extrapolation.

The sticks hummed dangerously.

They were dangerous when they hummed.

They were not humming.

Did that mean they were no longer dangerous?

Growling low in its throat, the Alpha stepped towards the sticks and slapped them with his hand.

They made a strange noise that made the Alpha tense, for a moment. But its hand was unhurt. The sticks were not humming dangerously. They were only vibrating noisily from his strike.

Bolder, the Alpha grabbed the sticks, and the cross-hatched structure of the wire wall that the not-so-dangerous sticks hung on.

Nothing. No pain.

No danger.

Beyond, the bleating of the Easy Prey made the Alpha's mouth salivate and spill over his chin.

It howled, long and loud, and its packmates howled with him.

Then it began to climb, and in the distance, the Alpha heard the many others howling back at him.

The Alpha had found all the prey they would need.

And the others were coming to feed.

***

"Are they fucking insane?" Peter hissed, peeking out the window, his fingers pulling the blinds away just far enough for him to see out. "They're gonna call every goddamned primal in the state to us with all that racket!"

Elsie crossed to the window with her stomach churning. She leaned into Peter to get a view out the window. His sweat smelled stale and stressful.

Beyond the blinds, she saw the street, and some of the neighbors' houses, and the neighbors coming out onto their steps, confusion in their postures. Concern. Fear.

Still out of view, down the street, she heard a soldier on a loudspeaker: "The Blackout Plan has been activated. Please gather each member of your family and proceed to the pre-planned rally area. This is not a drill. Please comply immediately."

It was a script, and he began to read it again, from the top, as he'd been doing nonstop, as whatever vehicle he stood in rolled down the neighborhood streets with excruciating slowness.

Elsie pulled away from the window, enraged to her core. "I can't believe Angela would do this. I can't believe she would stoop this low. She could've prevented all this if she'd just been willing to talk! But instead she's going to let people die!" Elsie looked back at Peter, and then at Claire who stood beside her. "People are going to die because of this!"

"Elsie," Peter said. "If we don't get out of here, we're going to die too."

"Not yet," Elsie snapped. "It's not over yet." She held up her satphone.

Claire nodded. "Call them," she said. "Get them involved."

Elsie began dialing. It was still early, but maybe Greeley's forces would be ready to move into action. And the Fort Bragg Safe Zone had never been riper for the picking.

***

Carl and his team drove right behind the pickup truck with the soldier in the back, hollering over his bullhorn. Carl had heard the announcement repeated so many times now, it wasn't even words to him—just squawking.

Carl was focused outward. First to the right, and then to the left.

Each side of the street. The houses.

Doors opening, civilians coming out.

Soldiers on the ground, walking alongside the two pickup trucks, addressed the worried civilians that approached them, always saying the same thing: Just take your family, don't bother taking your things, you need to get to the rally point immediately.

The houses were emptying out. Most people weren't waiting to speak to the soldiers. Everyone in the Fort Bragg Safe Zone was familiar with the Blackout Plan, and it was based on everyone getting their asses to a safe location *immediately*.

Everyone knew what a blackout meant.

No high voltage fences.

No protection from primals.

So as the trucks and their escort on foot made their way down the neighborhood streets—a scene playing out in all the neighborhoods in the Fort Bragg Safe Zone—the people streamed out of their houses and scuttled down the streets in an ever-thickening river of humanity, flowing before the soldiers, like sheep before the herders.

Except, not everyone was going to leave their houses, were they?

No, not if you were hiding from the military.

Not if you were Elsie and her Lincolnists.

The street they were on curved up ahead. In the stark light of the pickups' headlamps piercing the absolute blackness of the powerless night, adults towed children in firm grips, and everyone hurried, but they didn't run.

There was still a dazedness to their movements, like they couldn't quite believe it was happening. Which Carl found extraordinary, because couldn't they just remember back to the last time they felt this way? When society fell apart and the streets were swamped with infected, attacking everyone and everything they saw?

Why is it that people never learned?

From the driver's seat, Morrow leaned forward and pointed up to the right, towards another dark house front. "That one." He pulled his rifle from between his knees and rested the muzzle on the dashboard and hit the house he was referring to with a visible laser. "No one came out."

Carl nodded and turned out of his passenger side window. "Corporal Billings," he called, and the soldier that was walking on the side of Carl's pickup looked over. Carl gestured to the house that Morrow was still designating. "Check that one there."

***

Sam Ryder was just a few paces behind Billings, and he heard Master Sergeant Gilliard speak, and saw the laser flitter over one of the houses.

Billings looked over his shoulder at Sam, and then to the rest of his guys, who walked in file behind Sam.

"Squad!" Billings barked. "On me!"

Billings turned and pulled his rifle into his shoulder and started stalking towards the house in question. Sam followed at a jog. He glanced behind him, and saw Jones and Chris following close behind.

They were halfway up the lawn when the door opened.

Billings stopped, rifle snugged into his shoulder with one hand, the other waving at a man that froze in the front door and raised his hands, his eyes wide with shock. "Come on out!" Billings yelled. "Come out of the house, and kneel down!"

The man started forward on stilted legs. "I don't...you just told me to come out of the house?" he seemed confused.

Sam angled around Billings, pulling his rifle up as well and scanning across the front door, where two other faces appeared: a woman and a teenage girl, not much younger than Sam himself.

"On your knees!" Billings shouted at the man, louder because his commands were not being obeyed.

The woman and the girl at the door cowered back, then saw Sam.

Sam motioned them forward, and he tried to look reassuring, but he guessed that he wasn't, because he was pointing a rifle at them. "Billings, I don't think these are the people..."

Jones gave Sam a sharp elbow as he slipped around him. "Shut the fuck up, Ryder!" Jones pointed his rifle at the man and jerked it towards the lawn. "Go on now. Get going."

The man knelt, right in front of Billings.

The woman and the girl edged their way out of the front door, complying with Sam's gestures to come out.

"There anyone else in there?" Billings demanded of the man.

"I...No. It's just us! The other family already got out!"

Billings didn't take his eyes or his rifle off of the man. "Ryder! Jones! Clear the residence."

"Corporal," Sam began to protest.

"Clear that goddamn building or I'm gonna kneecap you, you insubordinate fuck!"

Sam looked to Jones and found the other man smiling at him as he started towards the door. "Jesus, Ryder. Why don't you stop trying to think so much? That's what people with stripes are for."

***

"They're sending troops into the houses," Peter said, his voice low and quavering with worry.

"Every house?" Claire asked.

"I don't think so. But if we don't send people out of this house, then they're gonna send troops in, I think. That's what they're doing. They're trying to flush us out."

Elsie stared at the satphone in her hand, the line now dead.

"Elsie, did you hear me?" Peter whined.

Elsie squinted at him. "What?"

Peter's face blanched when he saw the expression on Elsie's. "What's wrong? What did they say?"

Elsie stared at him for a moment, stumbling through an overgrown forest of thoughts. "They're nearby. They'll be ready in a moment."

But that wasn't what the forces from Greeley had said.

What they'd said was that they were waiting to engage until the "situation clarifies."

Cutting through the crap-cake, Elsie translated: "We're not going to commit the troops until it looks like victory is certain."

They were going to sit around and wait to see how everything played out.

The officer on the other end of the line, who was, presumably, somewhere nearby, had wished her *good luck*.

Good luck?

No such thing.

Elsie Foster made her own luck.

She snapped the satphone's antenna closed. Then straightened herself up. "Who here has never been interrogated about being a Lincolnist?"

Hands went up, tentatively at first, as though they weren't sure whether they were supposed to step forward, sound off, or simply raise their hands.

Elsie nodded. "Those of you who raised your hands are going to exit this building and join the crowds moving towards the shelters. That should give the rest of us time—make Carl and his troops believe this house had been evacuated." Then she looked at Peter. "The rest of us should load up. Just in case."

***

Sam stepped out of the house.

It'd been empty, just as the family claimed.

On the patch of weedy dirt that passed for a lawn, Billings and Chris still held the cowering family at rifle point. Billings looked up at Sam and Jones as they hustled down the front steps.

Sam decided to keep his mouth shut. He'd said enough.

Jones shook his head at Billings. "House is empty. All clear."

Billings stepped away from the people, and ported his rifle. "Sorry about the mix up, folks. Y'all better get going."

The family didn't say a word to that. They just got up and shuffled away, joining the rest of the people moving down the street, moving towards the center of Fort Bragg, like blood retreating back to the vital organs.

On the street, the soldier in the back of the pickup truck, issuing the announcement, was just abreast of them. Behind that truck was the truck bearing Carl and his team of operatives. Carl looked at Billings, who shook his head at them and moved to rejoin the other soldiers on the street.

Jones pushed passed Sam with a grumble that Sam couldn't make out over the rambling loudspeaker.

Sam looked down the street, in the direction that everyone headed.

It's odd how sometimes you can pick someone out of a crowd, just by the way they walk. You don't even have to see their face. You just see their frame, and their gait, and you know who it is.

But she did raise her face up, after he'd already identified her. She looked up, as though she knew that he was watching her. Her eyes locked right onto his as she hustled herself off the driveway of a house.

Charlie.

She looked away.

Sam did not.

He stared at her. Frowning.

This wasn't her neighborhood.

Those people with her weren't her housemates.

Sam's heart had begun to thud inside of him.

Something in his brain was getting close to connecting, and he wanted to make that connection, but simultaneously dreaded it.

"Ryder! You coming?" Billings shouted at him.

Who had told Elsie Foster about the colony of primals?

It could've been any of the guys in Billings's detachment. And rumors spread fast. Even when they weren't supposed to be talked about. Maybe even *especially* when they weren't supposed to be talked about.

But suddenly, Sam knew.

Felt like an idiot for *not* knowing.

The incessant questions. The group of people meeting outside the Fort Bragg perimeter. The secret meetings with Claire Staley.

Shit!

It all came together.

You stupid fucking idiot! He swore at himself.

That backstabbing little bitch! He swore at her.

"Hey!" he bellowed.

He watched her shoulders jerk at the sound of his voice. She'd been listening for it, tense and waiting. There was no other way she could have picked it out over the loudspeaker.

What was he going to do? Was he going to out her?

Would she be killed?

Would *he* kill her?

"Ryder, what the fuck're you doing?" Billings sounded on the edge of doing that knee-capping.

Sam watched the back of Charlie's head for another second, before he whirled around. He looked right past Billings to Master Sergeant Gilliard, who scowled at Sam.

Sam almost pointed at the house that Charlie had been walking away from, but stopped himself.

Be smart. Be smart FOR ONCE.

Sam sprinted for the side of the truck, his eyes jagging to his right, and every time they did, it took a little longer to reacquire where Charlie was in the crowd.

He slammed into the side of the pickup. "Sir! I know where Elsie Foster is!"

"Oh Lord," Billings said, clearly not believing him.

"Ryder," Jones hissed at him. "Shut the fuck up, bro!"

Carl's eyes shot Sam up and down. "Where?"

Sam nodded, discreetly. "That house. I can show you."

"How do you know?"

"I saw someone come out of it. A Lincolnist."

"Who was it?"

426

Sam's mouth worked with a silent syllable. And then: "I don't know their name. I just know they're a Lincolnist. I'll show you the house."

***

Charlie walked with her shoulders up, and her head down, and her sweatshirt hood pulled up.

He'd seen her.

She *knew* he'd seen her.

She'd heard his shout but she'd kept on walking, and he hadn't shouted again. Was he running after her? Was he going to grab her by the arm in a moment?

What was she going to do if that happened?

Fight him?

Surrender?

Her eyes were fixed in front of her, on the ground. The pavement. The heels of the man just ahead of her—another Lincolnist, trying to blend in with all the sheep.

A flash of rapid movement.

She snapped her eyes to it, feeling all of her insides tighten and rise towards her throat. A fleshy scramble of limbs. An inhuman snarl.

It all happened so quickly that Charlie didn't know what to do.

One of the evacuees went down, right on the sidewalk. A man. Screaming.

She knew what she was looking at, but she didn't have a framework to put it into, didn't have a plan of action, other than to do what everyone else did, to be a part of the herd and hope that there really was safety in numbers.

Her feet did a panicked dance on the concrete.

For a moment, that man's shocked scream was all that anybody could hear.

And then all at once, everyone was screaming. Everyone was moving. Surging. Away from the attack, away from the two houses, between which multiple shadows emerged, rapid and wraithlike in the gloom.

She let out a mewl of terror, and spun—right into Sam.

Sam, with a look on his face like she'd never seen before.

Sam seized her with his left arm and dragged her behind him, while he fired his rifle with his right—two rapid bursts of rounds. The rounds struck a primal that had been one small leap from sinking its teeth into Charlie's jugular.

It tumbled to the ground, but kept coming, kept gnashing its teeth until another flurry of rifle shots from Sam knocked those teeth back into its brain and it lay dead.

The people were screaming, and their feet made the noise of a stampede, and the primals were howling, and dragging the wounded back into the shadows.

Sam spun around, and his face was not the face of a saving angel. His eyes were like coals of fire and his teeth were bared, and his grip on her arm felt like it might crush her bones.

"You get the fuck out of here!" he growled at her, not sounding like Sam Ryder at all, but some stranger that had suddenly grown out of him. "I don't wanna see you again!"

He gave her a shove, and she almost lost her feet, but then recovered them and began running, her chest barely drawing air through the racking sobs that shook her.

Behind her—she didn't see it—but Sam Ryder planted his feet in the middle of the street, at the end of a driveway, and he activated the flashlight at the end of his rifle, and he blazed the beam across the front of one of the houses.

Marking it.

***

Elsie watched it happen.

"Shoot that little prick!" she snapped, and started scrambling for a gun, while the people around her chose windows and raised their weapons, all the while the light flashing against the drawn shades, like a neon sign:

They're here! They're here!

***

Carl saw and evaluated many things at once.

Primals attacking.

People running.

Sam, strobing the front of the target house.

A flicker in the blinds of that house.

Carl was already out of the truck. He swung himself onto the concrete and snapped his rifle up, scanning first to his right—towards the open street where the primals were coming from—then back to the left, towards the house.

Sam, still standing there, strobing it.

Definite movement in the windows.

"Ryder!" Carl bellowed. "Move!"

Carl was already starting to stride forward, the pickup was stopped, and he was twenty yards from the house, he and his team could form up on the side of the residence where there weren't many windows and breach through the back...

The windows shattered.

Muzzle flashes poked through.

Bullets pocked the concrete around Sam. He spun, then sprinted for the cover of the neighbor's house.

Carl turned his rifle and unloaded one long string of fire at the front of the house, tracing it from one side of the window to the other, watching siding and wood and glass come off of it in clouds.

He registered movement in the upstairs windows.

He pulled his finger off the trigger and ducked, just as those windows shattered and bullets struck the hood of the pickup.

Carl went into a crouch, teeth gritted, shoulders hunched. His team tumbled out of the truck, Morrow and Rudy tearing around the driver's side, and Mitch and Logan already taking cover on the passenger's, giving the other two covering fire.

They were pinned down by gunfire on one side, and primals on the other.

"Mitch!" Carl yelled. "Blow the motherfucker!"

Mitch had hit the ground near the rear axle. He looked up at Carl, just as a round smacked the pavement under the car. The concrete exploded, the puff of dust rocketing straight into Mitch's face.

He pulled backward and yelped, his hands going to his face.

Morrow rounded the back of the pickup truck, scrabbling into the space already occupied by Mitch and Logan, while Rudy duckwalked to where Carl crouched.

From the shadows across from them on their exposed side, Carl saw shapes flitting between the houses.

"Primals!" he called out. "On our backside!"

The deluge of gunfire coming from the enemy house continued to chew the truck to ribbons.

Carl's mind bounced back and forth to all the imperatives.

He glanced back towards Ryder, but couldn't see him anymore.

Goddamn idiot half-boot, standing in the middle of the street like that! What had he been thinking? What on earth had possessed him to run off in the middle of all of this anyways?

Carl snapped back to Mitch. "Mitch! Are you okay?"

"Yeah!" Mitch shouted back, but didn't sound completely sure.

"Can you see?"

"Kind of." Mitch pulled his hands away from his face, revealing half of it bleeding from a series of fine cuts and bits of gravel that had embedded just under his skin. His left eye was squinted shut and looked like it was bleeding.

"Can you blow that house?"

Mitch nodded. But his launcher was still in the truck. Hopefully not shot to shit. He'd bailed out with just his rifle. "Y'all give me some cover and let me get the launcher!"

Carl nodded. "Covering!"

He didn't wait. He bent into an awkward shooting position so that he was aiming at the house from around the front tire and under the front bumper. He let out quick bursts of three-to-five rounds. Focusing on the windows. The bottom window. The top window. Back and forth.

Behind him, he heard the others firing, too.

And then, roughly at the same time, they ran out of ammo.

Logan was the only one still firing.

Three of them shouted, "Reloading!" one after the other, ducking back into cover and swiping at their extra mags.

Mitch yanked the launcher out of the back seat and brought it up, aiming through the open doors of the cab.

Carl slammed a new mag into his rifle, saw movement dead ahead and rocked the rifle into his shoulder pocket as he sent the bolt home on a new round. He fired a burst, and the shape hurtling towards them puffed red, but didn't stop coming.

Carl kept firing, having to swing his rifle towards his teammates to track with the beast, and pulled his finger off the trigger just as the primal slammed into Rudy, crunching him against the side of the truck with a sound like a car crash.

Morrow reacted the second he was aware that Carl had ceased firing.

Rudy delivered vicious elbows to the primal's face while the inhumanly strong arms wrapped him up like a constrictor, the blows to the face the only thing keeping it from sinking its jaws into his neck.

Morrow rolled out, away from the truck, landing hard on his left side and sweeping his rifle up for the only bit of flesh he could find on the primal that wouldn't lead to Rudy being shot too, and he pumped five rapid-fire rounds into the things pelvis, breaking the bone structure, and causing it to lurch backwards off of Rudy.

Rudy spun with a cry and rammed the butt of his rifle into the stumbling primal's jaw, causing it to lurch sideways as it tried to force its crushed pelvis to support it. When he had the arm's length of movement, Rudy brought his rifle up and shattered its head.

Carl scanned. The street was clear. The houses beyond showed no movement.

They couldn't keep doing this.

They needed to get out of there, now.

"Hit it, Mitch!" Carl yelled.

But Mitch was already moving again. He'd been knocked out of his sights by the primal attack, but now edged back into position, sighting through the open back door of the pickup, between the two front seats, and out the open driver's side door, to the house beyond.

He fired his launcher with a heavy *ka-thump!*

At the same moment, a round zipped his collar.

Carl watched the cloth open up, and the blood spray off of him.

Mitch winced and jerked, but then came right back into his aim, his teeth grit, as though a bullet to the neck was something that only made him more angry.

His first round splashed, obliterating the second-floor window in a flash of fire and smoke.

He started firing as fast as the launcher could spin its cylinder.

Carl watched the blood spurting out of his neck.

The last four rounds went out.

The last four explosions rocked the house on the other side, and in the ringing stillness afterwards, there was no more incoming fire.

A quick look down the street revealed that the people had left, and the primals had gone with them, like a pack of hyenas chasing a herd of prey, picking off the slow and the weak.

Back to his team.

Mitch waggled around.

The anger had gone out of his eyes.

He looked scared. His bright red blood pulsed onto the side of the pickup, and across his hands, which were going to his neck to provide pressure.

"Get him in the truck!" Carl shouted. "Patch him! We gotta move, now! Morrow! Drive!"

Morrow hauled ass back to the driver's seat.

Carl and Rudy pulled Mitch into the back, Carl going into the truck first and backing across the seat, pulling Mitch up with him as he went. Logan stayed outside, covering them. Mitch made groaning noises, but Carl didn't think they sounded wet, or gagging.

At least it hadn't punched his windpipe.

Though the clip to the carotid was a huge problem.

Carl pulled Mitch's head into his lap and turned it so he could see the wound. The dome lights in the car were, somehow, still lit, and Carl evaluated the wound by the dim light.

Morrow slung himself into the driver's seat.

Logan hauled himself into the truck bed and slapped the side.

The second Rudy's feet cleared the pavement, he yelled, "I'm in! Move!"

The pickup lurched forward, all the doors closing on their own.

The truck still worked—miraculously—but for how long was anyone's guess. Hopefully enough to get them to the rally point.

Carl made eye-contact with Mitch. The man's eyes were wide and worried. And Carl didn't blame him. A shot to the throat induced panic like almost no other wound. "You're gonna have to stick your finger in it, okay?"

Mitch nodded, once, and his left hand came up, the index finger protruding.

Carl guided him to the hole in his neck.

He inserted Mitch's own finger into his neck

Mitch screamed behind clenched teeth, and kicked out with his legs, hitting Rudy, but Rudy didn't seem to mind, and kept calling encouragement to Mitch as he fended the boots off his chest.

Carl took one last look over his shoulder to see if there were any other troops in the vicinity, but this section of the neighborhood had turned into a ghost town. Elsie Foster's hideout poured smoke, and the dancing flames at the front of the structure were the only thing that moved.

Had they got her?

He couldn't say for certain.

At the moment, it didn't matter.

"Get us to the rally point," Carl said to Morrow. "I got a feeling this might turn into an evacuation."

TWENTY-EIGHT

DOWNHILL

OUT IN THE NIGHT a person screamed.

Out in the night a primal howled, and was answered by many more.

Sam Ryder watched the bullet-riddled pickup truck bearing Carl and his operatives tear around the curve of the neighborhood street.

"Motherfuckers," Billings whispered over Sam's shoulder.

"They didn't see us," Sam said, and pulled himself back in and shut the door as best he could, seeing as how there was no longer a door jam to latch to after they'd kicked it in.

"Yeah, no shit they didn't," Billings mumbled.

From the back of the house, Jones and Chris were yelling at each other.

"Fuck! That hurts!" Chris yelped.

"It's supposed to hurt! Quit moving!" Jones responded.

Chris had taken a round to the leg. Jones was applying a tourniquet for him.

There was a brief sound of scuffling.

"Don't you fucking hit me!" Jones seethed. "I'm tryna help you!"

Billings stalked into the kitchen where Chris lay against the back door, Jones kneeling over him. "Both of you shut the fuck up! You want the primals to hear us?"

Jones said something back, slightly quieter, but Sam didn't hear it. His attention had been drawn to a flash of movement in the darkness outside, lit only by the flicker of the fires burning in the house where Elsie Foster had been hiding.

"Hey. Corporal."

Billings looked at him, irritated. "What?"

Sam moved towards the kitchen window, pointing. "Look."

Staggering out of the back of the grenade-demolished house were three figures.

"Did they just come out of that?" Billings marveled.

Sam nodded.

It looked like a man and two women.

Sam didn't recognize the man, but he recognized the two women, although just barely. Their faces were covered in soot and blood. But he knew them well.

Claire Staley and Elsie Foster.

Something lit up in Sam's mind. It started between his temples, surged through his chest, and took control of his face. Gentle and kind and baby-faced Sam. His lips turned down. His teeth showed. It seemed like the child melted off of him in an instant.

The three figures staggered across the space between the ruined house and the next street over. Rifles in hand. Scanning around for primals.

Sam charged for the back door.

Jones held up a hand, but Sam simply reached over him and grabbed the doorknob. "Get outta the fuckin' way," Sam growled, in a voice he didn't even recognize as his own.

"Alright. Geez." Jones rolled out of the way and grabbed his rifle from where he'd leaned it against a counter. "Wait up."

But Sam wasn't waiting up.

He ripped the door open, even as Billings raised his voice, telling Sam to slow down.

The sound of Billings's voice made the three escapees turn towards him.

Sam erupted out of the house, his rifle raised to his shoulder. "Get on the fuckin' ground!" he shouted at them. "On the ground, now!"

Elsie Foster bolted.

Claire Staley and the man started shooting.

Sam juked sideways, firing off a clamor of rounds as he did. He heard the incoming rounds moaning as they passed close to him. Even over the slamming of the rifle reports, he could hear them thudding against the wall of the house behind him.

He looked for cover, but there wasn't any.

Stand and fight!

Sam skidded to a stop. If he'd caught a round after stopping, that would have made him stupid. But he didn't. And so he looked fearless. And in a way, he was. He wasn't thinking. He wasn't weighing consequence. And so he was a bit of both—fearless and stupid.

Claire and the unknown man were still firing at him when he stopped.

Their rounds tracking him...

A fusillade burst from the kitchen door of the house Sam had just come out of—Billings and Jones joining in, although their aim was wonky as hell, because even at twenty-five yards they didn't hit shit.

Claire and the man turned and ran.

Sam fired at them, lava in his gut, spurring him to give chase.

His rifle locked back on an empty magazine.

Sam screamed swears, and took off after them, yanking a spare magazine from its pouch and replacing the empty one in his rifle. He had the presence of mind to yell, "Crossing!" as he ran in front of Billings and Jones's line of fire.

He heard them yelling at him, but didn't hear what they had to say.

He was all forward motion now.

Claire and the man were getting away.

They were running for another house, nearly around the front corner of it.

They were going to hold there and try to ambush him as he came around.

Sam, heaving air and growling like a savage, peeled to the left, to the other side of the house. They thought they were going to waylay him when he came around that corner.

They were mistaken.

For a flash he imagined himself coming around the opposite corner of the house, behind them. He saw their backs. And he didn't hesitate. He didn't give warning. He just pumped rounds into their backs until they stopped twitching.

He didn't care that it wasn't right.

These people had to see.

That they shouldn't have fucked with him. That they shouldn't have fucked with his family, with his little sister—even if she wasn't really his blood.

That he wasn't weak. That he wasn't stupid.

That he could be just as downright savage as the rest of them, and God help you if you pushed him to it.

He came around the front of the house.

No one.

"Ryder! You fuck!" Billings screamed at him from somewhere in the backyard.

Sam wasn't listening. Didn't care.

The front door. It hung open, just an inch.

Sam ran for it.

When he kicked the door open, he saw two things.

He saw a man on the stairs, pointing a rifle at him, bleeding from the leg.

He saw a pair of feet, disappearing from the top landing into the second floor.

The man on the stairs fired.

Sam took the round with a grunt like he'd been punched. His chest plate stopped it. And then he fired back and slammed five rounds square in the center of that man's chest.

And all the while he watched the man's eyes, because they were wide with shock, and in Sam's burning heart, that felt good. That felt righteous. The man had underestimated him. And he had paid the price.

They had *all* underestimated him.

Well, fuck 'em.

The man wilted on the stairs, pouring blood.

Sam charged forward, his aching chest struggling for breath past his bruised sternum. He kicked the rifle out of the man's dying hands with something like happiness, and shot the man in the top of the head as he sprinted passed, making sure that he would never get up.

Up the stairs. He paused only once he reached the landing.

He spun, bringing his rifle up, expecting someone to be there.

His tactics sucked—he knew it.

But no one was there. If they had been, he would be dead.

His breath ripping in and out of his dry throat, Sam sidestepped his way across the landing, gun up, chest aching, muscles beginning to burn, heart thumping like the steady rhythm of an automatic grenade launcher.

He decided that it was best not to slow down.

He didn't know if that was a tactically intelligent decision or not. It just felt like the right thing to do. So he ran. He took the stairs in front of him two at a time, scanning about wildly as he reached the top.

"Claire!" he screamed, hoarse and winded. "Where are you?"

He had no idea why he called out to her.

Perhaps he thought she might say something and reveal to him which room out of the three doorways that faced him she had taken refuge in.

But she didn't. The hall with the three doors remained silent.

Sam picked a door at random.

It was all random. Like billiard balls bouncing off of each other from an amateur's break.

It was the door straight ahead.

He ran to it and didn't stop.

He went through it, shoulder-first, nearly ripping it off its hinges.

He lost his balance with the impact of the door, and went down. The doorknob caught him on the side of the face as it rebounded off the back wall.

Out of the corner of his vision, he saw her.

To his left.

Claire waited for him, her rifle up.

She fired, but she was aiming for the doorway, at chest height, and Sam was falling.

He hit the ground as her rounds pocked the wall above him.

They began to track downwards.

He fired furiously in Claire's direction.

One of the first few rounds found her foot, blasting it out from under her.

She lost her balance. Her shots lost track of where they were going.

Sam didn't stop firing. He was honing in.

She hit the ground on her side, staring at him with shock and anger.

He fired into her chest. Watched her twitch. Watched the mist come off of her, visible even in the darkness. She was still staring at him when his rounds found her neck, her jaw, her face, chewing it all up.

For some reason, Sam was surprised when she died.

He stopped shooting her.

He stared in the ringing silence, sucking air so thick with gunsmoke that he could taste it on his tongue. In and out, his breath went. Claire Staley's ruined face slumped onto the carpet, pouring its contents out like a broken pitcher.

"Claire?" Sam asked, and his voice wavered like a child's.

He heard yelling.

He heard feet stamping up the stairs.

Sam sat up. Leaned against the wall where the bullets that had been meant for him had left a trail of holes in the drywall. His mouth began to sweat. He spit it off to the side. He couldn't take his eyes off of Claire.

He felt horrified and elated.

It wasn't just elation at being alive.

It was elation that he'd killed her.

And horror at the elation.

They yelled his name. Billings and Jones.

Jones saw him first. "Christ! Ryder! What the fuck's wrong with you? Are you okay?"

Sam finally turned away from Claire's dead face and looked at Jones like he'd just woken up. "What?" he asked.

"Are you okay?" Jones repeated, coming to the doorway, then clearing it rapidly as he went through. He saw Claire's body. "Holy shit. Alright." He went down on one knee and looked at Sam. "You okay? You hit?"

"No," Sam said, his mouth lazy. Full of marbles. "No, the plates stopped it."

"Goddamn," Jones breathed. "Alright. Well. We need to get out of here."

Billings appeared in the doorway. Gave the scene a quick inspection. "Ryder, next time I tell you to stop running, you stop running."

"I got them, though," Sam replied, hollowly, as Jones helped him to his feet.

Billings nodded at the wreckage. "Yeah. You fuckin' got 'em."

Jones dusted Sam's shoulders off, grinning and tittering. Jabbed a finger at the hole in the fabric of Sam's plate carrier. "Damn, son. Hell yeah. Hardcore."

Sam coughed. As an afterthought, he checked the hand he'd coughed into to see if it had blood on it—maybe that round had actually penetrated his armor but he hadn't realized it yet. But no, there was no blood. He was good to go.

Sam looked at Billings. "Corporal, Elsie got away."

"Is that who that other one was?"

Sam nodded. "She got away. You need to contact command and tell them she's still alive. If they evac the Safe Zone, she might try to sneak out with one of the convoys."

"Alright, Ryder," Billings said, cracking a hesitant smile. "You fucking psychopath. We gotta go get Chris before the primals find him."

***

Captain Perry Griffin stood before the glowing monitor, one arm crossed over his chest, the other perched on his chin.

They were positioned in a small, abandoned strip mall, eight miles from the gates of the Fort Bragg Safe Zone. The monitor was perched on the bed of a pickup truck. A younger soldier sat before a complicated control apparatus that was attached to the monitor.

On the monitor there was a thermal-imaging view of the power substation in the Fort Bragg Safe

Zone. It was a bird's eye view, looking down through a screen of black pine boughs. But the images on the ground were clear enough.

Bodies. Shredded. Eviscerated.

They were already slightly dimmer than a human body should have shown. Growing cold. At least compared to the white-hot signatures of the creatures that fed on them.

Griffin's eyes coursed over the scene, looking for any signatures that didn't move in strange, animal ways. The way they moved...like a chimpanzee sometimes. And then other times like wolves.

There had been one human signature, huddled behind one of the substation's transformers. But he'd been sniffed out. The creatures had dragged him out. Latched onto his throat until he stopped kicking. Then a few of them had carried him off a short distance and fed.

That was it. There were no more humans at the power substation.

He wondered if Elsie Foster had foreseen that her little coup could end up like this? Those scattered bits of gristle, growing cold, were all the fighters she'd sent to take over the power substation.

Well.

She probably had anticipated a little more support from Greeley.

But Griffin had only ten men dispatched with him. He was not about to plunge them into the soup of carnage that Fort Bragg had devolved into. Elsie Foster should have thought a little harder about it before she cut the power. She'd held the Safe Zone hostage for her demands, and it sounded like Angela Houston had called her bluff. Yes, it would have made Elsie look weak if she *hadn't* cut the power. But looking weak was better than being dead, Griffin thought.

On the other end of an infected's digestive track, a weak man and a strong man both looked like a pile of shit on the forest floor.

Poor choices. All the way around.

Griffin waved at the monitor. "Alright. Fuck them. Zoom out. See where all the people are."

The soldier operating the small reconnaissance drone did as he was told. The image on the monitor zoomed out, then began to pan. It was high altitude, so it took less than a minute for the image to move into the center of the Safe Zone.

There, they could see how things were shaping out.

There was a large building—what appeared to be a hangar—that was surrounded by heat signatures. Upon zooming in, those signatures revealed themselves to be human soldiers. They had a defensive perimeter, and a steady stream of other signatures—civilians, Griffin guessed—flowed past them, and into the hangar.

Griffin let out a low whistle. "Shit. Couple Hellfires would solve a lot of problems."

The drone operator smirked, but said nothing.

The drone was for recon only. It wasn't big enough to carry munitions.

Too bad.

"Alright," Griffin said, with a sigh. "Pull it back. Charge it up. We'll check the situation out later."

Griffin's operations team leader leaned out from the other side of the truck. "We gonna move in tonight?"

Griffin shook his head. "Probably not. Earliest might be tomorrow morning. But I'm not putting us in there unless they evacuate." Griffin nodded to his team lead. "Post watch. Get a few hours of sleep."

"Hey Cap," the drone operator said.

Griffin looked over.

The operator pointed to the monitor. "Look at this shit," he breathed, a note of awe in his voice.

Griffin frowned at the monitor, and for a moment he wasn't sure what he was looking at. Some sort of thermal-imaging Rorschach test...

No. The operator had zoomed the drone all the way out.

From its high-altitude vantage, the monitor now showed a massive swath of the Fort Bragg Safe Zone. At the center of the screen, Griffin could see the box that was the hangar they'd just spied on, where everyone seemed to be gathering.

But at the edges of the darkness of that screen, there were blobs. Blobs of white, made by groups of eight, ten, sometimes a dozen heat signatures. And there were hundreds of these blobs. Moving like individual units, but also, as a whole, they seemed to be encircling Fort Bragg. They seemed to be following some basic strategy.

When Griffin squinted at the monitor, he could see the individual shapes. He saw how they ran, often on all fours, like wolves, and then sometimes like chimpanzees.

"Holy shit," Griffin whispered, then reached up with a single hand and touched his mouth. "It's gonna be a goddamned bloodbath."

***

Things had gone downhill at an alarming speed.

It had started with "You may want to keep evacuation in mind," and it had ended with "Angela, we need to evacuate. Immediately."

They were being overrun.

Maybe if they'd *told* Angela about the goddamned colony of primals living *right outside the gates*, she wouldn't have made the decision to call Elsie's bluff.

Or maybe she would have.

Angela didn't know anymore, and didn't care to analyze it. It did no good to her now anyways. The situation had devolved into shit, and she couldn't hand-wring it back to being okay.

The Blackout Plan had officially turned into the Evacuation Plan.

Angela stood in the center of the chaos, on the bed of a truck, in a hangar rapidly filling with people. All around her the people milled and formed lines, herded by soldiers. They argued with those soldiers, and yelled at each other, and sometimes at Angela, though she barely heard them.

Kurt stood beside her, tense, glaring out at all the people. He didn't like Angela to be surrounded like this. It was only a small sect of people around them that were hostile towards Angela, but even a small sect could do damage.

The huge main doors of the massive hangar were closed, but the man door on the north side of the structure was open, and a steady stream of people bustled through with terror-stricken faces, mouths agape and sucking wind from running here.

Outside, a strong defensive perimeter had been set up. But how long would that hold?

They would evacuate to the Butler Safe Zone. But they wouldn't be able to take everyone. They would have to come back. Which meant that there would be people stuck in this hangar overnight. Maybe longer, if the convoy had to fight its way back to the hangar upon it's return.

What did you do? Angela wondered, but she did not feel the self-condemnation that she once would have felt.

She watched the people being herded in, and she didn't see people, she saw cattle. She didn't hear their complaints and cries, she heard mindless lowing and bleating. They stared at her, and at the soldiers, and they didn't understand.

They never understand.

And she hated them.

She pitied them, and hated them all at once.

And somewhere out there, somewhere in that scrum of people jostling for a spot on the first convoy out, there were going to be Lincolnists. They were like a virulent mold spore. If only a few of them managed to make it out to Butler, then they'd begin to spread again.

Nearly a hundred people had failed to show up for work when Elsie Foster had initiated her plan to oust Angela. And based on the reports she was getting, her troops had encountered and fought half that many.

Which meant that they were out there.

In this hangar, right now. Trying to use Angela's evacuation plan to save their skins.

There was a list with all of their names on it, but that was back in the command office of the

Soldier Support Center. Which meant it was as good as gone, at this point in time.

A hand slapped the side of the pickup bed on which Angela stood. She jerked and looked. Marie stood there, her brown hair looking frizzier than usual.

"I got her secure," Marie said, speaking of Abby. "She's in that bus right there. Number three-twenty-two."

Angela looked and saw the bus, and then nodded. "Thank you."

Marie watched her for a moment, but Angela didn't notice. Her eyes went back to the crowd, back to watching them, scanning across them with a look of focus, combined with a seed of contempt.

"You need to get to a vehicle," Marie said.

Angela shook her head. "Not yet. I'm doing something."

Beside her, Kurt shifted. He wanted her out of here ASAP. He'd already made his case on that point. Angela had already shot it down.

Townsend, who'd received a temporary battlefield promotion to replace Lieutenant Derrick who'd been murdered, ran up to the side of the truck, and called up to her: "Ma'am, I got word from Master Sergeant Gilliard!"

Angela nodded and motioned him up.

Townsend climbed onto the bed with her, so that he could speak without shouting over the din of the hangar.

Out near one of the buses, a scuffle broke out, drawing Angela and Townsend's attention for a moment. There a burst of shouts, and then several soldiers piled on, and several other soldiers surrounded them and immediately started moving people back to what they were supposed to be doing.

That was the third time.

The soldiers were doing a great job keeping a heady situation from sparking into a riot.

Angela thought about if unrest started to happen inside the hangar. Thought about how it would slow everything down. How everyone would suffer, because a few malcontents, and she felt that ugly burning thing in her chest rekindle.

She pointed to where the scuffle was being covered. "Townsend, I want you to tell the troops that they're authorized to use whatever force necessary to keep people in line. If they have to drag someone to the wall and execute them to get the buses moving on time, then that's what they need to do."

Townsend blinked rapidly, processing what he'd heard.

Angela stared at him, waiting for his comprehension.

"O-okay. I mean, yes, ma'am. Um. Gilliard just called in."

"Yes?"

"And they're on the way right now. Mitch is wounded."

Angela's core tightened. "What happened?"

"Gilliard says they hit what he thinks was Elsie's house, and Mitch got shot during the firefight."

"Is he going to be okay?"

"I don't know, ma'am."

"Did they kill Elsie Foster?"

Townsend looked sheepish. "Unconfirmed, ma'am."

Angela nodded and looked out again.

How did this all happen? How did everything get so out of control? Why couldn't they stop themselves from being like this? Why couldn't a Safe Zone just be *safe*?

"These people," she muttered, her voice just a breath of wind in her chest, and she didn't think that Townsend heard her. Her eyes scanned over the crowd. A thousand people, forming lines, shuffling about, arguing, crying, yelling at each other, at the guards, at her, at the people that were trying to keep them from dying.

What was it in human beings?

Why were they like this?

Her eyes went over to the entrance again, but this time, about halfway across the crowd of people, she caught sight of a face she recognized.

It was that girl. Sam's girlfriend. What was her name?

Shit, Angela had only met her once...

Charlie.

Well, at least she was safe.

At least...

Angela's eyes narrowed.

Charlie squirmed her way through the crowd with her hood pulled up and her head down, like she was trying not to be noticed. And the line of people that followed her were doing the same thing.

Hiding in plain sight.

She might not have recognized Elsie Foster if she hadn't memorized the woman's face with the forced focus that only hatred can bring. Because Elsie's face looked very different now. It was a swollen and misshapen and smoke-smeared thing.

Blood and soot made half her face a mask. One eye was swollen shut.

Which explained how she got past the guards.

She looked so unlike herself, that for a moment, Angela just stared at her, and her heartrate hadn't even sped up, because she was half-convinced she'd made a mistaken ID.

But it was her.

Elsie Foster.

Trying to slip through the crowd, unseen. Trying to get away. Trying to escape the situation that she herself created. She was going to sit on a bus, and take a seat from someone who might actually be worth a shit.

She was a goddamned parasite. She was a cancer.

She needed to be cut out.

Without speaking, Angela slid off the tailgate of the truck. She pushed into the crowd of people, rudely breaking through their lines. Sometimes they scooted out of the way, and sometimes she had to shove them, but she kept her eyes on the last spot she'd seen Elsie, and she kept marching forward, making a B-line there, with Kurt marching after her, protesting.

"Ma'am? Ma'am." His voice became sterner. "Angela."

Angela ignored him.

She didn't even look at a man that cursed her out as she passed him.

She didn't even feel a hint of satisfaction when he cut off his foul-mouthed diatribe against her as he saw her draw the pistol from her hip.

She was the bow of a ship, slicing through water.

She lost sight of Elsie for a moment in the scrum of people. She raised the pistol so that it could be seen by everyone, and the crowd parted away from her the way oil parts from water.

"Angela!" Kurt went on. "What are you doing?"

Angela saw Charlie first, unaware of Angela's approach. And all she had to do was look back in line, three hunched figures behind Charlie, and there she was.

Still, Angela said nothing.

Still, Kurt kept protesting.

Angela's whole body shook with the pounding of her heart, as she finally laid eyes on this woman, and she watched as Elsie laid eyes on her. Face to face.

"Elsie Foster," Angela said, and the only way to keep her voice from shaking was to speak loud, nearly yelling.

And everything got very quiet.

Even Kurt finally shut his mouth.

From the epicenter of these two women, the quiet spread through the hangar like a silent shockwave.

Elsie's eyes jagged in a hundred directions, but they all told her the same thing: She was penned in. She thought she'd been clever sneaking into the hangar. But now all eyes were on her, and there was no way she was going to get out.

Backed into a corner, she became defiant.

A sneer crept up to the woman's mouth.

Crinkled the corners of her nose.

She tilted her chin up, looking down her nose at Angela with her one good eye, the other purple, and oozing red from what looked like a smattering of glass shards embedded in her skin.

And yet, she looked at Angela with contempt.

She looked at Angela like *she* was the piece of shit.

Elsie brought her hands forward, wrists together. As though inviting handcuffs. "Guess you got me, Angela," she said, loud and calm and confident. "Guess you got the one person who was willing to speak out against you." A smirk, hiding in the sneer. "What're you gonna do, Angela? You gonna—"

Angela shot her in the face.

The bullet struck Elsie Foster in the corner of her right eye.

Her head snapped back.

Her body wilted.

Hands still held out, with the wrists touching.

Angela didn't hear the gasp that went through the crowd.

Her ears were still ringing.

No one moved for a moment, too shocked. Too surprised at what Angela had done. This weak woman. This housewife.

Angela took a breath, and found that it entered her chest easier than before, as though she had been trying to breathe past a heavy weight for the last several months, and suddenly she could.

Not because the weight had been lifted, but because she'd suddenly grown strong enough to bear it.

With that breath, she projected her voice. Loud and calm and confident. "Get on your prescribed buses. We are evacuating to the Butler Safe Zone." She looked around her at all the people, at their fearful faces. She looked at them as though she were the only person in the world that knew what to do in that moment. And they listened. "If you do not like that, you are welcome to stay here at Fort Bragg. But *do not* get in the way."

Then she strode back through the crowd to where she'd come from.

They needed to get moving.

And they needed her to lead them.

TWENTY-NINE

DEATH LEAVES NO DOUBTS

JOHN BELLAMY STRODE through the dark streets of the Greeley Green Zone, out to the edges, where the Yellow Zone began.

He wore a pair of khaki workpants, a gray hoodie, and a black backpack. The only things that marked him as military were the tan watch cap on his head and the tan boots on his feet.

And, of course, the identification badge around his neck.

He tried not to walk like a guilty person. He tried not to seem like an escapee.

He was avoiding the checkpoints on the main thoroughfares. The border with the Yellow Zone was porous as hell, but they made up for it with a lot of roving guards that had the freedom to stop and question anybody in the Green Zone.

Being safe in the Green Zone was a privilege, not a right.

Fact was, there weren't many rights in Colorado anymore.

Up ahead, two soldiers walked, one of them with a canine on a lead.

Bellamy tried not to make eye contact with them, tried to look down the street with a neutral expression on his face, like he could care less that he was being approached by guards that might be on the lookout for him.

Out of the corner of his vision, he could tell they were looking right at him.

Shit.

He felt the weight of the pistol shoved in the front of his waistband. It would be one quick move. He could take them if he did it now. The one with the canine had only a pistol strapped to his thigh, and his companion still had his rifle slung.

Bellamy reached up and pulled his watch cap lower, so that the edge of it covered his eyebrows. Perhaps it would obscure his features. Make him less recognizeable.

"Excuse me, soldier," the guard with the canine called.

Shit, shit, shit.

Bellamy stopped walking and tilted his head back. "Marine."

The soldier with the canine was wrapping his dog's lead around his hand several times, shortening the leash. The two soldiers and the dog stood about five feet from Bellamy. The dog sniffed at him, but made no aggressive movements.

"What's that?" the soldier with the canine asked.

"I'm a Marine." Bellamy tried a cocksure smile. "Not a soldier."

The two soldiers exchanged a glance that turned into an eye-roll. "Roger that, Marine. See your ID?"

Bellamy took the ID from around his neck. He had to clench it between his thumb and all four of his fingers to keep them from trembling. He pushed it into the soldier's waiting hand, rather than holding it up for inspection, knowing that they'd see the shake if he did.

The soldier gave the ID a very cursory glance, then handed it back. "And where you headed, Sergeant Gilmore?"

Bellamy was almost shocked. He didn't think he looked much like the Sergeant Gilmore he'd swiped the ID from—that guy had been ten years younger.

He recovered quickly. "Yellow Zone."

"Yeah. What for?"

Bellamy sighed. "Get my dick sucked, if you must know."

The two soldiers snickered to each other.

The soldier with the canine lifted an eyebrow. "How much you paying?"

Bellamy shifted. "A thousand k-cals."

The soldier cringed. "Double wrap that shit, my friend. Anyone cheaper than two thousand is definitely got the herps."

"Definitely," agreed the other soldier.

Still chuckling to themselves, the two soldiers continued on their way.

Bellamy let out a long, shaking breath, then put the ID around his neck again.

He had no more run-ins with patrols.

The coyote waited for him three blocks into the Yellow Zone, right at the street corner he'd promised to be at.

It was a man that had maybe five or ten years on Bellamy. Balding on top. The rest of his hair cut short. A week's worth of graying stubble on his weathered face. His eyes were suspicious and restless. They hit Bellamy's face, recognized him, then continued to scan.

"Payment first," were the first words out of his mouth.

Bellamy nodded, then pulled a ration card from his pocket. The coyote snatched it up like he was afraid someone might see it, then, holding it surreptitiously between him and the wall of the building at which he stood, he perused it.

"This is five thousand a day. Two adults, two kids." The way the coyote said it—like he was displeased.

Bellamy frowned at him. "That's what we agreed upon."

"Yeah." The coyote glared at him. "That's before you were wanted by Lineberger and Cornerstone."

Bellamy swallowed. "How'd you know about that?"

"I've got sources," he growled.

"Well, it's gonna hafta be good enough," Bellamy said, finding his temper rising along with his urgency to get out of there. "That's what the deal was for. That's what I brought. I can't just go back and get more at this point."

The coyote pocketed the ration card. Looked Bellamy over. "You armed?"

Bellamy tightened up. "Why?"

"Because I might could trade you for it."

"No fucking way."

The coyote held up a placating hand. "You'll still have a weapon, cool your tits. It just won't be as nice as the one you probably got in your keester." The coyote looked momentarily worried. "You don't actually have it in your ass, do you?"

"No."

"What is it?"

"Glock 19."

"Mmm." The coyote seemed to be considering it. "Fine. I'll take the ration card and the 19. I got a revolver you can have."

"You gotta be fucking kidding me."

"That's the deal."

"No, the ration card was the fucking deal."

A shrug. "That's the deal," the coyote repeated.

Bellamy was up against a wall, and the coyote knew it. He let out one more venomous curse and then nodded. "Fine. Deal."

The coyote held out a hand. "Payment first."

"Fuck that. We'll exchange the revolver and the pistol at the same damn time."

The coyote's eyes bounced back and forth between Bellamy's for a few seconds. Another shrug. "Alright. Let's go, then."

The coyote spun on his heel and started walking away.

Bellamy went after him.

He watched the man's back, and he looked around himself, feeling warier now that the deal had been done. Like he was more exposed. Perhaps it was simply the fact that they'd almost not made a deal at all. Maybe that was making Bellamy feel like something had gone wrong.

The coyote, one step ahead of Bellamy, turned his head, glancing across the street.

Bellamy followed the look.

A man stood outside of a building. Had he been looking at them? He wasn't now—he gazed off down the street, as though waiting on someone else to arrive.

One of the coyote's men, perhaps?

Ahead of him, the coyote looked like he was angling for an alleyway.

Bellamy didn't like alleyways.

The mouth of it opened up to the left. A narrow one, sandwiched between two brick-front buildings.

Bellamy didn't want to go into that alleyway, and he was about to say something about it, but the coyote didn't slow his pace, nor did he turn into the alley. He kept walking. But as he stepped across the opening, his hands went up.

Tugged at the collar of his jacket.

In any other circumstance, it might've seemed like a natural move.

It stopped Bellamy dead in his tracks.

About three feet from the corner of the alley—one step.

The coyote took another two strides before turning back and frowning at Bellamy, and almost looking natural at it. "You coming?" he said. But there was a tremor in his voice. His eyes darted again.

In the direction of the other guy across the street.

The one that looked like he was waiting for a friend.

Bellamy stared at the coyote.

The coyote stared back.

Perhaps it was Bellamy's imagination, but he thought the man across the street was staring at him too.

In a flash, Bellamy ripped up the front of his hooded sweatshirt and snatched the Glock from his waistband.

The coyote was moving.

So was the guy across the street.

Bellamy punched out, two-handed, and fired three rounds, all of them hitting the coyote square in the chest as he tried to draw his own pistol. He failed, with the pistol not even out of his waistband. He died with his fingers still wrapped around the grip, his legs going out from under him and his body toppling to the curb.

Bellamy spun in place, forcing his feet to move.

Across the street, the other guy came up with a weapon. Bellamy didn't wait to see what it was. As he cut sideways across the street, diagonal to the man and away from the alleyway, he fired in a steady, controlled rhythm and managed to land four out of the eight shots that he made.

The man across the street slumped against the building, a pistol-grip shotgun in his hand.

Bellamy ran.

He knew he only had a few bullets left in that magazine. He needed to change it. He angled for another alleyway that would be about twenty-five yards from the one that the coyote had tried to lead him across, and started digging in his pants pocket for his spare magazine.

He never got it.

A bullet hit him square in the back, severing his spine.

He hit the pavement, face-planting out of a full sprint. His arms and legs were useless. He stared at the concrete in front of his face, and he tried to breathe, but he couldn't. He couldn't move. He wanted to look up and over, to where that shot had come from, to see where the threat was.

He wanted to fight back.

He hadn't even had a chance to fight.

He'd spent all this time sneaking around, and he'd never had a chance to fight!

The last seconds of John Bellamy's life were spent staring at the same bit of concrete, trying with every fiber of his being to get his head to turn, to feel the pistol in his hand, to *fight*.

The next round, wherever it came from, put him down forever.

***

Daniels strode out into the street. The denizens of the Yellow Zone were already gathering like the curious little monkeys they were, hooting and hollering back and forth as they stared at the dead body that lay crumpled on the concrete.

You'd think they'd never seen a dead body before.

My God, how quickly people regressed to their former, softer ways.

"Get these fucking people outta here," Daniels snapped at one of his Cornerstone operators, who turned and relayed the same barking command out to a few others, and they in turn began to push the crowd back, not-so-subtly threatening them with force.

He came to a stop at the feet of John Bellamy. The leak.

The traitor.

He was already dead.

Daniels was intimately familiar with the look. Death left no doubts.

The man on the ground was slumped and limp and boneless, like he'd been poured there out of a sack of liquid rubber. His eyes were half open. Bits of concrete dust sat on the surface of his eyes, and they'd already gone dry and filmed over. No more blinking for old John Bellamy.

"Self-important prick," Daniels murmured to himself.

His satphone rang in his pocket. He'd begun carrying it with him everywhere, as things had been heating up to the point that it was impractical not to.

He grunted in irritation as he dragged it out. Goddamned Lineberger, nagging him for a sitrep, when Daniels had *clearly* told him that he would contact him when the operation was concluded...

But when Daniels looked at the number that was calling him, it wasn't Lineberger.

It was Mateo Ibarra.

***

The head of the *Nuevas Fronteras* cartel stood amid smoke and death, at the Comanche Peak Power Plant.

He stood at a high point, on the very top of the main building, because it provided him a good vantage of everything that was happening, although, in the darkness of the early morning hours, there wasn't much to see but the flashes of his men's weaponlights and headlamps.

All around him the smell of spent propellant still managed to hang in the air. Something about the rain that made it stick around. And the tang of high explosives. Not yet the rot of bodies, but that would come soon enough. Mateo wasn't going to trouble his men with disposing of this many bodies. Let the *locos* have them.

The earpiece of the phone he held crackled faintly as the connection opened.

A slight hesitation.

"This is Daniels," the man answered. Cautiously.

"Hello, Mister Daniels," Mateo smiled as he spoke. "This is Mateo Ibarra. I'm afraid I have some bad news for you."

Another pause. "And what's that?"

Mateo looked down from the rooftop at the bodies below. Dozens of them. Dark against the light-colored concrete. Some of them were in pieces. His men moved between them, checking faces—if the body had a face to check.

Looking for Terrence Lehy. Or Lee Harden. Or Abe Darabie.

So far, they had not been found.

"Well, if you were waiting for your Mister McNair to contact you, I'm afraid that won't be possible."

***

Daniels didn't notice his grip on the satphone tightening until his fingertips started to ache. And his ear. Which he was vigorously pressing the phone against.

Mateo Ibarra's words bounced around his head.

What was that supposed to mean?

"Did you...?" Daniels husked, but didn't finish his thought.

"Oh, no," Mateo said over the line, his voice sounding like he felt he had made some sort of social gaff. "I don't mean to imply that I had them killed or anything like that. Although..." and here, his voice became harder. "...I will express to you that I'm not very pleased with how this was handled. I would have liked your man McNair to explain to me that my men's lives here at the power plant were disposable bait. I might have chosen less valuable individuals. But, as it stands, since McNair is no longer among the living, I guess we'll call it even."

Daniels found his respiration increasing. Hissing in his throat. He closed his eyes tight and pinched the bridge of his nose, feeling like the floor had been removed from underneath him. "What...what are you saying right now, Mateo?"

"I'm saying that, with the exception of your two helicopter pilots, the entire team of soldiers you sent down here is dead."

"How did they die?"

Mateo actually laughed. "Well, that is most strange, Mister Daniels. I cannot tell you exactly how they died, since my men are dead themselves, and your helicopter pilots have orders not to speak to me."

Daniels still couldn't bear to open his eyes. Phantom lights sparkled behind his eyelids. "Did Lee Harden take the power plant?" he asked, incredulous.

"No, no. Nobody took the power plant. It was quite the massacre, as I'm sure your pilots will outline for you, once they re-establish contact. Everyone died." Another chuckle, but this time there was something voracious behind it. "Well, not everyone. Because it appears that several very important bodies have yet to be found. Namely, Lee Harden, Abe Darabie, and Terrence Lehy. Strange, don't you think?" Mateo's voice dropped to a deadpan growl. "Nearly a hundred people dead. Except for the three motherfuckers that were *supposed* to be dead."

Daniels finally opened his eyes. Even in the darkness, everything seemed overbright. He swallowed. Gathered himself. "Mateo, once I speak to the helicopter pilots and get the story from them, I'll be sure to contact you and arrange—"

"Don't bother," Mateo said, quietly. "I've had enough of your help for today. For now, you should receive your last shipment of oil very soon, if you do not have it in hand already. Any future transactions between us will be on hold until I find and deal with this problem myself."

Daniels looked down at the body. Trying for a valuable card that might stave off *Nuevas Fronteras* cutting off the flow of fuel to Greeley. "We took out Bellamy. He was the leak."

A long hiss of breath from the other end. "Do you believe that this indebts me to you? John Bellamy was your leak. Your problem. I have not had any problems in my house, because my house is clean. I am glad you are getting your house in order. And yet it seems that business between us has not been profitable. I hope that you can correct that in the future."

"Mateo—" Daniels started to object.
But Mateo Ibarra had already hung up.

D.J. MOLLES

THIRTY

REBORN

Lee walked with Julia, *through the Butler Safe Zone, twenty minutes after everyone else had already gone to bed, and he was at peace.*

Inasmuch as he was able, given their circumstances.

But he thought to himself—and never said it out loud, because he thought it would be hokey—that on the other side of this thing, when the dust had settled and he was back at Fort Bragg and he was training the next generation of fighters, maybe they could just be together, him and Julia.

Maybe they could have peace.

***

He had died.

Somewhere between the mud and the air.

He was reborn in amniotic waters as black as midnight. As black as the space between stars.

His first breath was a primordial gasp.

473

And then he went under again.

Each breath formed him as he took it. A golem from the depths, gaining life as it breathed air. And after each breath, he went under and swam through the darkness. And in the darkness he wondered.

Why was he here?

He only knew of one thing, around which his very being had been formed. He knew only war and death. So that must be why he was here.

Eventually, exhausted to the brink of dying, he floated.

On his back, letting the tide take him.

At first, the sky above him was black and sightless. Formless and void. But then the rain stopped pouring, and gradually the blackness of the clouds parted, and the cold light of stars winked down at him, and the moon, a pale orb like a dead man's eye, stared at him.

The golem stared back.

***

Two men meet.

There is no one there to witness it. They are in the darkness of the pre-dawn hours, on a quiet shoreline on the north side of Squaw Creek Reservoir. All around them, the darkened world waits. Lurks. Hunts.

The one who had been watching the other from the shoreline, he leans down and grasps the other's arm. And the man in the water, not expecting it, lurches up and reaches for the other man's throat.

They halt in mid-combat with each other.

Recognizing each other as only brothers can.

Sodden and dripping and trembling, Lee Harden wilts. Abe Darabie catches his weight with a grunt, and pulls him out of the water and into the pine needle-strewn shore.

They had not expected to find each other, but neither are they surprised. Nothing could surprise them at this point. They are both beyond such things.

It seems that fate, or provenance, has brought them back together.

"They killed her," Lee whispers amid violent chills. "They killed everybody."

Abe is crying, and doesn't care. He clutches Lee's shoulders, weakened by the news. Lee holds onto him, and he cries too. But they do it quietly. Their breath seizes in their chests and it hisses out through their bared teeth, and their weeping is only a low groan from their bellies that might've been a gust of wind in the trees.

"It was a trap," Lee breathes, when he recovers control of himself.

Abe nods. "It was Cornerstone. They were helping the cartel take us out."

Lee looks out across the blackness of the lake towards the dim twinkling of the fires on the other side, the smoke still wafting above the flames like a bank of fog. A mile across the water, Lee can still smell the acrid stench of it.

"All of that just to get rid of us."

They are silent for a long while, staring at the flames.

"But they didn't," Abe says.

One man pulls the other up, black shapes in a shadowed woods.

And then two men disappear.

All around them the darkened world waits. Lurks. Hunts.

But they are unafraid.

They will also wait.

And they will lurk.

And they will hunt.

FOR UPDATES ON THE LEE HARDEN SERIES, MAKE
SURE TO FOLLOW D.J. MOLLES AT
FACEBOOK.COM/DJMOLLES
AND SIGN UP FOR HIS FREE NEWSLETTER AT
http://eepurl.com/c3kfJD
(If you're typing that into a browser, make sure to
capitalize the J and D)

READ ON FOR A PREVIEW OF D.J. MOLLES'
UPCOMING NOVEL

BREAKING GODS

PRE-ORDER YOUR COPY NOW!

RELEASES AUGUST 15, 2019!

BREAKING GODS

VIII And the gods perceived a great wickedness in humanity, and that every inclination of the thoughts of the human heart was only evil all the time, IX and that they would never be satisfied, and that they wished to swallow all the stars. X The gods saw what the human beings were building, and all that they had become, and all that they intended to become, XI and the gods said to themselves, "Come, let us go down to them and destroy everything they have built so that they will not swallow all the stars."

Translated from the *Ortus Deorum*

2nd Song, 3rd Stanza

Chapter 0
BEGINNINGS

He sits in prison and his sentence is death.

He does not know who he is, or what he is capable of.

And yet, destiny hurtles towards him whether he knows it or not.

Before we see who this condemned man is, let us look back to who he *was*, just a few days before. Let us go back to a battlefield, and a scavenging crew, and a series of events that will place this young man on a path from which he can never come back. A path to discovering who—and what—he really is.

If, of course, he manages to survive that long.

Chapter 1
SCAVENGERS

The Truth and The Light were murdering each other in droves.

Perry and his outfit waited on a dusty escarpment to pick over their dead.

It was the month of the Giver of Death. At night, the Deadmoon waned, and the days were short. The battle had begun later than usual today, and already the sun leaned westward. If it ran long, the crew might have to scavenge after dark. Boss Hauten did not like to scavenge after dark, and so he stood off to the side, fidgeting impatiently as he waited for the slaughter to be over.

Perry sat away from the ledge, his back against a comfortable rock. Around him, the rest of the outfit waited, holding quiet conversations and occasionally laughing at a joke. At twenty years old, Perry had already been on the crew for three years. That made him a middleman, with only a few others having more seniority than him.

First, there was Jax. He was a crotchety, white-bearded old fart that had been on Boss Hauten's crew since time immemorial. He held the job of "chief primer," and he guarded it jealously because it was easy work and he was ancient.

Second, there was Tiller.

Tiller was an ass, and he got along with nobody. Least of all Perry.

Lastly, there was Stuber.

While the rest of them waited, backed away from the edge of the cliff, hoping not to catch a stray round, Stuber stood at the edge in his battered armor and looked down at the battle that splayed out in the valley below. He watched the violence, always with an element of yearning, like a captured animal pines for the ferocity of the wilds.

The clasps on the back of his spaulders still had a bit of Stuber's old *sagum* cape.

The cloth was now sun-faded. Almost pink.

But it had once been a bright red.

Red for The Truth.

Staring at the ex-legionnaire's back, Perry felt a mix of unpleasant things rising up in his throat like gorge. Fear. Hatred. Loathing.

All things best kept hidden. It wouldn't do for anybody to guess Perry's past.

Stuber turned like he felt Perry's gaze on him. Those predatory eyes of his stared out from the rocky promontory of his face. A broad grin split the dark growth of his short beard.

"Shortstack," he beckoned with one massive hand. "Come watch."

Perry shook his shaggy, brown head. "Nah. I'm good."

Stuber's face darkened. "Come watch. Don't be bleeding vagina."

Perry grunted irritably, but rose up from his comfortable rock. It was probably the best seat on this ridge, and he was being forced to give it up. He dusted the back of his pants off and took a few steps forward, hunching his head down as he did, thinking about stray rounds from the battle below.

"You remember what happened to Hinks?" Perry griped, remembering how the poor girl's head had just seemed to cave in, like an invisible hammer had struck it.

"Hinks was an unlucky bitch," Stuber said dismissively. "She'd barely come back from the ants the day before." He snapped his fingers impatiently. "Come on. You're going to miss the best part."

Perry glanced behind him. Back to his comfy rock.

Tiller had already slid into place there. He crossed his booted feet and stretched himself with a great, dramatic sigh of pleasure. Then he smiled at Perry and mimed jacking off, completed by flinging an imaginary substance at Perry.

Perry's fingers twitched, and his brain tried to dip into the place where it always went when conflict was imminent—a place of flowing, red momentum that existed deep in Perry's brain—but the second that his body tensed to react to Tiller, a huge, callused hand grabbed Perry by the back of the neck and pulled him up to the edge of the cliff.

Stuber's hands were like iron wrapped in sandpaper.

"Look," Stuber commanded.

"I've seen it before."

"You've never seen *this* before."

"I have. Many times."

"Every battle is different."

"They look the same to me."

"That's because you're a peon. Here it comes."

Down below them, three or four miles away, the two armies prepared to converge. Blue on one side. Red on the other. Their *sagum* capes brilliant in the afternoon sun. Smoke coiled and wreathed them. Flak burst like black blooms in the sky above them. Mortars launched with a constant thumping rhythm and were shot out of the sky by the autoturrets. Gales of tracer fire scoured back and forth, lancing the crowds of men. Every once in a while a mortar shell would get through and a hole would appear in one battleline or another. Stuber didn't seem to care which side it was—when the bodies blew apart, he laughed.

The two armies were within a hundred yards of each other now. Their front lines were shielded phalanxes that inched towards each other, gaining ground stride by stride while bursts of bullets clattered back and forth, searching for a chink in the wall of shields. A body would fall, and the fire would concentrate on that hole, trying to kill more of the men behind it, but in seconds another shield would appear to plug up the hole, the dead soldiers trampled under their comrades' feet.

The two armies had closed the gap.

"Foreplay," Stuber said. "If the battlefield were a whore's bed, this is the part when you finally get to stick your dick in."

Below them, the gunfire intensified.

The mortars silenced, the two sides too close now for the shelling to continue. The autoturrets turned their focus on the front lines. Hammered shields. Created holes.

The space between red and blue was filled with bright muzzle flashes and glowing tracers and billowing smoke. It crescendoed, madly, and then, all at once, there was a break. A release.

The two sides crushed into each other.

"Haha!" Stuber thrust his hips. "Yes!"

Perry thought of the dead, crushed underfoot in the melee, in the stabbing, in the contact shots that would blow them open from the big .458 rounds. He thought about the way the mud would be a slick red-brown as he sloshed through it later, the dusty world watered by thousands of gallons of blood, but it would never be enough to bring the earth back to life.

At the rear of the two armies, further back than even the autoturrets, two armored command modules hovered on their turbines above blocks of troops waiting in reserve. On the deck of the modules stood the paladins.

Demigods.

They wore the colors of their side. Watching. Commanding.

Perry had never seen one of them die.

***

"Dogs and ants and spiders!" Hauten yelled at them.

Their buggy trundled its way down the rocky slope towards the valley below. A warm wind blew crosswise down the valley, buffeting in Perry's ears and making him squint against flying dust.

He could see the redness below. The floor of the valley had become a butcher's house. Bodies strewn about. Both The Light and The Truth left their dead where they'd fallen.

How many dead in six hours' worth of fighting?

Perry guesstimated that there were about a thousand bodies below.

Each body containing five liters of blood.

Draining.

Five thousand liters of blood in that valley.

"Dogs and ants and spiders!" Hauten bellowed over the wind and the rumble of the buggy's tires, and the struggling whine of the electric drive.

The buggy teetered at a steep angle that made Perry's insides feel watery and he clutched the roll bar nearest him.

"Keep your eyes peeled!" Hauten continued. "Watch what you grab! Watch where you put your feet! Don't die, because I can't afford to bury you!"

"What does he mean?"

Perry, still clinging to the rollbar as the buggy now listed to the right on what felt like a forty-five degree slope, looked over his tense shoulder at the girl riding next to him. Her name was Teran. She was new to the outfit. She'd come on with them at their last stop in Junction City. She claimed to have experience. Perry had discovered that that was a lie.

Perry doubted that Hauten had been fooled. Probably he kept her on because he thought he had a chance to fuck her. She was what they called "outfit pretty." Which was to say, in a town amongst other women, you wouldn't look twice. But in an outfit full of guys…yeah, you would.

"The crows come first, but they won't do anything," Perry answered, his voice wobbling with the shaking of the buggy. "Then the dogs. They smell the blood. They're mean, but they won't attack you unless you're alone. Then the ants come up from underground. Don't step on their hills—they'll tear you up. Almost lost a girl a few months back because of that."

Poor old Hinks.

"What about the spiders?"

"The spiders sometimes make nests in the shell casings. They jump out and catch the flies. But they'll catch a finger too."

Teran blinked a few times, facing forward. "Aren't we supposed to collect the shell casings?"

"Yes."

She processed this with a frown, and then seemed to hunker down. Her lips flattened into a grimly-determined line. The wind whipped a bit of her sandy hair into her eyes. She pulled it back and tucked it behind her ear, where it promptly came loose again.

The buggy lifted itself over a rock, and then started to tip.

Stuber, who rode on the backend of the vehicle slid to the left side and leaned out as a counterbalance.

Perry clenched down hard, knowing that if the buggy started to tumble, he'd be meat by the bottom. They all would be. Except for Stuber, who'd simply hop off the back.

Why did Hauten have to drive like such an idiot? There were a million other routes off the damn ridge, but of course, he had to take this one, because it was the shortest, and he was in a rush to make a profit.

All four tires touched the ground again.

Perry let the air out of his chest slowly.

A moment later, the ground began to level out.

"Why are you doing this anyways?" Perry asked her.

He half-expected a sharp response from Teran. Most women that he'd seen come onto the outfit knew that they were the outsiders and that Hauten was probably trying to fuck them. Hauten rarely hired a female that wasn't outfit pretty. They were always a bit defensive, and Perry couldn't blame them. That didn't make them very pleasant to be around, but then again, there weren't too many people on the outfit that were.

But Teran just shrugged. "All the places to make an honest living in Junction City were full up. So I figured I'd get on an outfit. This happened to be the outfit."

"You gonna ditch us when you find a steady town job?"

It was loud enough with the wind and the tires rumbling, and other peoples' shouted conversations that Perry wasn't concerned about being overheard. He didn't really think Hauten would care anyway. Turnover on the outfit was high amongst greenhorns, and nothing to balk at.

"Depends on how much Hauten pays," she replied.

"You ever goin' back to Junction City?"

This time she did look at him. "I dunno, Perry. You ever going back to what you did before?"

Perry stared at her. He didn't care for the way she said it. Like she knew about Perry's past. But that was impossible. No one knew. He'd never told anyone.

He quickly changed the subject. "When we get to the bottom, stay with me. Do what I tell you and watch where you put your feet and your hands."

The smell of blood was palpable now.

Perry could taste it on his tongue.

It was more humid down here in the valley than it had been on the ridge.

Despite it being the Deadmoon, out here where the earth had been scorched, the sun shone hot, no matter the time of year. And when it baked a pond made up of five thousand liters of blood, then it turned the valley into something of a steam room.

"Dogs and ants and spiders!" Hauten reminded them one last time, and then began to slow the buggy. As it rolled to a halt amid a cloud of dust, he looked back at them from the controls. "Work quick and we won't have to mess with any of that shit, yeah? Alright. Get to work."

Perry slid out of his seat and over the horizontal bar of metal. The black paint on it was hot to the touch. Flaking off. Rusty underneath. He went to the back, and Teran followed.

"Jax! Tiller!" Hauten called out, exiting his driver's seat. "Get some guns."

At the back of the buggy, Stuber had dropped to the ground. His Roq-11 .458 rifle was strapped to his back at the moment. He pulled a long, battered, black case out to the edge of the buggy's cargo bed. He undid the locks and lifted the cover.

Inside were two shotguns nestled next to each other, and a large, silver pistol.

The Mercy Pistol. Stuber left that where it was, but he grabbed the two shotguns in each of his meaty paws and turned, just as Jax and Tiller trotted up.

Tiller made it a point to shoulder past Perry.

Stuber shoved the shotguns in their hands. Jax ran his sunken, blue eyes over his, charged a round into the chamber, and then shoved his arm through the braided sling. He turned and walked off.

Tiller had the shotgun in both hands and he tried to pull it, but Stuber held on.

Tiller stared up at the ex-legionnaire, confused.

Stuber held the shotgun in his right hand. With his left, he jabbed in index finger like a dart into

Tiller's chest. Tiller let out an offended yelp and glared.

"Don't be an asshole," Stuber growled.

"I won't," Tiller grunted indignantly. He jerked hard and Stuber let him have the shotgun.

Tiller checked his action, just like Jax had, although the movements were not as sure. Tiller did most of what he did in an attempt to look as experienced as Jax.

When Tiller was satisfied that he had a loaded shotgun, he gave a baleful look over his shoulder at Stuber, and then marched off. He made another attempt to shoulder Perry, but Perry saw it coming and slid out of the way.

"'Scuse me," Tiller said anyways. Kept walking.

Perry felt that flowing river deep inside of him.

The blur of red.

As much as Perry enjoyed watching Stuber mess with Tiller, it only meant that Tiller was going to be more pissy than usual today.

"Come on," Hauten hollered, reaching the back of the buggy. "Buckets. Work quick. Quick, quick, quick. Lezgo lezgo lezgo."

There was a stack of buckets. They hadn't made it down to the valley in their original, stowed position. Perry grabbed two from the jumbled pile and gave one to Teran. He started towards the battlefield.

"We're here for the brass. Don't try to loot the bodies: some of the legionairres booby-trap themselves before they die. Besides that, we've got a delicate understanding with several other scavenging outfits—they let us have the brass, we let them have the armor, or the tech, or whatever their flavor of scrap is. All you gotta do is pick up brass. If it's severely dented, leave it. If you can see a spider web inside it, leave it—those things are poisonous. Don't try to move anything that already has an ant mound on it. If you notice anybody that's still alive, don't touch them, don't move them, and don't talk to them. Just call for Stuber."

The very first body they reached was still alive.

A man with half his face blown off.

His chestplate rose and fell with hitching breaths. His massive shield lay still attached to his left arm, dented and dinged, the edges chipped from thousands of projectiles that had skimmed by him.

But one had found him. And one was all you needed.

His blue *sagum* identified him as a legionnaire of The Light.

The dying legionnaire reached a hand towards them. He tried to speak, but couldn't.

Perry first eyed the man's right hand to see if he was still armed. Both sides left the bodies, but they were careful to retrieve the weapons. Funny how they did that.

Perry saw no weapons. He turned his head to project his voice back over his shoulder, but he kept his eye on the dying soldier in front of him.

"Stuber!"

The soldier knew what was next. Whatever he wanted, he forgot about it, and his outstretched arm fell to his side. He sat there with his chestplate heaving, his one good eye still looking straight at Perry.

Perry heard the sound of retching behind him.

He glanced over his shoulder, and saw Teran, doubled over with a thick rope of yellowy stomach juices issuing from her mouth and nose.

He turned back to the dying legionnaire.

The man's one remaining eye was a pleasant hazel color. The eye was nice and round. Thick lashes. He might've been a popular man with the ladies, Perry thought, though with half his face missing, it was difficult to tell if he was handsome. Maybe he just had nice eyes.

Stuber came over. Perry gestured to the dying soldier.

Stuber knelt before the man, as he would so many times that day. He put his hand on the soldier's forehead and he said the words that Perry didn't even need to hear, he knew them so well by now.

"In the eyes of the gods, it matters not the color of your banner, but the courage of your heart. Under the watchful gaze of Nur, the Eighth Son, all warriors are brothers. As your brother, I bear witness to Halan, the Eldest Son, that you have fought your fight. Be at peace. Accept this mercy, and go to The After."

The dying man closed his eyes as Stuber put the large, silver pistol against his head and gave him mercy.

And, as he always did, Perry watched, and thought, *That could have been me.*

And that made him think of the Tall Man.

END OF PREVIEW

PRE-ORDER BREAKING GODS NOW

ABOUT THE AUTHOR

D.J. Molles is the New York Times bestselling author of *The Remaining* series. He is also the author of *Wolves*, a 2016 winner in the Horror category for the Foreword INDIES Book Awards. His other works include the *Grower's War* series, and the Audible original, *Johnny*. When he's not writing, he's taking care of his property in North Carolina, and training to be at least half as hard to kill as Lee Harden. He also enjoys playing his guitar, his violin, drawing, painting, and lots of other artsy fartsy stuff

You can follow and contact him at:
Facebook.com/DJMolles
And sign up for his free, monthly newsletter at:
http://eepurl.com/c3kfJD
(If you're typing that into a browser, make sure to capitalize the J and D)